ACCIDENTS HAPPEN AND OTHER STORIES

RICHARD TOBABEN

DRACHIR PRESS

CONTENTS

Accidents Happen	1
Day Reclaimed	29
It's Only Business	49
Pilgrimage	69
Coffee Cake	95
A Christmas Visit	109
Extra Points	135
The Second Son	157
The Suitcase	169
Providence	183
Little Girl Lost	215
Tradition	229
Modest Heroes	257
Talent	285
Two Vigils	309
About the Author	335

ACCIDENTS HAPPEN

I

"Come in, Mr. Reynolds," the secretary said, giving him a friendly look. "Headmaster's waiting." She looked up at the clock on the wall. "Right on time," she continued. "That's good. He'll be with you in a minute." She was the overseer of the schedules and the gatekeeper to the inner sanctum. "Mr. Reynolds is here," she called.

"You may send him in, Mrs. Richards," said the voice from within, a little distant, a little bored maybe.

It was an impressive office with a massive, uncluttered mahogany desk, an Oriental carpet, and diplomas on the walls. Headmaster -Henry St. George Thatcher- stood gazing out the windows at the campus. He was dressed in a tweed sports coat and yellow sweater despite the warmth of the office and the unseasonably warm weather outside. He seemed in no hurry to begin the conversation.

Jim was there for his first contract talks as a master at Ravenwood Hall. He had not had a single conversation with the headmaster since he had been hired just before the start of the school year.

"Would you look at that, Mr. Reynolds?" Headmaster said at last, pointing outside the window with a yellow #2 pencil he had just been absently chewing on. Jim walked over but saw nothing in particular.

"Piles of dog manure," Headmaster continued. "There, and there, and there." He let Jim observe the defilement. "A regular triangle of poop." He tapped the pencil against his teeth. "I just don't know what to do about these faculty dogs. Is this the kind of folderol a headmaster should have to worry about? What if a visiting parent or board member were to step in a pile...?" He trailed off before the final phrase but continued to study the problem silently.

"Do you have a dog, Mr. Reynolds?" he finally asked.

"I do," Jim confessed, thinking it was hardly a promising start. "But he stays up on the mountain most of the time."

"Well, no matter. I'll never win the battle with the dogs." He cleared his throat by way of transition. "So, how has your first year at Ravenwood been so far?" he said, finally turning away from the offending dog manure and sitting at his desk.

"Pretty busy, sir," said Jim. "But I don't mind the routine."

"A good routine establishes good habits and good habits build strong character. It's what we believe here at Ravenwood." He paused. "From what I hear," he continued, tapping his pencil, "you're doing a satisfactory job."

He went through a checklist of what subjects Jim taught, what teams he coached, whose duty team he served with, and so on, getting help from Jim on the details. At the end, he said, "The athletic director tells me you got your bus driver's license. That's good. Bus driving is one of those jobs that make people useful. And everybody around here has got to be useful in lots of little ways."

"I help whenever I can, sir."

"I guess that's all we can ask of a first-year man," he said, looking at Jim directly for the first time as if in summative evaluation. "I think we can offer you a contract for next year. Provided, of course, all continues to go well between now and graduation."

They briefly talked about salary, and Headmaster offered him the barest of raises. "It's all I can afford to offer young faculty." He waited a moment, perhaps to see if Jim intended to negotiate, then said, "I assume you do want to return," and, without waiting for Jim to respond, added, "If not, let me know as soon as you can."

He stood up to signal the end of the discussion but didn't offer to shake. "I trust the rest of the year will go smoothly," he concluded as Jim headed to the door. "And keep being useful," he added, putting extra emphasis on the final word.

Outside the office, Jim met Cole Andrews, one of the more senior masters.

"Contract talk?" he asked. Jim nodded. "He likes to get them all in before spring break." He paused. "Everything go all right?"

"Well, we spent the first few minutes talking about dog crap. He hardly made eye contact. He asked me to fill in most of the details on what I do. But at least I know I'm useful because I drive a bus. Am I supposed to feel inspired now?"

"If you're expecting pats on the back, you've got a long wait. That's not his style. I've been here for twenty years and three headmasters. So far, he's the best I've seen. The first one had to stick his nose into everything you did. The next one thought everybody was in a conspiracy to undermine his authority. Thatcher sticks to his job. He woos the parents and the big donors. And he lets the faculty alone to do their job. He's there if you really need him. Otherwise, you're basically invisible."

"I guess invisible is OK," said Jim grudgingly.

II

Before dinner he took a long walk to unwind. To his eye, Ravenwood was the perfect image of a boarding school, the kind he had read about in novels. The academic buildings were built of local fieldstone; the headmaster's house was half-timbered; the chapel was English Gothic with stained glass windows. Beyond the scattering of faculty homes, there was a big fieldhouse at the bottom of the hill, practice fields on the far side of the road, and a small lake just inside the entrance gate. The campus had been dropped into the lap of a perfect natural setting. On one side, it was backed up against a mountain; on the other, it looked out over a panorama of rolling fields and distant blue hills, their crags eroded to rounded humps over a billion years.

Its distance from the distractions of the modern world made it a good place to realize the school's goal to "build young men in body, mind, and spirit." A bit idealistic perhaps. But he had to admit that the strict regimen of classes, study halls, athletic practices, and chapel services probably had turned lots of slothful adolescents into disciplined young men. He had grown to like the faculty and the boys and even, for the most part, the regimen. But the quiet beauty of the natural setting would be a big reason why he might stay for another year.

Jim sat with Cole and his family and a few other faculty members at dinner. It was a good time for some relaxed conversation and a chance to get away from the all-male atmosphere of the classroom and the athletic field. After dinner, he walked up the hill to his cottage at the foot of the mountain. It was a beautiful hike across a narrow stream and up a gravel road with woods on one side and pasture on the other. The sky was spangled with stars. He could now identify Orion and the Big Dipper and even a couple of planets. Tonight, in the dark, he could also make out some cows that usually grazed nearby.

There were only three houses on this side of the stream; his was the farthest up the road. By lucky accident, he had been assigned to it. When he arrived for the fall term, there were already enough masters in the dorm and all the families had bigger homes. It was his quiet retreat at the end of the day.

His dog, Magnus, a big, red Irish setter and golden retriever mix, met him near the top of the road and ran ahead to the porch waiting for his food bowl to be filled. He had inherited the hound from the previous tenant. During the day, Magnus generally roamed the mountain by himself. But at night he became the perfect indoor companion, snoring at Jim's feet while he graded papers or climbing up on the sofa with him while he watched television.

He liked the stability of the job. College had been a great four years. He had read his share of books and written his share of papers, drunk his share of beer, played his share of sports, and had a couple of romantic flings on the way to his degree in history. It was a fine college experience. But as graduation loomed, he realized he had no clear idea of what he wanted to do.

He first thought of applying to law school or grad school, but he had had enough of academia, at least for a little while. He decided to look for a job where he would be around people. He liked history; he liked sports. But with no obvious career skills, his choices seemed limited. A career counselor suggested teaching as something he could do for a year or two until he decided on a bigger plan. With no teaching certificate, the counselor suggested he apply to some private schools. Ravenwood eventually answered the call. Every so often, he thought how improbable it was that he had ended up at Ravenwood -a city boy who had never set foot in a private school and had never even thought of teaching as a career.

Just a fortunate accident, he guessed.

Even before the contract talk, he had pretty much decided to return for a second year. The fall term had been impossibly busy. Preparing for all the new classes, slogging through the routine of dormitory supervision and study halls, and driving the bus on long athletic trips had thoroughly exhausted him. He escaped from campus for the two weeks of Christmas break, wondering where he would find the energy to complete the school year.

But the winter, by contrast, had been downright relaxing. He had been assigned to supervise the winter intramural squad with no other responsibility than to be sure the boys got a little daily exercise. With Ravenwood's gym filled with basketball and wrestling practices, he usually had to take his boys outside. Most days it was too cold and snowy to play touch football or run laps around the track. Instead, he got permission to use the school's pick-up truck and chainsaw and took the boys out to cut firewood for the faculty woodstoves. He smiled to himself whenever he thought of his transformation from city boy to lumberjack and woodcutter. Before dinner, he and the younger faculty often had time to play basketball. In the evenings, he still had energy to prepare better lesson plans and grade papers. It was a routine that suited him perfectly.

The weekends offered more special treats. He got invited to dinner at the homes of his new faculty friends. For the first time in a decade, the school pond froze hard, and he learned how to ice skate. On Saturdays, he occasionally got to drive the boys on the bus to the local ski resort and, in return, spend the day gliding down the slopes for free. He could think of no more enjoyable way of being useful.

Life was good.

III

At the beginning of March, the boys headed home for spring break, leaving the campus nearly deserted. Jim had nothing in particular to do. He spent his first few days reading and hiking with Magnus and enjoying the solitude. It was just the break he needed. Everything was perfect. Perfect -except for the occasional sound of gunfire on the mountain. Though the booms seemed to be coming from high up the hillside, the situation made him uneasy. He mentioned it to Cole one day while they were fishing off the dock.

"It's the locals," Cole said. "They go hunting up there whenever school's not in session."

"Is it legal?"

"Technically, no. The mountain up to the ridgeline is all part of our property. But they don't go up there while the boys are on campus."

"The shooting is really giving me the creeps."

"Well, the school's only been here sixty years or so, and it was their land to hunt on before we arrived. So, I guess we shouldn't complain. Besides, it's most likely our folks up there."

"Our folks?" Jim said. "Who are our folks?"

"The Gregorys and the Campbells," he said. "The men at the carpentry shed, the groundskeepers, the women in the kitchen. Pretty much all of them belong to one family or the other. The school probably doesn't pay them much, so they supplement with venison or rabbit or whatever."

"In season?"

"Their season's whenever the boys aren't on campus."

"I can't believe nobody's tried to stop it."

"The previous headmasters tried. They called in the sheriff, but of course he could never figure out exactly who was doing the shooting. Folks up here practice the old mountain code of silence. And the sheriff had no intention of sending a posse up on the mountain. When Thatcher arrived, he evidently negotiated some kind of deal. Now you only hear the shooting when the boys are away. The locals seem satisfied to honor the agreement."

The news threatened to burst the little bubble of security that Jim felt in his cottage. At the foot of the mountain, he suddenly felt he was also on the edge of civilization.

The locals were still a mystery to him. Most of them lived in tiny frame houses bordering the school property or in trailers along the road up into the nearby hollow. He knew the ladies in the cafeteria by their first names and that some of them were married to the men who did the maintenance. They were pleasant and occasionally asked how his year was going. A couple of the men were friendly too. Old Henry liked to share jokes with the faculty men and included him in the group. Earl was even friendlier. He was a little guy, but wiry, strong, and hard-working. During the cold spell, he dropped off a load of split firewood from a dead tree the crew had just cut down. When the weather turned warm just before the beginning of spring break, he offered to plow up a garden patch for him. What was not to like about such helpful folks? Nothing - except for the shooting up on the mountain.

He brought up the subject of the locals again a few days later while some of the faculty men were having coffee together. Fine folks, they all agreed. Always ready to help. They each had a story about a particular favor, not just from Earl but from the other workers as well. Sharpened chainsaws, firewood, trucks of manure. Even an offer to get moonshine at the lowest price. They're good folks, everyone agreed. Really generous in their way. Salt of the earth.

There was a pause in the conversation, and Jim got the sense that they each were waiting for someone to tell him something more.

"You do know about the feud, don't you?" Mark Clemons of the English Department said at last.

Jim gave him a blank look. The others glanced at each other, smiled, and almost rubbed their hands in anticipation. Jim was about to learn a big community secret.

"These Gregorys and Campbells were regular feudin' families," continued Clemons, relishing his role as storyteller. "Part Hatfield and McCoy. Part Grangerford and Shepherdson. Part Highlander and Lowlander. I've done a little informal research over the years. First, I pumped Henry and some of the other friendlies for any colorful history or legend. It's pretty hard to separate the two. I even talked to Red one afternoon. We sat rocking on his porch while he shared a few tidbits."

"Red's the patriarch of the Gregorys," said Cole.

"More like the clan leader," said Clemons. "He lives in the house beside the back entrance to the campus, not far from you."

"You mean the hillbilly house that looks out on the road?" Jim asked.

"That very one," said Cole. "He's sharper than you might think. He owns the little grocery store down there at the intersection. And the cows that roam the pasture near your house are his also."

So, it was his cow, Jim thought, that had gotten across the cattle guard into his garden a while back.

"He's a real entrepreneur by the standards of folks around here," Clemons went on. "They respect him. When he speaks, his clan folk, at least, usually listen."

"Tell him more about the feud," one of the others said.

"Well, nobody really has any idea what started it. A jilted lover. Stolen cows. Most likely a territorial dispute over the moonshine business. I've talked to the county's commonwealth attorney and the county historian. Both confirmed that the feud is a lot more than legend but that most of the shoot-outs and such occurred back during the thirties and forties. It was a regular civil war for a while. A deputy was gunned down. They even shot up a courtroom and killed a judge during a murder trial. And, of course, they killed quite a few of each other. Estimates vary, but it's definitely in double figures."

"But that all died out years ago," said Cole. "In my twenty years here, there hasn't been a single outbreak. I certainly haven't seen any signs of hostility around here."

"Cole tells me most of the school workers are in one family or the other," said Jim.

"Far as I know, they're all related. Either directly or indirectly," said Clemons. "By marriage. By illegitimate parentage. Uncles. Nieces. Sisters-in-law. Cousins twice removed."

"How can you tell the difference?" Jim asked.

"For the most part, the Gregorys and their kin work in the kitchen and do the campus maintenance. The Campbells mow the fields, bush hog, and keep up the grounds. If you pay close attention, you'll notice the two groups don't mix much. They may not be shooting at each other anymore, but I'm not sure they've settled all the old scores. Once people get to hating each other over a few generations, they don't let go of those feelings any too easily."

So, there it was, thought Jim. People from two feuding families were shooting their guns up on the mountain behind his quiet little cottage. He just wondered what or who were they shooting at.

IV

A couple days after these revelations, he set off on a hike with Magnus that took them past Red's house. Red was sitting on his porch.

"Hey, young feller," he called. "I been seeing you and your dog walking past here most days. Why not come up and set a spell?"

Jim decided to take up the invitation to meet the clan chieftain.

"Anson Gregory," he said in a soft, husky tenor voice, getting up from his rocking chair. He stuck out a callused hand for Jim to shake. "Most folks call me Red."

He was seventy or so, Jim guessed, and completely bald, with a couple-day stubble and a big chaw of tobacco in his cheek.

"First year, right?" said Red. Jim nodded. "Fine school," he continued. "Yessir. Been a good neighbor to all of us up here on the mountain. Have a seat, son."

Jim eased into a creaking rocking chair. The small porch was littered with old tools, empty soda bottles, and assorted junk. They rocked a couple of minutes in silence. Perhaps it was in this very rocking chair, Jim thought with a smile, that Headmaster, dressed in his tweeds and tie, had negotiated terms for hunting on the mountain.

"Want to thank you for driving that frisky little heifer out of your yard and telling the boys," Red said at last. "She's a clever devil. Mighty neighborly of you."

"My pleasure."

"Where you from?" he said, scrutinizing Jim. "Not from anywhere around here, I reckon."

"No," Jim said. "I'm from up north."

"A city boy, too, I bet." Jim nodded. "Nothin' wrong with that," Red said, quietly spitting into a can. "You seem to like the country life pretty good."

"It's taken a while, but I like most things about it." They sat another minute in silence. "Have you lived here all your life?" Jim finally ventured.

"All my life," Red said. "In this here house. Raised my kids here. I'll probably die here." He spit into the can once more.

"Your kids still live in this area?" Jim asked, trying to find out how extended his family might be.

"All eight of my kids still live in the county. And their kids and their grandkids too. I got so many I lost count."

"Good spot for a house," Jim said. "You can keep track of everything going up and down the road."

"I been admiring this view for many a year. Very peaceful."

All of a sudden, there was a roar of an accelerating car engine from somewhere down the road. In a couple of seconds, a car - bright orange with racing stripes- went ripping past the house. Camaro? Dodge Charger? A big muscle car of some kind, Jim figured, but he couldn't tell which.

"Goddam kids drive like maniacs," said Red, spitting emphatically. "They all wanta be Junior Johnson and drive in the NASCAR. If'n I had a thirty ought-six by me right now, I'd have blown his tires out. Serve him right."

Jim was a little taken aback. "Do they drive like this all the time?" he asked.

"Naw. There's a few hot rodders. But it's mainly that kid in that damn orange soda-pop machine. Wish he'd drive the goddam thing into a tree."

The suddenness of the mood swing made Jim uneasy. What other anger was lurking inside Red? After a few more minutes, he got up to leave.

"Dog's waiting for me," he said by way of excuse. "It's been a pleasure."

"Come back again some time," Red said. "I enjoyed settin' with you."

V

As soon as the boys returned, the shooting stopped and life returned to normal. The spring term moved along quickly. He had used the break to plan ahead and no longer felt half-prepared for his classes. He was assigned to coach the field events for the track team and quickly took a liking to his group of young athletes. Most of them weren't especially talented, but all of them were friendly. After warm-ups, he watched them work on their technique, offering advice here and there. Between throws and jumps, he would often sit and chat with them, whiling away the time before they went inside to finish practice in the weight room.

Before he knew it, the season was over, and he was into his final reviews for exams. Graduation and summer vacation were just around the corner.

He escaped campus one beautiful Sunday to spend the day with a girl he had met recently, a grad student who would be staying around for the summer. He was in a buoyant mood as he navigated the winding road back to campus. He had almost survived his first year on the job, he felt sure that he had his contract for next year, and he had a whole summer of relaxation to look forward to. He thought about how unnervingly uncertain everything had been just a year ago when he was still trying to figure out what to do with his life.

Fortune was smiling on him.

It was almost dark when he turned onto the road that led up to the entrance to the school. He could just make out two cars, side by side, about fifty yards ahead of him. He slowed down, coming almost to a stop. It looked as though they had the road completely blocked. Be cautious, he thought. He could hear the revving of engines as though they were getting ready to race. He inched closer, squinting, trying for a better view. Suddenly, both cars peeled out.

He heard the roar of the engines and the squeal of the tires though all he could see were twin sets of taillights. The two cars seemed to be fishtailing across the roadway as they jockeyed for position.

He came to a full stop, his attention transfixed by the rapidly receding taillights. Suddenly, there was a sound like a giant explosion up ahead. A car horn started blaring. Then the taillights of the one car turned upside down again and again. He heard a tremendous crunch of shattered glass and grinding metal followed by a series of dull thuds. Meanwhile, the other set of taillights disappeared completely from sight, and the roar of the engine faded away.

He coasted up the road. Be cautious, he thought again. Go slowly. He saw the one car rolled up on its side and partially resting against an embankment down the road from the back entrance to the school. The engine had cut off, but the headlights still shone wanly on the embankment. He coasted nearer, then pulled off to the side of the road, put on his flashers, and got out to investigate. His headlights provided just enough light for him to see that someone was pinned under the car. He opened his trunk and groped around for the big flashlight he had recently bought just in case something unexpected -something like this- happened on one of these dark country roads.

He rushed over, wondering what he would do if he found someone seriously injured. He didn't know first aid or CPR. When he got to the car, however, he realized that any help he might offer would probably be useless. Right away he saw a victim. He looked to be a kid, maybe fifteen or sixteen, who had been the driver. When the car flipped, the door came open. The boy had fallen out, and the car had pinned him in its final rotation. His right arm was stretched out on the roadway; his left arm and his shoulder, chest, and legs were trapped under the car. His face was turned to the road. A little blood -not much- dripped from his nose; his jaw appeared to be broken. When Jim bent down to look more closely, he was surprised at how minor the injuries seemed to be. Then he noticed the gaping wound on the boy's chest. He was barely breathing, but Jim could hear faint moaning and saw him kneading his fingers slightly as though clutching weakly onto his fleeting life.

He wondered what he should do out there alone on this dark road. Nothing had prepared him for dealing with this kind of trauma. He had never seen a dead body before, except at a funeral. He had certainly never been near someone on the verge of death. He tried to use his cellphone to call for help, but he couldn't get a signal. He thought he should drive up to campus to have somebody call an ambulance, but he hated to leave the kid by himself. He got down on his knees and tried to feel for a pulse, mumbling a few words of comfort and staring into the boy's vacant blue eyes. He lowered his ear but could no longer hear even the shallowest sound of breathing. The boy's wounded chest was no longer moving; his fingers were still.

He pulled himself away, now sure it was time to alert people on campus. He rushed back to his car, then pulled up short at the sight of something even more chilling in the headlights. The body of another young man lay just beyond the shoulder of the road. He had been thrown out of the passenger side, and his head had smashed into a fence post. Jim needed just a quick look to feel certain he was dead already. He pulled back, repelled, but couldn't quite take his eyes off the body. The young man's face and shirt were covered in blood. His arms were thrown above his head by the force of the impact, and he had a look almost of surprise on his face. He had lost a shoe, which lay forlornly by his head. He appeared to be a few years older than the driver. Suddenly, it occurred to Jim that there might be even more bodies still to be found. He skirted the young man and peered into the field beyond the fence line, listening intently. If any other victim were still alive, he evidently wasn't able to cry out for help.

He stumbled, shaken, back to his car and as he was opening the door, he heard voices. A group of people suddenly emerged out of the darkness led by Red Gregory. He hesitated in indecision, trying to determine how to deal with the new rescuers. He couldn't very well drive away at this point without saying anything to them, even if it was just to say he was going for more help. A moment later, he heard a roar of vehicles and saw the glare of headlights coming from both directions toward the scene. One pick-up truck pulled up behind his car and another in front, boxing him in. In an instant, the road was swarming with people. At first, they paid no attention to him, as if he were invisible. One woman knelt down beside the driver, holding his hand and keening in the mountain way. Behind her stood a couple of other women.

"It's young Ethan Gregory," one woman called to the men. "Can't you lift the car off'n his chest? He might still be alive."

A troop of men gathered around to assess the situation and concluded that rocking the car to get it off might do more harm than good.

Another woman got down on her knees with her ear beside the boy's mouth. "Quiet, honey," she said to the weeper, "so's we can hear if he's still breathin'."

"Red, have somebody run up to your house to be sure the ambulance is on the way," said a third. The women had taken complete charge of ministering to the driver.

Meanwhile, the men wandered around the scene aimlessly, trying to figure out how to be useful. They soon found the young man smashed against the fence post.

"Hit's Ronnie Gregory, I think," one of the men called out and after a pause added, "'Fraid he's already dead."

Red hobbled over from the knot of people by the smashed car and confirmed the identity. "Hit's Ronnie, for sure," he said, gritting his teeth. "A good boy. A little wild, maybe. But a good boy."

A couple of the women moved over to look, but Red shooed them away. "This'll just kill Fay," said one. "What with her oldest already in prison."

Another pick-up truck pulled up, packed with people in the load bed. The driver jumped out and rushed into the melee. "Sweet Jesus," he said. "Bobby's wife called us to say she heard there was a wreck. My Elton is out somewheres, probably joyriding. Who was in the car?" He surveyed the scene and saw the two bodies. "Oh, my

God," he said, trying to hide his relief. "It's young Ethan and Ronnie."

A shout came from somewhere in the pasture beyond the fence. "There's another body over here."

The crowd, led by Red, flowed over in that direction, all afraid it was their son, their nephew, their cousin. "It's Trace Gregory, Abner's grandson," somebody called out.

The man who discovered the third body climbed back over the fence onto the road. He stood in the beam of the headlights, studying the road next to the overturned car. "Lookee here," he said. "Don't this look like another set of tire tracks? Red, take a look."

The men all came over, consulted, and agreed. There had been two cars. About this time, Red took notice of Jim for the first time.

"That your car, young feller?" he shouted, pointing at Jim's vehicle. He seemed unhinged by the carnage. Jim nodded. "You seen what happened, didn't you?"

Before Jim could answer, Red shouted to the crowd, "We got a witness. We got a witness. This feller was here. He saw the whole thing."

"Looks to me like there was drag racing goin' on," said one of the other men. "Ask him whether he saw any drag racin', Red."

Red turned to Jim. "You heard the man," he said in a voice ominous, almost threatening. "There was a drag race goin' on, wasn't there?"

Jim didn't answer either way, but his silence was enough for Red. "I knew it," he said in a fury. He thought for a second. "There's only one car I can think of fast enough to run these boys off the road. That orange piece of shit. You know the one I'm talking about?"

The other men consulted for a minute, trying to recall fast cars from around the county. "You mean that orange Camaro Seth Campbell's boy drives?" said one of them at last.

"The very one," Red shouted triumphantly. "I mighta knowed. Seth Campbell's boy, you say?" The man nodded. "That boy's trouble just like his daddy and his gran'daddy before him," Red snarled.

The others quickly accepted the speculation as truth. Soon they had all confirmed that they had seen the boy racing around roads in every corner of the county. The mood was turning uglier by the second.

Fortunately, just at that moment the sound of sirens could be heard in the distance. Help was finally arriving. An ambulance and the sheriff pulled up together. The attention quickly shifted away from Jim, but he still felt the threat. Some of their own had just died in a terrible accident, and they expected him to finger the killer. He wished he could don a cloak of invisibility and disappear. But as the EMTs began sorting out the carnage, Red went right over to the sheriff.

"This young feller," he shouted over the siren, "saw the whole thing." He pointed to Jim. "He's the one can identify who done this. Looks like murder to me."

Some of the other men moved over and crowded around the sheriff. Red took Jim's arm as though to escort him over to make his statement. "Here he is, sheriff," he said. "Here's your witness."

The sheriff, heavy-set and approaching middle-age, looked uneasy as though overmatched by Red and the crowd. "Take it easy, sir," he said to Red. "There'll be time for investigation after we get all this sorted out." He gestured to the EMTs, who were lifting Ronnie's body onto a gurney.

"We know pretty well who done this, sheriff. Seems like you'd be wanting to get the witness's story soon as possible."

"What's your name, sir?" the sheriff asked Red, looking him in the eye and trying to establish his authority as he pulled a notepad and pen out of his pocket. But Red wasn't about to be cowed.

"It ain't me you want to talk to," Red repeated, moving in close to him, his chin out, his jaw set, the image of primal rage.

"I'm asking your name," said the sheriff. "Just your name. I hope you don't mind if I conduct the investigation, not you."

The crowd had now gathered in hostile silence to hear the exchange. It looked like a face-off between county law and clan law.

Just then another car, long and sleek as a limousine, approached from the direction of the school, parting the crowd like the Red Sea. The crowd's attention now turned away from Red and the sheriff. The car stopped, and Headmaster emerged from the passenger side of the front seat. He walked directly up to the sheriff without looking either at the crowd or the overturned car. As he approached, he saw Jim standing nearby and paused to assess the situation.

"This is Mr. Reynolds," he said peremptorily, nodding toward Jim. "He is one of our faculty members."

The sheriff evidently recognized Headmaster without introduction. "Apparently, sir," he said almost apologetically, "he's the only witness to this accident. We'll need a statement from him."

Headmaster looked over Jim's way and considered for a moment. "I'd like to take him back to campus now," he said decisively. "I'm sure he'll be able to make a full statement at the appropriate time and in the appropriate place."

The crowd remained hushed. They looked at Headmaster, cool in his coat and tie, and at the sheriff, noticeably sweating under the pressure.

"Sheriff," Red's husky tenor voice sounded, intent on making it a three-way conversation. "There's no need for a fancy, formal investigation. This young feller saw it all. Tell 'em what you saw, son," he said, almost paternally now. "There was a drag race, wasn't there? And a orange car -what kind did you say it was?" He looked this time for help not from Jim but from the man who had discovered the tire tracks. "A Camaro? Well, anyway, this orange car run 'em off the road." He paused and pinned Jim to a spot with a stare. "That's what happened, wasn't it?"

"I can't honestly say," said Jim in a low voice.

"What did you say, boy?" asked Red, his voice rising again in irritation. "I can't hear you."

"I said I can't really say anything about the other car," Jim said, loud enough now for everyone to hear. "I just didn't see it." He was suddenly mad as hell that this old man should try to bully him into making up the truth.

Red looked as if he were about to fly into another rage. Jim felt Headmaster take him by the arm and lead him to the car. Just then a burst of sirens was heard back up the road. Hopefully, Jim thought, it was state troopers coming to the rescue.

"Why don't we wait till tomorrow for Mr. Reynolds to give you his statement?" said Headmaster as they got to the car door. "I can vouch for him." The sheriff nodded as though relieved to have the decision made for him and turned to the restive crowd.

Headmaster ushered Jim into the backseat and directed the assistant headmaster to drive Jim's car back to campus. Then before he got in, he turned and looked directly at Red. "Mr. Gregory, you'll have to be patient," he said, all diplomacy and ice. "We'll be sure the authorities have all the information that can be provided to get to the bottom of this. We'll do our part to see that justice is done."

Without waiting for Red to reply, he got into the car, and they drove off.

VI

Back on campus, there were lights on in all the dorm rooms despite the fact that it was almost time for lights out. News travels fast, Jim thought. Especially bad news. Headmaster barely said a word, evidently preferring to leave the details of the investigation to the police. He did offer to let Jim sleep in the guest room of his house for the night. When Jim politely refused, he quietly had him driven up to his cottage. At first, Jim was almost suffocated by the absolute darkness, but as he got out of the car, he heard Magnus's reassuring bark from the porch.

"Are you sure you want to stay up here by yourself?" Headmaster asked.

"I'll be all right," Jim answered. "I've got the dog."

"Come see me after breakfast, Mr. Reynolds," he said. "I'll have someone drive you in to talk to the sheriff." He paused. "Be assured that you have our support."

For some reason, Jim couldn't bring himself to say thanks. The car waited with its headlights on the front porch till he got inside and turned on the lights.

The formal interview with the sheriff and then with the commonwealth's attorney went fairly easily. He really had nothing much to tell them. He had seen two sets of taillights. There had been a race and a crash. Then the other car sped off into the distance. He thought the two cars might have bumped, but he couldn't say for sure. He hadn't seen anything that could help identify the other car. He had heard it peel out, its tires squeal, and the roar as it accelerated away. That was all. Several times he assured them he couldn't possibly be certain it was the same orange Camaro that he and Red had seen or any other orange hot rod for that matter. In the end, they seemed satisfied.

The faculty were tremendously supportive over the following days. He was almost surprised at how excited he felt to be able to tell the story in all its lurid details. But there was a sense of unease on campus. Though none of the boys asked him about the incident, he knew the story had made the rounds; whether they had gotten it accurately or not he didn't know. Headmaster let him know that he had talked to the commonwealth's attorney and that Jim almost certainly wouldn't be called to give any further testimony, unless perhaps there was a trial. Unless there was a trial, Jim thought. That left him far from relieved. The little nightmare wasn't over yet. Somewhere, the driver of the phantom car -orange Camaro or whatever- was probably still speeding around the county roads. And the victims' kin were still probably holding Jim at least partly responsible that the driver wasn't sitting in jail awaiting trial. The campus workers seemed to deliberately avoid speaking to him. He could only imagine what they were thinking.

A week before graduation, unease on campus turned to actual violence. Bright and early on a Monday morning, someone took a shot at one of the Campbells while he was across the road mowing the athletic fields. The bullet hit the rear fender of the tractor, ricocheted, and broke the driver's right arm. No arrest was made. The next day one of the Gregorys was cutting a dead tree just fifty yards behind the chapel when a bullet whizzed past him. Again, no suspect, no arrest.

Worse still for Jim, he was the target of some pretty obvious small acts of retaliation. As he and Magnus got to the house one evening after dinner, Magnus sniffed out something suspicious and began barking frenziedly. Someone had dumped a big possum onto his side porch, its blind eyes still staring out, and its needle teeth exposed. Revolted, Jim shoveled up the maimed carcass and carried it out into the trees well beyond his cottage. On the way, he discovered a break in the fence seemingly made by wire cutters. The next afternoon he found that someone had apparently led a couple of cows into his garden, where they had trampled his vegetable plot and torn up what little grass he had. Most disturbing, that evening just before sunset he heard a series of gunshots that seemed to be coming from just a little way up the mountain. Anger and fear competed for his attention. For the first time, he wished he owned a gun.

Magnus heard the shots also and went from door to door growling. Jim briefly considered going down to campus, but he didn't want to find himself in anyone's rifle range. Then he pulled himself up short. Someone, he thought, was up there playing games with his mind; he resolved he wouldn't give in to paranoia. The phone rang. A couple of the faculty had also heard the shots and wondered if he were all right by himself up on the mountain. He assured them he was fine. He wasn't going to let anyone drive him out of his own home. He shut off all the lights and sat awake listening for at least two hours, but heard no more gunshots. The quiet was unnerving. Magnus paced restlessly around the house; never before was he so thankful to have the dog. Finally, in exhaustion he fell asleep.

The next morning Headmaster called him to his office, sending one of the other masters to cover the last of his exams. He motioned Jim to sit down.

"Hold any calls for the time being, Mrs. Richards," he said. He looked at Jim without smiling. "I hear there has been some unpleasantry up at your house in the last couple of days."

"There have been some incidents," Jim said without offering any details.

"Mr. Andrews told me there were gunshots above your house yesterday evening. Is that true?" Jim nodded in affirmation. "I've made arrangements for you to move down here on campus for the near future, Mr. Reynolds. You should be quite comfortable. I don't want my faculty endangered in any way."

"I'll be all right at my cottage," Jim said. "I've got my dog there with me."

Headmaster looked at him skeptically but decided not to argue the point, at least for the time being. He sat for a moment in silence, tapping his pencil.

"You won't be surprised to know that this whole situation has created considerable unease. For you, of course. And for the whole school." He paused. "I've had calls from parents worried about their sons' safety. I've reassured them there's nothing to be worried about. The county law officers are working to solve the problem, and the campus is perfectly secure. But I can sympathize with their feelings."

Jim listened in silence. He suspected that some of the parents had threatened to pull their sons out even before exams were finished and perhaps not send them back next year.

"This morning," Headmaster continued, "I got a call from the chairman of the board of trustees." He started tapping his pencil again, perhaps the only indication of the pressure he was feeling. "He asked some mighty hard questions about what we intend to do about security." He paused, but still tapped the pencil. "We have got to ensure the safety of our boys," he continued. "It's our number one duty. You see our problem here, don't you, Mr. Reynolds?"

Jim nodded.

"I've talked to Anson Gregory. He has cooled down and seems to accept that there was nothing more you could have told the sheriff. But he doesn't necessarily speak for everyone in his family, much less those in the other family."

Jim began to see the direction the discussion was probably going.

"You've had a good year," Headmaster continued. "The faculty like you. The boys seem to like you." He looked up and paused. "But maybe with all that's happened, you might find that a change of atmosphere would be a good thing."

How rich, Jim thought, to be in the presence of the headmaster of diplomacy! He decided, then and there, not to engage politely in any negotiations to get rid of him. He flatly would refuse to accept the role of scapegoat with good grace.

"I know headmasters at some fine schools who would be eager to consider you for a faculty position," continued Headmaster, sensing resistance and not making eye contact. "Take your time," he concluded. "Think about things. We'll talk about your future again after graduation."

Jim got up and left without further word. As he went out the door, he heard Headmaster say, in a tired voice, "Mrs. Richards, get Mr. Churchill on the phone. We've got graduation plans to make." Jim realized that the situation was taking a toll on him as well.

He went dutifully back to the exam hall. Most of the boys had finished their exams and gone back to the dorm. They were underclassmen and would be heading out that afternoon. He wondered how they would remember him in light of all that had happened. One by one, the last of them turned in their exams and wished him a good summer vacation as they headed out the door to freedom. If they felt uneasy, they gave no sign. They were teen-agers eager for vacation. They probably had short memories.

He spent the afternoon by himself in his classroom trying to grade exams, but his concentration was short. He kept going back to his uncertain future. One part of him was infuriated that they wanted him out -parents, faceless board members, probably Headmaster himself. Another part of him, at some level, understood how they felt. Maybe leaving would be the best thing. He had never really expected to stay more than a year or two anyway. The teaching had been pretty good, but he wasn't sure he wanted to do it for the long haul. Besides, did he really want to spend another year on the edge of civilization among a bunch of murderous mountain people? But then his indignation and sense of injustice welled up again. Why should he have to be the victim? Why should he have to be the scapegoat?

He ate dinner quickly. Once again several of his friends offered to let him sleep in their guestrooms, but he was adamant. No one was going to drive him out of his home. Magnus met him part way up the road. Today they found no unwanted gifts, no dead possums, no cows wandering about. The break in the fence was still there, but it didn't appear any larger. Magnus went straight to his food bowl. Jim saw him sniff at something in it. Instinctively, in his firmest voice of command he said, "Here, boy. Here, boy. Get away from there." The bowl should have been empty. Magnus had finished all his food that morning before Jim headed down to campus. The dog pulled up his head and obediently came over. Jim saw something in the bowl -strong-smelling, greasy, rancid. Whatever it was, Magnus didn't seem inclined to eat it. Jim sniffed it carefully. Poison, he thought. Someone was trying to poison his dog.

He let loose a volley of expletives. Magnus looked at him with his head cocked in surprise, unused to hearing him raise his voice. He locked the dog in the house and took a box of plastic bags outside. There was no telling what else might have been left around. More tainted food. A hunter's trap. He scoured the underbrush but found nothing. Then he bagged up the food bowl and its contents, evidence for an investigation that would probably never take place.

It was time to air his feelings. It was time for justice. He put Magnus on a leash, grabbed the bag, and headed down to campus. Even though it was almost seven o'clock, there were lights still on in Headmaster's office. He strode into the administrative building without seeing anyone else. Magnus, though not used to being on a leash, followed behind him obediently. Mrs. Richards was still at her desk. She was about to reprimand him for barging into the office unannounced and daring to bring the dog with him, but decided not to speak. He walked right past as though she weren't there.

Headmaster looked up from what he was doing but hardly batted an eye. Unflappable. Cool in every situation. This reception drained away most of Jim's immediate anger. Now that he was there, he realized he didn't know exactly what to say. He had made up a garbled speech on the way down, but it seemed pointless to say anything. Instead of speaking, Headmaster waited for Jim to begin. The wait defused his anger even more. He laid out the litany of things that had happened over the past few days while Headmaster listened patiently. He held up the bag of evidence. What was the school going to do about this latest harassment? When would he get justice?

Now that he had spilled out his anger, his mind was suddenly clearer and more focused. He felt sure of his next step. It was time to pack up and leave, a few days before graduation. No regrets. No farewells. He certainly wouldn't be asking Headmaster for any recommendations. The break had to be quick and complete.

"Before you go on, Mr. Reynolds," Headmaster said, in his most measured voice, "I have a piece of information to share that might influence any immediate actions you are considering." He cleared his throat and tapped his pencil in his habitual manner. "I had a call just a short time ago," he continued, "from the commonwealth's attorney. He's a Ravenwood graduate himself. It was, you might say, a professional, not a social call. He told me that the sheriff had gotten an anonymous tip about an accident just on the other side of our mountain. It seems that when the sheriff arrived at the location, nobody was around. But there, twenty yards off the road and smashed headlong into a big tree, was a car. An orange Camaro, to be exact. The driver, a young man, was dead inside the car, his chest crushed by the steering wheel. There was no definite sign of foul play, according to the sheriff, but they are investigating. The story will be in tomorrow's paper, but he thought I would want to know as soon as possible."

Jim felt a chill along his spine.

"It appears," Headmaster continued, "that justice may have been served after all." He let Jim process the implications. "Now I assume that you came here to tell me something more than you've said so far. Before you do, I want you to think over the situation. Your job's still here if you want it. If you don't, that's your choice. Either way, you've earned my support."

Jim suddenly felt his anger drain entirely away. "What about the locals?" he said.

"Well, I can't speak for them. We know they've got long memories. And I suspect some of them probably used the accident as an excuse to settle unrelated personal grievances. I've talked to Mr. Gregory again. He's fundamentally a reasonable man. He swore once more that he doesn't hold you responsible. And as you certainly saw, he's got influence."

Jim stood there in silence, holding onto Magnus's leash and the bag of tainted food. Absurd, he thought. The whole situation was so absurd. Then he said the most absurd thing himself. "So, what you're saying is that if I stay, you can be sure I'll be safe." He knew as soon as he said the words how absurd they sounded.

Headmaster fixed him with his blue eyes. "You should know as well as I do, Mr. Reynolds, that the world isn't a safe place. Not here. Not anywhere. There's a possible accident around every corner."

He paused, then added, "Think about what you want to do. No need to give me any answers right away. Take your dog and go on vacation for a while. We'll talk when you get back."

He stood up to signal that the conversation was over but walked Jim to the door. When they got there, he reached down and gave Magnus a single pat on the head. "Good dog," he said.

"Thank you, Headmaster," Jim heard himself say as he stepped out the door. They were words he couldn't have imagined himself saying ten minutes before.

As he walked back up the mountain, Jim began to put the big picture a little more clearly in focus. Though he almost hated to admit it, Henry St. George Thatcher had handled the whole situation with a masterly mix of authority and diplomacy. And he had offered up a small but useful nugget of wisdom. The world isn't safe, and it's often only accidentally just. That was as true here as anywhere.

He would just have to learn to deal with it.

DAY RECLAIMED

I

Tom Wolfe sipped his coffee, browsed the morning headlines, and eased into meditative repose in the warmth of the morning sun. It was a routine he had followed in his inner sanctum most mornings since his retirement. At almost three score and ten, he could afford such idle pleasures.

Actually, he would have preferred a more active life. Not that he was sedentary. He went to the gym most days and exercised as vigorously as his stiff joints allowed. He volunteered in the community. He met old friends at the coffee shop to solve the world's problems. He traveled. But still he felt his life getting smaller and less vital. It was partly the little health issues that had become more numerous and sometimes chronic. Partly that his desire was burning less intensely. And partly that he seemed to be filling his time without a credible sense of accomplishment.

Yes, retirement is great, he assured his younger friends who were still happily burdened with careers. But in reality he was obsessed by the existential reality of aging. His prayer dialogue with the Creator -was it dialogue or monologue?- always seemed to return to the same question: Why have You saddled your creatures with such a long slog through old age to death?

Today, one headline captured his attention: "Astronomers say 8.8 billion Earth-size planets could support life." He wasn't quite sure how to feel knowing that there might actually be billions of other inhabited worlds and untold millions of billions of creatures perhaps on the same pilgrimage from life to death as he was. Were they all struggling with it as much as he was? Or did they have other natural laws and follow life cycles less inexorable, if not less final?

His mind drifted to an idea that had been part of his prayer dialogues for a few years now. Lord, why not grant your creatures periodic pauses along the path to old age? Or better yet, why not let us periodically relive days from our childhood, our youth, even our middle years -happy days preferably, or even mundane ones- but days when we were not so aware of age and decay? He occasionally lapsed into reveries about which days he might want to relive, trying to call up not just the bare events but the entire state of body, mind, and soul. It was a meditation exercise in reverse, recreating an earlier self instead of extinguishing the present one.

As usual, his effort broke down fairly quickly. His previous selves all seemed beyond the reach of his current one, except perhaps by divine intervention. As he sat trying to lose himself in fantasy, he intoned the words, "Happy memories, happy thoughts," under his breath in a mantra he occasionally relied on when the dialogue broke down. He put the paper on the coffee table. The clock said 9:30, the time he usually roused himself to some more productive task. But he felt overwhelmed by a sensation of heaviness and a desire to sleep. "Happy memories, happy thoughts," he intoned.

"Just what I've come to bring," he heard a voice say out of his fog.

He looked up to see a stranger bathed in a pool of light sitting in the one chair in the room normally out of the range of the sun. The stranger had a long face with a high forehead, white blond hair, sharp features, intensely blue eyes, and pointed ears tight to his skull. He had his feet propped on the coffee table and the paper spread out on his lap.

"My, my, what a violent and argumentative world you live in! Civil wars, religious strife, government shutdowns, not to mention murder, robbery, and rape. How can you stand to read about it each day?"

Tom stared speechless.

"My apologies," the stranger continued. "Sylvanus Engel, at your service." And seeing amazement yield to suspicion and fear, he added, "Just visiting from the planet Terrapax. Actually, not just visiting, but on a specific mission."

"Terrapax?" said Tom incredulously.

"Yes, quite a few light years away, but definitely within the galaxy." He scanned the paper again. "Quite an interesting article about the billions of just-right planets. Have you been unaware up till now of all the rest of us living out there?" He gestured vaguely toward 'out there.'

"Engel?" Tom asked. "Are you..."

"Not an angel, Tom. Just a mortal visitor from one of those 8.8 billion planets. The Creator sent me to help you as His Son is redeeming a world in another galaxy. You can't imagine how busy He is."

If this were a dream, Tom thought, it was the most curious one he had ever had.

"We on Terrapax have been studying you Earthlings for," the stranger calculated a bit, "thousands of years. You've made some progress toward becoming civilized. Let's see. No more human sacrifice. No more slavery. No more executing heretics, at least in your country. You're a little less violent -except in your movies and sports. A little less dishonest -except in the world of finance and politics. A little more concerned about the welfare of the under-privileged -except in certain states of your country."

"But a pretty woeful world nonetheless," said Tom.

"Actually, better than a number of others I've visited."

"Is life so different than on Terrapax?"

"Yes, Tom, it is. We've lived through all your stages and isms over the eons: the hunter- gatherer stage, the tribe, the clan, the kingdom; feudalism, mercantilism, capitalism, socialism, the technocratic state. We've mastered the art of genetic engineering, the discipline of self-control, the science of managing resources, the art of cooperative living. We've evolved a lot faster than you. And as our reward, we live long, happy, vital, and passionate lives."

"Eternal lives?"

"No, not eternal. The Creator won't permanently override His own basic law of nature. Everything that is born must eventually die, at least in the impermanent and temporal form in which it comes into existence. But we're able to stay healthy and vital till the very end and approach death without anxiety."

"Sounds as if you've managed to create the utopia we paltry Earthlings have long sought."

"Not quite. But we're working on it. With the Creator's help, of course."

"So why have you come to our hapless little world?"

"As I said, I'm on a mission. The Creator has recognized one of the newest challenges to finding happiness in your world. Not the biggest, but one He would like to address. He used to hear over and over again the same complaint: Life is too short. Disease, war, famine kill most people long before their bodies have time to wear out. Only recently has He begun to hear a new complaint: Life is too long. Advances in medical science, an abundance of food, and wars fought on a smaller scale by professional soldiers have all extended life without extending health and vitality. Anyway, the Creator has kept an ear open to your prayers, Tom, and rather likes one of your ideas. He listens more carefully than even the strongest believers realize."

"Which idea?"

"Why, the idea of letting you relive a random day from your past every now and then to reverse temporarily the ultimately irreversible process of aging."

Tom reflected for a moment. "So you're saying He's willing to override one of his laws of nature just to give an ordinary guy like me a little extra happiness?"

"Precisely. He's always been ready to perform a miracle when the occasion warrants it though He's disciplined Himself to use the power sparingly."

"And the Creator is going to let me travel back to the past. Is that it?"

"That's the plan, Tom. But just, of course, for a single day. Are you ready and willing? The Creator wants you to decide. You know, free will and so forth. It's no go unless you agree."

It was wish fulfillment unlike any Tom could imagine. Damn the details. How could he refuse? He looked his visitor in the eyes and said, "All right, then, beam me up, Sylvanus."

II

Young Tom Wolfe wakes up in sunshine. It's nine o'clock Saturday. The school year's ended; exams are done. No hurry to get up - except it's his week off before the summer job starts. It's his beach week. He kicks off his covers and leaps up with a burst of energy, revitalized after the usual night of uninterrupted, seemingly dreamless sleep.

In the bathroom, he shaves and admires himself in the mirror, flexing the biceps and the pecs a bit. Gotta look good for the beach babes, he thinks. Then he throws some underwear, some tee shirts, a couple pairs of shorts, and his surfer's baggies into a duffel bag along with his shaving kit. Keep it simple. That's his mantra. But he throws in one nice striped pullover shirt just in case.

Downstairs, his father is sitting at the kitchen table, scanning the headlines.

"So, what's in the news, Pops?" he asks. It's the usual morning conversation opener.

"NASA's gearing up for another moonshot, Tommy Boy. Can

you imagine? Won't be long before we're exploring other solar systems."

He could care less about men on the moon or men from outer space, not with a carefree week at the beach waiting.

"What time are you leaving, sweetie?" his mom wants to know. "I'd like to make you a good hot breakfast before you go. You probably won't eat anything but pizza and burgers while you're away."

"No time, Mom," he says. "Gordon will be here any minute now."

"Did you pack everything you need?" she asks, looking at his slim duffel bag.

"Check."

"Are you sure Ricky's parents don't mind you staying by yourselves at his place?"

"They're totally on board."

She's going through the maternal checklist now. "Did you take suntan lotion?" "I won't use it." She frowns but says nothing. "Towels?" "Check." Toothpaste?" "Check."

"Money?" his father chimes in.

"Enough to hold me," he says.

"Here's a little extra," his father says, "For a special occasion." He reaches into his wallet and pulls out a twenty. "Don't blow it all at once."

"Thanks, Pops," he says, "You're an ace."

He hears a honk outside the house. "Gotta run."

"I know you'll have fun," his mother says, and he knows she's thinking, 'Please don't get into trouble.'

He grabs his duffel, and she walks him out. Gordon's out in the driveway, making room on the rack atop his VW bus so Tom can load his surfboard.

"Hey, Mrs. W," he says in his always loud and overfriendly voice. His mother always says he reminds her of Eddie Haskell. "I'll take good care of your boy."

Then they're off. Untethered. Gordo -Gordon Fletcher Chilton the Fourth- drives like a madman. But then he is a bit of a madman:

long, white-blond hair flying whenever he swings his head, mobile features, constant chatter, weird mannerisms, a regular perpetual motion machine. Annoying at times, but entertaining and mainly harmless. Still, he makes Tom wonder sometimes exactly how people pick their friends.

Out on the highway, he cranks up the volume on the staticky radio. Top 40 Hits: Motown, the Rolling Stones, the Beatles, and best of all the Beach Boys crooning "Good Vibrations." With the windows rolled down, the wind whips through their hair. Two girls in an MG convertible pass them. Gordo honks the horn and calls out, but they don't even give him a glance. Guys in VW buses evidently don't rate with girls in sports cars. "Your loss," Gordo bellows as the bus belches smoke trying to catch up.

In another hour, the familiar landmarks begin to appear. In the distance they can see the causeway across the bay and smell the salt in the air.

"Bayshores," yells Gordo as they pass the most popular dance club. "I know a guy who can get us in." His attention is all over the map.

"Right turn here, doofus," says Tom as they're part way into the intersection beyond the bridge. Gordo takes the turn on two wheels.

They pull up in front of Ricky's house on the bay. He's in the yard waxing his board.

"Party central," announces Gordo.

"Not likely," says Ricky.

They drive across the island to a beach that usually has pretty good surf. Today it isn't pretty good. It's just about perfect. A nice little land breeze is holding up the waves, which are breaking well offshore in a beautiful tubular curl. Beyond the break, the ocean is glassy and sparkling. It is September surf but in late June instead.

Gordo is first in the water, first on a wave, and first to make a spectacular wipeout. Ricky eases in next; the water is cold, but he has nature's best wetsuit, a little body fat. Tom paddles out beyond the break and sits for a while, rocking on the gathering swells and enjoying the sun on his shoulders. Then he catches his first ride, just a two-footer or so but with perfect form and a concentrated energy. He barely has to shift his weight to keep the board trim and maximize his speed across the face. He makes a perfect kick-out at the end and celebrates with a whoop before padding back out.

After that, the wave sets keep rolling in, providing one good ride after another. Between rides he watches pelicans glide just above the water, gulls wheel and squawk overhead, and flying fish break the surface by his board. He is in perfect harmony with nature. He goes up and stretches out on the beach for a while, letting the sun knead and uncoil the muscles in his shoulders and drive the chill out of his body. Then he heads back for more rides.

Time stands still...

Until Gordo announces, “Chow time. The girls at the Grill have been aching to see me since last summer. Free food’s on me.”

A wild ride, trailing plumes of exhaust, and they are at the boardwalk. The inside of the Grill is all knotty pine, college pennants, booths with vinyl-covered benches, sizzling burgers, and a bevy of good-looking waitresses.

Their waitress comes around to take their orders. Something about her attracts Tom right off: long brown hair pulled back in a ponytail with a few stray wisps escaping, nice blue eyes, pretty features, and no make-up. In her waitress’s uniform, he can’t tell too much about her figure, but she moves in a graceful, confident way. An athlete maybe.

“I don’t remember you from last year,” Gordo begins, ready to try out his moves. “First year at the shore?”

“First year here,” she says a little coolly, instinctively feeling the flow of testosterone. She doesn’t offer Gordo even a hint of a smile as she takes their orders.

While they wait, he overhears her talking to a middle-age couple in the booth behind them and quietly gathers useful information. She goes to college upstate, not far from where he goes. It’s her second week on the job. The tips are good. She only wishes she had more time to work on her tan.

Soon she's back with their plates of food. Gordo tries a few more lame witticisms. Even Ricky tries to impress her with some surfing gabble. He, however, plays it cool. They inhale their burgers, fries, and cokes. Hungry heroes of the surf, their bodies effortlessly convert the calories into energy. She comes back to refill their drinks, and he notices the name on her identity badge: Samantha. She waits on the other tables but never seems to drift too far away. She comes back to refill his drink once more. Does she deliberately brush against him as she pours?

Gordo orders a banana split. Manic metabolism at work. While he devours it, they talk, but not really about anything important. The past year in school hardly exists in their memory. They exchange a few fantasies about last summer's big waves and big conquests. They hung out together most of the summer, but no one wants to puncture the balloon of anyone else's lies. Best of all, they laugh about the shared memories of things that actually happened: when they took the boat up the cedar creek and ran aground in front of the nudist camp; when they almost got nabbed by the cops during the beer party on the beach; when they took the great surfing safari to the beaches to the south. Nobody could have better stories. No buds could be tighter.

Finally, they call for the check. Though his wallet isn't exactly bulging with bills, he discreetly leaves a nice tip, then deliberately pulls up the rear at the cash register. On the pretext of having to take a leak, he lets them go outside without him. He's not usually very forward about asking girls out, but he has a good feeling about Samantha. She walks over to clear the table and, it seems, takes the long way there right by the register. Does he dare? If she refuses, it might make future visits awkward. But he feels confident.

"Samantha," he says.

She seems complimented that he knows her name, slows down, and gives him a sidelong glance.

"I couldn't help overhearing where you go to college," he begins, playing the only card he has. "I go to State. I was up your way for the football game last fall."

"Really," she says with a smile. "I was at that game too. You killed us if I remember right."

He shrugs as if in apology. "I can't say I remember much about the game." The conversation is threatening to go nowhere. "Funny. The one thing I do remember is that your team wiped out half our marching band when they came running out of the locker room for the second half."

"What a disaster!" she laughs. "It was definitely the highlight of the afternoon."

He laughs too. It was just the accidental icebreaker he needed. He can't quite figure out what to say next so he decides to be straightforward.

"Since we sort of know each other so well, how would you like to go out?" He pauses. "Sometime," he adds.

She considers.

"How about tonight?" he says, seizing the moment.

She tilts her head back and considers further. "I've got to work till nine, but maybe for a while afterwards."

"I'll be back at 8:55," he says, with perhaps a little excessive enthusiasm, and turns to go.

"Aren't you going to tell me your name?" she asks before he gets to the door.

"Tom," he says, a little embarrassed, but her wry smile says she likes the fact that he obviously isn't a player.

"Just call me Sam," she says. "See you tonight."

Sam, he thinks. He likes the simplicity of the name. A girl with no phoniness or frills.

"Sure took you a while in the john," Gordo says suspiciously when he gets outside. Tom considers but decides to savor his little secret.

Some clouds have rolled in, the wind has shifted off the ocean, and the surf is choppy. They try another surfing spot by a pier, but the morning's perfect surf is breaking somewhere else. "Sucks," Gordo concludes, and they load up their boards for the day. Tom could care less. Too many perfect waves eventually get boring. Besides, he has other things on his mind.

They head back to Ricky's house. It has a dock to crab off, a boat with a key, and not a single adult. They crank up some tunes. Gordo heads for the refrigerator and discovers three six-packs of beer. "A friend generously procured them for us," Ricky says. "Three bucks should pay for your third. Don't drink it all today."

Gordo considers this limit on his freedom. "How'd you convince your parents to stay away?" he asks.

"They trust me," says Ricky. "Have fun, my old man told me. Just don't make me come down to bail you out." Ground rules set, Tom thinks from the deck.

The hours slide by. His brain is idle. The clouds have drifted off to other places, leaving the dock windless, warm, and quiet. A few cars cross the nearby causeway. A few boats churn up a wake that splashes against the bulkhead. Gulls settle on nearby pilings; an egret stalks crabs in the shallows of a marshy island. He's hungry, but dinner's almost too much trouble. Ricky, the master of the castle, is checking out the boat. "Tank's full," he announces with satisfaction. "We can take 'er out tomorrow." Gordo is fidgety as always. "What's for dinner?" he asks. Nobody has a plan till Ricky, the practical one, offers to go for pizza. "Pony up, boys," he says. "Let's see," three bucks each should do it." Gordo starts to protest. "Gas and tip included," Ricky adds. Then he's gone.

By 8:30, the sun is a red half-circle oozing out pastel pink and blue along the horizon. The pizza's gone; so are most of the chips and a third of the beer. The other two are bored and still hungry. What to do? The lights from the clubs across the causeway are blinking on and off and beckoning. But can they get in? Gordo reassures them with bravado: "I know people. A bouncer, one of the bartenders. They won't card us. You'll see." He's already seen Gordo's assurances fall through, but Ricky's willing to give it a try. In five minutes they're ready to roll, but then he tells them he's not going. They eye him suspiciously.

"Going to bed early?" Gordo mocks him.

"I've got plans," he says mysteriously.

"You hit on the waitress," Gordo says in pretended outrage. "I knew you were up to something."

"Maybe," he says, enjoying the moment, their surprise, their small jealousy.

He's at the Grill at 8:55 sharp and wearing the new striped pullover he threw into the bag at the last moment. He hangs around outside while she finishes her shift. The crowd on the boardwalk has already begun to thin. Families with kids are heading home to bed. So are the old folks, he guesses. That leaves the place mostly to the young folks who can't get into the clubs. He stands looking over the ocean, which has barely a ripple. An early moon is part way up the sky. The air is still fairly warm, almost balmy. He hasn't even thought about a plan for the night. His mind is pleasantly blank.

He feels someone poke him in the ribs. "You look lonely," she says playfully. "Care to take a stroll?"

"Is this a pick-up?" he asks and she laughs. "You look nice," he adds and indeed she does. She has changed out of her waitress's uniform somewhere and has let the ponytail out of its corral. The short-shorts and short-sleeve top show off her slim waist, long legs, and nice shoulders.

The conversation begins a little formally. Where are you from? How do you like college? What's your major? The usual questions. She's a chemistry major. Serious stuff, he thinks, particularly for a girl. He wonders for a second if she's going to be too smart for him. His major? English, he confesses, with a minor in history. What's he want to do? Actually, he hasn't thought too much about it. Law school, he offers as a possibility. Or maybe work on a political campaign. Or grad school. Fortunately, she doesn't pursue the topic too hard.

"I was at State a couple times last year," she says to lighten things up.

"Really?" he says. "What for?"

"The first time was a blind date my roommate arranged." He waits for more information. "A party at Zeta something something."

"Ah, Zeta, the House of Snobs," he says and then wishes he hadn't passed judgment so quickly.

"Right on," she says with a laugh. "The parties were kind of a bore." She pauses. "Needless to say, I never heard from the guy again."

"Are you a sorority girl?" he asks.

"Not me," she says. "Too much gossip. Too much drama. How about you? Are you a frat boy?"

He tries to read the tone of 'frat boy.'

"Loyal member of the Lambdas," he says. "A band of brothers devoted to the three pillars of brotherhood: drinking beer, playing sports, and letting the good times roll. Such is our lofty ideal." She seems to like the answer.

"When else were you on campus?" he asks.

"I came over during the winter for the Smokey Robinson concert."

"Was that not the most amazing concert ever!" he says.

"He's got a voice like velvet," she says. "And somehow when he delivers the lyrics, you believe in his sincerity."

"So you were at that concert too," he muses. "Did you notice me in the crowd?"

"I think I heard you singing 'Tracks of my Tears'," she says with a laugh and hums a few bars in a pretty good voice.

By now he's feeling really comfortable with this first date. They're actually communicating, laughing, not trying too hard to impress each other. It's starting to get chilly at last. They move over to the store side and walk along, chatting about the opening of their summer vacations. Most of the stores are closing so they can't go in to get warm. She moves closer to him, and he puts his arm around her, feeling the chill on her lovely bare arms.

"You're cold," he says.

"A little," she answers with a slight shiver.

"And probably hungry."

She doesn't deny it.

"Want to patronize the competition?" he suggests.

In ten minutes, they've walked over to the Chatterbox, a couple blocks off the boardwalk. It's still bustling at ten o'clock. They get a booth and order, then decide on their selections on the jukebox: three for a quarter. The first one, of course, has to be Smokey Robinson. It's warm inside. Her face is a little flushed from the chilly air, the walking, and maybe the excitement of the night.

They eat, enjoy the tunes, and feel comfortable just with each other's company, not for the moment needing more than idle chat. He feels he knows her well enough already not to force the conversation. They each get an ice cream sundae and sample each other's; the waitress keeps refilling their coffee cups. He feels like he could stay there forever just listening to the music, laughing at her comments about the people in the other booths, sipping the sundaes, and looking at her pretty face.

But he suddenly realizes that almost everyone else is gone. He looks at the clock above the register: 11:45, almost closing time. He signals for the check. For the first time, he wonders, what next?

She gives him a questioning look, then says, "My car's still at the Grill."

He hesitates, but she seems to divine his problem. "Can I give you a ride?" she asks, emphasizing the word 'you,' and gives him a lovely smile of amusement -full of pretty white teeth- as if to say she's comfortable with the role switching.

As they walk back to the Grill, he asks the question he's resisted asking all evening. What are her summer plans? She's staying with her girlfriends from the Grill for the week, she tells him, till her family opens up their summer place. It's her week of freedom too. Her car is an old Chevy, big and clunky with three on the column and bench seats. She gets behind the wheel while he climbs into the passenger seat.

He has her pull up a few houses short of Ricky's place and looks at his watch, which says 11:58. She turns off the engine -a good sign- and he slides across the seat.

"I had a great time," he says with perfect sincerity.

"So did I," she says.

"Can I see you again?"

She nods and smiles.

He puts his arms around her. She eases comfortably into the embrace.

Their lips meet...Their tongues...

III

Tom wakes with a start. Has he already fallen asleep so early in the day? He wife looks in the door to tell him she is off to run errands.

"Napping already?" she asks. "You look like you were lost in space." She looks at the newspaper spread out on the coffee table. "Do you always read the news upside down?" she asks with an amused look.

When she is gone, he turns the paper right way around and checks the stories on a few pages. He sees nothing he hasn't just read. And the date? Same as when he nodded off. The clock on the bookcase says 9:31. He hasn't zoned out for long.

Suddenly his mind is flooded with the most vivid images of the past. He gives himself up to the fantasy that is unfolding in his imagination. It's not the usual jumble of unrelated shards of memory. It's like a movie with a sequential narrative. Even better, he not only can see the events but feel the experience with all five senses. It gives him a rush of vitality at the very core of his being.

For the rest of the day, he feels unusually energetic, centered, and serene. At the gym, he pushes past his usual limits on the treadmill and the stationary bike. He's definitely leaving the young guys behind today. The burst of vitality continues over the next few days. His wife notices; even his buddies at the coffee shop notice. And he can hardly sit still for a moment without those vivid images and exhilarating feelings effortlessly filling his mind.

But soon the yearning to return to the fantasy becomes a kind of addiction. By the end of the week, he feels worn out by his overheated imagination. He is grumpy and distracted. Perhaps worse than that, however, the images have begun to fragment and the feelings are losing their immediacy. Irritability is beginning to turn into depression, and he just wants to retreat into himself. His regular routine -his most dependable source of satisfaction- has begun to seem mundane and boring. The mood swing and the energy collapse don't escape the notice of his wife.

"This isn't like you," she says. "It's as if you're in another world and I can't get in touch with you."

As usual, she is right. But what can he do?

A few more days pass. He's back in his morning chair with the paper spread out on his lap but his mind lost in a fitful reverie. It is 9:31. A noise of someone clearing his throat brings him back to consciousness. There, glowing in the chair across the room, is the angel, the messenger, whoever he is. Though he hasn't thought of him over the past week, Tom somehow feels he has been expecting his return.

"You're having some troubling side effects from your day's stay in the past," the visitor says. "The Creator has noticed."

"So, it is you," Tom says. "The Engel from afar."

"Yes, Tom, back for a follow-up visit. How are you?"

"Not so well," Tom says. "Last week I thought I was out of my mind, but in a good way. This week I think I'm out of my mind, but definitely in a bad way." He pauses. "And now my number one hallucination has returned." He puts his hands over his face as though to banish the vision.

"As you've probably figured out, "the visitor continues, "the Creator decided to try out your suggestion."

So, I've been traveling in time and space, Tom thinks to himself sardonically.

"Indeed, you have, Tom," says the visitor. "You entered a wrinkle in time." He sees Tom's confusion. "Sorry," he continues. "I forgot to mention that I am empowered to read minds -but only on a limited basis. I can also fill you in on some background details about the experiment."

Tom thinks for a moment. "Well," he says, "I do have a few questions. One thing I'd like to know is why I was chosen. I'm just an ordinary guy, even by the standards of this ordinary planet. I'm sure I'm not the first to have this idea. Why did the Creator choose me?"

"Good question," says the visitor. "His choice is still a mystery to me as well. But as we both know, the ways of the Creator can be difficult to fathom."

"And why that particular day? I mean, of all the happy days of youth, why that particular one?"

"Again, a bit of a mystery. But I believe the Creator likes the way you handled that day. Even though you didn't do anything to advance humanity, it was a day of harmless, basically unselfish pleasure. Humans probably deserve a decent measure of those. And it ended before you got yourself into trouble, so to speak."

Tom sits quietly for a time.

"Tell me more," the visitor pursues. "How did you like the experiment? Was it a success?"

"Well, of course it was a thrill. Who wouldn't want to relive a great day? But why does the memory have to fade so fast? Why after only a week am I more dissatisfied than before? Why can't I relive lots of days? Pick my own? Even invent a few?" The questions just keep tumbling out.

The visitor smiles ruefully. "Naturally, the Creator expected this might be your reaction. It's the age-old human problem He's seen since the Garden: how to be satisfied with what you have, even for the shortest time. You humans are always striving, always wanting more, always dissatisfied." He pauses. "The Creator does take partial responsibility for endowing you with desires far beyond your ability to gratify them. But it was the only way to get you to strive to improve yourselves and make progress. Still, your excesses do provoke the divine temper on occasion."

"Does this mean I'll never get another day to relive?"

"That's for the Creator to decide."

"But you have His ear."

"So do you."

"Can you put in a good word for me as well? I've already thought of four or five other days I'd like to relive. It's all I'd ask for. And maybe to let the memories last a little longer."

"I'll do my best to help," says the visitor. He pauses. "But now I've got to get back to Terrapax. Is there anything else you might like to know before I leave?"

Tom thinks. "Yes," he says. "There's one other thing, since you probably know all the details of my day." The visitor nods. "Tell me. Whatever happened to Sam? I distinctly remember going back to the Grill each day for the rest of the week, but she was never there. That might have been a serious relationship." He chuckles to himself. "I think I've earned that much of an explanation considering the ribbing I had to take from my buddies."

"Ah, yes," says the visitor, with a look as though gazing back in time. "Kind of a sad story. The next morning she found out that her father had a heart attack. She had to go home right away. The family never did get to the beach that summer. Beyond that, I know nothing."

"Well," Tom muses, "life moved on. And quite satisfactorily too, I would say."

The visitor pulls a pulsating instrument out of his pocket and looks at it. "My chronometer," he explains. "It reads time in light years." He puts it back and says, "Well, I must be off. More tasks to carry out. I hope the whole experience wasn't totally disappointing. The Creator certainly had the best intentions and may try to tweak the experiment in the future."

In an instant, he has dissolved into being, leaving behind just a faint, whispery glow.

Tom stands up in the prosaic morning light.

"Fly homeward, Engel," he says to himself.

His eye notices the clock on the bookcase, which still reads 9:31. Time, he thinks, is such a mystery. We take it for granted when we're in it. We wish it away when it hangs heavy, and then we can't get it back when we want it. Except perhaps under extraordinary circumstances.

He pulls a dog-eared volume of poetry from the bookshelf, leafs through to a poem that always mystified him in his younger years, and reads aloud.

There was a time when meadow, grove, and stream,
The earth and every common sight
To me did seem appareled in celestial light,
The glory and the freshness of a dream.

But the ecstatic opening is followed by a lament for that lost visionary time: "The things which I have seen I now can see no more." The poet refuses to mourn and instead takes solace in the "philosophic mind." Somehow, the philosophic mind doesn't offer Tom much satisfaction at this moment. He is thankful that he had the exhilarating respite in the past even if it didn't last long, but he still feels the weight of age on him.

Then he thinks of the infinite unknown possibilities of those eight billion worlds, the complex promise of a future life, and the wonder of the Creator's power beyond all human comprehension.

His spirit lifts a bit, and he heads off to the rest of his day with a lighter step.

IT'S ONLY BUSINESS

I

George Abbott felt more rested and relaxed than he had in years. The bags were gone from under his eyes. For the first time in a couple months, he slipped into his tailored gray suit and dress shirt, taking three tries to tie his tie properly. Putting on the old uniform was almost like slipping back into the old life. He looked at himself in the mirror. Every inch still reflected the confident and successful man of business. He guessed he hadn't lost anything in retirement.

Lunch at the Hamilton Grill was always a pleasure, but why had Winslow invited him? He hadn't spoken to him or anyone in the company since his retirement dinner. Everyone seemed surprised when he told them he was stepping aside at only 62 from the firm his grandfather had started so long ago. But he felt the time was right. He was leaving the firm in good financial condition and, just as important, with a reputation for being a responsible corporate citizen concerned about the welfare of the community as well as the bottom line.

He had gotten out because he was tired of it all. Tired of the hustle, the competition, the hype, and the hard-sell that existed even in the most reputable real estate firms. He had promised himself early retirement years ago when he first realized he was actually going to become a success. And he had followed through. With his kids both well-established in their own careers and his ex-wife now safely remarried, he was ready. He had sold his big house in the suburbs and moved into a nice townhouse downtown.

He and Winslow had been pretty good friends over the years. But during the day, Winslow was all business. He wouldn't be wasting a lunch date just to talk over old times. He heard Winslow's voice calling to him from halfway across the restaurant, setting up an anxious tinkle in the crystal. He was already on what probably was his second martini. His face was as red as usual, and his neck threatened to burst his shirt collar.

"How's the leisure business?" he asked. For a while, George crowed about the pleasures of escaping the pressure cooker of the office, but it wasn't long before that line of conversation was exhausted. Winslow never had been much for small talk.

So quite naturally George was pulled back into the world they had both shared. Nobody was better at recreating it than Winslow. Nobody knew more than he did about who had made a killing on this deal or taken a bath on that one. He was carrying the whole world of New Zenith Commercial Realty around in his file-cabinet mind.

In no time, George was transported back into that world of telephones winking madly ('Tell them I'm out and I'll call back later'), a stack of contracts waiting to be signed, and three big decisions waiting to be made before lunch. Push. Stall. Think. Act. Hurry. Worry. But if everything went right, he would close the deal. It was frantic, of course, but challenging too, now that he thought about it. It was a world with its own laws, its own ethics, its own risks and rewards. He recalled with pride how completely he had mastered it.

Today, Winslow wanted to talk about a new deal, not rehash old ones. "Listen, George," he said, coming to his main point, "We've got an issue with that big parcel of land over near the airport."

"You mean the one you insisted we'd never be able to sell?" George said, reminding him of a strategic disagreement they had a year ago. "The one you were afraid wouldn't be worth the investment?"

"Yes, George," he said. "That one. But now, according to a very reliable source inside city hall, it will soon be worth big money. Rumor is the airport authority has almost gotten funding for a big expansion. I guess we're finally considered an important metropolis now. And with a bigger airport, big money from outside investors will start flowing in pretty soon. The city's on the verge of a growth spurt, and New Zenith is going to be a part of it."

"So why are you offering me the inside scoop on the expansion?" George asked.

"Well, I bet you still have the interests of the old company close to your heart." He paused, then added cagily, "By the way, did you know that Oldham and Stuart are looking for a new site for their distribution center?"

"And they're looking near the airport is my guess," George said.

"They have definitely been talking in those terms. But I've been pushing that even bigger parcel over in Patterson Park."

"The one we haven't been able to move for three years now."

"The very one, George. I think it would be just right for them. It's close to the interstate; it has infrastructure already in place. Seems like a perfect fit."

"Have you even mentioned the parcel by the airport? It's close to the interstate too."

"I haven't. It's still off-market. I'm almost certain Oldham isn't even aware it might be available. At any rate, I'd like to hold on to it a while longer -you know, just in case something really big does happen." He gave George a deeply innocent look. "I've already got some big ideas for it up here," he confided, tapping his finger against his temple. "Right now, it's just another piece of real estate. But if we hold on to it a while longer, it could be big. It could mean a big profit for your old family business."

George looked at him with eyebrows raised. "So, tell me again exactly why I rate all this inside information," he said.

"Well, Oldham says he doesn't want to move on Patterson unless he talks to you. You've worked with him before. He trusts you. Of course, I told him you're retired and probably not in the loop on all our properties. But he says he wants your opinion. He'll listen to your advice."

So, there it was. Only a couple months retired and already he was being put back in the very type of situation he had always tried to avoid. What was good for the client wasn't always good for the company. And vice versa. It was the worst kind of divided loyalty.

"I don't know," he said uneasily. "What do you want me to tell him?"

"Just play up how good the Patterson property is. You can do this. You wrote the book on how to persuade the reluctant buyer."

"I'll see what I can do," George said. "But I won't make any promises."

"Thatta boy, George," said Winslow. "I knew I could depend on you. I knew New Zenith could depend on you." He checked the armored Rolex on his wrist. "Well, gotta run. Let me know if there's anything I can do for you," he added, emphasizing the final word.

Right away, George regretted having committed himself. Oldham was a good guy. He had grown his business in the city for thirty years or more. The company employed over eight hundred people. Not high wage jobs, he knew, but lots of them. George had helped him not once but twice to find a new location for his growing business. He had been a valued client of New Zenith and deserved good advice and a good piece of land.

But he still had the welfare of the old company to think about too. No matter what advice he offered, somebody might end up unhappy with the result. It was rare that both parties in the deal got full benefit. But that was business. The fittest were the ones who walked away with the biggest profits.

He waited a few days before making the call, then tried to be as non-committal as possible, just letting Oldham air his thoughts without attempting to steer him in any particular direction.

Another month passed and he heard nothing about airport expansion or Oldham and Stuart's plans to relocate. But several stories in the business section did seem to point to Winslow being right. Big things were on the horizon for the city. Big things he wasn't going to be part of. He sensed an energy in the air that really excited him and just for a moment almost wished he still had a hand in the game.

II

"You're in a rut, George," she said.

She was Vera Diamond, a divorcee George had recently met in the coffee shop where he liked to read the morning paper. She commented on the problem not long after they began getting together there a few times a week just to talk.

"Here you are retired, but you're still wrapped up in the world of real estate deals.

You've got to figure out how to move on."

She was right, of course. After his conversation with Winslow, his brain had gotten locked into all the real estate prospects for a city on the move. It was all he wanted to think about and all he wanted to talk about. Old habits and old obsessions, he realized, were very hard to break.

Instead of being offended, he was pleased by her concern and by her honesty and forthrightness, traits most of the people he knew in the business world definitely didn't have.

He also liked her zest for life and her entertaining conversation. She wasn't beautiful, what with her hairstyle that sometimes looked like an abandoned birds' nest, her stocky figure, and her wardrobe of warm-up suits. But she more than compensated in other ways. She was good company.

"I felt the way you do now after I cut loose the old ball and chain of my ex-husband," she said. "I just couldn't seem to move on.

Finally, I had to have therapy. Then I realized that I was unhappy because I had always been living for someone or something else. I had no idea how to live for myself.

"It took a while before I found other things that really gave me satisfaction. I had to experiment. I tried out for parts in the Curtains Up Playhouse. Just imagine me, cutting up onstage. I have a natural talent for acting, you know.

"I did some traveling too. Exotic places like Marrakesh and Rio, not your standard touristy spots like London and Paris. I learned how to cook all over again. Spicy Middle Eastern dishes. Chinese cuisine. I even got into yoga and learned how to meditate at the Krishna Temple. I just kept discovering sides of myself I never knew existed. Suddenly, I felt free. Free to discover. Free to meet really different people.

"It's been wild, George. Now I feel like it's my mission to help other people like you get beyond their old, dead routines and discover themselves."

They had conversations like this a couple times a week. He told her, not without pride, about his family's humble beginnings and about their success in building a successful family commercial real estate firm that he had helped quadruple in size. She listened but sometimes seemed a little bored.

"That's the old you," she reminded him. "But aren't you bored with that George Abbott? Aren't you ready to move beyond him?" Reluctantly, he agreed. "He's going to be a hard old self to get rid of," she went on. "But together we can do it. Just look around you. This city has all sorts of opportunities other than real estate for a man with your energy and talent. This isn't Hicksville, you know."

He guessed she was right. After all, the old George Abbott, real estate tycoon, no longer existed. But who was he really? All this self-discovery seemed pretty vague, not like selling real estate.

Naturally, she had lots of ideas. "You need a new image," she said. "Clothes are a first step. No more stodgy George." She took him shopping, not at Norton Stockman, where he usually bought his suits, but at Tommy Brower for designer jeans and khakis and sporty shirts. Then she set up an appointment for him at a hair stylist for the next step in his make-over.

Next, it was physical fitness. She signed him up for a membership in her health club. For him, exercise had always meant riding around in a golf cart to play eighteen holes with his buddies from the Board of Realtors. But that was not her definition of fitness. She arranged to have him work out with a personal trainer who kept pushing him through complicated stretches and sets of crunches, balancing on the exercise ball, lifting weights, and walking on the treadmill. 'Aerobic fitness. Core strength. Balance. It's all important for a man of your age,' the trainer counseled him at each workout.

While he suffered through this personal torture, she rode an exercise bike, reading a magazine or watching the cable news on the tiny television. The workout hardly seemed to be trimming any extra pounds off her ample hips. What he enjoyed most was climbing aboard the exercise bike next to her at the end of his workout and pedaling off into oblivion.

Being free to discover yourself, he thought, was sure a lot of work.

After that, she moved on to eating. "People who care about themselves," she said one day, "are careful about what they put in their bodies. It's time for you to stop clogging up your arteries with all that cholesterol." That evening, she brought over her wok to cook Chinese for him. He had never realized there were so many vegetables. Water chestnuts, bamboo shoots, snow peas, and broccoli, all spitting and sputtering as she stirred them in the wok, along with the skimpiest little strips of chicken. She showed great dexterity in the preparation and even more in consuming an abundant portion of the fried rice and veggies with chopsticks. All the soy sauce, garlic, and ginger burned his palate, but he ate heartily to please her.

After a few glasses of rice wine, however, it suddenly seemed as if he were eating the food of the gods. For dessert they had black tea and fortune cookies. "Read yours, George," she encouraged him as he broke open its secret wisdom.

'Show honesty in all you do,' it said. 'Then your future look bright.' She beamed with pleasure. "See, George. All you have to do is be honest with yourself. Success will be guaranteed."

That night she stayed. He felt terribly bumbling in making the proposal. But she accepted so matter-of-factly that he lost his feeling of embarrassment and, at the same moment, a little of the element of mystery. Nonetheless, he felt tremendously freed by the experience. It was as if, for the first time since his divorce, he realized that he actually could have an affair completely without the need of deception or the fear of guilt. He was a mature and free adult who could have an intimate relationship with any woman who wanted him.

The next morning she petted his ego. "You certainly are the last of the red-hot lovers," she said. She didn't spend a whole lot of time prettying up or show any false modesty. During breakfast, she said, "I just want you to know I can't afford to be tied down to any relationship. I like to be honest with a man right away. I've got too many things I want to accomplish to let myself be tied down." As soon as she finished her coffee, she was on her way.

In her wake, he assessed the night before. Dirty dishes lay all over the kitchen counters. She was an impetuous chef who worked best amidst chaos. His ex-wife, dressed in an apron, always did the dishes as she went along. Her cooking was bland; it was neatness that she really served. But Vera cooked the way she was -sloppy, spicy, and full of different flavors. In all things, she had a good appetite. He wasn't surprised at her hasty departure. In the contemporary world, he had heard, women didn't usually ask for commitments or declarations of eternal love.

Nevertheless, he felt she would be back. After all, she had left her wok.

III

Instead, she disappeared without notice for what seemed like weeks. Once again, he was bored and at loose ends. With all his best friends from the Rotary and the Board of Realtors still working, he didn't have anyone to talk business with over coffee. He thought about taking a course at the community college, but nothing in the catalogue looked interesting. He thought he could make friends at the health club, but he despised the workouts and didn't want to face the trainer's accusatory looks.

With nothing else to do, he bought himself a ten-speed bicycle, and whenever the weather was nice, he would pedal over to the Greenway near his townhouse and ride all alone. The bike path was level and well-paved and riding magically soothed him. It was just his speed. He only wished he had someone else along for the ride.

Then, suddenly, the phone rang. Vera was back.

"I was in India," she gushed at the other end. "Just got home. You can't imagine what it was like." She invited herself over to cook Indian for him.

That Saturday night she showed up, her full figure wrapped in an Indian sari, carrying bags of Indian spices and a CD of sitar music. While she cooked, she described her adventure in a vivid stream-of-consciousness monologue. "You just can't imagine how absolutely frantic it is," she said. "When you aren't dodging motorbikes, you're dodging cows and stepping around cow pods. Of course, I took a tour to see the Taj. Did you know Sultan somebody or other built it just to be a tomb for his favorite wife? What a hubby!"

While they ate, she talked about the festivals and the meditation and the yogis who looked like Rastafarians and the filthy water of the Ganges. "They swim in all that filth, George, just to purify themselves. You know, that's the one thing I can't forget -all that filth and all that poverty. Riches and poverty, side by side, especially in the big cities. Shiny condominiums right next to hovels and people living on the streets. It's like nobody really has a clue about what to do to make things better. It's like nobody has a vision."

The image and the insight gave her pause.

"So that was my trip," she said at last. "What about you? Did you have any exciting times while I was gone?"

She read boredom in his face. "You know what you need? You need to get away and have an adventure too. I bet you've never traveled, have you?" Realtors' conventions in Las Vegas and summer vacations at the seashore didn't count, she confirmed.

They talked about possibilities. He admitted he didn't feel comfortable going any place where they don't speak English or drive on the wrong side of the road. He definitely preferred somewhere in the good old United States.

"Why not Alaska?" she offered. "Glaciers, mountains, moose, and bears." He thought about it but preferred someplace warm.

"Hawaii," she decided. "It has to be Hawaii. It was my first big trip after I got my freedom. I can just imagine you in a flowered shirt, drinking mai tais and ogling the hula dancers."

"Sounds wonderful," he said, now caught up in her enthusiasm. "When should we leave?"

"Oh, George, I can't go back to Hawaii. This is your trip. I just want to help you plan it."

Well, so much for Hawaii, he thought after she left. He was hardly interested in going by himself or as part of one of those packaged tours.

He was wondering when she would give up on her mission to transform her stodgy old George.

IV

The next week, however, she called to invite him to a lecture at the civic center. "The speaker is wonderful," she said. I started listening to his motivational tapes soon after my divorce, and he really helped get me out of my doldrums. He'll give you a whole new perspective on life."

The auditorium at the civic center was full. The speaker was Dr. Wayne Werden, whose book *The Freedom to Become* had been on the best-seller list for the past twenty-five weeks, according to the program. From years of attending banquets, George knew what made a good speaker, and right away he liked Dr. Werden. He was youngish, dynamic, and smartly dressed with his cuffs and cufflinks protruding just the right amount from the sleeves of his suit. He told a couple of jokes -good ones- in his introduction to put the audience at ease. But when he got into the heart of his lecture, he became quite intense, almost like an evangelical television preacher, but not in an obnoxious way.

Instead of staying chained to the podium, he moved back and forth across the stage, his coattails swinging around each time he turned to confront the audience with an important new idea. He could speak like a professor, quoting different psychologists and experts, chapter and verse. But when he really wanted to make a point, he had real-life anecdotes and examples that certainly made an ordinary person sit up and listen. He certainly had style, George thought. And he certainly could sell an idea.

Little by little, George began to pick up his message. It was possible, he was saying, for a person to see himself in two different ways. Either he was a weak creature -limited by his genes, his background, or whatever, and therefore fated to lead a meaningless life with hardly any real achievements. Or he was someone born with unlimited potential in energy, talent, and desire, whose whole life was an adventure in creating himself. It was up to the individual to determine which kind of person he would be. Then he had to look deep inside to discover his various talents. Once he did, he could develop a vision for the future. Then, he could seize life by the horns. He could take on any challenges.

By the end of the lecture, George was a true believer. He had always seen himself as being a mover and shaker in the real estate business. But maybe there was more to it. Maybe he hadn't discovered other areas of himself just bursting with potential that was waiting to be tapped and talents waiting to be used. Wasn't that basically what Vera had been telling him?

The next afternoon she called him bursting with her own great new idea.

"I've been thinking about your future for a while now, you know." she said. "At first, I was stumped. But now I know what you should do." She paused as though waiting for a drum roll. "Politics," she said. "You should go into politics. You'd be a natural."

She waited long enough to let the idea sink in a little. "Listen, George, I've got to run now, but I'll bring dinner tonight. We'll talk about things then."

Around seven, she showed up with Thai take-out and a whole new vision for his life.

"City council, George," she said. "I think you should run for city council." He looked at her skeptically. "I've thought this idea over carefully," she went on and jumped right into selling it. "You know lots about how the city operates, don't you? You have to know about zoning laws and taxes and sewer systems and public utilities and stuff like that if you want to sell commercial real estate. Am I right?"

"When you're right, you're right," he agreed, slowly warming to the idea.

"And you know you're good at sales. Just look at how successful your business is. That doesn't happen unless you can persuade people to buy your goods." He rubbed his chin, still looking a little skeptical. "And you know people," she went on, undeterred. "People in the right places." Yes, he had to admit, he had good connections on the Board, in the Chamber of Commerce, and in the Rotary. "All you need is a vision," she went on. "Remember what Dr. Werden said."

They talked into the wee hours, and little by little George became infected by her enthusiasm. He began to see himself running for office, offering his ideas to people in high places, but also listening to the voters. "Think of all the things this city needs, George," she said, and together they laid out a list of projects: a new baseball stadium, renovations to the civic center, a campaign to attract new high-tech industries, an arts center. "If this city is going to progress, George, it needs big thinkers. You could be one of them. And it needs help from the government. The right kind of help."

She spent the night filling his mind with visions of the future before they fell asleep. In the morning, he awoke to find her gone. But she left him a note that read simply, "Go for it, George."

V

For the next few weeks, he was in a state of nearly continual enthusiasm. He awoke each morning with a full day's plan springing full-blown from his brain. He got together with old friends and business associates in search of advice, and they all agreed he would be a good candidate. Somebody who would keep the interests of the business community firmly in mind. But he would need plenty of help on how to get a campaign rolling, how to develop a platform, and how to raise campaign funds. They could steer him to the right people who knew about such things and could give him the proper guidance.

He did some research into the ward he might represent. Now that he had moved into the townhouse, he was living in what the experts would describe as a very diverse demographic area. He wouldn't represent just the middle- and upper middle-class strivers with young families who had dominated his old suburban subdivision. Instead, he would have to try to advance the interests of people from a broad spectrum of ages, races, ethnicities, and income levels.

There were wealthy retirees, empty-nesters, and upwardly mobile young singles who had discovered the conveniences and pleasures of downtown living. They, of course, would be eager for things like a new downtown ballpark and a new performing arts center.

A little farther out was a modest, middle-class neighborhood filled with hard-working teachers, small business owners, and nurses who were doing reasonably well economically, if not exactly prospering. They probably wanted more practical things like new sidewalks, repaved streets, better parks, and, of course, lower taxes.

Farther out yet -and often invisible- was a neighborhood of the working-class poor, many of them struggling to keep their heads above water.

As he drove around this area, he was embarrassed to realize how little he had cared to know about certain parts of the very city where he had lived and sold real estate for so many years. He had read that there was a lack of affordable private homes, but the housing stock, he discovered as he drove about, was even worse than he had imagined. There were blocks in which every other house was falling down or boarded up. Even the best of the apartment complexes were shabby and in dire need of updating. But because New Zenith had only invested in commercial real estate, he had paid no attention to the market for private homes or apartment complexes.

He had heard about the existence of something called food deserts, but it was only as he began to drive around that the true meaning of that term become vividly clear. The only places to buy groceries were convenience stores; the only restaurants served fast food.

His real estate professional's eyes opened wide at the potential for investment. Where were the developers willing to take a risk to build better housing and accessible shopping malls? But then, he wondered, where were the decent paying jobs -jobs that would put enough money in the pockets of the people who lived there to offer them at least the hope of becoming responsible homeowners and good consumers?

Developers, he reasoned, could only be expected to take on a certain amount of risk. New Zenith Realty, he recalled, had never been among those willing to gamble on low-end retail development. He tried to imagine himself persuading Winslow and the other partners at New Zenith to invest. It wasn't very likely they would be interested.

Maybe, however, it was just a matter of offering the right incentives to attract the right new businesses and the right developers. To make this happen, the city needed elected officials with vision and an understanding of the ins and outs of real estate. He could be one of them.

If he wanted to get elected, however, there were lots of difficult promises he would have to make.

By summertime, the campaign seemed to be going fairly well. He had spoken with his party's chairman and some of the other bigwigs, all of whom seemed agreeable to his making a run, particularly since the incumbent had decided not to stand for reelection. He had visited various precinct chairmen in his ward and attended meetings with volunteers. He had filed early for candidacy, and amazingly no one else in his party had thrown in his hat. And with only a couple months to the election, he really felt as if he were making connections with his people. His people, he said to himself, liking the phrase.

He went to meetings with members of the Chamber. Vera helped arrange a cocktail party with some well-heeled potential contributors on the tenth floor of a condominium with a panoramic view of the city skyline. They had come up with an extensive wish list of what they wanted for the city.

The following week he spoke at a meet-and-greet barbecue in the shelter at the ward's largest park. Everyone was friendly. Their wish list was much more modest. Perhaps these folks had already learned not to expect too much from government.

Then two days later he addressed a townhall-style meeting in a Black church on the precinct's farthest side. The turnout was disappointingly small despite the fact that the neighborhood's needs were so great. He hardly felt at ease with this group. What promises could he realistically hope to keep? He told them that the Chamber was working hard to attract new employers and that a couple of neighborhood revitalization projects were in the works. The only questions he got were about what he proposed to do to deal with the rising crime rate and the problems with policing. He went away more than a little uncertain about his vision for the city.

Nonetheless, he felt exhilarated as well as exhausted. Running for office was no easy gig. But everything seemed to be going well.

VI

Then two news stories broke in quick succession. The first was a stunner. Oldham and Stuart had finally purchased property for their big new distribution center with major implications for the local economy. After weeks of negotiation and deliberation, they had finally found the perfect location near both the interstate and a regional airport. The new facility would eventually employ over twelve hundred workers.

Unfortunately, the new site was not in the city; in fact, it was in another city a couple counties away. George read the article with consternation. Twelve hundred jobs would soon be disappearing. Good jobs. Not tremendously high paying, but steady and dependable. Men and women who had been with the company for twenty years and more would be thrown out of work.

George felt a sinking sensation. He thought back to the call he had finally forced himself to make weeks ago. He hadn't exactly tried very hard to persuade Oldham to buy the Patterson property. But he hadn't exactly tried to talk him out of it either. He did push the proximity to the interstate, but he could hear in Oldham's voice that the site was far from ideal and that he wanted to be nearer the airport. And he had never, even once, mentioned the possibility of the other site -the secret site that Winslow had been reserving for a bigger client. He had done the company's bidding. He had been loyal to Winslow and to New Zenith Realty. But now the company still had the Patterson property on its hands. And worse, hundreds of people would soon be looking for work.

A few days later came the second news flash. The airport finally had received official approval and funding for expansion with construction due to begin the following spring. In a separate news brief in the business section was the announcement that a local commercial realtor was in final negotiations with a manufacturer of small private jets to purchase a large parcel of land bordering the site of the airport expansion. George shook his head in disbelief, then picked up the phone and called Winslow. He had a hard time persuading the secretary to put him through.

"George, old boy," Winslow said when he finally picked up. "Long time, no hear. You're a busy man out there wooing the voters." He paused an instant, sensing the direction the conversation would take. "Let me guess why you're calling. It's probably not for a campaign contribution."

"Tell me about Oldham and Stuart," George said. "Tell me why you held out on offering them the airport property." He could feel his voice rising in anger. "I know you must have a good reason."

"We talked about this before, George. I told you we were playing the long game at New Zenith, looking for a really quality buyer for that property."

"And what was wrong with a company that's been a bulwark of the community for thirty years?" George asked. "A company that had eight hundred-some employees and wanted to add lots more?"

"It was a business decision, George. All business decisions require some risk to go along with the reward."

"Did the gamble really pay off? You still have that Patterson property that you may never be able to sell. What did you get for your reward there?"

"Keep your shirt on, George. You're missing the reward part entirely. Beacon Air Jet is paying top dollar for that airport property. More than Oldham and Stuart could ever afford, I can assure you."

"And bringing, what, seventy-five jobs?"

"A hundred, George. Maybe one hundred and twenty eventually. But the big thing is they're high-paying jobs. Very high paying. That means wealth flowing into the community and pumping up the tax base. And as a high-tech company, they'll be bringing prestige to the city."

"But what about the eight hundred soon to be unemployed?"

"Collateral damage, George. You've just got to have faith that some other lower-wage employer will show up soon." There was silence at both ends of the line for an uncomfortable time.

"And you don't really have to worry about the Patterson property after all," Winslow finally continued. "The city has already approached us about buying it for a new landfill. They offered us a good price, but we're still negotiating. I know you're upset, George," he concluded. "Like I said, it was just a business decision. And we're just a business, looking to make a profit."

He guessed he should have known it would all play out this way. He liked to think that he would have done better by Oldham if he had still been in the business. He wondered if he were kidding himself that things were decided any more high-mindedly by city council.

To vent his anger over what had happened, he decided to call Vera even though they hadn't talked for a while. Somehow, she already knew some of the details about the airport expansion. Did she have sources of information that he didn't? She listened silently for a minute or so while he unloaded his frustration, then abruptly interrupted.

"Calm down," she said, "and start thinking like the old George again. Winslow was right. The city needs a makeover -just like you did. Where do you start if you want to improve your city's image? By adding some glitz to downtown. Build the new arts center. Attract people to open some fine restaurants to appeal to foodies. Build more nice townhouses. And a new baseball stadium.

"And, don't forget, renovate and expand the airport to open the city to the wider world. That's how you can begin attracting high tech businesses and smart young professionals. Little by little, the prosperity will trickle down to the people you suddenly seem so worried about."

She let him digest her message.

"You've got to have a vision," she concluded at last. "You've to keep your eye on the prize, George. The big prize."

Somehow, he wasn't surprised that she was less than a sympathetic listener. She liked men who made quick decisions, who took risks, and who didn't worry too much about certain kinds of consequences.

He couldn't think of anyone else to talk to, anyone who might understand the anger that he felt. But he couldn't just sit around and stew. Instead, he got out his bicycle and pedaled toward the Greenway, oblivious to traffic and the late afternoon heat. He rode on and on, ignoring the relentless sun. Despite his headband, sweat gathered in his burning eyes and bloomed in flowers on his tee-shirt.

At first, his mind kept churning in anger at Winslow's deceptions and Vera's unconcern. When he arrived at the lake at the far end of the Greenway, he stopped to rest for a while on a bench in the shade. He watched a couple of fishermen on the other side casting their lines into the water. They were older guys, probably retired like he was, but probably not nearly so well off. But they didn't seem anxious about the future, wrapped up as they were in casting and reeling in little fish. Finally, when his mind became totally blank, he mounted his bike and headed home.

He pulled up his driveway, let the bicycle collapse into a clump of bushes, and sat in the advancing shade of his front porch, taking the final swigs from his water bottle. He had been there perhaps fifteen minutes when two young men stopped in front of him on the pavement. They were neatly dressed in black slacks, white shirts, and black ties and didn't seem to be sweating at all despite the heat. When George offered them a friendly look and a word of greeting, they approached to talk.

"Can I help you?" he asked.

"No thank you, sir," one said. "But perhaps we can help you."

George gave them a look of surprise.

"We're here on the Lord's business," the other said.

In the shifting, filtered light, they took turns telling George about the end of the world, about the great books of prophecy, and about a community of the holy elect. They spoke with such a sense of inner peace that George decided they must be angels. He listened, gathering in an idea here and there, asking no questions and making no comment, but mainly enjoying the unpretentious sincerity of their voices.

They were offering him something they obviously believed to

be beyond all earthly value. And they were offering it for free. As he sat there, he felt as if he couldn't resist their offer. He thought it must be the most extraordinary act of salesmanship he had ever witnessed.

When they asked if he had any questions, he looked up from his abstraction and shook his head. "Not right now," he said. "But please, tell me more." They were in no hurry to go and went on to speak of the love of the Savior and the importance of doing the work of God's Kingdom. "We have to tend the Lord's vineyard," one of them concluded at last. "We have to prepare a harvest for all, not just the few. We have to stand against the doers of selfishness and the speakers of deceit."

Finally, reaching into his backpack, he offered George a handful of booklets. "Read these," he said. "They'll tell you many hidden things." Then, bidding him 'peace,' they journeyed on their way.

George took the booklets inside and laid them on the table beside his bed while he took his shower, thinking he might browse over them later. He spent the evening quietly, lost in the strangest of thoughts, oblivious to the mindless programs on the television. He went up to bed earlier than usual.

As he prepared to turn out the lights and go to sleep, he looked at the cover of the top booklet that he had left on the night table. On it, in bold letters, he read,

"Be not deceived. God is not mocked. For whatsoever a man soweth, that shall he also reap."

PILGRIMAGE

I

White Rock Apostolic Holiness Church was truly rocking that Sunday morning. The choir began lifting the spirit by opening with a new gospel number, then roused the congregation nearly to spiritual fury with one of their favorites, "I'll fly away, oh, glory." Soon everybody was swaying and clapping and raising up their voices to the Lord. As always, Sarah stood tall in the women's section and sang out in her rich mezzo voice, losing herself in the emotion and letting the sound flow out of her then wash back over again. Her voice wasn't as strong as it had once been, but the music still touched her soul.

After "I'll fly away," they moved on to more hymns, following no particular order, sometimes responding to requests called out from the congregation or the inspiration of the keyboard player and old Dr. Samuel, the conductor. She knew all the words by heart, loving best the old standards sung in the old-fashioned way. But she was tolerant of the new versions, dressed up and restyled for the younger generation.

After a soul-comforting rendition of "It is well with my soul,"

Elder Leroy seated them and launched into a long prayer, praising the Lord and thanking Him for the gift of His Son. It was a good time to rest her seventy-five-year-old knees and catch her breath before they rose up again to sing "He wrote my name way up in glory." The congregation got so roused by that one that Dr. Samuel kept them singing the verses again and again.

When they had finally sung themselves out, it was Elder Leroy's turn to build them back up by preaching the Word. He began with his usual exhortation to all the sinners in the pews. "Look around at your brothers and sisters," he said in his lowest bass voice, preparing for the emotional build-up but not wanting it to come too soon. "Look at your neighbors. Just like you, they done stuff they been ashamed of," he rumbled. "They been places they ashamed to tell about. You all got that in common. You know you do. But," he paused, preparing for the crescendo, "you all got something else in common too. You got Jesus as your savior. You got Jesus to pull you out of the muck and mire. You got Jesus to make you clean again." Murmurs of 'Praise the Lord' and 'Thank you, Jesus,' began rising from the pews. The Spirit was really moving among the people. But this part of the service sometimes dragged Sarah's spirit down. She was tired of being reminded of her sinfulness. She had mounted up sins aplenty, she guessed. But why dwell on them?

As usual, Elder Leroy's sermon made the prayer seem short. This one, like many, was on the sins of the flesh. She didn't have that much flesh on her bones anymore and not many forbidden desires either. He read from somewhere in the Old Testament about beautiful Bathsheba and how she almost caused David's downfall. It seemed like the women were always getting blamed for being lustful and devious, at least in some parts of the Good Book. What about Solomon and all his concubines?

She tuned out for a while but then started listening again when he read the story about the Samaritan woman at the well and how Jesus was ready to forgive her despite all the men she had been with. "You can have five children with five different men," the Elder was saying, "and still be forgiven 'cause Jesus will forgive you not just five times or seven times or even seventy times, but seventy times seven times." But then he went on to the greater sin. "You know what that is?" he asked. "It's getting rid of a child you conceived by the grace of God and not just by the pleasure of the flesh. It's getting rid of a child you gave life to just because you don't want the responsibility of caring for him. That, brothers and sisters, is a dark sin indeed."

She was relieved when they finally got to singing again, this time one of her favorites, "Just a closer walk with Thee." This was about a forgiving savior she could truly love. Surely any savior that could inspire such beautiful music must be divine indeed. After a longish testimonial by one of the new young members, some prayers, and a final hymn, it was time for lunch. But Elder Leroy held them for a few parting words.

"Brothers and sisters," he said, "I know praising the Lord and hearing His Word have worked up a powerful appetite for the Spirit." He paused to set up his joke, "And, yes, for the delicious lunch awaiting us in the fellowship hall as well. Today, I have a surprise. A special surprise for one of our own. For one of the most faithful in our flock. So, I don't want none of you sneaking away early for lunch somewhere else. Today especially we want everybody joining us for our food and fellowship down below."

Sarah had been thinking about escaping early. She was tired and not in the mood for noise and idle chatter. She hadn't even brought a dish to contribute to the meal. But as she changed out of her choir robe, the other ladies were making a big fuss about the surprise. They sure wouldn't miss it for anything. "You going, ain't you, Sarah?" said one. "Sure wouldn't miss if I were you," said another. "Sure enough," added a few more. All the enthusiasm seemed a little strange, but she couldn't politely resist being included.

In the fellowship hall, everybody had loaded their plates with fried chicken, macaroni and cheese, and cobbler. Elder Leroy took the microphone to offer up a blessing. But before everybody could tuck into their meal, he said, "Don't y'all want to know what the surprise is? I promised you a surprise." He waited dramatically for all the buzz to subside, then continued, "I want Sister Sarah to come and join me at the head table. We got an extra seat specially reserved for her. Sister Rachel, would you escort her up to the place of honor."

The crowd, forgetting the food for a moment, oohed and aahed as the preacher's wife led Sarah to the table. When all was quiet, Elder Leroy said, "Fifty years ago, when I was still a boy and White Rock Apostolic Holiness Church was hardly ten years old, Sister Sarah joined our flock. She's been part of us for the better part of her life. And what a life it has been! Fifty years she has devoted to serving our congregation, to being a faithful servant of our brother Jesus, and to lending her beautiful voice to our soul-inspiring choir. I myself didn't know about this anniversary. Sister Sarah certainly was too modest to tell me. Maybe she didn't realize it herself. But her old friend, Sister Martha, back there, she remembered." Everybody turned to acknowledge Sister Martha with polite applause. "Now I don't want to keep y'all from eating, but I sure don't want to miss this opportunity to commemorate this glorious occasion either. So, while you get started, I'd like to recall some highlights from our beloved sister's life."

While the congregation ate, he reeled off a list of little tidbits, some of which he had probably collected from her friends -the kind he usually offered at funerals. Valued employee of the local public library. Faithful wife to Brother Henry, who had been called home twenty years ago. And, of course, loving mother. At this point, someone ushered out her daughter Deborah, who, he let everybody know, had driven a hundred miles that very morning just to be part of the ceremony.

After a couple little speeches by old friends, lots of tinkling of spoons against iced-tea glasses, and a few rounds of applause, Elder Leroy presented her with a gilt-edged Bible inscribed with her name and the morning's altar flowers. At the end, she struggled to find the words to acknowledge her thanks. Then all the choir members left their seats and formed up to sing her favorite hymn, "Precious Lord, take my hand."

II

By the time she got home, she was exhausted and sat for an hour just staring out the window. She should have been thrilled. They had just offered up her life as a model of virtue. At least the last fifty years of it. So why not be proud? But the last fifty years were hardly the whole of her life. If the nice folks knew things about her first twenty-five years, Elder Leroy would have had a different story to tell. She had secrets from those years that nobody knew. Sometimes she wished she had someone to confide in, but listening to her lady friends gossip, she knew she couldn't trust a single one of them to keep her secrets.

She looked at a picture of her late husband and thought ruefully that he would have been the last person she would have confided in. They had been married for twenty-some years and hardly shared much more than meals and a bed. He was older by ten years and married as much to his used-car business as to her. He had been a good provider for her financial needs. They had a nice little house in a neighborhood with pretty good schools. He bought her a nearly new used car every other year even though she hardly ever drove. He even provided her with the daughter she so much longed for.

But as for tenderness and understanding, he was incapable of providing them. Besides, he was a jealous man, not quick in forgiving. And he surely had secrets of his own. He was often away two or three days a week looking for used cars to buy -and who knew what else.

After he died, she thought about talking to Deborah. She had always been loving and devoted and had made Sarah proud by graduating from high school and then from college. Now she was happily married with children and a career of her own. Sarah didn't want anything upsetting their relationship.

She tried watching television to settle her mind, but that didn't work. Then she tried reading her new Bible, but that was even less successful. Instead, she did what she often did to drive off the blues. She traveled back in memory to a few months of sublime happiness long before she became a pillar of White Rock Apostolic Holiness Church.

Getting to those months wasn't always easy because her growing-up years, for the most part, had been far from happy. She remembered the house she had lived in far more clearly than most of the people she knew in the neighborhood. It was a five-room bungalow in Greenville with a tiny kitchen, a tinier bathroom, and her own tiny but private bedroom. The lot was scrubby, the grass scratchy and weedy, but in the back was a tall shade tree that provided a place of retreat when her mother's foul moods made even her bedroom too close to find peace.

About all she remembered of her father was him coming home from work too tired to be bothered with her. He wasn't a playful man; he didn't seem much interested in the things little girls liked to do. When she was about five, the fights between her parents started up. By the time she started going to school, there were daily battles, sometimes hot and loud, sometimes icy and silent. Soon after, he was gone, and she rarely saw him again. Her mother took it hard, but she was determined to put food on the table, keep the house clean, and keep Sarah in line. She worked as a nurses' assistant in a nearby clinic, proud that she was smart enough and ambitious enough not to have to work in a factory. And she was ambitious for Sarah.

After her father left, her mother went through a series of men, never making any effort to let Sarah get to know them. After a while, the suitors stopped coming around. Mama seemed to have had enough of men. But learning how to deal with them became a core part of her motherly advice. Periodically, she gave Sarah her standard lecture on the importance of making right choices. Of studying hard and getting her high school diploma, and maybe more. Of hanging around with the right crowd. And particularly of dating the right boys and waiting for the right man to marry. A girl, she would say, has only one flower to give away.

All in all, most of the memories of this time were pretty dismal.

But there was one set of memories that she went back to quite often. They were her secret, guilty pleasures.

She was sixteen, a junior in high school, and finally getting her breasts after years of being awkward and flat-chested. A few of the boys had begun to notice, but she was shy and had no particular talent for flirting. In October, a new boy had arrived at school and was assigned to most of her classes. Right away she was attracted to him. She thought she had never seen a prettier boy. He had a long face, big dark eyes, milk-chocolate skin, fine features, and a thin body, a little gangly but with a kind of quiet grace.

For the first couple weeks, she never heard him say anything in class other than 'present' or 'yes, ma'am'. He was just as silent around the other kids. It was the teachers who first revealed his name -Joshua- a nice name that none of the other boys at school had. At first, the other girls seemed to feel the same mysterious attraction to him. They tried out their best flirtatious devices, but he seemed uninterested, and they soon lost interest as well.

Then one day she bumped into him outside a downtown store. He gave her a look that she could still see in her imagination and then introduced himself, amazing her that he could actually speak. They walked together for a while, looking in store windows and mostly staying silent at first though without any sense of awkwardness. Even though she rarely initiated conversation, she started telling him things about herself. He seemed interested and even asked her questions. Only after they went off separately did she realize that he had told her almost nothing about himself.

Over the next month, they began meeting regularly after school just to walk, look in store windows, or sit on a bench in the city park. Little by little, she picked up a few facts about him. He had come from some town further south that she had never heard of. Why the family moved he never said. He lived in a neighborhood she had never been in on the other side of town. He had brothers and sisters, but how many and what they were like he never said. And he seemed to deliberately avoid any mention of his parents. His vagueness probably should have made her wary about their future, but she was just living in the moment and enthralled by his milk-chocolate skin, his long, lithe body, and his gentle ways.

Even before Thanksgiving, it had gotten too cold just to walk the streets and sit in the park. Soon she worked up the courage to invite him back to her house for the afternoon. Her mother wasn't home; the house was quiet and fairly warm. Joshua could stay till it was time for her mother to leave work. She had to plan things right, however, because the neighbors would be nosy. One night she lay in bed thinking how to work that problem out. There was a little alley behind her house; he could climb the low fence and come in through the basement door. So began a few magical months of daily visits that still brought her secret pleasure almost sixty years later.

At first, they observed the proper rules of courtship, sitting at the kitchen table with the blinds closed and just talking. She taught him how to play a couple card games. He often brought treats for them -Little Debbie cakes and Nehi sodas in bottles, which she had to dispose of secretly so her mother wouldn't find them.

Soon they began stretching out together on the bed in her room, fully clothed and snuggling to keep warm because her mother kept the heat low. Before long, they moved on to new and more wonderful intimacies. She always remembered that he had never tried to make her do anything she didn't want to. He had been the most wonderfully patient lover. And for her that had been the very secret of the intensity of their pleasure. Afterwards, they would lie together -wordless- for as long as possible. Never before had she felt so inwardly calm as though floating on a cloud or on a sailboat -she could never think of just the right way to describe it. Then their inner alarm clocks would both sound at exactly the same instant. They would dress quickly, share a lingering kiss, and he would make his exit the same way he had come in.

By late May, she was starting to show. She tried to keep everything secret as long as she could, but she couldn't hide her changing body from her mother's watchful eyes. The reaction was just as she expected. Disbelief, then anger. How could she have been so irresponsible? Who was the boy? Didn't she know the sacrifices that had been made for her? Did she have any idea what it was like to have a baby? What about her education?

She had turned in on herself during that time. At first, she dreaded going to school, but she began to wear looser clothing and nobody seemed to suspect, not even Joshua. Even harder was having to shut him out. She told him that her mother was getting suspicious and they would have to stop spending afternoons together for a while. Though it almost killed her, she decided not to tell him about the baby. She didn't return a couple notes he sent to her in class or respond much to his looks.

Despite missing some days, she still managed to finish the year with good grades. On her final day, she arrived home to find her mother waiting for her. She had already made a plan for Sarah for the summer. She would leave the next day on a bus for her aunt's house somewhere farther south where she would have the baby. Then she would come back in the fall to finish her final year of high school. All the details had been worked out, at least the ones for getting her out of town before anyone else knew her secret.

She remembered throwing a fit and making all sorts of threats she knew she couldn't carry out. But the next day she was at the bus station bright and early with a little suitcase and a ticket to nowhere.

Summerville. Sumterville. She couldn't exactly remember the name of the town anymore. Mostly she remembered it was plopped down in the middle of cottonfields and tobacco farms and smelled of hogs and a chicken processing plant. The town itself was just a few streets long with ugly little houses, a general store, a tiny post office, and a church. There were no young people she might want to hang out with, not that she would likely have done any socializing anyway, being over seven months pregnant.

The aunt -younger than her mother by ten years- lived with her husband and a brood of kids in a little bungalow not far from the chicken plant. The husband worked there and came home each day with the foul smell of the place on him. Her aunt certainly knew about having babies and the basics of caring for them. There was no doctor in town, but her aunt arranged for regular visits from a midwife, who examined her and advised her on getting ready for the delivery.

The summer had been sweltering, and the house noisy with the kids running about. She felt sick most of the time and languid, dragging around her bulging belly and the little life inside. The aunt was patient and provided for her pretty well, surely with help from money inside the envelopes from Greenville that occasionally arrived at the post office.

Just a week before she delivered, her aunt and the midwife sat her down to discuss the options for the baby. It was a topic she herself had been refusing to think about. Her aunt told her that her mama wanted the baby put up for adoption somewhere down there. The midwife said she could talk to an agency that was working with some nice young couples nearby who had been wanting a baby for the longest time. She could start up the adoption process right away, get the paperwork from the county courthouse, and so forth. By the time the baby came, it would just be a matter of signing the papers. They would say she was eighteen. It would all be for the best, they had said. The baby would have a secure home, and she would be free to move on just as if nothing had happened. She couldn't remember, however, signing any papers.

Even if she had really wanted to keep the baby, she figured there was no way she could care for it. So, she agreed. Then during the next few days, she felt, for the first time, the maternal tug. The baby inside her was a part of her. And it was a part of Joshua. Her labor was long and hard. The curse of Eve, she now guessed. When the baby finally popped out, the midwife asked her if she wanted to know whether it was a boy or a girl. She turned away without a word. They cleaned the baby up and asked Sarah if she wanted to try to nurse. Something inside told her that if she said yes, she would never want to give the baby up.

As soon as she was able, she got out of the dirty little town and headed back to whatever awaited her at home. Her exile was over. Her mother asked almost nothing about her time away, about the delivery, about the baby. She was ready to have the incident disappear from their lives. They had a brief period of frostiness, then started the fighting began.

She got back to school a few weeks into the school term and had to make up a story about where she had been and why she had gotten back late. It was a pretty poor lie, but no one asked any questions.

She inquired as casually as possible about Joshua. No one seemed to know for sure though one girl said she had heard the family had pulled up stakes and moved elsewhere as soon as the school year ended. 'Sorry, honey,' she remembered the girl saying. 'I know you had kind of a thing for him.' It was the last news she ever had of him.

To help her forget, she took a job and earned some money. She turned eighteen that January and decided it was time to be free. Her mother wouldn't hear of her living on her own in Greenville, so she took her little bit of savings and headed out of town, north for a bigger place.

She tried to forget most of the following years. She worked a series of dead-end jobs and went through a series of no-account men. She wasted money on fancy clothes trying to imitate the styles in Hollywood fan magazines. She tried out marijuana and drank her share of liquor at dens of sin like the Kit Kat Club. She even went to see a woman to get rid of another problem she didn't want. She kept moving from one place to another, each time hoping that if she went missing from one place, she'd find herself in another. But once she had lost her way, it seemed impossible to find her way back.

Then she found Jesus. Or maybe it was Jesus who found her. He had been waiting for her in a little church that her friend Martha had invited her to visit. At first, she wasn't sure that she wanted to go. She had rarely gone to church when she was young and mainly remembered the praying and the sermons dragging on and on. But she liked the spirit and the friendliness of the people at the new church. So, she kept going back, trying to make up her mind whether to offer herself up to the Lord and become a new member.

The thing that finally decided her was the picture of Jesus on the cover of the church bulletin one Sunday. He had such nice features, such a gentle expression, such deep brown eyes and smooth, almost chocolate-brown skin. It was certainly a face unlike the faces of all the shiftless men she had recently known. He seemed like the kind of savior she could love. He would win her by gentleness and let her gradually reveal her secrets. Most of the stories about him showed his gentle side though she did notice that he showed a temper on occasion. His story about the virgins who didn't get into the wedding because they had no oil for their lamps disturbed her. But otherwise, he seemed to like and respect women, especially Mary Magdalene with her sinful past.

She also really liked the music and discovered, to her surprise, that she had a good singing voice. So, she made her testimony of faith to the congregation and joined. Nobody asked any questions about her past. They just seemed interested in helping her get where she wanted to go in the future. At Martha's urging, she even decided to go ahead and join the choir.

All that was fifty years ago.

Lately, though, she had been thinking more and more about those first twenty-five years. Her mother was long dead, and Joshua was just a treasured memory. But what about the baby she had borne? What had its life been like? That question had been nagging her for a while. She had prayed many times over, asking Jesus what he would have her do, and he seemed to be giving her the same answer each time.

III

The bus ride south was going to be long. She had found a town called Sumterville on one of her late husband's Rand McNally road maps. The helpful people at the Greyhound terminal had gotten the route all planned out for her -a long ride to Columbus followed by a local bus to Marietta. From there, they said, she would probably have to hire a cab. She sat with her little suitcase next to her on the seat, planning exactly what she would do. She would have to spend two nights in a hotel if she wanted to accomplish everything. She just hoped she had brought enough money, what with the hotel and meals and a cab and who knew what else. She figured she would start at the county courthouse in Marietta looking for records of some kind. Then she would spend part of a day in Sumterville trying to find -well, she didn't know what. It was all very vague.

As the bus rolled along the mostly featureless highway, she tried to imagine what her daughter would be like. She had already decided it must be a daughter. She would be in her late fifties by now. Had she had a happy life so far? A good life? Did she have a husband and children and maybe even grandchildren already? Was she church-goin'? Did she even live anywhere near Sumterville?

Between her imaginings, she nodded off occasionally, ate the lunch she had packed, and read some passages from the little Bible she had tucked into her pocketbook. It was almost dinnertime when she arrived in Columbus. The nice man at the ticket window sold her a ticket for the next morning's ride to Marietta and directed her to an inexpensive hotel nearby and a homey restaurant along the way.

She got up in the morning and put on her nicest dress, her Sunday hat, and her white gloves. By 6:30, she was at the terminal bright and early for the seven o'clock bus to Marietta. The road passed by fields of corn and cotton, ramshackle houses only a little closer to collapsing than they probably had been fifty-eight years ago, and an ancient service station with a bunch of broken-down cars and pick-ups sitting in front. In Marietta, she found her way to the big brick courthouse with its dome, its columns, and its Confederate soldier still standing guard on the lawn. An official-looking woman in the front office barely looked up as she waited for Sarah to speak.

"I'm trying to find information on a child," she started in, then paused. "That is, a woman who was a child...who was born in, let's see, 1962." Her awkwardness in formulating the request was magnified by a twinge of nervousness, wondering if the woman would need to know why she wanted the information. The woman, youngish, with her hair pulled up so tight in a bun that it seemed to strangle any possibility for a smile, gave her a patronizing look.

"This is Licensing," she said curtly. "You probably want Records. Down the hall." Sarah gave her a brisk thank-you, refusing now to be intimidated. She had worked in a library and knew a few things about records.

The clerk in Records was more helpful. He was older, just as unsmiling, but not so puffed up and condescending. After her first awkward effort with the other clerk, she was able to explain herself more clearly. He scratched his head and frowned slightly. "You say you're trying to find the *name* of a baby born here in this county on August 29, 1962," he said blandly, slightly raising an eyebrow at the oddness of the request.

"That's right," she said. "I know the birthdate for sure. It's just I don't know the baby's name."

He eased off his stool and disappeared into the stacks of records, reappearing after a few minutes with a big, dusty-looking, thumb-indexed ledger labeled 1962. He laid it on the counter and browsed through it. "Here it is," he said at last. "August twenty-nine of 1962. I do see we've got some births registered for that day. Three, to be exact. A banner day for a small county like ours," he concluded with just the hint of a smile.

"I'm specifically looking for babies born in Sumterville on that day," she said. "Just in Sumterville, sir."

"I'm sorry," he said, "but county records don't list the town where the babies were born."

She felt a mixture of hope and disappointment. "Are you sure they were the only ones born on that day?" she pursued.

"Can't say, ma'am. Some folks, especially from out in the country, didn't always get the date registered exact. Most of the babies weren't born in the hospital back then, you know."

The needle of her disappointment moved higher. "Well, sir," she said, "May I have a list of those names."

He pushed the ledger in her direction. "You're welcome to copy them," he said. "You can sit at that desk over there. Do you need a pencil and paper?"

"Thank you, sir, I've got my own," she said, gesturing to her pocketbook. She sat down and carefully copied out the names - three girls- and tried to imagine which one might come to life in the form of her mystery daughter. None of the names sounded like one she would have given to a precious new life. She read the names of the parents. There was no 'Sarah' listed as the mother of any of the babies, and she couldn't even remember her aunt's name. Who, she wondered, had gotten credit for all the pain she had gone through birthing that baby?"

When she finished, she brought the ledger back, thinking her research was done. Then another idea occurred to her. "Do you, by any chance, have a list of adoptions around that time, sir?" she asked.

The clerk considered a moment, checked the table of contents, and leafed through to the back of the ledger. "1962," he said to himself. "Let's see...August." He adjusted his glasses and ran his finger down the page. "No," he said. "No adoptions listed for August or September or October, for that matter." She must have shown her disappointment. "It's not unusual," he said. "Back then, if a girl wanted to give up her baby, it was often done without any legal fuss. No papers. No lawyers. The girl or her mama or the midwife just turned the baby over to the people who wanted it."

Sarah felt herself blush, believing he must have divined why she came around making such strange requests. What if he did? she thought. Why should she feel any shame in front of a man she would never see again.

"Sorry I can't help," he concluded matter-of-factly, closing up the ledger. "Our records is as accurate as they can be. But they sure don't tell the whole story of all the babies that came into the world way back then."

"Thank you kindly for your help," she said. She put the list of names into her pocketbook and headed out the door.

It was late morning by the time she left the courthouse. She ate a quick lunch in a sandwich shop near the terminal, trying to formulate in her mind the next steps in her search. Outside the terminal, she found a lone cab driver eating his lunch in his cab. She tapped on the window, and he put his sandwich back in the bag. He was a hulking fellow bursting out of his short-sleeve white shirt, but he showed a natural politeness in helping her into the backseat. When she told him to take her to Sumterville, he gave her a curious look as if to ask whether she was sure that was where she wanted to go.

The ride took her past another forgettable stretch of farmland and houses. She sat wrapped in her thoughts while he whistled absently. For her morning's work, she had gathered three names. Three names of real people, one of whom might be carrying a bit of her own flesh and blood. The baby's existence now seemed more real than ever, but almost as elusive. She had a whole afternoon to fill in at least a few particulars of that reality. But she still could think of no clear plan for her search. So, she decided just to put her trust in Jesus. If he wanted her to find her child, he would show her the way.

A half-hour later, the driver pulled into a tiny town and stopped in front of a hardware store with a comfortable bench in front. "This is Sumterville, Mrs.," he said. "You got family in town?"

"Maybe," she said. "At least I think I might." He studied her curiously as she opened her purse and counted out the fare and a small tip. After he helped for out of the backseat, he said, "Is there anything else I can do for you?"

"Well, now that you mention it," she said, "I'll be needing a ride back later this afternoon. Can you pick me up?"

"About when?" he asked.

She looked at her watch. "Let's say five o'clock."

"Five o'clock it is," he said, and they agreed to meet at the same spot. He waited briefly just to be sure she hadn't changed her mind about staying, then said, "Why don't you write down my phone number. Just in case you want to leave early. You could probably make a call from any of these stores." She wrote the number on the paper with the three names and thanked him for being so thoughtful.

After he drove off, she studied the town closer. At first, nothing looked particularly familiar, but she figured she had deliberately wiped away almost all memory of the place. On the opposite side of the street were railroad tracks and beyond them the sagging remains of an old factory, its cinderblock walls overgrown with vines and its corrugated roof collapsing inward. It did seem vaguely familiar. Along the main street beyond the hardware store were a Piggly Wiggly, a hair salon, and a handful of other nondescript buildings. Though none of the stores set off any specific memories, the place did seem vaguely familiar. She decided to go into the hardware store just to get the lay of the town. It smelled pleasantly of fertilizer and seed.

"Can I help you?" said the clerk, noting her white gloves and Sunday dress with a curious expression.

Once again, she was confused about how to start. "I used to stay in Sumterville," she began. "Long, long ago. I was in the area and decided to come back and maybe even find some people -some old friends and such- who used to live here." The little lie had spilled out accidentally, but she realized right away how useful it could be.

"Doing a little family research?" he suggested.

"Oh, yes," she said, happy to follow up on the suggestion. "I'm doing a little family research." She paused a moment then said,

"I've mostly forgot what the place looked like. But some things do look kind of familiar like that old, falling-in building across the railroad tracks."

"That used to be a chicken processing plant," he said. "Employed lots of folks around here at one time. It closed down years ago."

"Left a lot of people out of work, I expect," she said.

He nodded. "Probably so. From what I've heard, Sumterville was almost a ghost town for a while after the plant closed. Then a big agricultural products company located nearby bringing a bunch of new jobs. Folks started to move back to town; some new houses got built. That's when my father decided to open up the store. But nothing much else has happened since then. We're hanging on, just barely, though there's rumor another company has plans for a new plant.

She thanked him for the information, thinking how everyone had their own worries. What he said about the plant closing certainly diminished the prospects that her daughter had grown up in town.

"Hope your family research goes well," he said. "The ladies in the Piggly Wiggly may be able to help."

She walked up the street in the gathering afternoon heat, reminding herself to keep trusting in Jesus. The Piggly Wiggly was mostly empty at that hour. She stood by the empty carts for a minute, working up her courage. No matter how she started, the inquiry would still sound awkward. She chose to talk to the older of the two cashiers, probably in her late fifties or early sixties. Her identity badge said her name was Raynelle.

"I'm looking for some old family and friends. People who were born here in Sumterville a long time ago," she began, reaching into her pocketbook and pulling out her list. "You wouldn't, by any chance, recognize the names of any of these folks?" she continued a little more confidently, showing her the list.

The cashier scanned it and read off the names silently with her lips. "I don't reckon I do," she said. Then she called over the other cashier, a younger, pretty girl with chocolate skin, for a consultation. "We don't know a June Robinson, do we?" said the first cashier. "We know a Louella Robinson who shops here. She lives out of town. But not a June Robinson." The other cashier nodded in agreement. "It's a big family, them Robinsons," she said. "Maybe one of them's a June."

They talked about the connections a bit, then the younger one said, "You looking for white folks or colored folks? 'Cause all the Robinsons we know is white." Seeing Sarah's disappointment, they went back to discussing the other names, hoping to be able to find a clue in one of them.

"You sure all these girls don't have new names. You know, married ones?" the older one asked. Sarah acknowledged it was something that hadn't occurred to her.

"I'm sorry, honey," she said at last. "Wish we could help you." She handed back the list. "It's always nice reconnecting with folks that you knew growing up."

"I was really close to one of them in particular," Sarah said. "But we haven't been in touch since she was very young."

"Well, good luck in your search," she said. "You might try Ella in the hair salon. She been in business here a long time."

When Sarah got back out into the heat, she felt more than ever the futility of her search. What even gave her the right to find her lost daughter? Much less to expect that she would be willing to talk. And here she was telling little lies to try to find out the truth. But she wasn't quite ready to give up.

Ella was a big, black woman with a hearty voice. Her beauty shop had three chairs, a bank of mirrors, bottles of haircare products, a tiny refrigerator, and, standing watch over a rack of ladies' magazines, a picture of Jesus, knocking on the door of someone's home.

Ella's lone customer was sitting under a hair dryer, and Ella's big voice welcomed Sarah over its noise. "Pleasure to see you, Sister," she said. "Are you new to town? I do the best cuts and styles in the county."

Patiently, over the mechanical roar of the dryer, Sarah explained again her reason for being in town and once again produced her list of names. Ella scrunched up her eyes as she read. Then she took the list over to the customer, who was thumbing through a fashion magazine while the dryer whooshed away. She turned off the dryer, and the two of them studied the names together.

"Can't say either of us recognizes any of these folks," she said at last. "Strange, too. I been cutting hair thirty-five years in this town and thought I knew just about every lady in the area. All the ladies comes here to have their hair done."

Seeing Sarah's disappointment, she said, "Lots of people have come and gone from this town over the years. My own children they moved away soon's they were able. Yes, we've seen hard times here, and folks went off in search of opportunities in other places. Lots of businesses followed. Maybe you remember the barbecue restaurant used to be a couple doors down. It's been gone a while. And the ladies' clothing store. Gone too. Why even the post office pulled up stakes and moved five miles off to Clinton."

Then noticing how hot and tired Sarah looked, she said, "Listen to me goin' on and on and not asking you to set a while. Why don't you rest here by the fan before you head back out on your search? I'll get you a cold soda pop to cool you off."

Sarah eased down into the welcoming chair, feeling the weariness set in and wishing she were home in her own living room. After fifteen minutes, she checked her watch. It was getting late. Her driver would be coming back for her before too much longer, and she still had a little more to do. She thanked Ella for her hospitality and her sympathetic ear. Then, feeling revived enough, she headed back outside.

The street began to look a little more familiar now that Ella had jogged her memory. She now remembered the restaurant and even a soda shop just beyond where the local kids with a little money to spend had hung out. And she remembered walking down to that post office to pick up the mail from Greenville, all the while trying to conceal her swelling belly from prying eyes.

At an intersection just past a vacant lot, she turned off the main street and made her way back to the narrow lane where she remembered her aunt's house had been. Years ago, it had been lined by little old bungalows with peeling paint, crooked porches, windows with no screens, and outhouses in the back. Most of those bungalows were gone now, replaced by little brick ranch houses, most in need of considerable repair. The only people stirring in the afternoon heat were kids playing kickball in the yards and chasing each other among the sheets and underwear hanging out to dry. Farther up the street was a big plot of ground planted with corn, collards, and tomatoes and, just beyond, the place where she thought her aunt's house should have been.

There was one old bungalow that looked like the place where she had suffered through that long hot summer and given birth to her baby. She remembered the house had a big sweetgum tree in the front yard that dropped stickerballs that jabbed into her bare feet when she wasn't careful. She remembered a wide porch where she tried to find peace and quiet from all her little cousins. This house, however, had scrubby bushes in front but no stickerball tree and a porch that didn't seem quite so wide. If she had gotten her bearings right, it might be the house where she stayed. But it might not. Perhaps it was where her daughter had spent her early weeks - or even years. If so, Sarah hoped she had escaped to a better place before she got too old. Standing there, she felt a twinge of guilt that she hadn't been there to provide the mothering and had shown so little gratitude to the aunt who probably had done her best to deal with a difficult situation.

She walked back to the main street, expecting to sit on the bench outside the hardware store for the forty-five minutes till her driver arrived. Her knees and feet were sore, making her wish she had worn more sensible shoes. But she knew she had to look respectable if people were going to take her seriously. Clouds had piled up on the horizon, emitting distant rumbles of thunder, and she was afraid of getting caught in a sudden downpour.

She emerged at the little clapboard church at the far end of town, one of the few buildings that she did remember clearly from the past. It was still balanced a little precariously on the brick piers of its foundation. Her aunt used to go every Sunday and usually took along at least a few of the children. She had always invited Sarah to come too, but she was too self-conscious and too hard in her heart to go. She hurried on in order to stay ahead of the storm. Then a thought came to her. Had her baby ever been baptized? It was a thought that had never occurred to her before. Her aunt had been a God-fearing woman. She might have seen to having the baby baptized. It would surely ease her mind to find out. Maybe there was a record in the church.

As providence would have it, the preacher was just coming out the side door as she passed. He was a pleasant-looking older man, at least in his sixties. He greeted her with a friendly voice and listened patiently while she told her story about doing her family history.

He gave her a curious look. "Is there anything I can do to help?" he asked.

"Could I possibly look over the church records?" she asked. "Baptisms and such would be especially helpful."

"We do have some old books with lists of baptisms, confirmations, and weddings," he said. "How far back you need to go?" When she told him the date, he gave her a look of uncertainty. "We don't have many records that old," he said.

"Would you mind if I took a look at what you got, just for a few minutes?" she asked.

He led her into the unadorned sanctuary, still a little cool despite the afternoon heat, and back into a musty room filled with choir robes, candlesticks, and old hymnbooks. He searched a bit before coming up with a slender volume with a leather cover.

"The oldest entries would be in here; they're arranged by year," he said. "Mostly the 1950s and '60s. You're welcome to browse." He quietly slipped back into the sanctuary to give her privacy.

There were not many entries, just as he had said. She leafed through the pages till she found ones from the 1960s, then scanned the names and dates of the host of baptized souls. She came upon a promising entry for a baptism on November 2, 1962. The mother's name was Sara -not exactly the right spelling, but close- but there was no last name and no father's name. There was, however, a name for the infant. Precious. The baptized girl's name was Precious. Perhaps this was her baby. Somehow the name seemed right. The more she thought, the more convinced she became. She had a daughter. A daughter named Precious. Sensing that she had no more need to search, she closed the book and went back into the sanctuary.

The preacher was gazing out the door. "Looks like the storm may be moving off to the east," he said.

Some rays of the late afternoon sun had escaped the cloud cover and set aglow a single stained-glass window picturing the Good Shepherd.

"A beautiful window, isn't it, Sister?" he said. She nodded her agreement. "It cost a lot. At first, some folks in the congregation was against it, thinking it was too expensive. Some of them wanted to use the money to shore up the old foundation instead. But the rest of the folks persevered, and we got our window. Now we couldn't live without it."

He paused, trying to read her expression. "Well, Sister," he said, "did you find whoever you were looking for?"

"I believe I have," she said. "I believe I've found a lost lamb."

He smiled. "Just like the poor widow who wouldn't give up till she found her lost penny," he said. "Well, be blessed."

Together they made their way back down the steps to the sidewalk. "Are you staying in the area a while?" he asked.

"No," she said. "I have to be on my way today." She paused a second. "It's been a good visit though. Folks in town sure have been helpful and nice."

"It is a nice town," he said. "Do you have you a long way to go?"

"A lot of miles," she said. "And a lot of years."

"Well, have a safe journey home," he concluded, heading off to his car.

IV

So, she thought, her search was over. She had done her best, and she thanked Jesus for whatever truth she may have found. She slowly made her way back to the bench in front of the hardware store and eased down in exhaustion. Her mind went blank as she waited for her driver to return.

He arrived right on time and got out to open the door. As he turned the cab around and slowly headed back to Marietta, she tried to fix an image of the town in her mind. One by one the old chicken plant, the straggling line of stores, and the little clapboard church receded from view. The lifting of the spirit that she had felt when she saw the name Precious had collapsed again, leaving her not exactly depressed but not elated or even fully satisfied.

A couple miles out of town, the driver asked politely, "Did you find what you was looking for?"

She shrugged her shoulders but conceded, "I think I might."

"This is the first time I ever brought anybody to this town," he went on. "How long ago did you live here?"

"Many, many years," she said, now glad for the conversation. "At first, I hardly recognized a thing though it probably hasn't really changed much."

"I expect it hasn't," he said.

She was quiet for a minute, then said, "So I guess you're wondering why I wanted to come back."

"I don't want to pry, Mrs."

"Well," she said after a pause, "I came out here to find a daughter I haven't seen since the day she was born. Fifty-eight years ago." She stopped a second, amazed at what she had just revealed, and amazed that just those few words seemed to have begun lifting a burden from her. He said nothing, but she sensed he was listening, not just politely letting her fill the conversational void.

Suddenly, she felt eager, even compelled, to offer him more details. She didn't tell him the whole story, not by any means; she certainly didn't reveal any intimate details. She could never imagine herself saying such things to anyone. But it was enough to satisfy her that she had finally told her story to someone. When he seemed sure that she had finished, he said that it was a brave thing she had done, coming so far to a place she hadn't seen in so long just to find someone she hardly knew.

"It was something I just had to do," she said. "At least if I want to regard myself as a Christian woman."

They were quiet for the rest of the ride. When they got to the hotel, she fumbled in her nearly empty wallet for the fare. He turned to face her. "The trip's on me, Mrs.," he said. "Anybody going to all the trouble you went to, well, they at least deserve a free ride for the final mile."

All she could say as he opened the door to let her out was, "The world don't have enough people like you. You're a true Christian man."

During the ride home the next day, she felt awash with conflicting feelings. Disappointment, of course, that she never would know the answer to the mystery of her own daughter. But also a sense of finality. She had actually done all she planned, and she was satisfied that there was nothing more she could do. She let her mind drift for a while, feeling neither happy nor sad.

After she ate the small lunch she had bought with the last of her money, she felt revived enough to read her Bible. She did as the elder sometimes did, opening to a passage at random, believing it might offer her a key to help unlock the door to salvation.

Closing her eyes, she turned right to one of the *Psalms*. "Blessed is he whose transgression is forgiven," she read, "and whose sin is covered...I acknowledged my sin to Thee, and I did not hide my iniquity." She said a little prayer to Jesus, hoping she had done enough to have her old transgression forgiven. But then and there she decided she didn't need to confess it to the rest of the world. Just so long as Jesus knew, she trusted that would be enough. Some secrets, she reasoned, were best left secret.

It was evening when she got home. The answering machine was blinking with unanswered calls. No sooner did she set her suitcase down than the phone rang.

"Sister, where you been?" said the voice, a bit breathless. "We been worried. You ain't never missed choir practice before. We was getting ready to call your daughter."

"I had the laryngitis and couldn't speak a word," she said, after the briefest pause, amazed at how easily she came up with another useful lie. "But I'm doing fine now."

"You absolutely sure, sister? Ain't nothing troubling you?"

"I'm fine," she affirmed. "Good as I been in a long while."

Then she had to listen to a summary of the new music they would be singing on Sunday. "We even got ourselves a funky, upbeat new arrangement of 'Amazin' Grace'."

"Amazin' grace," said Sarah. "Yes, indeed. It sure can come in lots of amazing forms."

Afterwards, she deleted all the messages and stretched out on the sofa to rest. She thought about the ancient Hebrews setting out from Egypt on their journey to the Promised Land and how tired they must have been after forty years of traveling and with lots of battles still to fight. She was bone tired after just the three days of her journey. But she had done what she needed to do. It was enough.

COFFEE CAKE

Raymond Knight shook out his umbrella in the hallway before entering his apartment. He held up a white baker's bag so that he wouldn't drip any water on it. Through the door he could hear the faint sounds of music.

The apartment was warm, even slightly stuffy. He opened out the umbrella again to let it dry, hung up his raincoat, and hid the bag on the shelf of the coat closet before making his presence known. He was tall, fair, and sturdily built, but there was a refinement about him that was reflected in his fine features and small, almost delicate hands. He pulled on the gray cardigan sweater that he usually wore around the apartment on chilly nights.

"Smells delicious," he called out above the rippling sounds of *La Mer.* His wife Lydia peeked out of the entryway to the kitchen. "Is that roast chicken?" he called.

"Yes, dear," she called back. "And wild rice."

"My favorites again, sweetheart," he said wandering into the kitchen. He kissed her and nuzzled her cheek softly, taking in the lemony scent of her perfume. She was, he thought to himself for the two hundred and fortieth time, the most beautiful girl he had ever seen. So petite, so refined, so well spoken. Imagine her still wearing jewelry for dinner, and with her perfume as fresh and pleasing as it had been in the morning. So perfectly and ideally feminine, he thought, and so perfectly right for him.

"You're going to spoil me," he said.

"Only because you deserve it, Ramon. Besides, today's our anniversary. Remember?"

"How could I forget?" he said. "Just think. Eight months already. You look so fresh," he added. "Did you have your nap today?"

"I simply had to," she said. "You must be really tired, dear. Just look at the circles under your eyes." She traced them with a well-manicured finger. "Were you worried about your work last night?"

"A little, I guess.

"Talk to me while I'm cooking," she said. "I want to know all about your day. Did everything go smoothly at the office?"

"Oh, for the most part," he said resignedly and then allowed her to pull out the usual list of petty annoyances. "I guess I just have to get used to frayed tempers when big deadlines are coming up."

"They just don't know how to treat anyone as brilliant and dependable as you are," she said.

"How about your day, darling?" he asked.

"About the same as usual," she said, dropping a handful of French-cut beans into the boiling water. "Some of the sophomore boys were impossible. They were supposed to be finding books to check out for a research project. You can just imagine how well they were keeping on task. I wish their teacher had been better at keeping them under control. But she's new and still learning how to manage adolescents. I think it was one of them that wrote something obscene on one of the tables. In ink, which is almost impossible to erase."

"Boys will be boys," he said.

"I guess that will never change," she said with a smile. She sighed as he gave her a hug. "I'm just so glad I have my mature man to come home to."

"And I have my tender-hearted and tolerant woman," he said. "Everything will be fine just as long as we have each other." He gave her another protective hug. "Now, why don't I set the dining room table."

He laid out the dishes to the shimmering sounds of a Beethoven violin romance and poured the wine, their favorite Chardonnay with just a hint of sweetness, catching the drips with a dish towel. "Dinner's ready," Lydia called from the kitchen.

"Just a minute," he said, disappearing into the living room.

"Hurry, darling, everything is just right."

He reappeared in an instant with the baker's bag and helped her pull her chair to the table. "Sweets for the sweet," he said, showing her the assortment of cheese and fruit pastries. "Happy anniversary."

"Oh, Ray, you never forget."

They dined leisurely, accompanied by the atmospheric strains of a Chopin nocturne. According to their ritual, they did not speak of work or any unpleasant topics during dinner. All of those topics had been banished to the kitchen. Raymond admired the delicate manner in which Lydia lifted tiny forkfuls of food to her lips. He refilled their wine glasses during Beethoven and helped her to seconds after the beginning of Chopin. When the last strains of music had died away, they sat back and sighed quietly.

"Wonderful meal, as always," he said. "And don't forget, we still have dessert."

"Of course, your present," she said. "But I just couldn't now." Instinctively, he frowned slightly. "And after the trouble you went to. I'm so sorry," she said, patting him on the hand and forming her mouth into an expression of sympathy. "I know. We'll have it before we go to bed. You know how hungry my needlework makes me."

They cleared the table and did the dishes together, then settled into their usual routine of evening activities. He read the newspaper aloud while she worked on the little dog in her giant needlework picture of a girl carving her initials into a tree. Fragonard was their favorite artist. They discussed the articles he read, and Raymond thought once again that she was as intelligent as she was beautiful. Afterwards, they watched the first part of a new British production of *Sense and Sensibility*. Tonight, he yawned several times during the show, apologizing each time. "We mustn't stay up for the news," she said. "You're much too tired."

About ten o'clock, the phone rang, and Ray started perceptibly in his chair. They always hated to have phone calls interrupt their evenings.

"I hope that's not you-know-who from upstairs," said Lydia apprehensively. It turned out to be a wrong number. "She wouldn't dare call again, would she?" Lydia asked as Ray sat back down.

"I hope not, darling."

"How could she have bothered us that way after we were so nice to her?"

"Now you know you made a promise not to talk about that anymore. It gets you too upset. Besides, she hasn't called in almost two weeks."

She was Mrs. Hamilton, the woman who lived in the apartment above them. And she had gotten into the distressing habit of making late evening phone calls to them. The acquaintance had all started quite innocently. For their first few months in the building, they had never spoken to her and, in fact, rarely seen or heard her. She seemed to be a respectable, middle-aged woman, widowed or divorced probably and living alone. The only thing unusual was her penchant for moving furniture -or something heavy- at odd hours of the night. The noise occasionally woke Lydia, who was a light sleeper, and that, in turn, woke Ray, who could not sleep without her by his side.

Then, about four months ago, there had been a knock at their door at almost eleven o'clock. It was Mrs. Hamilton, dressed only in a housecoat with Oriental peacocks on it and obviously intoxicated. Even Lydia had noticed that. She claimed to have locked herself out of her apartment and requested, quite politely, to call the manager. Even in her embarrassing predicament, Ray noticed that she kept her dignity. The next morning in the parking lot she gave them a crisp hello but made no mention of the evening before.

That night, however, she invited them up for dessert. They went, partly out of curiosity and partly from a feeling of obligation. When Lydia had objected at first, Ray overruled her on the grounds that everyone deserved the opportunity to make a proper apology. The apology was proper, if brief, but the visit lasted a good deal longer. She set out a fine dessert on elegant china and kept an air of formality, but at the same time she was a probing conversationalist. Ray and Lydia found themselves telling her a good deal more about their lives than their natural modesty usually allowed.

Having decided to stay a half hour at most, they ended up staying for two. They talked about her till bedtime in place of their regular conversation. Lydia was impressed by her exquisite furniture; Ray, by her distinctly high-toned manner and the Southern accent he had never detected before. They speculated about her age. If, as she had said, she had a full-grown son, she kept herself very well. She was, Ray thought, highly attractive, at least for an older woman, though he never said so to Lydia. They even talked about the possibility of having her down sometime, but they never did. In fact, she disappeared from their lives once again except for the occasional late-night bump of her furniture.

Then, a couple of months later came the first of the phone calls. Right away Ray felt sure that she was drunk. This time there was none of the former reserve. She talked on and on, incoherently at times, about her life and her troubles. This call was followed by others, longer and even more personal, in which she complained about her loneliness and about the faithlessness of men. Ray was too embarrassed to tell much of the conversation to Lydia. Once - sometimes twice- a week she would call, often as late as ten o'clock, and no matter which of them answered, she always managed to end up talking to him. Usually, she was just maudlin and self-pitying, but sometimes she would pick fights with him, bait him with insults, and then, just when he was about to hang up, apologize profoundly.

She told him things about her relationships with men that he knew he shouldn't listen to. But he couldn't hang up. It wouldn't be gentlemanly or right. Besides, she sometimes told him things he wanted to hear, such as how beautiful Lydia was and how lucky they were to have such a perfect marriage. One night she told him that he was the only one who cared enough to listen to her troubles and the only one sensitive enough to understand. She called him her cavalier. She was drunk. But he listened and was fascinated.

The problem, however, had gotten out of hand. He was aware of that. He and Lydia even had a fight about it, almost the first one they had ever had. She had a tantrum while he was on the phone and forced him to hang up. The phone rang soon afterwards, but he didn't answer. "I don't want you talking to that woman anymore," Lydia had said. "You're not her psychiatrist." He had never seen her that angry before. Was she a bit jealous of a woman as old as Mrs. Hamilton? They talked about things in bed for a long time. There were tears, but they made up before they went to sleep.

After the argument, the calls had stopped. But then, just last night, she called again. This time she didn't seem especially drunk, and she didn't seem eager to talk about her personal life. Instead, she said things to him, some of which embarrassed him and others which horrified him. This time he was able to hang up, and she didn't call back. Fortunately, Lydia had been in the shower when the call came, and he didn't tell her about it. How could he? Maybe it really was his fault that she kept calling. Maybe he was somehow leading her on. He felt guilty. Just knowing that they were carrying on this "affair" over the phone filled him with remorse and fear that his own marriage might become tainted.

At ten o'clock Lydia carefully gathered up her yarn and put it in the plastic bag, then rolled up the mat with the half-finished Fragonard girl. "Time for a shower," she said. "Why don't you get out our special treat? I really do have a craving for something sweet. And would you make some of the lemony herbal tea tonight?"

The sounds of the water beating against the shower stall and the tea kettle clattering musically on the burner soothed him. He always drank whatever kind of tea she asked for, and they often fancied themselves enjoying a little tea ceremony. Lydia usually wore her Japanese print bathrobe. He put the cakes on an Oriental style plate they had gotten as a wedding gift and poured the tea to steep. Just as Lydia was coming out of the shower, they heard the wail of a siren right near the apartment building. They both froze for a moment then edged toward the window looking out on the parking lot, but with the drapes closed, they couldn't tell if the noise came from a police car or an emergency vehicle. Next, the outside door of the apartment banged twice. There was a clatter of footsteps on the stairway in the hall and a muffled sound of urgent voices followed moments later by loud thumps as though someone were banging on the door of one of the upstairs apartments.

"Whatever could be making that noise?" Lydia said nervously. "Do you think you should peek out and see what's going on, Raymond?"

"I guess I ought to," he said doubtfully."

"It could be dangerous," she said. "Maybe you shouldn't."

"I have to. It might be something serious," he said.

"It might be," she said. "But you do have to think about your own safety," she added, perhaps sorry she had made the original suggestion. "What would I do if you got hurt?"

"I'll be careful," he said, making his way toward the doorway.

"You should at least take a weapon or something," she said. They looked around the apartment till Lydia noticed the umbrella still opened up to dry. "This should do," she said. He folded it up, wondering whether he should slash or stab with it.

"Keep the door locked," he said. "Don't open it unless you hear me tell you to."

He peeked out. The stairwell by then was empty. In the distance, he could hear more sirens. Suddenly, two men came hustling down the stairs and brushed past him without acknowledging his presence. He looked outside and saw them unload a stretcher from the back of an emergency vehicle just as a police car pulled up behind. He held open the door as the two re-entered and began hefting the stretcher up the stairs. A pair of police officers got out of their car and followed them in. Ray realized that he was now inescapably part of the situation.

"Are you the son?" asked the first officer, a big, beefy fellow.

"I beg your pardon," said Ray.

"We got a report of an attempted suicide. Middle-aged woman. Her son called." Ray mutely signified his ignorance. Without further word, the officers headed upstairs.

Instead of going back into his apartment, Ray decided to walk upstairs also to make a discreet investigation. The door was open, and he walked into the living room. All the drapes were pulled, and the only light came from two small lamps set on the lowest power and covered by ornate, colored glass shades. The living room with its fancy furniture looked as if it had scarcely been lived in. The only signs of disorder were a whiskey bottle and some dirty glasses that had been left in various places around the room. There was a sour, unclean smell about the place. The apartment manager, bald and tired-looking, arrived soon after. From a back room came the sound of someone retching. Then Mrs. Hamilton's voice became clearly discernible.

"Oh, God, that's all," he heard her gasp loudly, a little hysterically. "There couldn't be any more."

"Are you sure?" said a man's voice more quietly.

"I'm sure," she said, more controlled this time.

There was the sound of a toilet being flushed. Though he couldn't hear any further details of the conversation, he assumed that she had taken an overdose of something. The rescue workers suddenly appeared in the living room, carrying Mrs. Hamilton, dressed in her peacock bathrobe, on the stretcher. Her make-up was smeared and her face was blotchy, but she was firmly, almost regally in control, her pride taking over when outsiders intruded.

She looked at Ray momentarily as the stretcher bumped against the doorway but said nothing and gave no sign of recognition.

Ray ended up acting as the doorman as the procession moved onto the landing. There ensued an argument outside the door that he could only partly hear. The rescue workers' voices were garbled, but Mrs. Hamilton's was clear and a bit contemptuous, demanding to be let off the stretcher to walk down on her own. The rescue workers evidently acceded to her demand. Last in line was a respectable-looking young man in a tweed sport jacket, presumably the son. As he walked by Ray and the manager, he seemed about ready to say something but thought better of it and mutely followed the procession down the stairs.

The manager closed the door, checking to be sure it was locked, and Ray, still clutching the umbrella, followed him down the stairs. Halfway down, he thought he saw the door to his apartment softly closing, and when he tried the knob found it unlocked. Lydia, he realized with distress, had probably seen the whole thing. She was standing behind the door when he came in, anxiously holding her arms as though chilled.

"Hold me, Ray," she said, huddling against the security of his presence before he could even put down the umbrella. He switched it to the other hand and let it fall. He could feel her shiver, but she made no sound.

"I think she took some pills," he said quietly.

"Don't tell me," she said with sudden vehemence. "I don't want to know. I don't want to know any of the disgusting details."

Ray was taken aback by the forcefulness of her words. "She at least seemed to be all right when they were taking her out," he said placatingly.

"I don't care," she said. "I hope she's really sick. She deserves it."

"But darling," he said.

"I saw her come down the stairs. She looked so ugly and old. Like a washed-out hag."

"Don't say that, Lydia," he said, shocked by the harshness of her tone.

"She deserves to suffer."

"But we know so little about her problems."

"Some of us know a lot more than others," she said, stiffening and drawing away from him with anger and resentment.

"Well, I do know for a fact that she's had a rough time lately," said Ray defensively.

"Don't defend her. She had no right to drag us into her problems. How dare she call at all hours of the night!" Ray reached out to hold her again, but she pulled farther away. "And how dare she do whatever she just did up in her apartment! She had no damn right to do that." Turning away from him, she stepped on the umbrella then petulantly kicked it against the wall. Then she stalked off into the kitchen. He could hear her crying softly, but he stood rooted, unable to decide what to do. He stood by the dining room table where the tea was getting cold. She was leaning against the refrigerator and wouldn't look at him. Finally, after working up his courage, he walked over and took her in his arms again. This time she didn't resist but rested limply in his embrace. Then, she looked up at him with a pained expression.

"I'm so sorry, Ray. I just don't know how I could have said such nasty things to you." He petted her hair but said nothing. "I want you to tell me you forgive me," she said, looking squarely at him. He kissed her on the eyes but said nothing. "Right now," she said firmly. "I want you to tell me you forgive me." She paused a moment to be sure he was taking her seriously.

"I forgive you," he mumbled, trying to find the right tone.

"And promise, right now, that you'll forget all those nasty things I said about you. You have to erase them from your mind as though I never said them." He looked down at her red-rimmed eyes. "Say you promise," she said again, more forcefully.

"I promise," he said. She buried her face in his chest and would not raise it for a couple minutes. He was at a complete loss of what to do. Finally, he said gently, "Darling, don't be so upset." He paused to consider the next avenue of comfort. "You know, we still haven't eaten our special surprise. Why don't I reheat our tea? That might help you feel better."

"No," she said. "No, I couldn't. Not after all that's happened. I just couldn't eat a thing."

She went into the bedroom while he put the coffee cakes back in the bag and poured the tea down the drain. It was almost the first day they had missed their tea ceremony since they had been married. Afterward, he put on his pajamas and brushed his teeth. When he got into bed, she was sniffing quietly.

"Why the tears?" he asked, pulling against her in the spoon position. She turned over to face him, lifting herself up on one elbow.

"Because," she said, still sniffing.

"Because why?"

"Because things aren't perfect anymore," she said. He looked at her quizzically. "Once upon a time, everything was perfect for us," she continued. "At least at home. But now things aren't perfect here either."

"You have to forget that any of this ever happened."

"But what if I can't?"

"You just have to." He said some forgettable words of consolation, and they held each other in separate silence. Finally, she turned over out of his embrace and went to sleep on her side of the bed. He lay awake thinking about the loss of Eden.

The next morning she was quiet and remote. At breakfast she picked at her poached eggs and nibbled at her toast but hardly ate anything. When he asked her what kind of tea she wanted, she said she didn't care, and he was forced to make the decision by himself. Choosing the tea had always been her job. He felt oppressed by the reality of the night before. He put on the kettle and, as he was making his own toast, noticed the bag of coffee cakes still sitting on the counter.

"Won't you have something more to eat, darling?" he said. "You're going to be awfully hungry."

She shook her head. Her face was so pinched and unhappy that she didn't even look like his own Lydia. He felt he would give anything just to get her to smile again. Their silence made the whole meal seem unreal. The whole of the last ten hours, he reflected, were unreal, a violation of the intimate routine they followed in the perfect little world they had created for themselves.

"I'm really hungry," he said mainly to himself while buttering his toast. "It must be because of all those strange dreams I had."

"What did you dream about?" she asked politely, responding to the unspoken pact they had of never ignoring the other's conversation.

"To tell the truth," he said, "I can't remember. I can't remember any details at all. But last night was one stormy night."

For the first time that morning, Lydia really looked at him. "Did you really forget all those dreams?" she asked.

"Everything," he said, not returning her look. "All I remember is that we were so tired, we went to bed early without watching the news." He paused. "And without even having our treat," he added, smiling and glancing at the bag on the counter.

"Raymond," she said. "One of the things I love about you is that you can't tell a lie with a straight face." She studied him intently. "I know I can't forget what happened last night. I'm not even sure I wish I could." She paused to collect her thoughts. "I have to admit I'm ashamed of the way I acted. "

"You don't have any reason to be ashamed," he said.

"Let me finish, Raymond," she said. "I am ashamed. That woman obviously has her problems. Maybe there's nothing we can do about them. But it was wrong of me to condemn her. And then to be upset with you when you were brave enough to try to help. That was wrong too."

"You were just trying to protect me," he tried to argue.

"No, Raymond, I was just being selfish."

They sat in silence, while the kettle whistled insistently, each of them separately turning over the conversation in their minds. There seemed to be nothing else to say on the subject. At least not for now.

"Are you ready for your tea now?" he asked gently. She nodded. "What kind would you like? I simply can't make up my mind."

"Lapsang souchong would be nice this morning," she said with a smile.

While the tea steeped, he noticed the coffee cakes still sitting on the counter. He got out their special plate, neatly arranged them, and put them on the table.

"They look just delicious, Ray," she said. "Does that one have an apricot filling?"

He poured their tea, then watched her eat the pastry with delicate bites, admiring her long, slender fingers and carefully manicured nails.

"The cakes are a bit stale, aren't they?" he said.

"No, darling," she said. "Everything is perfect. Or at least almost perfect."

A CHRISTMAS VISIT

I

The neighborhood was declining gradually and not without dignity, but declining nonetheless. Everyone who had grown up there said what a wonderful place it had been to live. So clean. So law-abiding. So neighborly. The experts had catalogued the main causes of its woes: closed-down factories, a lack of convenient supermarkets, underperforming schools. Whatever combination of factors, the result was that few young people with families and steady jobs wanted to move in, and ambitious young people wanted to move out.

All the nice old stores on the Avenue had closed long ago, giving way to cut-rate clothing and jewelry shops, chain drugstores, fast-food places, and hair and nail salons. A few long-established businesses, scattered throughout the neighborhood, still survived. At John and Ralph's barbershop, the two brothers still carried out the same ritual of trimming and shaving just as they had done for decades, but almost all their customers were old men. Gertrude still eked out a living from her variety store by selling cheap school supplies, flowery greeting cards, and fake flowers. A few did better.

Bartleman, the grocer, made a comfortable living selling fresh rye bread, deli meats and cheeses, and a limited variety of produce and boxed and canned goods. But even he had begun to stock items to appeal to an ethnically more diverse clientele. And Beckenbauer, the butcher, still did a good trade in pork roasts, lamb chops, freshly ground beef, and bad jokes.

The economic distress and transience of the neighborhood were not everywhere obvious. Only on the fringes did the illusion of order and respectability give way to a darker reality. Here the unemployed, uneducated youth hung out during the day at corner stores and on front stoops. And at night, they moved into the increasing number of abandoned houses to use drugs, to have sex, to plan crimes.

Fortunately, this group seemed far removed from Cumberland St., which was still a pleasant thoroughfare lined with a few aged sycamore trees that had once given it a little bit the look of a small-town street, especially during the height of summer.

Still, the brick rowhouses looked much the same as when they were built. Though the doors needed painting, the granite steps had gullies, and the brick needed pointing, there was an air of respectability, even pretension, about the street. It was, after all, the block with larger houses, fancier doorways, and ornate cornices. It was even said to have more churches per block than any other street in the city, from onion-domed St. Athanasius near the river to the gothic Church of the Holy Visitation just beyond the Avenue.

A half-block from the Lutheran church was a brick rowhouse just like all the others. It needed some repairs, but the sidewalk was always swept and the steps scrubbed. An old woman could always be seen at the first-floor window. She -Edith- was the eldest of three siblings who lived together in the house. She had lived there all her life. Her brother and sister had married long ago and moved away, and after the parents died Edith had remained in the house by herself. But a decade or so ago, the other two, their spouses now deceased, had found their way back home.

Now in her eighties, Edith seemed as fragile as an eggshell. Her face was a masterpiece of interwoven wrinkles. Most days she sat propped in a chair at the front window. With her wispy white hair tied up in a bun and her black dress pulled demurely over her knees, she kept watch over the regular comings and goings of the neighborhood. At mealtimes, Fred, the second eldest, would interrupt her watching to take her arm and lead her through the living room and the dining room to join the younger sister, Anna, at the kitchen table.

Anna was the youngest by ten years and still vital and energetic. She did all the cooking and almost everything else of importance in the house. Fred would set the table before going in to help Edith, but he usually forgot the napkins or laid the forks on the same side as the knives and spoons so that Anna had to make official corrections. For her, it was important that the table be exactly right, even though the dishes and silverware came from a half-dozen different sets that they had accumulated in their separate households over the years. Mealtimes were the high points of the daily routine, and every part of the ritual procedure had to be observed punctiliously.

Though their food budget was small, Anna was a frugal shopper. Her favorite menu items included pork sausages with mashed potatoes and sauerkraut, vegetable soup served with chunks of stewing beef, and boiled potatoes with liver and onions. These were the filling and economical foods they had learned to eat as children in this same house. Breakfasts and lunches were lighter, but substantial nonetheless. They had been brought up to believe that eating is a serious business and wasting food a cardinal sin. Nonetheless, every meal ended with a dessert because it was also a part of their deepest mode of thinking that every life deserved its ample share of little treats.

The rest of their day was just as structured. Fred worked hardest at just keeping a routine going. He was a skinny man with a darting, hawk-like face and nervous energy that kept him moving about restlessly. Every morning he rose early and after breakfast read the paper, looking down through his bifocals and humming tunelessly. How much he understood or remembered was unclear; however, he liked to think of himself as well-informed. Then he would putter about on projects that he believed needed to be done. In the early afternoon, he would take a stroll if the weather were nice and occasionally stop at Wally's Taproom for a beer and a little male conversation. The regular customers didn't pay much attention to him, however, and he usually returned a little insulted to watch *I Love Lucy* reruns or do an easy puzzle.

Anna's routine was more strenuous, but she was built to meet the challenge. She was a big-boned woman with thick wrists, strong hands, and thick, iron-gray hair. She spent her days in a complex round of duties. Each week every piece of furniture in the house had to be polished, every floor scrubbed or waxed, every knickknack dusted. And the house was filled with furniture and knickknacks. There were tables and cabinets crowded with figurines, old family photographs, ceramic robins, and pendulum clocks. All these solid chunks of the past had to be preserved from dust and disorder. This was what kept the world a reasonable place in which to live.

Then there were errands to be run. The round of activities never ended. And no matter what other task she had begun, there were three meals a day that had to be gotten ready on time. Fred, at least, would notice if they were ten minutes late. In the evenings after her bath, Anna would read the paper and sip a cup of coffee while the other two watched television. Over its sound, she would tell them interesting or humorous facts from the articles she was reading. Fred usually nodded or made some short reply. Edith rarely heard, often because she had dropped off to sleep in a cozy corner of the sofa.

In this fashion, their lives went by.

II

The days before Christmas always found Anna working harder than usual. One wintry morning, with the holiday less than a week away, she was busily setting out the ornaments and the Christmas cards when the doorbell rang.

"It's the old man with the funny eye," Edith said, referring to one of the itinerant panhandlers who had regularly visited them for years.

Through the blinds Anna saw the wizened face with its white flecks of beard and the strange eyes, one of which remained fixed while the other wandered independently in its socket. As always, she invited him in though he made her feel uneasy. And as usual, he simply asked for a glass of water, which he drank greedily, dribbling some down the sides of his mouth. Then, he sat for a while longer, half-listening to Anna's attempts at conversation. Finally, he interrupted her in mid-sentence to say,

"I'd be careful if I was you, Mrs. There's been a bunch of boys on this street the last while. I've seen them myself as I been walking about." After that, he got up, accepted a dollar from her, and returned to his mysterious rounds.

His message annoyed more than upset Anna. She had shopping to do for her Christmas baking and refused to be intimidated by vague warnings. She went back to the decorating, storing away her Thanksgiving knickknacks to make room for the Christmas ones. On the larger table, she set up the wooden stable with the artificial straw and the manger with the hand-painted Baby Jesus surrounded by the Holy Family, shepherds, and Wise Men. Around the scene, she arranged all the family Christmas cards. Most of them had not been received that year or even the year before. They were from dear old friends, most of them now dead. The only new ones she got were beautiful, flowery ones from her two children, who lived several states away.

On the smaller table, she set out her special treasures: three circus performers, which had been hand-made years before she was born at the old toy factory. There once had been a full troupe of performers: a colorful lead lion tamer and lion, a ringmaster, some clowns, and a striped circus tent. Now only a wooden horse and two ceramic acrobats remained. The horse's limbs were held to the torso by elastic bands that had lost their stretch, but it could still balance on its tail ready to prance. The shapely female acrobat, dressed in painted-on tights, could no longer keep her arms up to hold onto the trapeze. Neither could the male acrobat though he still looked handsome with his painted-on handlebar mustache.

After she finished, she put on her warm coat, scarf, and hat, wheeled her shopping cart down the steps, and pushed it in the direction of the church. The weather had suddenly turned much colder, and a few flakes of wet snow tickled her face. At the corner, she turned onto Trenton St. and headed toward the market, staying close to the wall of the church for protection against the wind. A sudden gust lifted up her hat, and she barely saved it from being blown off.

As she adjusted it back in place, she heard the slap of running feet behind her. Before she could turn, she felt her arm being wrenched and her pocketbook torn from her hands. The motion jostled her against the wall and knocked her hat askew again. A group of figures rounded the corner before she could see them clearly. She stood paralyzed for a few moments, buffeted by the wind and holding her cart firmly to use as a weapon in case they came back. Once she fully realized that she had been robbed, her surprise turned to anger. Never before had such a thing happened to her, and it made her especially upset that it had happened so near her own house. She looked around for help, but the street was deserted. Apparently, no one had seen the incident.

She began to wheel her shopping cart around to go back home. As she did, three boys rounded the corner, one of them holding her pocketbook. A wave of fear made her heart flutter. The three of them walked right up to her, led by the one with the pocketbook. They looked to be sixteen or seventeen, maybe a little older. She did not recognize any of them.

"Excuse me," said the leader, a smallish boy wearing a knit hat and a raggedy jacket. "Is this your pocketbook?" Anna took it wordlessly, feeling instinctive distrust even in the face of the boy's politeness.

"My friends and I," he continued, gesturing to the two behind him, "were coming down the street when we saw a bunch of kids hotfoot it around the corner. One of them was carrying the pocketbook. I called him on the spot. He dropped the bag, and the three of them raced off together. I got a pretty good look, but I've never seen any of them before. They sure don't come from this neighborhood."

Anna didn't know quite what to make of the story. She wanted to check inside to see if her money was still there, but she didn't quite dare. Instead, she mumbled her thanks, wrapped her coat around herself protectively, and steadied her hat as another gust of wind came sweeping down the street.

"Why don't we walk you to the market?" the boy continued, "You know, just in case those hoodlums are still lurking around."

Without asking, he took hold of the shopping cart and began wheeling it down the sidewalk. He looked harmless and boyish, Anna thought. His ragged jacket seemed too big for his slight frame, and the wool hat was perched, elfin-like, on the top of his head rather than pulled down over his ears. His cheeks were flushed and his nose running with the cold. He moved along with a bouncy stride, chattering away and sniffing back mucus from time to time. She could not see his friends, but she felt their presence, lurking silently behind her like an armed guard. They all walked along for a couple of blocks while the spokesman prattled on about how the number of muggings increased during the Christmas season, citing figures from a newspaper article he said he had read. Meanwhile, the blank wall of the church gave way to another blank wall of the old textile mill. Its chained door made her heart sink.

"Things just aren't as good as they used to be in this neighborhood," the boy was saying. "Only the other week, my own grandmother was robbed. Some boys broke into the back of her house. Fortunately, she was able to run upstairs before they saw her. They stole all her silverware and her TV. She couldn't even call the police because she couldn't get to her phone. By the way, you do have a phone in your house, don't you? I mean, just for safety's sake."

Anna was barely following the drift of his conversation, keeping an eye out for a familiar face, or better yet a patrol car. But she heard the question and instinctively answered with the truth. Yes, of course, she did have a phone. Immediately, she regretted having made even this small revelation. Why did the boy really want to know? But he hardly seemed to pay attention to her answer and went on pushing her cart and talking quite cheerfully.

In a few more minutes, they arrived at Bartleman's market. She went inside, relieved that they didn't follow her, and checked her wallet but found that none of the money was missing. She got out her list but was so flustered that she wheeled down aisles right past items that she needed and ended up taking twenty minutes to do the same amount of shopping she normally did in ten. At the checkout, she considered telling someone about the incident and maybe asking him to give the police a call. Unfortunately, old Bartleman wasn't there, and she didn't know his new assistant very well. He checked out the groceries without initiating any conversation, took her twenty-dollar bill, and wordlessly made change, ending their transaction by banging the cash drawer shut.

She decided not to make her other stop at the butcher shop but go home instead. Tentatively, she wheeled her cart to the door and looked out but saw no one. She rolled the cart out the door, searching up and down the street. Light swirls of snow shrouded her vision. She decided to take the opposite sidewalk. Instead of the abandoned mill, she would at least have a row of houses. She had hardly gone half a block when someone appeared magically from an alleyway and fell into step beside her.

"Let me give you a hand with that," said the same overly friendly voice. "I used to do this same sort of thing for my grandmother till she passed away a year back."

Anna was startled but not so confused that it didn't occur to her that he was contradicting himself. Didn't he say that his grandmother had just been robbed? At the intersection, the other two boys appeared as well and fell into line again behind her. The leader wheeled the cart along the uneven bricks past the long row of dark houses, whose occupants were probably at work. They passed an old man whom Anna thought she recognized, but he gave no sign that he knew her and failed to return her nod of greeting.

"I'm one of fifteen grandchildren, you know," the boy was saying. "My grandmother was kind of lonely because all of her family had left the neighborhood except my mother and I." The cart bumped down the curb as they turned onto Cumberland St. and headed past the empty steps of the church. "How about you?" the boy was saying, "Do any of your family still live in the neighborhood?"

Again, reflexively, Anna offered the truth. No. She had no family nearby. She realized, even through the confusion of her fear, that he may again have found out what he wanted to know. As they neared the house, Anna no longer was planning or fearing. Let them do what they wanted. She could hardly resist. But when they arrived, the boy stopped and handed her the cart.

"Well, my friends and I will be off now," he said. "Take care of yourself, Mrs. And be careful."

She felt so relieved she didn't know quite what to say. Perhaps they weren't really thugs after all. She fumbled at the clasp of her pocketbook and pulled out her wallet. Inside were several crumpled dollar bills from her change. She took one and gave it to the boy.

"Thank you," she said nervously. "You're a nice young man."

Nonetheless, once inside she felt more vulnerable than safe. She decided not to tell Edith and Fred about the incident, at least not until dinnertime. Instead, she made herself a cup of coffee to warm up and steady her nerves. Then, she plunged into the afternoon round of baking. Later, as she was pulling a tray of pfeffernusses out of the oven, the bell rang.

It was Billy stopping for one of his regular afternoon visits. He was the son of long-deceased friends of the family and now lived with his older sister a few blocks away. He was chubby and balding with fat cheeks and blue, extremely crossed eyes. The coarse bluish stubble of beard always seemed incongruous with those child-like features. Each morning, he went to work at an outdoor stand on the Avenue, selling newspapers, magazines, candy, and chewing gum. Around his waist, he always wore a metal money changer. When he got inside. he beat his sides to warm up and then pulled off his knit hat.

"Golly, it's cold out there. And that snow is slushy and wet," he said. "I gotta get old Brickhouse to put a little heater inside the stand. He shouldn't be so cheap." This was the way he had begun almost every conversation on cold days for the past ten years. He took his gloves off and blew into his hands. "I sure could use something to warm me up," he added.

As usual, Anna gave him some hot chocolate and cookies. He blew on the chocolate, then paused for a moment with an intent look on his face. "Before I forget," he said, "I saw Pastor George on the way here, and he told me he can't come to visit this week. Too busy with Christmas and all. He also told me to remind you," he paused in thought, "to remind you about church on Christmas Eve." As he sipped the chocolate and nibbled the cookies, he told her a joke he had heard and then described the excitement of the holiday shoppers on the Avenue. He was enjoying the warmth and contentment so much that Anna hated to burden him with her worries. But finally she decided to tell him what had happened.

"The bastards," he said when she finished. "You see these young punks over on the Avenue all the time now, trying to snatch a magazine or giving you a lot of lip. But what are they doing over here?" He scratched the bald spot on his head. "It just don't make any sense."

They talked for a while longer while Anna made him a second cup of hot chocolate. "Will you come over and join us for a while on Christmas?" she asked as she did every year. "What's a holiday without guests?" With a mute look, he asked an unspoken question. "No, Billy," she said. "The children won't be bringing their families this year." Then, he waited to be persuaded a bit to stop in for dessert. It was all part of the ritual. He finished his chocolate and got ready to leave. As always, he was enchanted by the toys and picked up the horse lovingly.

"You don't see anything as pretty as this no more," he said. "No, sir, they don't carry nothing like this over on the Avenue." He delicately placed the girl acrobat on the horse's back with his pudgy fingers and danced the two of them around the room. "Look at them," he said delightedly. "I bet she could ride all the way around the ring on her hands."

Finally, he was ready to leave. It had begun to clear up outside, and he left his coat open and set his hat lightly on top of his head. He was in excellent spirits. At the door, Anna took him firmly by the arm. "Billy, I want you to do us a big favor," she said. "You remember what I told you about those boys? I want you to find a policeman and tell him what happened. Then ask him to come see us. Ask him to come right away. All right?" She waited for a moment to see if the message had registered. "Remember, find a policeman and tell him to come see us."

She was hoping the horse, the acrobats, and the Christmas treats wouldn't make him forget. He promised to do everything she asked and even to stop the next afternoon to make sure they were all right. As she cleaned up his dishes, she noticed that he had forgotten to take his gloves. She looked out the door, but he was already out of sight. She did, however, notice the old man with the funny eye sliding by on the opposite side of the street with his long, silent gait. It seemed strange because she rarely saw him more than once a week on his wanderings and sometimes not for several weeks together. Even Edith remarked on the fact.

As Billy went down the steps, he was thinking about the message he had to deliver. A couple inches of fresh snow had fallen, but the sun had come out and its reflection made him squint. As he walked down the block, a snowball whizzed toward him from behind and plunked him on the shoulder. 'Damn kids,' he thought and looked around but saw no one. As he walked on, a couple more snowballs came flying at him from different directions. One of them knocked off his hat, and as he bent over to pick it up, another skimmed over the back of his head. When he picked up the hat, he realized he had left his gloves at the house. But another snowball from behind convinced him not to go back.

He became frustrated, then infuriated that he couldn't see who was throwing the snowballs at him. When he turned to look in one direction, he would get hit from another. One especially hard-packed ball of ice hit him square in the forehead, drawing blood. His mind became confused and, as often happened when he became too confused, he began to sputter out a string of curse words. He kept walking faster, hoping to get beyond the barrage, but his tormentors kept pace. Soon, their snowballs had driven away all thoughts of finding a policeman. His mind was occupied solely with his own personal task of survival.

He ducked into a corner variety store for a few minutes and watched some boys play pinball, but when he emerged, the firing began again. Bewildered, moving heedlessly on his stumpy legs, and muttering strings of curses, he finally arrived at his house, getting pelted one last time as he reached the front door. His sister had rarely seen him so livid, but when he tried to explain, he could only bring forth a confused and garbled account. At last, he relapsed into a brooding silence, and his sister got nothing more from him.

III

At first, Anna thought she would call the neighborhood police station herself if no policeman showed up within an hour. But she didn't want to trouble the police with a trivial complaint. At dinner, she told the others what had happened, trying to make the situation sound unimportant. At this point, she was trying to make herself feel that way. Fred grumbled a bit about how society would be better off if kids were sent to work younger so that they wouldn't be hanging out on the streets causing trouble, but otherwise he didn't seem upset. Edith hardly seemed to hear, but she pushed her food around on her plate distractedly, even though she normally finished everything.

After dinner, they watched television together for a while, but Edith complained of feeling unwell and retired early. In helping her up the stairs, Anna thought she seemed more unsteady than usual. As she disappeared under the great comforter on her bed, she gave Anna a wan smile but said nothing. Afterwards, she and Fred watched a Christmas special. Near the end of the show, they heard a siren nearby; a few minutes later, the bell rang. Anna got up instinctively feeling that Billy had done his job and an officer was finally at the door. She stepped into the vestibule, released the dead latch, and opened the front door a crack. A body filled the crack, pushing her back into the vestibule. It was not a big, blue policeman whom she had expected to be standing on the steps.

IV

The three boys swept her back into the living room. At first, Anna considered screaming, but she knew no one outside the house would hear. "Good evening, good evening," said the boy in the knit hat. "We noticed earlier today where you live and decided to pay you a visit. After all, I feel like we know each other pretty well now." He blew into his red hands. "Hey, you know it's really getting cold out there."

He pulled off his hat and shoved it into his pocket. "How are you, Pop?" he said. "We're the ones who rescued your wife's pocketbook today."

Fred looked dumbfounded, unable even to correct him. The boy took off his coat and laid it neatly across one of the wing chairs. The other two stood around silently and let him do all the talking. One looked ill and was convulsed every few moments by a wracking cough. Anna realized she should be terrified. Three boys - or young men- had just broken into their home. But the earlier encounter had dulled her fears slightly. They already had had their chances to hurt her or at least rob her, and they hadn't. Now she was trying to fathom what they could possibly want.

"Where's the old woman?" the boy asked. Anna explained that Edith didn't feel well and had gone to bed early. "That's a shame," the boy continued. "Carl here is under the weather, too. He needs a good place to get warm." As if on cue, Carl succumbed to a terrible coughing fit. His eyes looked feverish and haunted, and he kept his jacket wrapped around himself. "By the way, my name is Nick," he said. "And this is Alex," he added, after a slight pause, gesturing to the biggest boy.

As they talked, the boy's eyes wandered about the living room. Without the hat, Anna could make out his features better. His blond hair had been mussed and flattened into a peculiar and unstable equilibrium by the hat. He had a long nose, a thin mouth, and blue, darting eyes that neither missed anything nor studied anything too long. His slender body was in a constant flurry of motion. He soon began to move about, investigating and picking up everything in the room. "Don't worry," he said. "I won't break anything. It's just that I can't tell about things till I've touched them. You know what I mean?"

Meanwhile, the boy with the cough had huddled in the corner against one of the steam radiators and waited in a state of near catatonia. He was like a frog or a snake that, finding a warm place, seems suddenly to be put under a spell. Tall, muscular Alex, on the other hand, had disappeared. This made Anna feel more nervous than when all three of them were in the room at the same time. She had seen enough of them now to make a few judgments. The boy with the cough was weak, and the one with the hat was mainly a charming talker. The only one who seemed really threatening was the tall one. She broke her silence to ask where he had gone.

"Oh, don't worry," said Nick. "He's a big feeder. He just went to check out the refrigerator."

For some reason, Anna felt a little relieved to hear this. Could they possibly just be boys from broken homes who needed a little attention and a chance to see what a real home is like? She looked over at Fred to see if she could read any of his thoughts, but he sat on the sofa, looking utterly helpless.

Nick continued his tour of the room and kept up a steady patter of talk. She listened a while and then, working up her courage, interrupted to ask why they had picked this particular house to visit. She had to pause to search for the word 'visit.'

"Well, you know," he said, "I've been watching this house for quite a while so I've gotten to know your routine pretty well. I've seen the old woman looking out so serene every day. And you always washing the steps and carting back groceries so regular. And the old man always taking his walks and everything. So I figured it was the kind of family that might be nice to get to know."

He gave Anna one of his direct and winning smiles, but she was more chilled by the revelation that they had been under observation than by the seeming sincerity.

"I bet you don't believe me when I say that," he went on. "And I don't blame you. But lots of other houses in this neighborhood are dumps now. Isn't that true?" He made a reflective pause. "I've always known your place wasn't a dump. And I've even imagined what the inside must look like. With the furniture and the knick-knacks and stuff. And now that I'm here, it's even nicer than I imagined."

At this point, Carl broke into a terrible coughing fit. "Where's your bathroom?" he asked between gasps.

"Would you like me to find you something that could help soothe that cough?" Anna asked.

He looked at her directly for the first time and said, "I didn't ask for tender, loving care, lady. All I want is the bathroom." She directed him upstairs.

"Keep it quiet on the way up," said Nick. "The old woman is asleep." He paused and then said confidentially, "You'll have to excuse him. He isn't well at all. He's had this thing off and on for a month or so. But he hasn't really got anyone to take care of him at home." Sympathetically, they watched him shuffle up the steps.

"Like I was saying, though," he continued, "I could always tell just by looking at the outside that this was a nice place. I really like old furniture and that sort of thing, and yours is kept up so well. I bet some of this stuff is really old."

"A few pieces have been in the family a long time," Anna said with pride. No one had ever admired the furniture before.

"And I bet they're valuable too," he added. She felt a moment's suspicion, but he changed the subject with protean swiftness. "That's a wonderful picture," he said, pointing to a charcoal portrait of a young girl in a ruffled blouse with her hair piled on top of her head and a few wisps trailing delicately down her neck. "Who is she?"

V

"That," said Anna, "is my grandmother. And the picture was drawn by my grandfather before they were married." She was warming to her subject. "He drew her to look like a Gibson girl, but I guess you wouldn't know what that is." They gazed at the picture.

"My mother was pretty like that, too," he said in a hushed voice.

"*Was* pretty?" she asked.

"Yes. She died when I was just a young boy." He paused, as though collecting his thoughts, and then continued. "My father wasn't an artist, however. He didn't leave any beautiful drawings of her. He was a doctor, and a good one. I can remember my mother telling me that he could have practiced anywhere and even been a great surgeon. Instead, he became a family doctor. He came to this neighborhood because he believed he could help more people here than he could in a fancier neighborhood."

He was so silent for a while that Anna felt compelled to ask, "Is he still practicing nearby?"

"No," he said after a pause. "He and my mother were both killed in a tragic car crash."

The revelation completely took her aback. "Who do you live with?" she asked, no longer fearing she was being too personal.

"I've lived with my aunt ever since then. She's OK, I guess, but she's got her own kids to take care of. And her husband doesn't really like me. I mean, I understand. After all, he doesn't make much dough. I'm just an extra mouth to feed."

"Oh, my God!" she heard a voice say. "Get out the shovels. Better yet, call out the bulldozers." It was big, blond Alex returning from the kitchen. He was tearing at a roll and spoke with his mouth half full.

"If you don't mind," Nick said, "the lady and I were having a nice chat until you arrived."

"I'm only warning you, lady. You don't look like a person who's been around much. Don't trust cuddly, little boys with big blue eyes and a sad story."

"You have about as much sensitivity as my dog's rear-end," Nick shot back. "That's the part I kick."

For a moment, it looked as if there might be a fight. Fred cleared his voice as though preparing to intervene. But just as quickly, the whole problem blew over. It was Alex, who called off the confrontation. "Don't you have anything decent to eat?" he said. "Most of the stuff out there made me gag."

"I was just about to admire your Christmas display," said Nick, instinctively changing the subject. He picked up a few of the cards and read them. "You must still have a lot of friends."

"Those are from very old friends," Anna said. "But most of them are dead now."

He picked up the horse and examined it. "Very pretty," he said. "It's a shame it doesn't stand up very well."

"It's been around longer than any of us," she said. "I guess it's rather feeble."

Nick handed the horse to Alex, who put it on the table and manipulated its limbs with his big hands. But he couldn't get the horse to stand in a prancing position. In a burst of irritation, he tore the elastic band that fastened one of the forelegs.

"Do you have to break everything you touch?" said Nick, taking back the horse. "Say," he continued, looking around, "Where's the TB patient? He's been upstairs an awfully long time."

He looked at Alex. "Why don't you go up and see if you can find him?"

A couple minutes later, Alex returned down the stairs with their friend and gestured back at him with his thumb. "I found Goldilocks asleep in one of the bedrooms."

Nick looked at his watch when they were all in the living room. "Well, it's getting late, old people," he said. "Time for both of you to be getting to bed. My friends and I will watch television for a while and let ourselves out when we're ready." He offered Anna his arm to escort her to the stairs and noticed the look of alarm on her face when he announced that they were staying. "Don't worry," he said, "We'll treat everything exactly as if it were our very own." He gave her a kiss on the cheek. "And remember," he concluded, "it will disturb us very much if you come down again before we leave."

In his politeness, there was no choice. Now Anna began to worry in earnest. The anxiety of the evening had worn her out, but the thought of sleep never crossed her mind. Upstairs in her bedroom, she sat in her rocking chair, fully clothed, thinking about the evening and trying to decide what course of action to take. The situation remained unclear. Obviously, this was more than a simple prank though she couldn't be sure if there were any definite plan behind what they were doing. They would have to leave sooner or later. But how long would it be before they decided to return? The thought that these visits might occur periodically was too disturbing, and she drove it from her mind. She tried to come up with a plan, but her mind was blank. With their only phone downstairs, there was no way to call for help. And Billy seemed to have failed them. Though the boy in the knit hat -Nick, if that really was his name- was ever so polite, he certainly seemed devious and probably dangerous.

After a while, she got restless and looked out the window. Perhaps she could call out to someone down below for help, but there was only an old man hobbling down the street, small and feeble in the darkness. She stood and watched a little longer. Several times the door of the corner taproom opened, and a few people issued out into the arc of the streetlamp. But they were all quickly sucked back up into the darkness. She felt such a tightness in her throat that she wondered if she would be able to call out even if the opportunity presented itself. She was overwhelmed by the desolation of the street, which seemed to echo in the rumble of a lone truck passing by. Where were the good people when they needed help? Probably they had all left the neighborhood years ago without telling her. Or maybe they also were too feeble to help.

She looked into Edith's bedroom and saw that she was buried inside the womb of her comforter. How much did she know of what was going on downstairs? In the next room, she could still hear the steady squeak of Fred's rocking chair. She knocked on his door and went in, but he continued to rock as though oblivious. The stubble on his cheeks and chin made him look craggier and more determined. "They've got us cornered," he said grimly. "If we don't take action, they're going to have the whole house."

By now, she believed he was probably right, but she said, "They must have somebody somewhere who wonders where they are. Somebody must be keeping account." It was still hard for her to conceive of mere boys who were on their own. Then, she remembered the one part of the boy's story that probably was true: the uncle-stepfather who had too many kids of his own to worry about.

"I've been thinking," continued Fred. "And the way I see it, we can't depend on Billy, let alone any of the other neighbors for help. We've got to do something ourselves. Now they won't listen to lectures or reason. But there is one thing I think they will pay attention to."

He planted his slippered feet, stopping the chair in mid-rock, and stood up. Then, he went to the closet, opened the door, and looked on the shelf. On top of a pile of summer clothes was a .38 revolver, which he had kept at the service station where he had worked for years. He took it down, checked it over carefully, and spun the cylinder to make sure it was empty. Over the years, he had kept it well-oiled, shiny, and carefully maintained. “It hasn’t been fired for a while,” he said. “But it’ll do the job.”

The idea that someone could be shot roused Anna to action. She realized immediately that a single shot from that revolver would probably shatter their existence. If anyone got hurt with it – either one of them or even one of the boys- they would be the victims. They would be judged too old and too irresponsible to live on their own. They might be considered menaces to society, firing off a revolver at a bunch of young pranksters. She had read of more outrageous incidents in the paper. Her own children had already told her they would be better off in a retirement community of some kind.

“Not yet,” she said, placing herself in the doorway. “It isn’t necessary yet. We’ll give them till morning to leave and then decide what to do.”

“All right, we’ll wait,” he said. He walked over to the bureau, opened the bottom drawer, and took out a box of bullets. “We’ll wait till morning and no longer.” Then he sat back in the rocking chair with the gun in his lap and continued his creaking vigil.

Instead of going back to her bedroom, Anna decided to sneak part way down the stairs to try to find out what they were doing. At first, the talk was garbled, but gradually her ear began to pick up the conversation. They were arguing in low voices. She moved down a few more steps till she could hear everything they were saying.

“It may take some time, but I think we can overcome most of their suspicions.” It was Nick speaking. “The only one we really have to worry about is the younger lady. But she’s starting to trust me a little. She was eating up my story about my childhood misfortunes till you arrived. She’ll come around pretty soon and keep the old man in line for us.” There was a pause punctuated by a coughing fit by Carl. “Above all,” Nick continued, “you’ve got to be polite and give them a nice word once in a while. I don’t believe you broke that horse. I told you how important all those little possessions are to them.”

"By the way, I'm pretty sure I finally found a buyer for some of this junk." It was Carl's voice now. "A guy way up on the Avenue who just opened a consignment store said this is one of the last neighborhoods with a supply of old stuff still owned by people who don't know its value. There may be a thousand bucks worth here."

"Did you line up a truck?" asked Nick.

"It's ready whenever you are." The voice belonged to Alex.

"We'll take our time on that," said Nick. "First, let's give them more of a chance to get used to us being here. Besides, we still need to figure a way to smuggle stuff out."

The design now began to be revealed. She suddenly recalled an article she had read a couple of weeks before about some older people in another part of the city who had been victimized the same way. Somehow, knowing their plan gave Anna a sense of relief. The worst was being in suspense. But what was to be their fate? Did the boys honestly believe they could move in, imprison people in their own house, and carry off their furniture without the neighbors, the police, or anybody knowing? Just maybe they could. She wanted to go back upstairs but feared to move in case they would hear her. She heard Nick say, "We'll leave before they get up tomorrow morning and let them have the day to think about things. If they go to the cops, we just disappear for a little while but keep our eyes open. Then, when things settle down, we make our grand return."

"The more I think about this, the crazier it sounds," said Carl. "I just don't think we can pull it off. The old people aren't that stupid."

"It's not stupidity we're depending on," said Nick. "These people simply won't have enough imagination to figure out what we're doing till it's too late. They're so used to trusting people they don't know how to be suspicious. The important thing is to let them get used to things gradually. It's all psychology." He paused and Anna could imagine him flashing his winning smile in appreciation of his own cleverness. "Besides, who's going to help them out?"

"What about the idiot?" asked Alex. "What do we do when he comes around?"

After a silence, Nick said, "Right now, I don't know. We'll just have to figure that out when we come to it. But don't forget," he added contemptuously. "He's just an idiot."

VI

Silently, Anna crept back up the stairs. As she reached the top, the light below was switched on. "Look through all the drawers," she heard Nick say. "There's got to be an extra house key in here somewhere."

Before returning to her room, she decided to check on Edith. She was still buried deep beneath her comforter, but her breathing was perceptible and regular. Trying to wake her would make no sense. She quietly pulled her rocking chair into the hallway and began a vigil outside Edith's room. Sometime later, she drifted into a light sleep and, when she awoke, was startled to see that it was already 6:50, twenty minutes past her normal wake-up time. She peeked inside Edith's room and was relieved to hear that Edith still held on to sleep with the same delicate intensity. Then, she decided to investigate the situation downstairs.

She crept past Fred's door, expecting him to be awake, but to her relief, he was snoring lightly in the rocking chair with the gun still on his lap. She crept down the stairs, listening for sounds coming from the living room. Halfway to the bottom, she heard the bell ring. Who, she wondered, could possibly be at the door so early in the morning? The bell rang again and then again. Finally, she heard one of the boys say, "Get up, you loafers." The voice was Nick's. "Turn on the TV and look like guests or something."

She heard him hustle to the door and the door being opened. "Oh, hello," she heard him say in his politest voice. "Are you a friend of my grandmother?" There was a pause and the sound of another voice she couldn't identify. "No, she's not awake yet. My family just got in late last night from Toledo, Ohio, where we live. Only my brothers and I are up yet."

There was another pause and then Nick's voice continued. "No,

I haven't seen a pair of gloves around. You probably didn't leave them here. Listen, I don't think my grandmother would want you coming into the house. Why don't you come back later if you want to see her?"

It must be Billy, she thought. She heard him say something she couldn't make out and then the door was closed again. She crept back upstairs, then hustled to the front bedroom, but by the time she got there he had already disappeared. They had lost yet another opportunity to be rescued. She sat in a chair feeling weak from anxiety, her mind struggling to deal with the situation. A few minutes later, the bell rang again. She looked out the window but couldn't see who was on the steps. As she walked out of the bedroom, Fred came to his door. He too had heard the bell.

"I'll get it," she said as calmly as she could. "You get dressed."

"Are the boys gone?" he asked suspiciously.

"Yes," she lied, making her way down the stairs.

From the dining room, she could see the boys clustered in the vestibule. "I told you she's our grandmother," Nick was saying. "Listen, if you don't believe us, why don't you come in so she can tell you herself. I'll go upstairs and ask her to come down."

The three backed out of the vestibule allowing Billy into the living room. He stood there, squat, blinking, and looking both bewildered and determined. When Nick turned around and saw Anna, he was momentarily startled, and Anna could almost see his mind make the swift operations to cope with the situation.

"Grandma," he said with a practiced look of perplexity. "This man says he knows you. But he doesn't believe you're our grandmother." He gave her a look too complex to interpret. Billy, meanwhile, stared intently at him while he was talking. Then, he turned to Anna.

"After I left the first time," he said, "I remembered what you said yesterday about your family not coming to visit you. So I started to wonder."

He looked at her with his blue, crossed eyes, formulating a question, but Anna said nothing. Then, he looked around the room from one boy to the next, trying to figure out the contradiction. Finally, Alex stepped in front of him, put his spread fingers on Billy's chest, and pushed him backward toward the door. He loomed over Billy by half a foot.

"Don't you get the message, idiot?" said Alex.

Suddenly, he backed up a step and spit. A gob of saliva arced down onto Billy's cheek just below his eye. Billy said nothing and didn't even flinch though the hit was registered by the increased quivering of his lower lip. "My God," Alex said with an irritated laugh. "We don't have to worry about him. He's not even conscious."

Without even wiping the spit from his cheek, Billy looked past him at Nick. "I know who you are," he said. "You used to steal candy bars off the rack of my newsstand. You always thought I was too stupid to see. But I did." He paused and thought for a moment. "Your mother lives around the corner from me. I know her pretty good. She even told me what you did to her before you left home."

He caught the cuff of his coat and used it to wipe the spit off his cheek as though he had just noticed it was there. "You always thought I was so dumb, but I know a lot about you."

"Let's go," said Nick suddenly. "There ought to be a law against letting idiots like this stay on the street."

In a couple minutes, the boys had collected their stuff and were prepared to head out the door. "Good-bye, Grandmother," said Nick on the way out. "Wish the old people a Merry Christmas for us. And tell them we'll be back for a visit soon."

Even to Anna's ears, it sounded like a hollow threat. When they were finally out, she locked the door behind them and collapsed into a chair. She felt such a violent flood of emotions that she thought she would be sick. Her forehead and hands were clammy and her heart palpitating. She tried to thank Billy for coming to their rescue, to commiserate with him for what they had made him suffer, and to tell him that he was not an idiot but a rare species of creature -a caring human being. Somehow, she just couldn't find the words.

Fred, too, was downstairs, holding the gun, sleek and dark, in his hand like a Christmas toy he didn't know how to play with. He looked embarrassed, but, even more, diminished and withered. "I was going to come down," he said. "Several times. But I didn't want to till it was absolutely necessary." He paused, then went on, "I'm sorry, Billy. I let you down. You just lose all your nerve when you get old, I guess."

Then, Anna remembered the one still upstairs. Edith was still awake, sitting propped up against her pillows but still wrapped in her comforter. "Are they gone?" she asked weakly. Anna gave her a look of mild surprise. "I heard the boy with the terrible cough last night." She paused, then went on, "I knew there were terrible things going on downstairs." Anna offered just the barest summary of the situation.

"Those boys," Edith said. "I think they're the ones I've seen outside the house for the past few weeks." She looked utterly crestfallen. "It's my fault. I'm so sorry. I should have said something." She paused again near tears. "But they were just boys."

"You mustn't blame yourself," said Anna, sitting on the edge of the bed and rubbing Edith's arm. "How could you have known?" How, she wondered, could anyone have known?

Back downstairs, she called the police. While she waited for them to arrive, her mind was suddenly filled with thoughts of all the things she needed to do to prepare for a Christmas dinner that they surely wouldn't enjoy in the usual state of happiness and security. The thought made her angry.

Billy, meanwhile, seemed to have moved back into the moment and wandered about admiring the decorations again. "How can we possibly thank you for being so brave?" she said. He looked up, pleased. "What they did to you shouldn't have happened to anyone." She watched him continue his tour. "Maybe we shouldn't be allowed to live on our own anymore," she mused. "I guess we're just too stupidly trusting."

"That ain't something to be ashamed of," he said in a burst of indignation, looking up from the carnival figures. "Nobody should have to worry about being too trusting."

Then, he sadly pondered the damaged horse. "Look at this," he said. "The front leg is busted. And I bet there ain't nobody around who will know how to put it back together."

EXTRA POINTS

As the boys wandered into the fieldhouse and took seats in the bleachers, Jack Elliot sized them up, trying to guess which ones would be good ball players and which ones wouldn't. This group looked bright and hopeful, like all the others, though perhaps a little bigger than usual. They quietly filled out 3x5 cards with their names, a few vital statistics, and the positions they hoped to play. As usual, he made a special pitch for linemen. Then they listened politely while he made his opening speech on the qualities of a good football player: aggressiveness, love of contact, and above all discipline, teamwork, and sportsmanship.

After the talk he took them outside and put them right to work. They were slow getting organized for calisthenics, but that was to be expected. They were new to school and probably overwhelmed by all the rules they had just been told. He talked about what they could expect from daily practices and even demonstrated some of the types of drills they would do. This year he had to do everything by himself. For the first time, he would be coaching on his own. His old buddy Ross, his loyal assistant coach for years, had taken a new job at the last minute, and the athletic director hadn't been able to find anyone to replace him. Ross was good. He was easygoing and knew his role as coach. The boys liked him, and he got on particularly well with them. Together, they made a good coaching partnership. He was usually the disciplinarian and the details guy, but Ross had a special gift for motivation.

After the short practice, there was equipment to be given out. He took them to a large room and turned them loose to rummage through boxes of equipment. For many of them, it was the first opportunity to experience the intricacies and mystique of the uniform. In this room, he had his first chance to watch the boys interact in a less structured situation. He spent the next half-hour in the middle of a mob of slightly sweaty bodies in various stages of undress, explaining above the babble of voices how to insert knee pads and thigh pads and wiggling and jiggling helmets and shoulder pads to see if they fit. It was here that he first met Wes.

The good equipment had already been thoroughly picked over, and only a few dawdlers were still rummaging through the remainders. As the manager began sorting the discards into the proper boxes, Jack sensed someone standing behind him. "Looks like this is all that's left," he said, figuring the boy had come to ask him to magically produce a better pair of shoulder pads.

"I've got all my stuff," the boy said. "I was just wondering if you need any help cleaning up."

"Thanks. The manager will get all of this."

"That's all right," the boy said. "I'll help anyway."

He was tall and gangly and comically dressed in a tee-shirt, a pair of football pants that were too short and too baggy, and a helmet that tilted forward over his eyes. Everything about him was long, especially his arms and legs.

"That helmet doesn't look like it fits very well," Jack said, wiggling it back and forth. "Didn't you have one that fit better a little while ago?"

"Well, yes, but another guy had this one and it didn't fit him at all, but it sort of fit me," he said by way of explanation. "Anyway, we traded, and this one's fine." He took off the helmet, revealing a narrow head balanced on a long neck, fine features, and a mop of blond, curly hair.

"I bet you're an end," said Jack, figuring the boy had waited to lobby for a position.

"An offensive end," the boy said. "At least that's what I put down. But I'll play wherever you think I'll be most helpful to the team." He began to put the last few pieces of equipment into their proper boxes.

Jack was amused and a little curious. "Ever play the position before?" he asked.

"Last year," the boy said. "But I never caught a pass."

"A blocking specialist?" Jack asked playfully.

"No," the boy said without looking up. "The quarterback just never threw me the ball."

"Maybe we'll get one to you this season," Jack said, but the boy didn't respond. Maybe the subject was a touchy one for him. "What's your name?" he asked.

"Wesley McCaffrey," the boy said, wiping his hand before extending it for a formal handshake. "Actually, just Wes."

"McCaffrey." said Jack. "Any relation to Vince?" He was thinking of the powerful two-way end who had graduated a few years back and was playing college ball.

"He's my brother," said the boy.

"No kidding."

"I know," he said smiling. "How did he get all the muscle in the family?"

"You going to be as good as he was?" Jack asked and right away knew he shouldn't have asked the question.

"No," the boy said. "I'm no great football player." He seemed genuinely unoffended. "I just like being on teams if I can be useful."

All the others had departed by then, and Jack moved the boxes of equipment back into storage while the boy put his own into his locker. When he went into the gym to unwind by shooting some baskets, the boy trailed after him. After taking a few shots, Jack passed him the ball, but he passed it right back, seemingly satisfied just to retrieve Jack's misses. As they got ready to leave, Jack said, "See you tomorrow. And thanks for your help."

"No problem," the boy replied. "You know something?" he added seriously. "I really think we're going to have a good season."

"We sure are," Jack said, trying to complete his escape. "We sure are."

The first week of the season, however, didn't go very well. Right away, equipment was a big problem. Every day before practice, he was greeted by a line of customers with complaints. Occasionally, it was a helmet that didn't fit, a loose buckle, or torn pants. But more often, it was missing gear, which they lost with disturbing insouciance. Each phase of practice had its own special problems. The exertion necessary to run a couple warm-up laps around the field seemed to some an irrational expense of energy when they would never run that far in a game. He had to patrol the lines of players during calisthenics to keep them from just going through the motions. He had always had to do some of this in seasons past, but this group seemed to need closer supervision than most.

The round of drills that followed was the biggest test of his patience. The boys had apparently been conditioned at least to accept the ritual of calisthenics. It was part of their image of how a football team should operate. But many of them simply couldn't see the importance of all the emphasis on stances, blocking the push bag, and tackling the dummy. They were out to play football, and this wasn't football.

Drills, however, were the key to his coaching style. Scrimmaging was enjoyable and gave them a chance to learn under fire. But drills were the time for the most effective teaching. They were repetitive and maybe boring, just like most of life experience, but they imprinted techniques and responses at the very deepest level. His dependence on them, he sometimes thought, probably indicated his strengths and his limitations as a coach. But without them, he hardly felt he was a coach at all.

Over and over, he demonstrated the proper stance and then watched them offer their versions of the crouch or the squat that seemed to imitate his own. He maneuvered them, prodded them, pushed and shaped them. But still a foot or a knee would stick out in an awkward position like a stubborn cowlick. He tried to teach them the correct way to throw each of the different blocks, the correct way to take hand-offs, run pass patterns, cover receivers. The problem was that he had too many things to demonstrate. When they performed the techniques correctly, he tried his best to praise them. He even enlisted the better players to demonstrate for him. He had the team run simple offensive plays again and again as he had been taught to do by the coaches he had learned from. Repetition. Repetition was the key. But even at the simplest level, things seemed to keep breaking down. All they really wanted to do was scrimmage.

Perhaps most frustrating were his attempts to teach proper tackling technique. He showed them how to move up aggressively, stay low, and drive through the opponent. But many of them insisted on stepping aside from the charging runner and jumping on his back like a rodeo rider wrestling down a steer. It was a natural inclination, but the players on his other teams had fairly quickly gotten beyond it. Most of this group couldn't, and they knew each other well enough by now to take keen delight in each other's failures.

One of the boys, Riggins, was especially fond of the technique. Pretty soon, the other boys nicknamed him "Cowboy Bob." He was tough and had lots of potential, but Jack couldn't get much cooperation from him. One day Jack lost his patience and singled him out for a personal demonstration. Even though he was directing every word at him, the boy was looking impatiently off into space. When Jack was finished, the boy looked at him, as if to ask if that were all, and said, "My coach last year said that defensive ends should tackle high and try to strip the ball." A dozen angry replies tumbled to the brink of expression, but he stopped them all short of words and instead went on with another drill.

There were certainly bright spots too. Many of the boys really were friendly, and some stayed around at the end of practice to work on punting, practice running pass routes, and especially to talk. They were a little self-conscious and the main message seemed to be: 'Do you think I can be a receiver?' or 'How did I look at tailback today?' But he enjoyed the interaction. On days when a half-dozen or so were there, he really felt himself bonding with the team. Wes was among the little group that stayed most frequently and seemed to have formed a band of comrades.

Some of the boys came with lots of talent, and he hoped they would emerge as team leaders. Others were definitely showing improvement and especially team spirit. Wes, in particular, was always on time and paying attention. In the drills, he always tried his hardest to do the techniques correctly. After determining that he didn't have a receiver's speed, Jack tried him at defensive end. During scrimmages, the boy was dependable and surprisingly strong though he lacked fierceness. If he continued to improve, however, he might earn a starting position.

As the first game approached, Jack didn't feel very confident. The team was still rather undisciplined and unpredictable with equal potential for success or disaster. There were still so many question marks, so many things he hadn't been able to cover in practice, and so many players who still didn't know what they were doing.

He really didn't expect to win.

Naturally, the team went out and proved him dead wrong, winning not just their first game but their first two. In enjoying the victories, Jack tried not to pay too much attention to the lack of beauty in the way they won. The games were marred by penalties, mental errors, and sloppy technique. And yet, there was a concerted energy in their scoring drives that was impressive. And there were perfect images of Churchman, his tailback, slashing through briefly opened holes, and Fox, his inside right linebacker, following the ball with the instinct of a veteran and making crushing tackles. He therefore chose to forget that Arnold, his quarterback, fumbled too many snaps and botched too many handoffs and then came off each time to blame somebody else; or that his defensive backs could not get their zone coverage straight; or that Riggins still played defensive end the wrong way.

Jack hoped these victories would improve discipline at practice, but they didn't. In fact, they helped establish more firmly the quirky identity the team had been forming since the opening practice. Leaders were emerging though not necessarily in a positive way. Riggins was elected one of the captains. The fat Nugent boy had emerged as the team jester. And Eddie McManus, enthusiastic, sincere, but somehow the master of the inappropriate word and gesture, had already taken on the role of goat. Unfortunately, the best players, who ordinarily would have emerged as leaders, were being pushed into the background. Jack tried to convince himself that all these guys were just a bunch of free spirits who were forging a winning team, but that illusion was shattered in the next game.

Right from the warm-ups, he knew the team wasn't ready. It was a blustery day with occasional rain showers, and the field was muddy. As the boys went through their drills, he could read on many of their faces discomfort and a desire to be anywhere else except on that nasty field. When they ran through a few basic plays, Arnold kept fumbling the ball. He tried to psych them up in his pre-game talk, but they scarcely listened, preoccupied with their own discomfort.

The game was basically over by the middle of the second quarter. The other team was neither big nor particularly fast; they were just clever and well-drilled. They scored in a variety of ways: on a sweep, an inside trap, and a pass play. With a 20-0 lead, the other coach was already beginning to play his second team. At halftime, everybody was miserable. If he had asked for a vote, Jack suspected most of them would willingly have called off the second half. They played anyway, managing a touchdown on a long run by Churchman, who refused to give up. The defense tightened up a little, at least keeping the score respectable. The second and third-team players sat glumly on the bench rather than milling around asking to be put in. At the end, they straggled into the locker room concerned only with the prospect of a hot shower.

Instead of being depressed, Jack felt relieved. Now at least, he had a clearer idea of how good they were. This would teach them a lesson, he hoped, and put him more firmly back in control so he could get on with some more serious teaching. As he waited for them to turn in their dirty uniforms, however, he overheard several of them talking. "Boy, this weather really stinks," said one. "We shouldn't have to play games on days like this." Over the clatter of equipment being shoved into lockers, he heard another say, "Did you see number 54 for them?" A few affirmative grunts. "Dirtiest sucker I ever played against. All he did was hold."

On the way out, they moved past him wordlessly, perhaps a little accusatorily. Obviously, they had seen the game a little differently than he had. He complimented the ones who had played well, but there weren't many and the silence was awkward. When he thought they were all finally gone, he saw Wes, still standing in front of the mirror combing his hair.

"That manager sure is quick," he said, glancing over at the already filled laundry hamper.

"Everybody likes to get home early," Jack said. "Especially after a game like this."

"Want to shoot some baskets?" the boy asked hopefully.

"Sorry. I've got some things to do," Jack said vaguely, gathering up his stuff to leave.

"I understand," he said as he put away his comb. "By the way, Coach," he asked in an offhand tone, "Do you think that team we played last week was pretty small?"

Jack scrutinized him, trying to read what was on his mind. "They were kind of small," he said. "Why?"

"Oh, nothing," he said. "I was just wondering. Anyway, I hope we do better next week.

The look on the boy's face when he asked the question stuck in Jack's mind. Apparently, he had been willing to look straight and clear at things even before Jack had. They walked down the hall in silence. As Jack let the boy out, he said, "Good game, son, though he couldn't quite remember any particular plays for which he could compliment him.

"Thanks, Coach," he said, sounding genuinely pleased. "I didn't think I was going to be any good on defense, but I'm really getting to like it."

After he locked the door, it occurred to Jack that he actually had played fairly well even though he had only been in for a few series of downs. He had made no flashy tackles, but he had strung out a couple of plays by knocking out the interference, just as he had been taught, allowing the linebackers to make the tackles. It seemed just like the boy, he thought, letting somebody else get credit in the scorebook. Maybe it was time to play him more.

During the next week of practice, Jack went back to work on the fundamentals, but with little success. The loss had had no effect on them. They were still as disorganized and lacking in concentration as ever, and they saw the drills as totally separate from actual game experience. They were the coach's time fillers used to delay the reward of a scrimmage at the end of practice. The system was something that could only have been invented by an adult. He sure wished Ross were around. He had been the one who could invent ways to make the drills more fun.

Unfortunately, getting them ready for their next opponent would require more than fun and games. The scouting report he got from another coach indicated the team was good, not fancy but strong and fast. It would be a team that had to be beaten with technique and discipline. On the day before the game, he asked Churchman and Fox, his top players, to stay after practice. They were both quiet and self-motivated, but he encouraged them to be more vocal leaders; the rest of the guys needed to hear them on the sidelines and especially in the huddle. After they left, he began turning over in his mind another challenge: how to handle Riggins, who had made more mistakes than good plays in the last game. While he thought, he watched Wes fielding punts. With his long legs and the facemask on his helmet jutting way out, he looked like an egret high-stepping in a grassy marsh. But once he got to the ball, he never dropped it. In a few minutes, Jack called him over.

"You've got good hands," he said. "I almost forgot you used to be an offensive end."

Wes flashed him a grin. "An end who never caught a pass," he reminded Jack.

"How would you like a starting job?" he asked. Wes looked surprised and pleased. "I need you at defensive end," Jack went on, realizing he probably would be disappointed. "You're the end who knows how to play the position best."

"Starting defensive end," said Wes tentatively. "I guess I can handle the job.

"You'll do fine," Jack assured him though the boy's reaction made him feel unsure about the wisdom of the decision.

The boy looked pretty well convinced, but then considered for a moment. "Which side will I be playing?" he asked.

"Left."

"You mean instead of Cowboy Bob?" Jack nodded. "Why him?"

"Because I think you can do a better job," Jack said.

"But he's one of the captains," the boy said as though searching for a better reason. "Besides, football is more important to him."

"He already plays both ways," Jack said. "But more important, I can't depend on him. He makes a great play every once in a while, but for every good play he messes up two others." It was a bit of an exaggeration, and Jack could see the boy wasn't fully convinced. "Wes," he continued, "I know I can depend on you." He knew the boy would now feel obligated.

"OK," he said, still a little doubtfully. "I'll give it a try."

. . .

The scouting report had been accurate. The other team was big, strong, and above all mean. He would never forget his fullback coming off the field in the first quarter, ripping off his helmet, and saying with genuine astonishment, 'God, those guys can hit!' Nonetheless, he thought that if they had been playing together and playing right, the game would have been closer. At halftime, everybody was subdued, almost in shock. He heard no talk about how the refs were making them lose. They were being beaten very straightforwardly, and nothing he could say would change that.

Wes played as well as could be expected, helping to string out a couple of sweeps and making one tackle on his own. He got his shoulder in on some inside power plays as well and a couple of times ended up as one of the players dragged along by their powerful tailback. Midway through the third quarter, on a sweep, he lunged for the ballcarrier as he cut back and got knocked backward in a heap of gangly limbs. Another player piled on top. When the play was whistled dead ten yards downfield, Wes got up slowly, holding his right arm limp, and shuffled back toward the huddle. Jack looked around for a substitute. Riggins sat sulking on the bench, and by the time Jack found him it was too late to make the change.

"Get ready to go in," he said, and Riggins slowly put on his helmet and walked huffily over to where Jack was standing. "Remember what your main responsibility out there is," he said. "Contain. Shut off the outside."

The boy said nothing, carefully protecting his pride. The next play was a dive into the line, and Wes came off without further contact. "Just twisted my shoulder a little," he said, heading toward the bench. "It'll be okay."

For the next quarter, Riggins played inspired football. He was the only one who seemed willing and able to give out as much punishment as he took. Even Fox had begun sliding off tackles, and

Churchman was no longer putting his head down for extra yardage. But Riggins was obsessed with accomplishing two goals: reestablishing his image and proving coach was a fool. Not only was he playing fearlessly; perhaps unconsciously, he was playing correctly. Near the end of the final quarter, with the rest of the team demoralized, he broke up a fourth-down sweep and brought the ballcarrier down for a two-yard loss with a perfect form tackle. As he came off the field, he walked near enough to Jack to be overheard and said to one of his buddies on the bench, "Maybe we wouldn't be losing if he hadn't started that damn stork." The remark might have been worth a couple of laps at the next practice, but instead Jack walked over and complimented him on his perfect tackle.

On Monday, for the first time, a good many of the boys were nursing little injuries. Jack used the injuries as an excuse for easy workouts for the next couple days. By Wednesday, the last game had been forgotten, and they were back to their old ways. But he had gotten away from the old drills and team talks. They pressed him to scrimmage more, and he gave in. Fatalistically, he felt his resolve weakening. He would have a tough time getting back to the old discipline. He was in limbo with this team, trying to figure out an approach that would work with them.

Being slack, however, wasn't the answer. The less he yelled at them, the more they picked at each other. He tried to cultivate the friendship of a few more of the popular players, but almost nobody was staying after practice anymore just to talk. He began to feel alienated, even from his best players. His leadership and their leadership had been rejected. With the purpose of the team in doubt, they silently questioned him now, too.

Everyone seemed to have deserted him except for Wes. Each day Jack could depend that he would stay after practice, fielding punts in his egret style, catching passes, and hauling in blocking dummies. Sometimes he was talkative; other times quiet. But his presence was something Jack had really come to depend on. All week Riggins had been particularly tough to handle during practices, and Jack had almost decided to start Wes again. But he certainly didn't seem to want his job back very much. He knew benching Riggins might cause dissension, but he felt he had to draw the line somewhere. Wes solved the dilemma for him by mysteriously reinjuring his shoulder in a light workout the day before the game.

The next day they were beaten badly again. This time it was not by speed and power but by finesse. Granted, Jack had rarely seen even a varsity level team that could execute plays with such timing and deception. But his team was bigger and should have made a much better game of it. Unfortunately, they were not only sloppy and undisciplined; they seemed to have lost the will to play. They had one real scoring opportunity early on when they drove to the opponent's thirty yard line. Jack had noticed that the safeties were sneaking up to stop the run. His right end came out with a minor knock, and Jack looked around to see whom to send in. Wes was sitting nearby on the bench. "You're in at right end," he said. "Tell Arnold to call a play action pass and look for you on a ten-yard square out. You should be open." Arnold's fake pulled the safety up, and Wes ambled past him with his long strides. But just as Arnold was about to release the ball, Wes got tangled up in his own feet. Jack could see his quarterback hesitate, try to adjust, then throw the ball anyway. It fluttered weakly in the air -a classic wounded duck- and the safety, badly beaten, was in perfect position to intercept.

The game went totally downhill from there. The linemen, despite a size advantage, laid down after one half-hearted hit. The defense stood around and watched the plays set up, then reacted reluctantly and too late. Even Churchman had lost his will to play. After the blocking broke down yet again and he was dumped for a five-yard loss, he took himself out and disgustedly slammed his helmet into the dirt beside the water bottles. Every time the team got any kind of drive going, it broke down because of offside penalties, illegal formations, and other mental errors.

At halftime, Jack didn't know where to begin. It would have been impossible to list all they were doing wrong in so short a time. It was not a matter of making fine adjustments in execution or position. He needed to explain the whole game to them again. He decided to ask them at the very least to concentrate on avoiding penalties. It would be a place to start. He keenly felt he had completely lost contact with them, something he dreaded more than losing. He concluded with the traditional loser's motivation speech about playing the second half just like the first half had never taken place. But they went out and played the second half even more sloppily than they had played the first. They were penalized a half-dozen more times for mental errors, and two of them had picked up penalties for unsportsmanlike conduct. Not only had they disappointed him they had made him ashamed.

At the end, he gathered them all on the sidelines. Instead of berating them or scolding them, he coldly informed them that practice on Monday would begin with ten laps around the field, one for each of the ten offside and motion penalties they had committed, with further penalties for the two guilty of unsportsmanlike conduct. The locker room was quiet as a tomb, and everybody cleared out quickly. Everybody except for Wes. Jack was ready to go home and spend the night with just himself and maybe a few beers. But there the boy was after everyone else was gone, hanging about with a certain 'there-ness' that couldn't be ignored. It was as elegantly expressive as any of his spoken communication. Jack realized that, as usual, the boy was there for a purpose. He was, at the very least, restating their solidarity. They were outsiders together.

'How's your shoulder?" he asked.

"It feels a lot better since I rested it," he said, with only a half-hearted attempt at deception. "But I feel like I let you down today."

"Because you didn't catch that pass?" Jack asked.

"I know I should have had it," he said. "I just looked over the wrong shoulder." He didn't seem too upset. "Actually," he said, "I mean that we let you down. The whole team. It isn't your fault we're playing so bad. We'd be doing all right if we just listened to you."

"It's always the coach's fault if the team isn't doing well," he said wearily. "But let's say you're right. What am I supposed to do?"

"Don't let us get slack," he said seriously. "Keep up the drills. A lot of us really do want to win."

Ordinarily, it might have hurt his pride to be given such advice by a boy, especially because he knew it was correct. But this wasn't really a boy he was talking to, at least not at this moment. The buried adult in him was emerging. They were, for the moment, equals in wisdom. He waited in silence for Wes to finish putting his uniform in the hamper.

"By the way, would you like to know where I went right after you gave us that talking to on the sidelines?" Wes went on. He gave Jack a look, part proud and part mischievous. "I made a little scouting trip." Jack guessed it was time for yet another surprise. "My family knows the coach of the other team," he went on, "so I thought I'd stop by and say hello." He had a big grin on his face. "I hope you don't mind, but I picked up a little information for next week's game." Jack gave him a quizzical look. "They already played the team we're going to play and beat them by twenty points."

"Well, they beat us by twenty-five," Jack said, "so I guess the outlook isn't too good."

"He told me the other team wasn't very good and that if we played like we did in the first quarter we could probably beat them." He gave Jack one of his profoundly innocent looks. "They have a pretty good option quarterback," he said, "but not much else. And they don't play good defense." It was good information, Jack thought, even if Wes didn't exactly sound like a professional scout. "By the way," Wes concluded. "What's an option quarterback?"

"So you think we can beat those guys," Jack said, trying not to laugh.

"Why not," the boy said. Why not, Jack thought. How many reasons does he want? "We can do it if we work together," the boy concluded. "I bet every team goes through times like this."

"But how many survive to be winners?"

"Anyway, Coach," he concluded, "I'll be ready for those laps on Monday."

At this point, Jack knew it wasn't really in the plan for him to spend the whole evening alone. After all, loyalty did require a reward, and the boy had to be paid.

"What are you doing for dinner?" he asked. "How about the two of us going someplace together. It's on me." The boy looked very pleased. "Would your parents be upset if you get home late? You can call them on my phone."

"That's all right," Wes said. "They won't be worried."

Over burgers and fries, the boy reverted to his other, child-like self. He talked about his family: about his father who owned a successful business but was rarely at home; about his mother who had decided to go back to college; about his older brother, the star athlete; and about his younger brother, who was often his responsibility. "He's the one I get along with best," he said. As they talked, Jack felt the disappointment of the game and of the season fade away. There was something different about the boy's conversation. Perhaps it was his openness and his willingness to talk about his personal life. Perhaps it was the absence of bragging and the desire to impress the adult world with the variety of his experience. At any rate, the conversation was completely natural, if slightly dull.

He let Wes do most of the talking, but when he did ask a question or recount one of his own experiences, he could tell the boy was listening respectfully. Soon he just relaxed in the secure knowledge that he could mainly be an attentive listener. The season, he realized, had produced at least one minor success.

Jack arrived early to greet each one of them as they arrived for Monday's practice. He spoke to them briefly, reminding them of why they were running the laps. The penalty remained at ten, but they could run without their helmets. Then he gave them the order to start. Wes jumped up to lead the pack without looking back. A few got up more slowly to follow, and a few more followed them. He was only a little surprised to see Riggins near the front of the pack. The boy did like to play football.

Finally, all but five had been dragged into action by the mysterious force of peer pressure. The final five included a couple of expected holdouts but also a few others he was disappointed to see. Together they walked off the field and into the locker room. Round and round the others jogged. Nobody dared to horse around. After the last stragglers had made their way across the finish, he held a long team talk. He didn't lecture. The incident, he felt, was now behind them. He talked football instead. When he gave them Wes's scouting report on their final opponent, their interest perked up. "We were winners twice before," he reminded them. "We can win again. The season really rides on this last game." He wondered if this were just a coach's cliché to gloss over an otherwise worthless season or whether, in this case, it might actually be true. He would only know when he saw how they handled themselves in the final game.

The talk had the desired effect. For the first time in a long while, they finished everything he had planned for them without grumbling even though it was almost dark when they finally quit. Part of the reason the practice went so well was that he didn't have to do all the disciplining himself. Churchman and Fox finally assumed leadership roles. When someone was out of line, they got on him quickly and firmly. And they were applauding good plays. The spirit was infectious. As the afternoon wore on, Jack was able to focus more and more on just where individual players needed to improve and figure out how to make corrections.

After practice, he asked Fox, Churchman, and the two captains to stay and talk. For the sake of unity, he wanted them to give the five walk-outs the chance to rejoin the team. They would be given a suitable penalty if they decided to come back. The next afternoon all five of the prodigals presented themselves to apologize to him and to the team. Though none of them was key to the team's success, Jack felt satisfaction in having them back. Once forgiven, they began the long penance of laps, puffing through all ten with their helmets on, as stipulated by the captains, while the rest of the team watched in silence. As he watched, Jack thought ruefully of all the stages this group had had to come through just for the chance to end up, hopefully, as an average team. Turning out winners was a lot less work. With the slate wiped clean of penalties, it was back to work.

The final practices were long but organized. He kept to the routine of drills, but still reserved time for a closing scrimmage. They raised no objections to the workouts. He suspected, however, it was not really his leadership that was responsible for the changes taking place in them. The dynamics of this team were more subtle. Most of them had suddenly become ready for each other and for football. They had grown up enough to accept discipline from him -or probably from anyone who could teach them how to win. But who could say why? Perhaps the main contribution he had made was to be persevering, and Wes deserved some of the credit for that.

During the week, Wes remained in the background. Though he stayed after practice each day, others did too. But the boy didn't seem to mind being swallowed up in the larger team identity. Sometimes, Jack would notice him looming at the periphery of a conversation and feel the boy's comfortable 'there-ness' once again even while he was concentrating on what some of the others were saying. The boy was not asking for the exclusion of anyone else, but just the inclusion of himself. At the end of the final practice, after everyone else had gone, he had a catch with Wes, sending him out on a variety of pass patterns. The boy still ran the patterns a bit awkwardly, but he never dropped the ball. There was no doubt about it, Jack thought, the boy did have good hands.

The entire final game was etched sharply in his mind. He remembered them organizing warm-ups pretty much on their own and breaking into groups quickly so he could run them through basic plays. The first half was close. Though his boys racked up lots of yardage on a couple of drives, the score was still 6-

6. Jack felt they were the better team. If they continued to play as well, they would finish off enough drives to win.

Midway through the final quarter, they had an eight-point lead, but the other team had begun a scoring drive of its own. For the first time in a while, he had the pleasure of feeling actual tension on the sidelines. Something was riding on this game – a half-decent record and pride. He watched the other team rip off a seven-yard gain on a sweep and shouted at Riggins to knock out the interference. A tie wouldn't be so bad, he thought, but they really needed a win. He watched the other team gain six yards up the middle, moving into their territory. He shouted to his inside linebackers to plug the inside gaps.

Their option quarterback picked up eight more yards on a keeper and had to be dragged down by a safety. By now, he was starting to worry and wondered if he should call a time-out to reorganize. They had had a good week of practice but probably needed a few reminders on shutting down the run, particularly since the other team so far had shown virtually no passing attack. He shouted to his outside linebackers to contain, but the opponent's tailback picked up ten more on a pitchout. At the end of the play, he spotted a receiver wide open on the twenty yard line. The safeties had all started coming up to shut down the run. He looked around for somebody, anybody, to send in and found a defensive tackle.

"Get in there," he said. "Tell the safeties to watch out for the option pass and tell Fox to blitz. Watch out for 85. He was wide open on the last play." The boy would never remember all that, he thought. "Call timeout," he shouted, but nobody heard him. The substitute appeared in the defensive huddle. There was a long pause before they broke. Evidently, some message had been delivered.

The other team broke out of its huddle and lined up. The quarterback took the snap and rolled to his right. Sure enough, he pulled up short, looked downfield, and prepared to unload a pass. Just as he released the ball, Fox crashed into him from the side. The ball wobbled in the air as though the shock waves from the concussion had upset its flight. Number 85 was at the fifteen yard line waiting, but there was his left safety just drifting into the picture. He stepped in front of the receiver, neatly picked off the pass, and spurted up the sidelines to the twenty-five.

Jack let out a whoop of joy. Pandemonium broke loose on the bench. With just a couple minutes left, the game seemed to be in the bag. "First offense," he shouted. "No fumbles. No offsides." All they had to do now was run out the clock.

After two dives into the line for no gain and two time-outs by the other team, Jack realized they might have to give up the ball again anyway. He certainly didn't want to punt, but he certainly couldn't give up the ball on downs on their own twenty-five. He figured he should probably play conservative and pray. But he had noticed that the other team was really crowding the line and their ends were pinching. Then he thought, why not call a sweep? It was something Ross would have advised him to do. The other team would never expect a sweep. It was time to take a risk.

He sent in the play. The snap was fine, the pitch was perfect. The defensive ends were playing way too far inside, and the outside linebacker evidently was napping. Churchman turned the corner and saw nothing but open field. Jack felt himself glide along with his tailback stride for stride past the surprised linebacker and the astonished cornerback. The safeties gave half-hearted pursuit, but Churchman was gone. Effortlessly, he gulped in the seventy-five yards by fives and tens and twenties. Jack wanted to put it all in slow motion to keep the image perfectly fixed in his mind, especially the moment the boy crossed the goal line.

When he turned away at last, there was Wes standing by his shoulder cheering. Jack realized he had played very little that day. Then his mind made one of those sudden, successful synapses leading to decisions that only later seem obvious. "Wes," he shouted though the boy was right next to him. "You're in at right end for the extra points. Tell Arnold to call a square out right and be sure to tell him *right.*

When the play started, he momentarily lost sight of Wes in the shuffle of bodies. But suddenly he emerged, by himself, in the corner of the end zone. It seemed like an interminable time before Arnold released the ball, but it got there. And Wes, sure-handed Wes, did not drop it.

The game ended after the ensuing kick-off. The players all mobbed Churchman and even Jack himself. It was, he realized, one of those moments of acceptance that ordinary people experience only rarely in their lives. As they shouted and clapped and shook hands with him and with each other, he noticed Wes hanging at the fringes of the crowd. His achievement had been an anticlimax, its timing causing it to go unnoticed in the shuffle and bump of the world. But as he stood there, helmet-less, his narrow head looking small above the bulky shoulder pads, Jack could tell he was happy. He had done what he wanted to do.

The locker room was noisy and sweaty and joyous. Even before everyone was dressed, he had begun to be hoarse. He had heard or recounted every important play. He had managed to dredge up a compliment for almost every player. Now he wanted to sit back and savor the quiet feeling of success. For a moment, his tranquility was disturbed by that familiar irony that a season often ends just when the team has learned how to play. But one thought back to all those weeks of chaos convinced him it was just as well the season was over.

When the crowd finally cleared out, there was Wes sitting by his locker, now looking a little dejected. Looking at him, Jack suddenly began seeing the season in a different perspective. The victory itself, which had seemed so important only a few minutes ago, was reduced a little in scale. There were other, perhaps more important things that had been accomplished. Jack went over and offered some idle conversation to cheer him up, asking what he would be doing now that the season was over. The boy said he might play basketball, trying to make the prospect sound interesting. Then Jack thought about all those long-awaited free afternoons in front of him and, at the moment, felt the emptiness that inevitably follows the euphoria of the season's end. This year that feeling was accompanied by a more personal sadness.

He knew -and he could tell that Wes knew also- they would see very little of each other now. The motive was gone. They had been thrown together by chance, and the boy had reached out and offered Jack something more than he would share with anyone else on the team. But now they would go their separate ways.

"We'll keep in touch," he said sincerely.

"Sure," said Wes, brightening for a moment. "We'll keep in touch."

"That was a good catch at the end," Jack added.

"Thanks," said Wes. "I just needed someone to throw me the ball."

THE SECOND SON

Phone calls of late were bringing nothing but bad news, thought Phil Grant as he hung up from a brief conversation with another of his son's teachers.

He stood by the desk, leafing through a magazine for articles he hadn't read and trying to decide what to do. Stalling, he thought. Just like the boy would do if he had a problem he didn't want to deal with. Last week it had been Ramsey's civics and economics teacher calling to say that he just didn't seem to be comprehending the big concepts. This week it had been the boy's eighth-grade math teacher calling to say how worried she was about Ramsey's progress.

The arc of the garden sprinkler caught his eye, and he went outside to shut it off. The grounds, with the dogwood in bloom, the dense new stand of bluegrass, and the beds of multi-colored tulips, looked especially beautiful this year. He had put out a little extra for the best seed and bulbs, fertilizer and lime, not to mention the large investment in hard work and know-how. But the results were worth the effort. He could depend on getting a high-quality product.

In other areas, however, his investment didn't seem to be paying off. At least, not in his dealings with his younger son. Such calls were nothing new. Other teachers in past years had called to say that the boy didn't understand long division or had trouble memorizing the names of all the state capitals or was having trouble concentrating and had poor work habits.

Each time, Phil had felt that the boy just needed a little motivational talk. All children, after all, were naturally sloppy and lacking in concentration from time to time. Good parenting was, in large part, just a matter of overcoming these tendencies by routine and persistence. As for the boy's particular difficulty with math, a couple of educational psychologists had long ago assured Phil and his wife that the problems were purely developmental. His handwriting too would improve as soon as he got better fine motor coordination. And his spelling would improve as soon as his visual recognition improved. It was just a matter of time.

Unfortunately, Ramsey was not improving. At least not fast enough. In fact, according to today's conversation, he was in danger of failing eighth grade math. And his performance had also deteriorated over the past month in social studies and language arts, subjects in which he ordinarily did fairly well. Phil had sensed bewilderment and concern in the math teacher's voice. "Ramsey is as cooperative as ever," she said. "But he's simply in a world of his own. I doubt if he follows a tenth of what I say." She was a competent teacher, and Phil fully believed the accuracy of her observation.

So he and Ramsey would have to have a talk. Not a pep talk like they usually had, but a real talk. He wasn't looking forward to it because he had suddenly begun to feel that he really didn't know what was going on inside his son's mind. Until recently, he had thought of Ramsey as an extension of his own identity, unique in his own way, but still very much a Grant young man. It was the way that Phil always felt about his older son, Clark, who was just finishing a successful first year at college after a brilliant high school career. But Ramsey evidently was different, and communicating with him had become a special challenge.

. . .

The phone call had surprised him, but it was really only the culminating event in the reevaluation he had recently been making of his son. It was a process that had actually dated back to an incident on the baseball diamond a couple weeks before. It had been a mild early spring day. The puddles had dried up and the turf was springy, so he took Ramsey and a group of his friends out for a little fielding practice. Tryouts for little league were coming up soon, and he really hoped Ramsey would make a better showing this year. There was no pressure, just high hopes. All the kids were a little rusty, letting easy rollers go through their legs and making wild pegs to first. But Ramsey was the worst. He couldn't do anything right and didn't even seem to be trying.

Ramsey had never been very good at baseball or really at any sport, except perhaps for backpacking and camping, which could hardly be called sports. But he looked so much like a ballplayer - tall and well-built for his age- that he had evoked great expectations from his previous coaches. Unfortunately, he didn't have very good coordination, and he didn't have the instinct for competition. He would always be in cloud cuckoo land when the ball was hit to him. Obviously, this year's extra physical maturity hadn't changed that. The other boys had begun needling him a little. Then, remembering that Phil was there, they had looked over at him to see his reaction. He was angry and embarrassed that his own son could be so inept and ended up criticizing the boy also, more sharply as the morning went on.

There were other signs that the practice would not end well. At one point, Ramsey had run in to complain privately that the sun had given him a headache and ask if he could sit out for a while. Phil persuaded him to continue. Later he had taken an awkward tumble and bruised his elbow slightly while reaching for a grounder, then spent fifteen minutes behind the batting cage quietly playing games on his cellphone. It was a small blunder, however, not an injury that caused an embarrassing scene. Phil was spraying grounders and fly balls and had put a couple of kids on the bases to add some competition to the drill. He hit a line drive toward left field. Ramsey, who always had trouble with line drives, misjudged the ball but recovered and, with an awkward lunge, made the catch. The runners, expecting him to miss, were both caught off base. But Ramsey hadn't been able to make up his mind what to do and stood there holding the ball while both runners scrambled back to safety. Phil had just stood at the plate silently shaking his head in frustration. How many times had he told the boy to think out the situation before the play started? He said nothing, but the other boys took the expression on his face as the signal to work the needle a little more.

Normally, Ramsey had been able to handle such situations. He was used to little humiliations. But he had been unpredictably sensitive of late. Without a word, he threw down his glove and walked off down the left field line with his hands in his pockets and that annoying slouch he had developed recently. To save pride, Phil kept on playing, stepping up the pace of the action and increasing his enthusiasm. All the while, Ramsey's glove lay out in left field like a lump of dog dirt that all the boys carefully avoided stepping on. At the end, one of the boys brought it in and handed it to Phil with an embarrassed look before fading away with the others.

Phil realized as he headed home that he had just lost a large measure of respect for his son. Sure, the boy had made ridiculous errors and even lost his temper on other occasions, but he had never just quit. Phil had looked at these earlier incidents as little missteps in his slow movement to maturity. Now he began to see them as part of a pattern rather than an exception. For the first time, he was looking at his son with true detachment. He was a nice boy, not sneaky or disrespectful and certainly not bullying. But he completely lacked some important qualities of character that he was supposed to have developed by this time. They were the very qualities that had made Clark such a good high school athlete and enabled him to get accepted into the business school after just his first year at college. It was time to sit down and have a long, serious talk with his younger son.

He carried the glove into the house with him, slapping it rather noisily against his thigh, but Ramsey didn't even notice. He was sprawled on the couch in the den playing a video game. The coffee table was littered with orange peels and there were crumbs on the carpet. His jacket and ball cap were thrown in the corner. He objected mildly when Phil asked him to shut down the game but seemed quite unaware that he had seriously embarrassed his own father. It made Phil angry that he seemed able to put the incident behind himself so easily. He was just about to start the man-to-man talk when Ramsey interrupted him to say that Bruce Baynes, his best friend, had called to invite him on a camping trip the next weekend. Bruce Baynes, thought Phil. He was a nice enough boy, but unathletic and only in the seventh grade. Ramsey's mother would surely support him in his desire to go despite the fact that next weekend would be the first round of workouts for the upcoming little league tryouts. He decided, however, not even to mention that fact, at least for the time being. He also decided that neither of them was probably ready for a serious talk.

Since that day, everything the boy did or said seemed to reveal some deep-rooted flaw in his character. His sloppiness and forgetfulness were no longer attributable just to childish indiscipline but were the result of an inadequate supply of the mental energy needed to organize his life. His easygoing temperament became simply a lack of will, while his poor academic achievement was the result of some minor cross-overs and short circuits in the wiring of his brain. In trying to be objective, Phil realized that he had probably gone overboard in finding weaknesses. For years, he had seen the boy only through the screen of his own hopes and illusions. Now a more clear-eyed view was necessary to help him get a little more distance and perspective. In time he would find a more balanced and realistic image that he hoped he could learn to admire. Until then, he didn't intend to stop loving the boy. But obviously he was going to have to find a way to love him a little differently.

Some questions, however, gnawed constantly at his peace of mind. First, he wondered who was really responsible for the boy's failure to become good at his studies or good at sports or good at anything really important. He tried to think back to where he and his wife might have gone wrong. They had always given the boy attention and intellectual stimulation. They had let him try out new experiences and sent him to good schools. When he ran into difficulties with his studies, they had hired tutors. He himself had always exercised a firm and steady hand in discipline and trained him to have good work habits, though his wife, he often thought, had tended to coddle him a bit too much. It was, he rationalized, a woman's role and her prerogative. In return for this careful investment in parenting, however, he expected Ramsey would live up to the same high expectations for success that he had set for Clark.

Perhaps that's where the problem lay. Were they -was he- guilty of setting up extravagant expectations? It should hardly have been surprising that he would have misjudged the boy's potential. After all, both he and his wife came from very good stock. He had already made a highly successful career for himself in business and become a community leader of sorts. His wife had graduated from college and even begun pursuing career till they started their family. Didn't it make sense that all of their offspring should be at the very least above average? He found himself looking at other families they knew and calculating the ratio of above-average children to average and below-average ones. It gave him some consolation to realize that, mathematically, the chances were fairly high that he would have one child of average ability. But natural ability didn't have to limit potential, he believed, not if one were willing to make the extra effort. It was all about the extra effort.

Nonetheless, it would probably be necessary to scale down expectations, at least until the boy found himself. That way, they wouldn't be too disappointed if he weren't a big success and doubly satisfied if he turned out to be a late bloomer as the educational psychologists had been predicting. He hadn't talked over all these thoughts with his wife. He felt uneasy at the prospect. He had always assumed they were fully in agreement on how they viewed their children, but lately he hadn't been so sure. In the meantime, maybe they just needed to give him a little space and even a different kind of positive reinforcement. Perhaps the promise of a new bike or some new backpacking gear would convince him to work harder though somehow that seemed too much like a bribe. He would just have to think of other options.

All these thoughts of how to motivate the boy pointed to other big questions that upset him more. Never before had anyone in his family needed to be persuaded to strive for excellence. The desire to achieve was in the Grant blood. So where did the boy get his passivity and his lack of ambition? What factors had created this image he had of himself as a loser? And whose fault was it that he was so willing to fail? Phil had no answers for any of these questions.

His arguments with himself over the past couple of weeks had always gone this far and no farther. The only way he could learn anything more was to talk to the boy himself. He had been getting around to it for a week and couldn't afford to put it off any longer.

He strolled around the garden for a few minutes, trying out in his head a few opening gambits for the conversation, but none seemed adequate. Finally, he looped up the garden hose, took in the sprinkler, and headed inside, deciding to let the conversation take its own course. He hoped the boy would talk a little for a change so that the conversation wouldn't be so one-sided. He reminded himself to be patient and understanding, but decisive. The boy had to come to the realization that he couldn't be passive. He had to begin taking responsibility for his own future.

He opened Ramsey's bedroom door halfway and then, absurdly, stopped to knock. "Mind if I come in?" he asked.

As usual, the boy's room was cluttered but not exactly messy. Everything at least was organized in piles that had some semblance of order. The camping equipment, the fantasy novels with the garish covers, the biking and car magazines, even the set of *Star Wars* figures he had held on to with precocious nostalgia, all had their own place. His bureau and walls were covered with his drawings of fantasy characters, his carefully detailed renderings of floor plans for little houses, and his watercolor paintings of woodsy nature scenes. Most of the art was not especially to Phil's taste, but the boy's art teacher had convinced his mother that they were good enough to enter in some local art shows. The ribbons he had won were still attached to the bottom of a few pieces. Ramsey was sprawled out on his bed with his sketchbook, listening to some wild music on his I Pod.

"Why don't you turn that off?" Phil said, but then, hoping to avoid a bad start, added, "Just so we can talk." While Ramsey fiddled with the I Pod and closed the sketchbook, Phil surveyed the scene, thinking of it almost as a foreign landscape, unfamiliar terrain through which he always had trouble finding his way. "You know we haven't had any chance to sit down and talk over the past couple weeks," he said, clearing a place for himself on the bed. "How are things going?"

"All right, I guess," the boy said.

"I saw the surest sign of spring the other day," Phil went on. "You got your bike out. As soon as that happens, spring has officially sprung."

The boy smiled, temporarily redeeming the poor start. "I gave her the opening-of-the- season tune-up," he said with a smile. "I put on new brake pads, adjusted the cables, and cleaned off the old grease and dirt that were gumming up the derailleur. She runs like a champ."

"You've got a talent for mechanical things, I've got to admit," said Phil. "Maybe I'll finally pull the old ten-speed out of storage and let you give her the treatment." It was a promise he had made the last few years even though he knew riding a bike would just get in the way of his playing eighteen holes on the weekends. "How is everything else going? You doing all right in school?" He hoped that if he remained as casual and non-judgmental as possible, the boy would be willing to own up to the problems he was having.

"I guess so," said Ramsey.

"What are you studying right now?"

"Oh, lots of stuff," he said evasively. "You know, quadratic equations and the houses of the government and that kind of thing." He was always inarticulate in these situations.

"I just got a call from your math teacher," Phil said. He paused for an uncomfortably long interval, hoping for some kind of response. "She's really worried about you," he continued at last. "She says you're not doing well at all." The boy looked at a spot on the floor and unconsciously bounced up and down, causing the bed to shake. "Are you aware that you are on the verge of failing that course for the year?"

"I guess so."

"You guess so," Phil repeated, smoothing back his hair and waiting long enough for the rush of anger and frustration to recede. "You don't seem overly worried. Do you get along with your teacher all right?"

"I like her. I really do. It's just that she seems to think there's something seriously wrong with anybody who can't solve for all those x's and o's and doesn't get everything to come out neat and equal."

"And you don't think that's important, right?"

"I only mean that some people have trouble learning it," the boy said, looking up for the first time. "I just wonder how good she would be at fixing my bike."

"All right, maybe the work really is difficult for you," Phil said, ignoring the remark. "But she also said she doesn't think you're trying at all."

"That's not true," he said quite strongly and looked directly at Phil for the first time. "People always say I don't try," he continued, including Phil in the accusation. "But I turn in all my work at school and spend hours up here on my homework."

"What I mean when I say you don't try, Ramsey, is that you don't concentrate. You sit up here with all your textbooks open, but your mind really isn't in gear." He tried to keep his voice calm, but the pitch kept rising as he struggled to make his point clear. "You're surrounded by all this stuff," he went on, gesturing to the carefully stacked piles. "And you're always listening to music. Or doodling. How can you concentrate with all these distractions and all that noise going on in your head?"

"But, Dad," the boy answered in a surprisingly controlled voice, "the music and the doodling are how I get by. I'd go crazy otherwise."

"Is school really that bad?"

"It's not that it's so bad. It's just that I'm no good at it. And it all seems kind of useless."

"Don't you think you'd get a little better at it if you tried a little harder?" Phil asked, trying to swing the momentum back his way. "Maybe then you'd begin to improve."

"Maybe. Maybe not," the boy said with mature consideration in his voice. "All I know is that I don't do it very well, and I don't like it." He looked at Phil with his head cocked thoughtfully to one side. "If you felt that way about selling stocks and bonds, would you want to keep at it?"

Phil was taken aback. "But you have to do well in school if you want to do well in the world," he said. Stated aloud, the words sounded incredibly trite.

"And what if I don't care about doing well? What if I really am dumb," he said and paused, searching for the right words. "What if I'm just incompetent in school?"

"But you're not incompetent," said Phil, momentarily proud that his son even knew the word and, at the same time, personally upset by his poor self-image.

"Then why do I embarrass you so much?"

"What do you mean?"

"Why do I embarrass you so much when I don't do well in school or mess up playing baseball?"

"Does it really seem that way?" Phil asked, his voice trailing off as he felt the stab of truth in his heart.

"I know I'm not as good at sports as Clark."

"We've never compared you to your older brother."

"And I know I'm never going to do as well in school," the boy continued without listening. "But I don't care just as long as I get by."

"Ramsey, you know your mother and I love you just as much..."

"I know," interrupted the young man. "All I'm saying is that I've got to live my own life. Do you understand?" They looked at each other in silence.

"Don't worry," Ramsey continued, softening his voice slightly. "I've thought about this. I'll be all right." He paused. "Do you understand?"

Phil guessed he understood. The only question was whether he could finally come to accept his second son.

And perhaps whether the boy could accept him.

THE SUITCASE

A POSSIBLE FAMILY HISTORY

My great aunt Hettie died almost half a century ago in her eighty-seventh year. I was traveling and couldn't get to her funeral but a month later was back to visit when the family gathered to clear out the rest of her belongings before putting the house on the market. I took a piece of furniture, an old army uniform, and a battered suitcase filled with assorted photos and documents, which no one else even cared to look at. I gave the contents a quick glance, then stored the suitcase in the attic.

I wasn't really surprised at the family's lack of interest. I come from generations of people who have been uncurious about the family's past. Hettie was the last of her generation. Her three brothers had already passed away after quiet, unremarkable lives. Her life also seemed unremarkable if a little different from the pattern of many of her peers. I saw her whole generation as having lived in a black and white age, like her photographs, when people stayed where they were born, worked the same jobs, had big families, and died young. What history was there to record?

Hettie was born in the last decade of the nineteenth century and grew up in a working-class neighborhood of Philadelphia. She graduated from the sixth grade at Lucretia Mott Elementary

School, then went out and worked in one of the neighborhood knitting mills. At some point she escaped that dreary fate and got a job in the office of *The Evening Bulletin* and later yet in the office of a neighborhood attorney. She never married.

Decades passed.

Sometime during the early 1950s, she moved fifty miles east to a town near the Jersey shore to set up housekeeping with her brother Ted, he of the army uniform. It was then that I got to know them. She led a quiet life during those years of retirement. Each year she spent the month of August in New Hampshire with a friend to get relief from her asthma. When she returned, she hosted her childhood girlfriends for a week of gabbing and reminiscing. For Christmas, she came back to the big city to visit us for a few days.

So it went.

In old age she wore frumpy dresses, but she never impressed me as a typical old maid. She had dimples when she smiled and a twinkle in her blue eyes. She laughed a lot, and her laugh -hearty, wheezy, almost rumbling because of her asthma- was spontaneous and uninhibited, particularly when she got rolling on one of her stories. The repertoire was small, but we -my sister and I, especially- would always crank her up, like an old Victrola, to tell them even though we had heard them all before. Most of them involved practical jokes played on her by characters with improbable names like Jimmy Peacock and Fritz Stengel. The fact that she was always the butt of these jokes simply heightened her pleasure in retelling them. "Oh, brother," she would gasp between throaty guffaws, "would you believe it?" Was she aware of how often she told the same stories? She did seem a bit dotty by then. Still, we didn't care. We just enjoyed her style and gusto as a storyteller. We never thought to ask her more about her life. We were young and the young rarely think in past tense.

Besides, how much more could there have been for her to tell?

It was another twenty years before I rediscovered the suitcase while cleaning out the attic. This time I looked through it more carefully though I wasn't expecting to find more than a few scraps of her past. Not surprisingly, the contents were in complete disorder. Some of the photos were pasted in leather-covered albums; most were just loose. There were random scraps of paper, a few old newspaper articles, greeting cards, and a few letters. It was literally a mess of memorabilia. The documents, however, did catch my attention. At the bottom, neatly rolled up like an ancient scroll, was the marriage certificate of her parents: Theodor of Hamburg and Maria of Schwerin, Prussia. It was a beautiful work of graphic art, all in German, with a pair of angels ringing wedding bells and a couple who looked a lot like Martin Luther and Katharina von Bora being joined in holy matrimony. The date is January 11, 1890; the place, Zion Lutheran Church in Philadelphia. Here, I thought with a frisson of delight, was the fount and source of the family gene pool, at least the part that began begetting in the New World. She had saved something worthwhile after all.

Next, I unrolled several baptismal certificates, smaller but equally elaborate, picturing the Baptism of Jesus, Jesus with the little children, and Jesus the Good Shepherd. Hettie's birthdate is listed as December 13, 1892; her brother Ted's certificate lists his as December 13, 1893. Most surprising was the certificate of Maria Alwina, born May 10, 1896, and baptized May 14, 1897. Here is an ancestor of whom I had never heard, a genetic stem evidently cut off short. How long had she lived? Had she even managed to see the new century? All I could surmise was that she had been important to Hettie.

The other documents were Hettie's. First was her certificate of confirmation along with a photo of her class of confirmands. Even at age fourteen in her white, high-necked confirmation dress, she was immediately recognizable. As I gazed at her, she seemed to be gazing back at me with a bemused and knowing look. Why had she kept this particular certificate and photo? She had never been particularly religious as far as I know -except, I soon found out, in keeping up with people from her past.

The last of her documents, the least attractive artistically, was a graduation certificate issued by the Philadelphia Board of Education on June 8, 1905. It certifies that Hettie "has completed satisfactorily the course of Instruction in Cooking at the Lucretia Mott Elementary School, has been regular in attendance and diligent in study, and has conducted herself with propriety and to the satisfaction of the teacher." It is signed by a whole roster of pedagogical bigwigs from the superintendent down to Sophia Axelrod, Teacher. Thus, at age twelve, she was deemed to be an adult by the Philadelphia Board of Education and ready to go out into the world with her cooking skills and her good character. It was hard to believe that so recent a generation had grown up in an age before the invention of adolescence.

Captivated by the beauty of some of these documents, I took a couple to be framed and hung them in the house. Little by little, the daily interaction with them began the mysterious process of binding me to the people whose lives they represented. Hadn't the ancients kept busts of their venerable ancestors in the house to honor their spirits and guard the home?

Another ten years or so passed before I got the suitcase out again. It was a cold, rainy Saturday afternoon just right for such a project. I began sorting the loose photos with no particular plan in mind for organizing them. I was pleased to see a few pictures with people I recognized and separated them from the much larger pile labeled "unidentified." Then I separated the more recent ones from those from the distant past and the group photos from the individuals. And so on and so on. Hettie had collected haphazardly and labeled very little, so no method boded success. I kept arranging and rearranging the piles. Plotting even the most general outline of the family history would require more than a little detective work and even then would probably leave mostly yawning gaps in the record. But I refused, at least for the time being, to give in and seek help on one of those ancestry databases. It was the suitcase or nothing.

I focused first on what seemed to be the earliest photos. I will call most of the folks in them "The Old World Ancestors." A few are vintage photos taken at professional studios overseas. One is of a man in his twenties in a military uniform. His hair, parted down the middle, is probably pomaded. He has a full face and lips, regular features, and a hint of a mustache. He seems full of quiet self-confidence and authority. The dark uniform, with epaulets, is fastened with brass buttons all the way to the high collar. Perhaps this handsome young officer -the uniform seems to say officer- served in the army of the recently formed Imperial State of Germany. The photo was taken at a studio on Bahnhofstrasse in Hamburg. Is this perhaps the Theodor whose name appears on the wedding certificate? Is he the adventurer who eventually left Germany to start a new life in America? Perhaps he had been born in some village in nearby Schleswig Holstein, part of the Kingdom of Denmark till the 1860s. Hettie had once claimed that there might be Danish blood in our veins. It was a whimsical notion that we all liked. We were the Great Danes. All in all, I was quite ready to adopt the officer as my great-grandfather.

More mysterious is a studio photo of an attractive young woman of about twenty with her hair pulled back and a dreamy look on her face. She has the aura of a romantic. I like her immediately. Was she perhaps Great-Grandmother Mary? The front of the photo lists the studio as C. Fisher of Orenburg. I googled Orenburg, Germany, and Orenburg, Prussia, but stubbornly Orenburg, Russia, kept coming up again and again. Then I noticed that printed on the back of the photo were several words in Cyrillic, one of which, the Web site revealed, spells Orenburg.

Today Orenburg is a good-sized modern city, located 1500 kilometers southeast of Moscow on the Ural River, with three-star hotels recommended by travel booking sites. But even by today's travel standards, it is a long way from Germany. Its history is rather exotic. It was founded during the 1730s as a frontier outpost from which the Cossack Host could launch attacks against the Turks and Kazakhs in defense of the Motherland's southern border. The photo bears the date 1882, a period, according to my source, when the city had become a railway junction and trading center, but when Cossack bands still controlled the outlying provincial area.

What would Great-Grandmother Mary be doing in Cossack Russia in 1882? Surely this wasn't a vacation trip. I searched for evidence that German forces might have been stationed there. Perhaps the young officer had been deployed there, and the pretty Jungfrau had followed him. But I found no evidence to confirm this hypothesis. My romanticizing imagination leaped to all sorts of possible scenarios, none of which seemed plausible. My rational inner detective was even more puzzled over what the photo would have been doing in Hettie's suitcase.

The next picture is more pedestrian and less pleasing to the imagination. It is a badly underexposed photo of a family of four. The father looks much like the youthful soldier, but no longer youthful. His hair is thinner, his face fuller, and his expression considerably more serious and perhaps disillusioned. Gone is that quiet self-confidence; life perhaps has beaten him down. His wife, matronly and sturdy, holds a baby enveloped in a white dress. She is definitely not the romantic young woman from Orenburg. An unsmiling girl about five, wearing a big kerchief, looks lost in unhappy thoughts. The photo has a message on the back, in German, that gives specific but exasperatingly incomplete details of their life. It is addressed to the ex-soldier's brother, who is evidently in America. The woman is probably his second wife and has brought children from a previous marriage though "3 of them are gone for good." Now they have a second family together. Their life in the Old World is a struggle. They obviously are not the couple who crossed the Atlantic and produced the first New World generation. I am disappointed. But still I wonder why this family has found a place in the suitcase.

There is one other candidate for great-grandfather among these studio photos. He is a man of about forty with a square chin, wispy mustache, and receding hairline. He is wearing a starched collar, striped cravat, and three-piece suit. He looks formal and forbidding and not nearly as appealing as the formerly handsome officer. Perhaps this man is Theodor before he boarded ship and headed off to found the New World line. Yet nothing about him resembles anyone in that first generation nor does he appear in any other pictures. I'm satisfied to reject him as patriarch. But why has he found a place in Hettie's suitcase?

The last of the Old World photos offers a glimmer of a revelation. It features another girl of twenty or so, rather full-figured and unsmiling, with pursed lips and hair pulled tight against her head. Her eyes bulge slightly, and she seems both severe and slightly fearful, perhaps unready for changes about to take place in her life. This, I reluctantly conclude, is probably Jungfrau Mary from Schwerin, Prussia (not far, I must note, from Danish Schleswig Holstein), shortly before she boarded the ship for America. Why do I arrive at this conclusion? The next group of photos, which I will entitle "In the New World," contains half a dozen photos of an older woman who is certainly Frau Mary, posing alone or with her sons. The resemblance between the unsmiling girl and the aging matriarch seems undeniable. The main difference is that the matriarch shows no signs of fear or uncertainty in her photos, but rather resignation and indomitable will.

The old photos offer genealogical teasers but raise far more questions than they answer. I'm beginning to wonder if I have to invent at least great-grandfather's side of my own family line.

The next photos are all from the New World. I will entitle the earliest of them "Childhood and the School Years," depicting the first generation of Theodor and Mary's brood. No one is smiling in any of these photos. It hardly seems to be the Gay Nineties for them. In one, little Hettie in high-top brogans and two of the brothers sit on the front stoop of their row house. All three are frowning. Perhaps they have just been punished for not doing their chores. In another -a studio photo- unsmiling Ted and Fred, in suits with knickers, stand on either side of Frau Mary. In yet another, Grandfather Herb, age thirteen or so, poses next to a pedestal in some studio. He is wearing a full suit with long pants and white gloves and resting one gloved hand on a book on the pedestal. He doesn't seem happy as though being pushed too quickly into adulthood.

What conclusions can I draw from this period? Was it an especially dark time in the family's life?

There is one amusing photo from this period. It shows Frau Mary and five of her most formidable friends, all in black dresses and enormous hats, standing in front of the same row house, probably waiting for the trolley to take them to the Avenue for coffee and kuchen. These were the women who ruled the home and the neighborhood. No hothouse Victorian ladies, they had rough hands and strong forearms and iron discipline. Peering out from among them is a little boy in a cap; I'll call him Fritz. So surrounded by matriarchal authority, there was no chance for him to get into any youthful mischief.

Hettie's signature photo comes from the end of this period. About fifteen, she is dressed up in a topcoat with a fur wrap draped over one arm and a white pocketbook dangling from the other. For the first time, I see the joyful smile that she would carry throughout the rest of her life. She is wearing one of those absurd hats that she may have borrowed from her mother and looks like a girl ready to step out into the world. The smile is still a bit uncertain as though she is wondering whether she is ready for the future. But I believe she is already dreaming about something more than the daily grind in the knitting mill.

The transitional photo from this era is the only one that is dated. On the back someone has scrawled in pencil 4-4-09. Taken in someone's backyard, it is a group shot of twenty-five or so people from the neighborhood. At the center is Great-Grandmother Mary in a high-collared white dress with her hair severely pulled back in a bun and with that look of long-suffering strength that comes through in all her pictures. Nearby are Herb, still unsmiling, and Ted, with an almost fierce scowl. On the front row is a man in his forties. He has a square jaw, penetrating eyes, and an almost threatening look. Is he the mysterious Theodor? If so, it is the only time he appears in any of Hettie's photos. Perhaps he was one of those many husbands, in this mythical age of strong families and family values, who went out for a loaf of bread and never came back. Or who spent his evenings in the corner taproom.

Hettie, on the third row among a group of teen-age girls, is now quite beautiful at age sixteen with a bountiful head of hair, fine features, and a self-assured smile. Does that smile reveal that she has made a big decision about her future? Behind her is the only other adult male. He wears a bushy mustache and towers over all the others. He looks to me like a giant Swede, maybe just off the boat from Stockholm. How does he fit into the group?

The photo somehow seems to lead into the most intriguing period of Hettie's life. It's all contained in a leather-bound album of about forty photos. The time is between 4-4-09 and perhaps 1915. The place is Valley City, North Dakota, as indicated on some of the photos. How, I wonder, did a girl in her mid-teens, out on her own for the first time, end up in North Dakota? Why did she leave the crowded blocks of brick row houses and brick knitting mills, the coal yards and cobblestone streets, the clanging trolley cars and hucksters' wagons of Philadelphia for the prairies of the Upper Midwest? All I could think of was the giant Swede. Perhaps he was a refugee caught in a big city but yearning to return to a simple life on a farm. Perhaps he had described to Hettie the endless, vast spaces of the countryside, its yawning quiet, its night sky filled with a million stars, and its families of reticent, hard-working farmers. Perhaps he had left family and friends in Valley City. No matter, the place apparently sounded like paradise to her.

She must have saved a long time to buy a train ticket. Most of the meager wages she made in the factory certainly went to support the family. I can imagine her going to the big library downtown to ask for a book about North Dakota and maybe an atlas with a map that showed Valley City, just west of Fargo and south of Bismarck. Then finally she got up the courage and bought a ticket for Chicago and Minneapolis and eventually points farther west.

She evidently traveled alone. None of her many pictures of North Dakota show the Swede or, for that matter, anyone from the family. The trip would have taken a number of days. She would have rolled past Lancaster County farmland and seen Amish farmers driving their plow teams, then crossed the Appalachians and passed through the coal fields and steel mills of western Pennsylvania and eastern Ohio till she saw the cornfields of Indiana and Illinois. A new world had opened before her. Had she already made plans on where she would live or what she would do? She left no word about that.

Once in Valley City, she evidently threw herself quickly into life on the farm. A few pictures show Valley City with its grain mill, its lumber yard, and its courthouse. Others show life on the farm. She was fascinated enough by this new place that, for once, she not only took pictures but actually labeled them. They show stacks of hay in the pasture and farm machinery like the separator, the thrashing rig, and the barley binder, all of it still powered by teams of horses. Other pictures show herds of cows and horses in flat expanses of pasture. There are workers in each photo. Was Hettie ever one of them? Did the city girl learn how to bind the barley and milk the cows? Or did she help keep the books and use the domestic skills she learned at Lucretia Mott Elementary School in working around the farmhouse?

No matter what she did, she made lots of friends. One picture after another depicts her with them. Mostly there are groups of young women: lined up atop a split-rail fence while the prairie wind blows back their hair, gathered together in a shaky pyramid atop a rock, standing waist-deep in a lake dressed in voluminous bathing costumes. Silly stuff mostly, but the one consistent feature is that she was always laughing or looking serene. Life on the prairie evidently agreed with her, at least for a while.

Other photos show her in family groups of all ages. Lots of towheaded kids in shorts or bathing suits are getting ready to play. There are clean-cut young men as well in these groups though most of them are standing with their wives and holding young children. Was this lifelong spinster thinking about a family of her own out there on the prairie?

I've saved the most intriguing pictures till last. The first shows

Hettie and another girl her age posed with a pair of sleek, black stallions. The other girl has a cocky smile, a masculine stance, and a rakish cap; she stands between the two stallions holding each by the halter. Hettie stands to one side petting the one stallion tentatively. The other girl is plainly in control of the horsepower. Underneath is the caption: "The Prize Team."

The next one shows a man in his early thirties in bib overalls standing between the same horses and holding them by the halter. He looks straight at the camera with an expression of manly confidence and control. The caption reads: "Ole, Louis, Sam." I choose to believe that Ole, not Sam, is the man's name. He appears in the next photo as well, standing in front of a barn, this time holding a colt by the halter. This caption reads: "The colt and its master." The final picture shows Hettie in dress coat and hat standing beside Ole, now in fedora and sport coat. He is obviously the master of horses and the sturdy provider. He has one arm akimbo and the other seems to be around her waist. Nonetheless, the caption reads: "Just friends." A couple scenarios suggest themselves. Were Hettie and Ole just friends or was she hoping for something more? And what about the unnamed girl with the two stallions so firmly under her control? Was she perhaps the object of Hettie's affections?

But here the North Dakota chapter comes to a close. There are a few winter snow scenes to go along with the spring, summer, and autumn ones, indicating she stayed for at least a year. But nothing more. Did the pastoral idyll end because of a love match that didn't work out? Or did she simply miss her family and life in the big city? Whatever the reason, all communication with these people and this place seems to have ended for good.

Back in Philadelphia, she was reunited with her brothers, but no more photos of Great- Grandmother Mary are to be found. A large group of photos feature friends in uniform. Ted was the only one in the family who went off to war. He looks especially proud in his uniform (the one, of course, that came with the suitcase). The smile fails to reveal what may have been the horror of his experience. In the pocket of the G.I.- issue overcoat, size 34, was an unmailed letter to the family from an Army hospital in New York, where he received treatment for breathing mustard gas in the Argonne Forest. It gives the barest of details in unemotional language. Back home, however, he looks healthy and smiling, evidently not especially damaged physically or psychologically.

The early twenties must have been a happy time for all of them. One picture shows Ted and a bunch of buddies with open collars and rolled-up sleeves, each with a bottle of beer, a hand of cards, and an impish grin. No loose women here, but I assume the returned warriors were sowing their wild oats. During this period, Hettie is usually pictured in big groups of women, often out in the country or at one of the nearby Jersey lakes. They're still young enough to revel in silliness, and they're always laughing. But there don't seem to be any men in her life.

By the late twenties, the photos get more subdued and domestic. Ted had gotten married and moved to Ohio; there are plenty of photos of the couple and their daughter. But the marriage didn't last, and he eventually moved back east. Hettie worked away in the office and gathered amusing anecdotes to tell us later. More years passed and Hettie continued to take her black-and- white snapshots, picturing the two of them with friends in middle and old age. I am pleased to recognize a number of the people in them. But none of the strangers is a candidate to be a forgotten ancestor or a distant cousin. Thus, I lose interest.

At this point, I believed I have gotten to the end of the story.

But one more discovery still remained among some letters and photos I hadn't previously noticed. And these, it turns out, did take me back to the beginning of the story in the Old World and the discovery of a new cast of characters with whom Hettie had been quietly communicating most of her life. They were from Great-Grandmother Mary's side. All the letters and photos had been sent by a cousin named Frida and fortunately were written in English -a bit fractured but still comprehensible. She was a little older than Hettie and lived in the old hometown of Schwerin. In one early photo, she is wearing a frilly dress and a big kerchief and, like seemingly all other children at that time, is unsmiling. She looks a bit familiar. Then it dawns on me that she is probably the sad stepdaughter wearing the kerchief in the picture with the disillusioned officer. In a much later photo, taken in 1921, she has an expression of even deeper sadness, bordering on despair. This time she is wearing a blouse with a kerchief fastened by a stick pin in the shape of a German cross. She had reason to be despairing. Germany was reeling economically in the aftermath of World War I, and life must have been a struggle. Perhaps also she had lost a husband or lover in the Argonne Forest, where Ted had inhaled the poison gas.

Hettie kept a few Christmas cards from her sent during the early 1930s followed by a long period of silence. Sometime in the late Forties, however, she sent a photo of two young men, fair-haired, slender, very German-looking, and dressed in naval uniforms. On the back she identifies them. Kurt, geboren am October 29, 1906; gefallen am June 10, 1944, just after D-Day. "Gefallen" sounds especially somber and final. For Werner, she just lists the birth and death dates: May 30, 1908; March 30, 1941. I assume he too was a casualty of war. What grim stories would these two distant cousins have been able to add to the family history? I apparently will never know.

Now I finally arrive at the final chapter. World War II took its toll on the family beyond the deaths of Kurt and Werner. Frida and her family stayed in Schwerin, which ended up in the occupied Eastern Zone, and tried to continue operating the family business. A lengthy letter, dated December 28, 1948, reveals the family's struggles. They have had to close the business for lack of coal to heat it, and Frida is now working in the shop of a Jewish jeweler and is thankful that she at least has a job. Many, she says, are unemployed, and "many others are suiciding." Worse yet, they live in daily fear that Soviet troops may occupy the city, a fate they assume would be worse than the pettiness and corruption of East German bureaucrats. There are a few bright spots. Her husband and daughters are well. One of them, Elena, has somehow gotten a visa to spend time in England.

Then, one final surprise. She thanks Hettie profoundly for helping her apply for immigration. She has been to see the American consul in Berlin and still needs an "affidavit of support" from an American citizen. Would Hettie provide it? I am amazed to think of Hettie -laughing, lovable, slightly dotty Hettie- reaching across the Atlantic to try to help these cousins whom she certainly had never met, contacting the American embassy, even writing a formal letter to help expedite their immigration. They apparently never came to America even for a visit, and Hettie certainly never went to Germany. Fortunately, life seems to have improved for these cousins over the next decade. A final group photo taken at their home some years later shows the whole family as well as "three ladies who help us in the shop," all smiling. This is the last of the communication from them that I found.

What more can be said? My research and speculation remind me that people's lives are often far fuller and more mysterious than the short and simple annals of the poor would have us expect. Hettie, in her quiet way, had lived a richer life than I could have imagined. Sadly, I never thought to ask her about it, and she probably never assumed anyone would be interested to hear. Fortunately, in her own haphazard way, she still became the preserver of the only portion of family history that I probably will ever know. Would she be offended by my modest attempts to explore her life and her generation from the scattered clues she left behind? I choose to think she would be pleased.

And what of my own generation? And future generations? With the technology to save anything and everything, will we do any better at saving our own history from oblivion?

PROVIDENCE

I

No doubt about it, Raymond Harrison was a gifted storyteller. It was probably the naturalness of his style that kept my attention. He didn't try to dramatize the essentially undramatic or impress me with improbable or sordid revelations. Instead, he filled his story with a wealth of vivid detail and an occasional exploratory reaching out for meaning that he may never quite have found. I say that only because I don't know the ending of his story.

I met him in the overnight shelter for the homeless sponsored by the church I attend. He was a big man whose shambling gait couldn't hide a natural sense of dignity. He always entered among the last of the twenty or so men who arrived to spend the night. They all received plastic storage bins filled with their meager overnight belongings, lined up for a hot meal, socialized a bit, then retired to their sleeping mats at nine o'clock sharp. Raymond was a regular during the winter I got to know him. After accepting his evening portion of whatever was being served, he poured himself a glass of iced tea and settled in at a table, usually by himself if possible. I don't think he considered himself superior or even unsocial.

He was friendly enough toward the other guys; he just seemed to be in a world apart from them.

I had talked to some of the other men at one time or another during my weekly volunteer evenings. For the most part, they were surprisingly willing to share their tales of woe: a sketchy, often confusing litany of lost jobs, broken marriages, drugs, jail time, and alcohol. Most of them had traveled a bit, hoping to reinvent themselves and start over. Most expressed some hopes for the future. I wanted to hear their stories. Was it mainly a desire to show empathy? To offer advice? Or just to satisfy my curiosity about a life so radically different from my own? We would talk for fifteen minutes or so, but I soon realized that I had little help or insight to offer. Raymond's story, I found out, was different. He hadn't stumbled into the life he had lived, but willingly chosen it, with all its freedom and radical uncertainty. He hadn't suffered from any of the usual problems of drugs, anger management, conflicts with employers, and broken marriages. Nonetheless, the longer we talked, the more I sensed his need to tell his story in its entirety as if to discover its meaning himself.

He first showed up in early December soon after the shelter opened for the winter season. He was new to us that year unlike a number of the other guys whom I recognized from the past. Because our space was limited, we accepted only the same twenty men night after night. After a few weeks, I decided to join him at the dinner table and introduce myself.

"New to the city?" I asked by way of openers.

He nodded and chewed on.

"Where are you from?"

"Well," he said after a ruminative pause that he would employ so often in our conversations, "Anywhere and everywhere, I guess you could say." I waited, hoping for a few more details. "How about you?" he asked instead. He paused briefly to dab his lips with his napkin, then added, "Let me guess." He sized me up. "Somewhere in the Philadelphia area, I'd say." I must have looked surprised in confirming his guess, and he seemed pleased at the success. "The accent gives you away," he continued.

We introduced ourselves though I don't know whether he stored away my name in his memory as he never called me by it.

"Quaker City," he continued. "The City of Brotherly Love."

"One of the everywhere places you've lived?" I asked.

"Philly born and raised," he said.

And thus began the childhood chapter of the life he would unfold to me little by little over the next months with only a little prodding from my questions.

"I grew up in North Philly when parts of it were still respectable. Take my neighborhood. It was working class, but people had jobs. Manufacturing was still strong in the city. So were the unions. My old man worked in the same factory for years and eventually became a supervisor. Not bad for a man who never graduated from high school. Most of the families I remember were pretty stable. My parents were actually married before I was born. They owned their own house. My mother worked for a while in the school cafeteria but stayed home after I was born. I was the only child. We were quite the up-and-coming Negro family. My old man made enough money to move up from a Chevy to a Buick. Every summer, we spent a whole week on vacation in a little hotel for colored folks in Atlantic City in the years before the casinos arrived.

"Life was good," he concluded, sitting back in his reflective pose with his hands folded on his belly. "Even for us Negroes." He pronounced the last word as though it were a foreign or archaic word, not distasteful but just peculiar.

"The neighborhood was safe, and my parents, like all the other parents, let us kids roam pretty free. After school I would be off on my own till dinnertime. The whole neighborhood was block after block of rowhouses filled with families with two, three, four kids, so there was never any lack of others to play with. They all gathered in the concrete schoolyard for stickball, basketball, and any other ball you could play in tight places with no grass. I myself was never any kind of athlete. You know, the pudgy, slow kid who always got picked last in choose-up. But I found other, more interesting stuff to do instead.

"As I got a little older, I started to range farther afield, sometimes with another friend but more often by myself. I always had a little money burning a hole in my pocket, and I knew all the best places to get cheap snacks. I even started venturing across the Avenue into the White neighborhood. I'm not sure why I dared. Maybe it was because the corner bakeries over there sold the best chocolate eclairs. The White folks gave me suspicious looks, but I never had any run-ins. I don't remember too many details from that time. Except maybe the time I walked all the way to the river and found a little produce stand that was selling huge watermelons. I bought myself one, pulled out the penknife I always carried, and carved up it up right there. In my mind, I can still taste that watermelon and see the ships floating by. Strange the random memories that end up summarizing whole periods of your life. I couldn't have been much more than thirteen during that period. But I think that's when I first developed my wanderlust."

He sat back and smiled, relishing the memory. With lights out coming in a few minutes, he gathered up the remains of his meal, bid me good night, and headed off to his sleeping mat.

I didn't get much chance to have a long conversation with him for a few weeks. We mostly exchanged a few pleasantries and comments on the weather. But I was eager for more of his story and finally gave him a subtle reminder of our earlier chat. He seemed pleased and even remembered where he had left off.

"High school," he said, picking up the thread, "That was a big transition time for me. It wasn't much fun. I never had many friends in the lower grades, but in high school I had even fewer. The building was in a different neighborhood with more crime. Drugs all over. Boarded-up houses with who knows what going on inside. Some gang turf battles. I never was very excited about school, but high school seemed totally pointless. I just drifted through classes, but with pressure already on teachers to keep up the graduation rate, I could get by without having to do much work.

"I got an after-school job stocking shelves in a grocery store, which paid me enough to do what I wanted with my free time. I spent hours riding the elevated train, gazing over the sea of rowhouse rooftops, the factory smokestacks, the church steeples, the graffiti scrawled on the walls. It was really soothing. Eventually, I would get off and go exploring downtown. I've always loved cities. I would stop in my favorite used bookstore and buy a couple cheap paperback novels, then head over to my favorite bakery for chocolate eclairs. Then I would sit on a bench in one of the parks, reading and eating an éclair with nothing to bother me but pigeons and an occasional panhandler.

"These trips were always by myself. I made the mistake one time of going with another guy who offered to pal around with me. Maybe I was flattered that he wanted to be friends. He was uninterested in taking the skyline tour on the El, so we headed right downtown. Soon after we got there, he pointed out a man wearing dreads who he swore was dealing drugs. I wondered how he could be so sure. At his suggestion, we browsed through the LPs in a record store, and he raved about some of his favorite new bands. Santana and Black Sabbath, he assured me, were all the rage. He talked about heavy metal and guitar riffs and other things I had never heard of, but added a little mournfully that there would never be another Jimi Hendrix. He apparently had just died.

"Next, we went into a newspaper and magazine store he seemed to know about. It was a little hole-in-the wall place with cigarettes, cigars, paperbacks, and a rack of magazines that included *Playboy* and some other sleazy issues whose covers he was eager to share with me. I eased back toward the news magazines, noticing the owner eyeing us. At last, he was ready to leave. 'Can I help you boys?' the owner asked in a cigarette-raspy voice as we passed the register. He followed us to the door and just outside, as luck would have it, a cop was walking by. My good friend, of course, had a copy of one of those magazines stuck inside his jacket.

"This was my first and only encounter with the law. Long story short, we both got marched a block to a patrol car and stuck in the back seat for a ride to the station. My father had to leave work early to come down and pick me up after I got a lecture from the sergeant. The old man was furious. We never had been exactly close. He never did seem to see the son he was hoping for when he looked at me. But this incident really opened up a big divide between us. He invented a little lie so that my mother never knew the truth, but he always seemed to hold it against me." He paused and a shadow came across his face as it did occasionally when he was reliving an unhappy moment.

"He didn't have to lecture me. I had learned some life lessons I needed to know. You've got to look out for yourself. Don't be too ready to trust your fellow traveler. Practice spotting trouble far enough away to avoid it. Over the years, I've witnessed more than my share of unpleasant confrontations involving the police, but always from a safe distance.

"My other great passion during that time was the movies. Saturdays when I usually had a couple bucks in my pocket, I'd head for the local theater for the double feature, the newsreel, and the cartoons. Since there weren't any theaters in my neighborhood, I had to walk to the Avenue. Usually, I was usually about the only Black person in the theater, sitting pretty much by myself up in the balcony. I watched whatever was playing. My preference was for action movies, especially World War II ones. I lost count of how many times I watched *The Dirty Dozen.* James Bond flicks were okay. But Clint Eastwood spaghetti westerns were better. It didn't matter, though; I was generally entertained by them all. Pretty odd tastes for a person of color, you're probably thinking. But they weren't making any movies for colored folks back then. If you wanted to see movies with Black actors, you were basically limited to ones starring Sidney Poitier or Sidney Poitier.

"But it didn't make any difference. I was mainly trying to escape having to make any decisions about my life. I really had no idea what I wanted to do. I just knew there was a big world out there, and I was curious to see it.

"My parents kept the pressure on me to make a decision.

Community college. Trade school. The factory where my old man worked. The military. I know they must have seen my eyes glaze over whenever they started in. About a month after graduation, we had a big row, and they laid down an ultimatum. I had to find a job with a real future if I wanted to continue living in their house. I had to be responsible. Responsibility. It was all both of them ever harped on.

"Well, I have a little voice that talks to me every time I have a choice to make. After the ultimatum, that voice helped me decide what to do, probably in a way my parents hadn't expected. I made up my mind to hit the road. It was at that point that I began turning my future over to luck or chance or fortune -whatever you want to call it. All I knew was that the only important thing was to live free and not be tied down to a boring grind."

The lights dimmed, signaling curfew and leaving me filled with curiosity about the next chapter of the story.

II

We began with the usual small talk the next time we met. I never wanted to rush him into the story, but I wanted to assure him I was eager to listen.

"Most of the next ten years were pretty boring," he began. "It's amazing how a decade can just get lost. I tried out some new cities. New York was too big and expensive. Boston was too cold and snooty. Atlanta just seemed to have no soul. I'd stay in each new place for a while to test it out. I usually was able to find a job fairly quick, bagging groceries or working in the kitchen of a restaurant, trying to make just enough money to rent a room or a cheap apartment. Life wasn't easy, but I was young and free to go whenever I wanted. That was the main thing.

"In Baltimore, I got my first experience of living on the street. It was early summertime. I had just quit one job to take a higher paying one doing manual labor for a construction company, hoping to finally get my own apartment. The work was brutal, moving wheelbarrows full of stones from one place to another, digging holes for footings, hauling sheetrock and plywood. My back hurt, my knees hurt, and I kept wondering why I was killing myself. After a few weeks, I picked up my paycheck and told the boss man I was quitting. 'The work ain't for everybody,' he told me without any sign of disapproval. I couldn't have agreed more." He held out his hands for me to see. "Look how smooth," he said proudly. "Not a callous. Comes from a lifetime of avoiding manual labor.

"Soon I couldn't pay my rent even for a boarding house," he went on. "So I thought I'd try sleeping outdoors. It wasn't so bad at first. The weather was still warm. The parks were full of benches. There were bridges to sleep under if it rained. The cops left you alone as long as you didn't hang around the Inner Harbor and panhandle the tourists. The local soup kitchen fed pretty good meals. The public library had comfortable spots to sit and read. I could even get a shower in the overnight shelter every so often.

"All in all, I was happy enough for a little while. I had to get by without much cash because I refuse to panhandle. It's a matter of principle. But pretty soon all the freedom got a little too much even for me. Besides, as the summer heated up, the streets got more dangerous. It was a bad time for cities in general and a really bad time to be homeless in Baltimore.

"So, I gave in and found work at a succession of grocery stores and restaurants. I'd work for a while to build up some spending money, most of which I spent going to the movies. It was a different decade for film. America was more dangerous, even in the movies. *The French Connection, Apocalypse Now, The Godfather, Serpico.* Pretty dark, but really compelling stuff. Black folks even got a chance to see a real Black action hero in *Shaft* and a Black comedian in Richard Pryor."

We spent a while trading trivia about movies we had seen. With his prodigious memory, he easily outdid me in his recall of actors and scenes -a fact that I believe secretly gave him great delight.

"After a few years," he continued, "I landed a job at yet another grocery. The manager really liked me and the way I got along with the customers. He offered to train me to be a cashier and maybe more. It meant more money, but more responsibility; more security, but probably less freedom. It was a temptation. Maybe I could finally afford a decent place to live. So, I said yes.

"I kind of liked the work. The store wasn't usually very busy, so I didn't feel rushed or overworked. Time flowed by. Other cashiers came and went. The new hires were often assigned to me to help them learn how to use the register and introduce them to the layout of the store. I have to admit, it made me feel important.

"One of the new hires was a woman about my age, maybe a little younger. Leona was her name. Not bad looking. A little overweight, but then so was I. And very well-endowed." He held his hands in support of an invisible bosom. "She wore very red lipstick all the time and lots of jewelry -big earrings and bangly bracelets that clinked against the register whenever she rang up a purchase. She was friendlier than any other woman in my experience. Soon I noticed she would try to time her breaks so that she could talk to me. It was pretty lame conversation, but then I didn't have any experience talking to women. I had never before thought about getting involved in a relationship. Too many strings. But since I had already signed away some of my freedom, I thought, 'maybe now.'

"One day she asked me if I wanted to take her to this nightclub in the neighborhood. I guess I was flattered. And pretty easily manipulated. She told me to meet her outside the place about ten o'clock, which was usually the time I went to bed. 'Why so late?' I asked. 'Well, honey, the action don't start till at least then,' she said. I should have been more suspicious, but about some things I was still pretty innocent.

"Well, the Black Panther Lounge was a revelation to me. I had to pay a $10 cover charge for each of us in order to get in. I got blasted right away by electronic music and strobe lights. It was a scene right out of a seventies disco movie. Even I realized there were drugs all over the place. Leona had poured herself into a spangly, rhinestone-covered dress. She had a big voice that cut through the noise. She obviously knew everybody, and all the men came to drool over her. After a few minutes, she seemed to forget that I was even there. I was just her ticket for admission. It didn't take long before I was in a different zone of reality. I was mesmerized by the DJ, who had studs in his nose and ears and an enormous Afro and spun out music with impassive efficiency. The flashing strobe and the pulsating rhythms put me as close as I ever would get to a psychedelic trip. All the people seemed to be blue and magenta; their outlines blurred when they danced. It was like a bad technicolor movie, but weirdly thrilling. Leona kept moving from one guy to another, flaunting her -well, you know, her goods. She was in her element. While I leaned against the bar, I dimly heard the bartender shout at me, 'You get a free one with the cover charge, homeboy.' But I was already high without a drink.

"Finally, around one o'clock, my survival skills kicked back in. During the DJ's break there was shouting on the other side of the room. I got alert real fast and started to ease toward the door as the shouting moved on to pushing and the pushing toward a brawl. I had lived on the street long enough to have developed a special sense when a fight was about to happen. As I slid out the door, I could hear furniture getting banged around and the voices getting louder and louder. There were no windows in the place, but the door was still slightly open, and I could tell things were getting more and more out of control. I waited around for a couple of minutes to see if Leona would come out. Then, I heard the first police siren, followed by another and another. I hustled down the street and turned the corner just as the first squad car pulled up in front of the building."

He leaned back, smiling wryly at the memory. "Like I told you," he continued, "I only ever had one encounter with the police, and I intended to keep it that way."

"The next day I worked the second shift. One of the other cashiers, who usually never spoke to me, sidled over. 'How was your date, honey? I heard things got a little wild.' I played dumb and told her I had left early. 'Cops took Leona and a bunch of others downtown,' she continued. 'News to me,' I said.

"Her girlfriend came over to join the conversation. 'You a big disappointment,' she said. 'We thought you were gonna be her new sugar daddy and keep her straight.' I gave her my best blank look. 'She's just looking for a man with a little cash who wants to have some fun,' she went on. 'Maybe she give you some candy if you're generous.'

"Well, I worked the rest of my shift," he concluded, "then turned in my apron and gave notice. The little voice was telling me it was time to move on." He took a reflective sip of tea and studied the ice cubes. "I reminded myself not to get involved in any relationships. At least not then. And certainly not with Leona and her crowd. Relationships sure can make life complicated. Too messy and troublesome," he said by way of summation.

The lights dimmed and he headed off to his sleeping mat, perhaps to mull over his memories.

III

He wasn't there the following week, and I was afraid he had headed off for another city and a new start. But the week after he was back again. We made a little small talk, and I asked him where he had been. "Oh, around," he said as if to indicate that the immediate past wasn't very important. "So where did you head after Baltimore?" I asked to get him started again.

"Well, I went to the Greyhound Station the next morning at dawn with no particular idea of where to go. Once again, I was just trusting to dumb luck. I'd tried out most of the East Coast cities and wanted a different destination. The next bus in two hours was headed west to Pittsburgh. I would go west, I decided just like that, and bought my ticket. I rode there with my mind on cruise control and spent the rest of my first day just wandering around the city. I walked from where the three rivers meet up to the Cathedral of Learning. It was a long walk, mostly uphill. I got to see all the city I wanted to see. The place just didn't quite seem right for me. Maybe it was because the skies were gloomy or the streets were too steep.

It's amazing how influential the first impression of a new place can be. All I know is the next afternoon I was back at the Greyhound station. The next bus out was for Cincinnati, Ohio, a state I'd never been in. I bought a ticket and climbed aboard.

"I spent my first night in a rundown motel, knowing I had to be careful with my money till some kind of job turned up. The next morning was sunny and warm. It was a good omen, I thought. During that period, I became a pretty strong believer," he paused a little dramatically, like he was waiting for a drum roll, "in serendipity." He smiled." Serendipity," he repeated. "What a fun word! I read it in a book somewhere, and it seemed to fit what happened in my life at that point. It meant something more than just dumb luck. It meant that if you didn't try to rush things and kept your eyes and ears open, sooner or later something good would be bound to turn up."

We bandied about that idea for a while, particularly in light of his current situation. He admitted that luck had been an inconstant companion for him but insisted that there was more to what happened in his life than just luck. "Let's just say that serendipity became my most valuable survival skill at that time.

"I spent the first morning roaming around downtown Cincinnati, which seemed clean and easy to navigate. Not far from downtown in a neighborhood that was a little seedy but seemed safe, I found a small, older hotel called the Corona. It was in a respectable red brick building with granite steps and a big blue awning over the front entrance. I wanted something nicer than the place I had stayed the night before. The sign outside advertised 'Great Rates,' which I hoped would mean cheap enough for me. What really attracted me, however, was the sign underneath that read 'Free Movies.'

"The desk clerk looked bored. When I asked about the free movies, he gestured toward a corridor. 'There's a VCR in the room down the hall,' he said. 'And a bunch of old tapes on a shelf.' The room rate was reasonable, so I decided to stay the night. I had heard of the VCR but never seen one.

"They were cutting-edge technology back then," I said.

"Indeed, they were. And to me, they were absolutely miraculous machines," he said, musing. "Just think, up till then if you wanted help escaping to a fantasy world, you had to leave the comfort of your own home. Now all you had to do was pop a tape into the hatch and press 'play'."

He paused as he often did before a major transition. "Well, I thought I'd stay the night," he went on, "but ended up staying for," he made a mental calculation, "let's see, at least ten years."

"Serendipity?" I asked. "Or the VCR?"

He thought a moment. "Probably a combination of the two."

"I found a job selling newspapers at a busy intersection. It was a bold, new career path for me," he said with a wry smile. "The tips and such enabled me to stay on a little longer at the hotel. A couple weeks later when I got back after work, the regular clerk, a real sullen character, wasn't behind the desk. Instead, it was the older gentleman I occasionally said hello to on my way to my private cinema."

"'Off to see another movie?' he asked in a friendly way, and I nodded. 'I guess you're one of the only ones who uses the room. Maybe I can add a few new tapes to the collection. Also, there's a Blockbuster just a few blocks away. You're welcome to rent something and bring it back to watch.'

"He seemed genuinely friendly and not just making polite conversation with a guest. Then he introduced himself. Abe Cohen, the manager of the Corona. He asked if I were happy staying there and satisfied with my room. During our conversation, I just happened to mention, by the bye, that I was between regular jobs and looking for new career opportunities. I wanted to sound impressive.

"I saw him again the next evening. When I asked what had happened to the regular clerk, he said he had to let him go, without offering specifics, and added that he was looking for a replacement. It turned out that the assistant manager also had recently moved on to another hotel. Abe was working at his regular job during the day supervising the housekeepers, dealing with problems with the elevator and the plumbing, and so on. Then, he manned the desk at the end of the day clerk's shift, checking in guests. The next day I asked him how the search for a new desk clerk was going.

"'It's been slow,'" he confided. 'We can't afford to pay much.'

"I was running low on money myself and realized I would probably have to find cheaper lodging within the next few days. The very next day he saw me in the lobby and motioned me over. After a little casual talk, he kind of sized me up, then asked if I would like the job as night clerk" He sat back and folded his hands on his stomach with a look of satisfaction. "About the best job I could have hoped for," he went on, "and just in time to keep me off the streets. The pay, as he had warned me, wasn't much. But we worked out a deal to let me continue staying in the hotel free of charge. Just like that, all my problems were solved."

"Serendipity?" I asked.

"It sure seemed like it to me. Like I said, I just had to be patient."

He went over to refill his tea before continuing. "The hours suited me fine. I came on around four o'clock and checked in guests for the night. I was surprised at how fast I got used to being a night owl. The job was pleasant enough. I enjoyed the little banter with the guests while I helped them fill out the reservation form. We had a nice mix of Black and White folks. It was during the time when everybody was beginning to pay with credit cards, and I had to give instructions to those guests who weren't comfortable with the machine. We eventually even got a computer and an upgraded phone system, which I had to learn how to use. But I did it.

"By 10 o'clock every night, my work was basically finished. We rarely had guests checking in after that. Sometimes there would be an emergency in one of the rooms -a faulty shower, a stopped-up toilet, something like that. I usually just had to move the guest to another room and write up a report for Abe. Mainly, I could sit back for the rest of the night and read and drink iced tea. That's when I developed my addiction," he said, holding up his nearly empty glass. "Often after my shift was done, I'd retire to the video room to watch movies half the night. It was my other addiction. It got so I would watch a good one so often that I could rattle off the dialogue by memory. Life was good.

"Abe and I got to be good friends during some of the dead time in the evening. The night manager came on around seven, but sometimes Abe would stay around for an hour or so just to spend time with me. He would help me check in guests if there was a rush or do some paperwork he needed to catch up on, but mostly we just talked.

"He liked listening to the stories of my travels, probably because he had never done any traveling himself. Every once in a while, he'd drop some details of his own life. He lived by himself, his wife having left him years before. He had no kids. He had worked most of his life in hotels and hadn't had much opportunity to have hobbies or develop friendships.

"Sometimes he'd say, 'Raymond, what's at the movies?' if he knew I had gone out to see a new release. I'd give him a quick summary of whatever I'd just seen and some critical commentary. I think he was mostly being a polite listener, but he really made an effort to show interest. He even created a little budget to update the hotel's video collection, telling me he thought the little theater was really helping pull in more business. Then he assigned me the job of shopping for new titles even though we both knew I was probably the only one who would ever actually watch them.

"He even taught me how to play backgammon, and we would play occasionally during evening lulls. I remember one year when a big snowstorm shut down the city for a couple days, Abe was stranded at the hotel. We must have played a hundred games of backgammon while we waited out the storm. I think he delighted in being my teacher.

"Like I said, he'd ask me about new movies every once in a while. Eventually, we got into a routine of going to see a new one every couple of months at one of the plush downtown theaters. We'd usually pick out a comedy, which was what he liked best. It was the eighties, and there were plenty of good comedies that decade. He'd treat me to the movie or to dinner.

"I had a week's paid vacation every year and usually headed off to explore some new place. But I must admit that for the first time in my life I no longer felt a great urge to travel. I had a friend. I had a steady job. I had security. I didn't need to go out looking for anything. During those years, it seemed like I didn't have a past or even a future. Just a present to fill."

He sat back to collect his thoughts as he often did when he was wrapping up a chapter in his story. "Then," he went on, "the hotel got sold to a group of investors. The new owners had big plans for the property, according to Abe. What they were he wasn't sure. They were talking about shutting the place down for six months to renovate and upgrade. They wanted to be more competitive in the higher-end hotel market. A team of management guys in fancy suits came in to look the place over. Abe tried to sound optimistic about the future, but I could see he was worried. Would the hot-shot new owners find a place for him in their swankier new hotel? He was in his mid-fifties, and new jobs would be hard to find. I felt bad for him. It seemed like for the first time in my life I was actually worried about somebody other than myself.

"But what could I do? Things were moving fast, and I figured I'd be out of my perfect job before long. It was all right, I told myself. I would do what I had always done before. I'd simply move on. When I told Abe, he half-heartedly tried to persuade me to stay. But we both knew he would probably have to move on pretty soon too.

"On my last day, he took me out for breakfast near the hotel, then walked me over to the Greyhound station. I promised him I'd send him a postcard or something to let him know where I landed. But I never did. And, of course, I never found out what happened to him."

He had a look of sadness that I had never seen before. "Relationships," he concluded reflectively. "They sure can make life complicated." He paused, then added, "They sure can make you feel empty when they end."

That, of course, was the end of the night's conversation. He rose slowly and walked over to his sleeping mat with what seemed a little loneliness in his gait.

IV

"Next-to-last chapter," he said as we opened our story telling the next week. "But probably the longest.

"That last chapter had kind of a bummer for an ending," he continued. "At the bus station I had to decide where to go next. Over the past years, I'd taken little trips to some other cities around the Midwest. All of them had some things I liked and some I didn't. There were departures for half-a-dozen destinations in the next six hours. I went to the cashier's window with my mind still a blank. There was a bus leaving for Chicago in two hours. I had never been there. I knew it was bigger than I usually like. I knew it had cold winters and a big crime problem. Logically, it wasn't a good choice. But that little voice I told you about suddenly began saying Chicago. So, Chicago it was.

"We pulled into the LaSalle St. Station around ten at night. The weather was windy and cold even though it was only late October. I had saved up some money, and Abe had slipped me fifty bucks at the station so I could afford to stay in a cheap hotel for a little while. I looked for jobs in a few older hotels, a couple restaurants, a few grocery stores, but nobody seemed interested in a middle-aged man with my particular credentials. There didn't even seem to be any jobs selling newspapers on street corners.

"After a couple weeks my funds were about gone. I was getting desperate. Homelessness was staring me in the face. That old magical serendipity seemed to have abandoned me. Even though I had been waiting patiently, nothing seemed likely to turn up. It was a pretty dark time for me."

"I spent a few weeks back out on the streets, eating in a soup kitchen, keeping warm in the library or the bus station, and sleeping in one of the shelters. It was a rough place, kind of dirty, and packed with a bunch of angry homeless guys. Nothing like here," he added, motioning to our big, clean room with the sleeping mats and tables spaced comfortably apart. "One night while I was lying awake, I sized up my situation and concluded that maybe I was finally going to have to pay the price for a lifetime of living day to day.

"The next day I was walking through a neighborhood I had never been in before. My feet were wet from plowing through dirty slush and snow. My knees hurt. For the first time, I was really feeling my age. I stopped in front of a small Catholic church and decided to try to get inside to warm up. The door was unlocked. I eased into a pew at the back of the sanctuary to rest. The room smelled a little musty, but it was warm. The day had been overcast, but soon after I sat down the sun came out and flooded the space with warm color from the stained- glass windows. It seemed like a good omen. Right away I dozed off. When I woke up, I saw a priest standing at the altar straightening things up. I thought he might be annoyed by my intrusion. But no. He came down and greeted me in a friendly voice. 'Father Francis,' he said by way of introduction. I started to apologize for barging in, but he said, 'Friend, the door is always open, not just on Sundays.'

"He asked what brought me there. Well, as you know, I don't have any trouble telling my story if I feel like I have the right listener. I gave him a few details about my recent woes and told him I figured my luck had finally run out. I even trotted out my theory of serendipity. He listened patiently, not interrupting to ask questions but clearly filing away the details.

"When I finished, he kind of studied me a second then said, 'I like to think life's not mainly about luck. Maybe it was providence, not luck, that brought you here'."

He paused to go over and refresh his iced tea and perhaps to refocus an idea that he couldn't quite accept or quite discard.

"Well, providence was a new way of thinking for me," he said when he got back. "Father Francis explained it as God working behind the scenes to help you along and find you an opportunity when you really need it. I politely agreed that might be the case for some people though the idea certainly didn't ring particularly true at that time. Why would God lead me to this place just as winter was setting in, with the wind always blowing off Lake Michigan, the snow and slush piling up, and no jobs for middle-aged guys with no particular job skills? Where was the hand of God in all that?"

He looked at me and waited, and I realized that he wasn't simply asking a rhetorical question but actually expecting a response. I didn't have any ready answers. It always seemed to me that believers in providence have a habit of cherry-picking a few select instances from history or personal experience that are not readily explained by coincidence or human planning as proof of its absolute sway. Still, it seemed to explain some important things. I wasn't sure what I believed.

"I guess I prefer it to mere luck," I said. "Or even serendipity."

"It is a nicer idea," he agreed, "if you can bring yourself to believe that God is always waiting nearby in this big, overpopulated world just to help you."

"Perhaps," I offered, "God has his human agents who are keeping their eyes open for opportunities to make His plans happen. They may be stationed in many places, even quite unlikely ones, just waiting for an opportunity to help. Or even actively seeking one out."

"Maybe so," he said. "Maybe so."

He drank the last of his tea in preparation for wrapping up for the night.

"Well, anyway," he said, "the good father went on to say that he had heard some unpleasant things about the shelter where I was staying but that the Catholic church ran its own shelter nearby. He fished out a little notebook and a stubby pencil from his coat pocket and wrote down the address, then gave me starting directions to get there. 'If you hurry, you can get dinner,' he added. As I walked to the door, he said, 'Don't forget, the church is open all day. Come back. We can talk some more.'"

It was almost time for lights out. "Guess I'll have to leave it there," he said.

He sat musing for a little longer as though still working out some inner problem.

V

I arrived the next week during a freak, tail-end of winter snowstorm. The guys came in smelling like damp wool. Most of them didn't show signs of being chilled, the result probably of months or years getting inured to long hours outside in wet, cold weather. As usual, Raymond arrived among the last, his close-cropped hair frosted in white.

"I thought Southern weather was supposed to be more hospitable," he said as I joined him for dinner. "This feels more like Chicago." He ate the last bites of dinner and walked his plate to the trashcan. Then he settled in with a comfortable sigh to continue his story.

"I started to tell you about Father Francis," he began. "I've never been the religious type and hadn't met many men of the cloth. My original idea of Catholic priests probably came mostly from the creepy priest in *The Exorcist.* But the Padre, he was the real deal. I took his invitation to come back and talk. I always felt he was really listening, not just paying polite attention. He asked me questions occasionally that made me really think about my life. He didn't try to offer me spiritual counseling or pass judgment on what I told him. I think he realized that I was probably learning more about myself just by telling my own story.

"I began to come in about once a week just to chat. He was never too busy to make time. He found it amusing, I think, to hear about all the places I'd visited and lived. He told me he had grown up in Chicago, gone to college and seminary in Chicago, and served in a couple parishes in Chicago. When I asked him if he had ever traveled anywhere, his eyes brightened. During his first year in seminary, he and his fellow students had boarded buses for New York City to hear the Pope say Mass in Yankee Stadium. Then there were a few religious retreats and a visit to Washington to see a different Pope. Each experience really seemed special to him. Other than that, he said, his whole life had been right there in Chicago. I asked him if he ever got tired of being there year after year. 'Not at all,' he said. 'Chicago is my home. St. Mary's is my home.'

"One time I mentioned that I had read lots of books while I was working at the hotel. Mostly detective fiction, spy novels, books on World War II, that kind of thing. He seemed impressed that I had done any reading at all. He told me that the church had a good little library and I would be welcome to borrow a book if I wanted.

Since he knew how much I had traveled, he began by recommending a book about St. Paul and all his journeys. Quite an interesting guy, St. Paul. Maybe a little fanatical, but very courageous. I enjoyed following him on his boat trips and his visits to all those exotic cities. We talked about the book and about all the gentiles he converted and how Christianity probably wouldn't have gained a following without him. I said I thought he could have used a few pointers on survival skills. A bad joke, I guess, but he chuckled and didn't seem offended. He mixed in discussion of some of Paul's ideas on sin. He sure set a high bar for ordinary humans to measure up to and maybe took the fun out of life. But I agreed that he certainly had been a great man.

"My favorite book, though, was a biography of St. Francis. We talked about his vow of poverty and how he wandered around Italy with his followers preaching and serving poor people. Even though he had grown up rich, he had given it all up for Jesus, and even more for other people. 'Your role model?' I asked him. 'I could only wish I had his devotion,' he said. I said it was appropriate that his parents had named him Francis, but he told me his full name was actually Gerald Francis O'Connell -Irish, not Italian, on both sides. He had been Gerry as a kid. But when he became a priest, he decided to call himself Francis in honor of the saint.

"It got so I really looked forward to our visits. But that was about the only bright spot in my life. One day, after at least a month on the streets, I stopped in mainly to get warm. It was like he knew I was coming because he was already in the sanctuary. He saw right away I was in a gloomy mood. Despair, he called it. But he greeted me with a smile, not a mournful look of sympathy. 'I've been expecting you for a few days, Raymond,' he began. He was trying to engage my attention, but I refused to look up. 'I've got a proposal for you,' he went on, then waited for me to make eye contact. 'How would you like to work for St. Mary's? We have an opening for a job as the church sexton?'

"He went right on giving me details about what the duties would be, kind of casually shuffling around hymnbooks in the rack. 'The church council has been after me for a while to find someone,' he said, 'and I think you're the man for us.' Well, I was surprised. As usual, I wouldn't make a commitment without thinking over how it might infringe on my precious freedom. 'Take your time,' he said. 'You don't need to let me know right away.' Well, even as I walked out, I knew I would accept. The next day I was back bright and early for a new beginning.

"The job turned out to be pretty easy. Cleaning. Setting up chairs and tables for meetings. A little groundskeeping. Being around when repairmen came. That sort of thing. The pay wasn't much, but I figured if I was careful, after a month or so I could probably afford a cheap apartment not too far away. I got to know the sanctuary really well as I dusted and mopped my way around. The Padre gave me the grand tour, explaining all about the panels showing the Stations of the Cross, the big baptismal font, and the little shrines to St. Mary and St. Francis. I particularly liked the carved wooden statues of the four Gospel writers that were set in the front of the altar. For such a small church in such a poor neighborhood, St. Mary's seemed to have some real treasures.

"It was a pretty active place even during the week. There were often people in the sanctuary, sitting quietly, or going in and out of the confession booth. A lot of them were old ladies, fingering their rosary beads and mumbling their prayers. But there were younger people too. I asked the Padre about the booth once, and he explained its strange design, with the little seats, and the grill in between. Then he went on to explain the whole business of confession. There were bigtime sinners in the world who probably felt no particular guilt much less a need to confess, he said. 'But deep down, most folks really do feel the need.' People often get hung up confessing to silly acts or a few idle, impure thoughts. The peccadillos, he used to call them. A lot of times, they miss the most important sins of selfishness and of failing to live up to their responsibilities. He always used to say, 'I believe most people are more guilty of the sins of omission than the sins of commission.' It was one of his favorite ideas.

"I asked him if he figured I had any sins I needed to confess. It was an offhand question because I'd never felt like I was dragging any sins around. I had never mugged anybody, run after loose women, sold drugs or even taken them. The Padre studied a moment as if he had something big to say, but simply answered, 'Raymond, we all have sins we probably need to confess.'

"Only later that day did I think about my relationship with my mother. After my old man died, I hadn't been around for her. Our relationship had been nothing more than an occasional phone call from wherever I happened to be living. Her life probably hadn't been easy. She could have used at least a little support from her only son. But staying away was just part of the pattern of my whole life -always trying to avoid responsibility. But by then, it was already too late to do anything. She had been dead for years.

"A couple weeks later, we returned to the conversation. I asked him what difference it made to confess if you couldn't undo the past. He said he saw my problem. But he insisted that each time you confess, the meaning of the confession sinks a little deeper into your heart and maybe makes you a better person in new relationships.'

"I asked him what the old ladies got from spending so much time repeating their Hail Marys. 'I pronounce people forgiven in the confession box,' he said, 'but I always give them something to do, whether it's repeating a prayer or, better yet, doing some kind of service for others. It helps people feel they have repaid whatever debt they mounted up by their actions. I prefer not to think of it as punishment so much as repayment,' he said. It all sounded reasonable enough. I especially liked the fact that he didn't focus so much on guilt the way religion usually does."

He paused to ask whether we practiced confession the same way in our church. I told him we didn't use the confession booth but that we all made a general confession of our sin aloud each Sunday morning. Beyond that, it was up to each of us to come to terms with our own individual sins in private conversation with God. He seemed to prefer that approach on an intellectual level though he remained noncommittal on the whole need for confession.

"How do you decide the right number of Hail Marys to assign yourself?" he asked, perhaps offhandedly, but I could tell the idea had piqued his interest.

"It's all a matter of individual conscience," I said. "I like to take a periodic personal review of my life," I went on, "looking for patterns of failure and focus on them. Saying Hail Marys is one thing. Actually changing how you live is more important."

The lights dimmed briefly, signaling the countdown to lights out. It was a good place to stop. He headed off to his sleeping mat perhaps with a few ideas to mull over, and I prepared to head out with some new thoughts of my own.

VI

When we got together the next week, he was in a mellow mood. The weather had been nice and newspaper sales good.

"I found a little bakery downtown that sells chocolate eclairs," he said. "Brought back some good memories of youth. I had a little extra cash in hand, so I treated myself."

We exchanged a few more pleasantries, then he worked his way back into the story. "The next part is the happiest and the saddest," he began.

"I had been working for a number of weeks but still wasn't able to lay aside enough money to afford to get out of the shelter. The old despair started to set in again. Then one day while I was gathering up the last Sunday's bulletins from the pews, the Padre came in. 'Raymond,' he said, 'I may have a solution to your housing problem.' He gave me one of his mysterious smiles. 'Mrs. Zorah Morgan, who sits right where you're collecting those bulletins, has a room in her house that she's willing to rent very inexpensively,' he went on. 'You'd recognize her. The Negro lady with the big hats and the big singing voice. She's in pretty good health but needs some help around her place. Best of all, she lives just a few blocks from here.'

"Well, long story short, I was soon a boarder with Mrs. Zorah Morgan. She was in her seventies and pretty gnarled up by arthritis and bum knees. The house was small and rather run-down, but she kept it neat. She and her husband had lived there for decades after they moved up from the South. She had been a widow woman for a long time. Her children and grandchildren had moved away long ago, leaving her on her own. Far as I could tell, they rarely got in touch.

"We didn't talk much. She spent her days watching revival preachers, soap operas, and game shows. We shared the kitchen but didn't eat together very often. She usually had her dinner in front of the television, watching *Wheel of Fortune*. I usually came down afterwards, cooked something for myself, and took it upstairs. She would fall asleep around eight-thirty in front of the TV, wake up around nine, and go to bed. Then I'd go downstairs and watch TV myself. Nonetheless, she seemed to like me all right. We got along.

"I did things for her. I helped out with cleaning and chores. Saturdays we'd make a grocery list and I'd do the week's shopping. Sundays I'd walk her the few blocks to church. She was unsteady on her feet and afraid to walk around the neighborhood by herself. Sometimes I'd stay for Mass. Most times I'd walk a few blocks for coffee and an Egg McMuffin, then come back to escort her home unless she was going out for lunch with her lady friends. I felt useful for a change.

"I asked her once how she became a Catholic, being from the South. She said she had been raised in a speaking-in-tongues Pentecostal church but wasn't happy with any of the ones she visited when she got to Chicago. She tried being a Baptist and a Presbyterian. Eventually, one of her friends invited her to St. Mary's, which she told me proudly always had lots of colored folks. She ended up staying because of Father Francis, who had just taken over as pastor about the time she joined. 'The most Christian man I ever met,' she called him, 'Colored or White.'

"I certainly had to agree with her. And nobody ever worked harder to put his faith in action. He was a very busy man. He always started the morning in the sanctuary in prayer with Jesus and Mary and, of course, St. Francis. Then he was in his study writing letters, working on his sermon, making phone calls to community organizers, reading reports about repairs that needed to be made to the church roof, and so on.

"After lunch, he was off to visit people getting ready for surgery or coming out of surgery or ready to die. Then it was visits to homebound parish members. Late in the afternoon he was usually back at St. Mary's counseling couples getting ready to be married or talking about divorce. After dinner, it was council meetings and committee meetings. Saturday mornings he taught the children the catechism and trained the altar boys. And Sunday, well, you can imagine the routine. It seemed like the work never stopped. Still, he always made time to stop and talk to me.

"But he wasn't too righteous or too busy to enjoy some fun on occasion. He told me how much he enjoyed the youth activities and shared stories of when he played on his church's basketball team as a kid. I don't think he did much socially. But every once in a while, he'd invite me over to the rectory for the evening. He usually ordered a pizza, and we'd spend the evening playing gin rummy or watching a ballgame. I've never been interested in sports, but it was fun watching him root for his beloved Cubs even though they lost the pennant year after year. It was even more entertaining watching Bears games with him. He was quite the animated fan, sometimes to his own embarrassment, especially when the home guys blew a big lead or made a spirited comeback. 'What would St. Francis think,' he once said, 'if he knew how much I love watching 300-pound giants bashing each other about?' I, of course, offered him full and complete forgiveness even though I told him I didn't believe he'd ever change his ways.

"Well, that was probably the most carefree decade of my life. I had spending money, a secure job, a secure place to live. I was free to explore Chicago, which I got to love. You know, it also has an El - not as good as Philly's, but an El nonetheless. It's a good walking city during the warm months, especially along the lake. Zorah let me hook up a DVD player and rent movies, but I had rather lost interest in the new ones coming out. Every summer during the slow period at the church, I'd take a bus trip for a week, making sure Zorah's pantry was stocked with groceries before I left. It was a good life all around.

"Inevitably there were some crises. Six or seven years along, the Padre had a health scare. He had been looking tired and pale for a while, and people had been asking him to cut back and relax a little more. But he couldn't. There was always one more person to counsel or one more saint's festival to prepare for. Then one morning he collapsed in his study. The secretary called an ambulance to rush him to the hospital. A heart attack, they thought at first, but after the tests and such, they determined it was just exhaustion. He was forced to take his first vacation in twenty years.

"Zorah also was having problems with her health. Arthritis, diabetes, high blood pressure. I began to have the old feeling that I might have to move on. But this time it wasn't accompanied by the excitement that came when I needed a change of scenery or even the fatal acceptance that nothing good could last. For the first time, it was fear about the future.

"Well, the Padre did recover and soon was back at work as busy as ever. A few more years rolled by, and I forgot that scare. I got the feeling that things could go on like they were pretty much forever. But, of course, that isn't the way stories go. Father Francis kept getting older and not slowing down. You probably have guessed that he didn't have long before he got to meet the Maker that he had been serving so faithfully.

"A massive heart attack took him down during the fall. They rushed him to the hospital in critical condition. The people in the congregation were devastated. I went to visit him about a week later. He looked pretty bad. Ashen. Exhausted. He could barely talk, but his face lit up with a smile when he saw me. We talked just a few minutes before I could see he was too tired to go on. Before I left, he said, 'Raymond, I wish I could guarantee that St. Mary's will keep you in the fold forever. You know better than most how insecure life can be. Try to keep the faith. Keep trusting in providence.'

"A few days later he suffered another heart attack and eased over into the next life. I have to confess I had feelings I never knew I was capable of. The bishop had the funeral in a big church to accommodate the crowd of mourners. It wasn't just the people from his congregation but rows of priests and lots of others I had never seen at St. Mary's. The bishop gave the main homily, but a few local civic leaders gave eulogies as well. I never knew how respected and how loved he was outside his own church. I took Zorah there in a cab. Though I had never seen her show much emotion before, she cried off and on throughout the service.

"The next few weeks were pretty tense. I knew St. Mary's was in some financial trouble. Not only that, the diocese was having trouble finding young priests to fill positions when older ones retired or died. Even if St. Mary's survived, my job probably wouldn't. Not only that, but Zorah was in really rough shape physically. The diabetes was so bad it was cutting off blood to her feet. I took her to a few doctor's appointments. They had to admit her to the hospital. Then came the dire news. She had to have one of her legs amputated. Things -bad things- were happening in a regular tidal wave.

"After the surgery she had to go into a nursing home. She hadn't any money to speak of. Her only real possession was her house. Social services got in touch with the son she had stopped speaking to years ago. He came and visited her in the nursing home, but mostly set to work selling off the house. When the money from the sale ran out, she would qualify for Medicaid."

He took a long pause to study his tea, then continued. "So, once again, I was homeless. A couple of days later the church council president made a day visit to the church to tell me that the budget didn't allow for a full-time sexton anymore. He told me how much Father Francis had valued my service, and he only wished he could keep me on the payroll. I suddenly realized that the Padre had probably persuaded them to hire me to begin with and then to keep me on full time even when they probably wanted somebody just part-time.

"So now I was also jobless. For the first time in a decade, I was a free agent. And now it wasn't just a little fear, it was downright dread about my future. I went to the nursing home to pay a final visit to Zorah. I think she was genuinely sorry that I had lost the job. Like I said, she never was a lady who showed her feelings very much. But I believe she was grateful for all I had done for her.

"It was already November and getting cold in Chicago. I headed off to Greyhound once again with no idea where I would go. I decided before I got there, however, that it would be somewhere south. There was a bus to Cincinnati later that day, but I had already been there. I needed a new destination. I hadn't once considered where else I might go during the past few weeks when everything had begun falling apart. Deep down I knew things wouldn't be staying the same, but I really wanted them to. So, I avoided thinking about what I would do. Not surprising, I guess, since I'd always depended so much on serendipity.

"I took the bus to Louisville, but the little voice didn't tell me to stay. I headed east to Charleston, West Virginia. But that place didn't call to me either. Finally, I boarded the bus for here. I hadn't really heard anything about your city before, but I liked it right away. Maybe it was because the weather was so pretty the day I arrived. Beautiful, warm Indian summer in mid- November. The people were warm too. Things seemed to be falling in place.

"I noticed right away there were guys selling newspapers at busy intersections. It was a job I had experience doing. Maybe I could earn a little cash till something better came along. Then I heard about the shelter here. Definitely as nice as the Catholic one in Chicago. You had one last vacancy the first night I arrived. So here I have stayed. Warm and fed."

"Luck or providence?" I asked.

He shrugged his shoulders, gathered up his plate, and prepared to head off to his sleeping mat. "Still to be determined," he said. Once again, I couldn't get a feeling for where he was emotionally.

VII

When I arrived the next Wednesday, Raymond wasn't there. I asked the volunteer coordinator about him. "Sad story," she said. "He was hanging around near the bus station a few days ago, probably waiting for our doors to open. Somehow, he got in the middle of a brawl and got beaten up pretty badly. The details are sketchy, but he seems to have accidentally walked in on a drug deal gone wrong. The police arrived soon afterward and got him to the ER. We contacted someone at social services who said he had been admitted to the hospital for observation but would probably be released in a day or two."

I felt like I had let him down. Or at least my hometown had. Instead of waiting till the next Wednesday, I returned two days later to see if he were back. He shuffled in as he always did among the last of the guests. He had a cast on his left arm and bruises on his face. One of the other guys had assumed the role of caretaker, helping him with his storage bin and carrying his dinner to the table. A few of the other guys came over to offer sympathy. I let him eat in peace, not knowing whether he would want to talk. But soon he looked my way as though to invite me over.

"Not your usual night to be here," he said as I sat down.

"I came to see how you are."

"I'm surviving," he said.

"Looks like you took a pretty bad beating."

He nodded. "They kept me in the hospital because they were afraid I had a serious concussion." He paused. "But I'm all right. No headaches now." He chewed the last bit of dinner with his usual thoughtfulness. "First time I've ever been in a hospital overnight."

"Did they treat you well?"

"First class, all the way. The nurses and the docs were really nice. And the food was pretty good."

"But not an experience you want to have again," I said.

"No," he said. "Once was enough."

Naturally, I was curious to know about the incident at the bus station, but I was afraid he might not want to talk about it.

He was quiet for a minute, then said, "All this comes from losing my edge, you know. After all those years living in civilized company, I just forgot my survival skills. Like I've always said, if you're going to live on the streets, you have to know how to spot trouble far enough in advance to avoid it."

I was tempted to ask him when he would finally accept the fact that he could no longer afford to think about life in terms of survival skills. Instead, I asked what he intended to do once the shelter closed later in the week.

"Well, the weather's getting warmer. I guess I could start sleeping outside." He paused. "But I'm getting too old for that. There's always the year-round shelter," he continued, "but I've gotten spoiled by the first-class treatment here."

We talked a little longer. I told him I was honored that he had shared his story with me, and he thanked me for being a good listener. Most people, he said, are much better talkers than listeners. Then he said that telling his story had somehow made him understand it a little better. "Sometimes I feel like the Ancient Mariner," he said. "That's about the only thing I remember from high school. The old guy who had to keep telling his life story over and over again till maybe he could really understand it.

"You know," he continued, "some of the choices I've made over the years haven't made much sense. I never was good at planning my life." He paused. "But I'm not sure anything a person does can really prepare him for everything life throws his way. So, no complaints."

"Are you really going to move on?" I asked.

"This is usually about the time I would," he said. "I was already thinking about it before this happened," he added, motioning to his broken arm. "But I did have a visit from a social worker while I was in the hospital. She said she would help me find subsidized housing and maybe some other benefits. She was pretty persuasive." He considered the idea a bit. "It's certainly a temptation," he added.

"So, you probably will stay?" I asked.

"Well," he said, "the future's still a little uncertain. I'll just have to wait to see what comes up."

We sat in silence as though we were both trying to figure out how to tie up the ending.

"Are you ready to put your trust in providence?" I asked at last.

"Maybe so," he said. "I hope so."

LITTLE GIRL LOST

Kristie sat near the front of the bus, slowly swinging her legs back and forth under the seat, hugging her Smurfs lunchbox, and looking absently out the window. It was Friday afternoon, the first Friday of the school year and the end of her first week of kindergarten. Behind her, the boys were being rowdy. The driver scolded them, but to no effect. 'Boys are stupid,' she thought. Next to her sat Merrie, her best friend, swinging her legs in excitement and wearing a Friday smile. She had on a gingham dress and a bonnet because it was pioneer dress-up day for first grade.

Kristie watched the black and white cows in the fields along the road. Some were standing and munching; some were lying under a big tree; a couple young ones were scampering about. 'Cows stink,' she thought. But they made her feel peaceful. So did the soft, green hills in the distance. They had two humps like the camels she had learned about earlier in the day. People rode the camels across the desert and lived in funny-looking houses -yogurts, she thought they were called- filled with magic carpets. She wondered why they rode on the hairy camels if they could fly on the magic carpets.

"I'm going to stay up late tonight," Merrie said, "and watch cartoons as long as I want tomorrow morning. Mom said I can."

When she smiled, her freckles smiled. "What are you going to do? Are you going to play with your new sister?"

"Maybe," Kristie said. "I guess so."

Having a day off was a new experience. Have a new sister was an even bigger one. She wasn't sure what either would be like. So far, things didn't seem promising for baby sisters. All this one did was eat and sleep and poop and cry. She looked out at the tall grass waving along the roadside and the big, lazy clouds. She didn't feel especially eager to get home.

Suddenly, a big wad of damp paper flew between their heads and thwacked into the window.

"Tony, did you throw that," Merrie said peevishly, peering around the side of the seat.

This time a spitball whizzed up the aisle, just missing her freckled nose. Merrie couldn't quite see Tony or Sean, her other brother, who were crouched down in their seats. They were being quiet. Sneaky quiet, she thought, like they were planning something.

A little farther down the road, the bus pulled off to the side to let them off at the campus of the boarding school where they lived. Tony and Sean burst up the aisle, jostling Merrie back into her seat and grabbing her bonnet before they clambered down the steps to the road. Merrie grabbed her lunchbox and raced after them. "Slow down," the driver said in his usual monotone. "Be careful on the steps."

Kristie moved up the aisle at her own pace, lagging behind her friend. By the time she got down the steps, the three others were already through the entrance gate.

"Dorky hat, dorky hat," she heard the boys cry as they passed the bonnet back and forth. Merrie tried to snatch it back, but Tony spun and feinted and dodged, then tossed it to Sean, who tossed it back. Then they began to run up the hill toward home, with Merrie squealing in protest and vainly pursuing.

Kristie slowly walked up to the gates, watching the bus head toward its next stop and her friends getting farther and farther away up the hill. She was tired and didn't want to run to keep up with them. In fact, she didn't want to be with them at all. She was tired of school; she was tired of stupid boys. She was even tired, for now, of Merrie. When she looked up the long hill, the others had already disappeared in the distance.

Sandy walked down the hill from her house, carrying the new baby in a snuggly. She had had plenty of visitors during the week, coming up to help with housework, to chat, and to play with the baby. By now, she felt cooped up and in need of getting out. She was still tired, and carrying the baby on such a warm day made her break out in a sweat. She couldn't wait till she felt energetic and vital again. How long, she wondered, would it take her to get back in shape? She couldn't remember how many weeks it was after Kristie as born till she felt like a young woman again, sexy and attractive.

Today, she just wanted to walk down to the school gates to meet Kristie at the end of her first full week of school. She had wanted to greet her at the bus earlier in the week, but the walk down and especially the walk back up had still seemed too much. Instead, each day Kristie had played at Merrie's house till dinnertime in the dining room. Dinner was always noisy and the children got easily distracted, so she hardly had a chance to ask Kristie about her day till they were heading back home. Even then, the baby often demanded most of her attention, and it was often Austin who got the summary of what had happened. So far, it had been a series of pretty short stories. She couldn't tell whether or not it had been an auspicious opening to the year. Austin had been the one to read to her and sing to her and put her to bed. She was relieved that the weekend had arrived so that they could spend some mother-daughter time together.

Down near the bridge that separated their faculty house from the main part of campus, she was joined by Clyde, their golden retriever. He was big and gentle with a powerful chest and noble head, but he smelled from swimming in the school lake and wandering on the mountain. She liked him well enough as long as he stayed mostly outside. Austin and especially Kristie adored him.

She got to Nancy's house half an hour before the bus usually dropped the children off, expecting to take her time walking down to the gates. Nancy had been her mentor and wise older sister since she had first arrived. She had been a tireless helper in the past week and a half since the baby was born, particularly helpful in watching after Kristie. But now Sandy was ready to assume her new role as mother of a kindergartner. She had come down to meet the happy students when the bus arrived and perhaps invite Merrie up to her house for the rest of the afternoon. She had already baked cupcakes that morning while the baby napped as a special treat for completing one week of kindergarten. While she waited, she browsed through Nancy's extensive library of paperback books.

"Take a few," Nancy said. "You haven't read anything new in weeks."

"Who has time to read?" she said.

"There's always time to read." It was Nancy's philosophy of life. There must always be time to read, to garden, to visit with friends.

"Maybe later," she said, looking at her watch. "Right now, I've got to walk down to the gates to be there when the bus arrives.

"It's too hot to walk down," said Nancy. "Besides, I usually walk down only in the morning to see them off. That's when they tend to dawdle and get into arguments. They're old enough to come back up by themselves in the afternoon."

Sandy supposed she was right. It certainly was hot, and they should be responsible enough to get back up on their own.

Instead of climbing the long hill up to Merrie's house, Kristie decided to take a different way back. On her right was the big school lake, looking cool and quiet in the late afternoon. She decided to sit by the shore in the tall grass and rest for a while before she went on. While she sat, a duck plashed down just twenty yards or so from her and began to swim in her direction. He had a green head and stripes on his wing. He swam a few yards closer, then lifted up and flew away. Maybe he wants to be alone too, Kristie thought. Suddenly she felt hungry. She opened her lunchbox, took out a half-finished peanut butter and jelly sandwich, and began to eat. The lunchroom had been so noisy that she had lost her appetite, but here by the quiet of the lake the sandwich tasted good. Next, she finished the apple slices and the animal crackers in the plastic bags. Also in the lunchbox was a page of art work with lots of stickers on it and, at the bottom, "Kristie," which she had printed by herself. There was also a picture of Baby Heidi that mommy had put in there in the morning. She looked briefly at the picture, then tossed it into the grass nearby. A gust of wind lifted the sticker art out of her lunchbox and blew it up toward the road, but she was too tired to retrieve it.

By now she was sweaty despite the little breeze that ruffled the lake. The water looked inviting. But she was not allowed to swim in it. That was the rule. Mommy said so. Daddy said so. Nobody was allowed to swim in the lake.

Nonetheless, she took off her sneakers, rolled her pant legs above her calves, and edged down toward the water, holding out her arms for balance. 'Nobody will ever know if I just cool off for a minute,' she thought. The water was warm like in a bathtub. The bottom was squishy, and blobs of mud oozed up between her toes. She stood there for a few moments and watched some long-legged water bugs land on the surface and row about. Then a swarm of gnats discovered her face, and she backed onto the shore again trying to brush them away. She sat on a rock and tried to wipe the muck off her feet with some leaves but got some of the nasty stuff all over the bottom of her pants. 'Now Mommy will know I was in the lake,' she thought. She put on her sneakers but left her pants rolled up. As she got ready to leave, she picked up Baby Heidi's picture from the tall grass, looked at it, and put it back in her lunchbox.

She looked at the wide road up to Merrie's house, then decided to follow a little trail along the shore of the lake. She just wasn't ready to go home yet. She liked the way the tall grass tickled her legs. Off to one side, she heard a frog croak and plop into the water. Overhead, the clouds had gotten bigger and fluffier, and the air became very still again. She continued along the curve of the lake and followed the trail as it headed up the hill.

In the distance, the big mountain rose up. She remembered one of the stories that Tony had told them about the mountain. An old log cabin was up there, and a man lived there all by himself. He was nine feet tall and had a beard that came down below his waist. He had a wolf for a pet and ate whatever he could kill with his bare hands. It was a stupid story. She didn't believe it. At least not all of it. But she wondered what really was up there. Her daddy cut firewood up there, and he said he had never seen a nine-foot man with a long beard.

Still, what was up there? Maybe she would find out.

The kids plopped their book bags and lunchboxes in a pile inside the front door and prepared to play.

"Where's Kristie?" Nancy asked, gathering up the gear and handing it to them to put away.

"Dunno," said Tony racing off.

"Dunno," said Sean racing after him.

Sandy was already looking out the door with an expression of mild concern. She and Nancy both looked at Merrie, flushed from chasing her brothers up the hill.

"I don't know," she said. "She was right behind us, I think."

Sandy made a beeline out the door and peered down the road but saw no sign. She came back, now having moved from concern to mild alarm. "Can you hold the baby? I'll just walk down the road and find her," she said, trying to sound nonchalant. Adrenaline flowing, she started to walk, stopping every twenty yards or so and shading her eyes to scan the distance. No sign of Kristie. She passed the campus lawn and a row of faculty residences on her right before she got to the lake. She scanned again but still no sign of Kristie. At this point, alarm turned to panic. On one side was the safety of the campus; on the other were the lake and the woods beyond.

She called Kristie's name again and again as she continued down to the stone gates. Little by little, she edged over to the lake side, trying to make her calls sound calm, not shrill or panic-stricken. Near the lower end of the road in the grass beside the lake, she found the page full of stickers with Kristie's name at the bottom. Her daughter obviously had been this far, but where had she gone from here? Seeing no sign, she turned and began running back up the hill, propelled by a burst of real fear. When she got to Nancy's, her breath was heaving.

"She's gone," she gasped. "Lost."

"Stay calm. We'll find her," Nancy said, drawing on all her own reserves of calm. She thought a moment. "I'll call down to the fieldhouse. She might have gone there to look for Austin."

"I can't believe I didn't go down to meet her," Sandy said. "I promised her this morning I would. I've got to be the worst mother."

"You're a good mother," Nancy said, futilely trying to comfort her. "You know you are. This is as much my fault as anyone's. You stay here with the baby. I'll make my way down to the fieldhouse and call back here to let you know what's going on." She called the three kids in a voice now full of authority. "Tony, Sean, Merrie. I need your help now. I want you to take me to the place where you last saw her." Her voice died away as they headed out the door.

Kristie followed the trail to a sluggish little stream that fed into the lake. It led behind the stone chapel at the far edge of the campus. She had never been here before. In front of her the mountain loomed large. The trail had ended, but the grass was fairly short. She was tired of carrying her lunchbox and decided to hide it behind the chapel and come back for it later.

The ground now dropped off again till she arrived at a narrow, rushing stream. Mom and Dad had told never to play in the stream near her house, but this stream wasn't very wide and it didn't look deep. Besides, she would have to cross it if she wanted to go up on the mountain and see if the cabin and the giant mountain man really were there.

She was sweating again, and the water looked very cool. She sat down and took off her sneakers. She put a little water on her socks and tried to wash the mud off her pants. 'Now,' she thought, 'Mommy will never know I was in the lake.' The stream bottom was filled with mossy rocks. She picked up a few and chunked them into a little pool downstream to see how big a splash she could make, then cupped her hands and sprinkled water onto her sweaty neck and face. Soon she felt revived enough to continue.

She picked up her shoes and socks and tiptoed across the stream. The middle was deeper than she expected, and she got her rolled-up pants wet up to her knees. Then she stepped on a sharp, slippery rock and fell, hitting her elbow and getting wetter yet. Two steps farther and she was across, but her elbow hurt and now she would never be able to hide the fact that she had been in the water. She sat down on another rock, getting the seat of her pants wet also, and slipped her feet into her sneakers. When she looked at her elbow, she saw it was bleeding. The whole adventure was going wrong. She wished she were back home. She just wasn't sure how to get there.

She was about to cry but bit her lip and gained control. She wouldn't be a sissy. She thought about going back across the stream, but she didn't want to fall again. Instead, she would go a little farther up the hill to the big meadow she thought was in front of the mountain. She had been somewhere up there with her daddy. Maybe she would recognize something when she got there. She wouldn't be a fraidy cat. If there was a cabin up there with a mountain man, she would sneak a quick peek at him, then turn around and go back. She just hoped the mountain man wouldn't smell the blood on her elbow.

. . .

Sandy paced back and forth across Nancy's living room, alternately looking out the front and back windows. This was all her fault, she thought, for not paying enough attention to Kristie. Sensing her anxiety, the baby began to get fussy. She concentrated on relaxing her breathing till she felt the baby calm down again. The phone rang. Nancy was calling to say they hadn't found Kristie yet, but the men and some of the boys had set off looking for her around the lake, down by the tennis courts and the pool, inside the dining hall, even across the road. "She can't have gone far," Nancy reassured her.

Sandy began to visualize the men and boys fanned out like a bunch of hunters flushing out foxes on the manor's game preserve. All to find her lost child. Her fear was now tinged with embarrassment. After a few more minutes, she could wait no longer. She called Nancy back to tell her she was heading back to her own house. She had a premonition that Kristie might somehow find her way there and dreaded the thought that she would find no one home.

"Wait where you are," Nancy cajoled her. "I'll come back and drive you up. I'm right nearby."

"You keep looking," said Sandy. "I'm heading out the door now."

"Can you at least wait and let me take the baby?"

"All right," Sandy conceded, realizing that she needed to focus all her attention on Kristie.

The hill was steeper than it looked from the creek and the trail ended a little way beyond, but Kristie kept on walking anyway. The grass was knee-high in some places and the ground rough and stony. It was quiet except for an occasional rustle in the brush. A couple of times she thought she heard distant voices, but she couldn't be sure. All that she did know for sure was that she didn't know where she was.

Just ahead, she saw a big boulder sticking up in the meadow. She decided she would climb up on it and then she would be able to see her house, but the boulder was taller than it appeared from the distance. She couldn't find places to put her feet, and after she had climbed a little way, she slipped and fell on her bruised elbow.

Finally, exhausted, she sat at the base and put her head on her knees. She was too tired to cry. She no longer cared whether there was a cabin and a giant mountain man or anything else up on the mountain. All she wanted was to be home. As she sat in the shade of the boulder, she fell into a kind of trance. Once again, she thought she heard voices calling out. She lifted her head to listen, but then they died away and she was alone again. She put her head back down, listening to the whirr of cicadas and the caw of a crow.

Suddenly, she felt something wet and cold touch her hand and then her face. She shot up her head in a panic. Was it the mountain man's wolf? Instead, looking her in the face with his great brown eyes and panting on her with his doggy breath was Clyde. "Good doggie," she uttered in an exhale of relief and put her arms around his sturdy neck.

As Sandy walked up to the house, she could feel her heart pounding. 'It's my fault,' she thought again. 'I should have been there to meet them.' She knew she was probably being unreasonably hard on herself, but it wasn't the time for being reasonable. She paused at the bridge to quiet her breathing. As she rested, she heard voices calling Kristie's name, but no one seemed to have come across the stream yet to search. She took a deep breath and called out herself, but the effort seemed futile. She walked on, the sweat stinging her eyes. She looked at her watch. Five o'clock. Kristie had been missing for well over an hour now. She imagined all sorts of horrible scenarios: drowned in the lake, lost in the woods, bitten by a copperhead.

Just as her imaginings became most lurid, she saw two figures emerge onto the road a hundred yards or so ahead of her. She called out in a voice not loud but filled with hope. By now, she could discern that one figure had to be Kristie. The pair kept on walking. She broke into a slow jog, closing the gap. Then, closer up, she saw the swish of a tail and realized that Clyde was walking by her side. When she got even closer, it seemed that Clyde had Kristie's sleeve in his mouth and was leading her on. She called again, and this time they heard her and turned around.

Sandy ran on, but Kristie hung back and didn't come to meet her. She felt yet another pang of guilt to go along with intense relief to see Kristie standing, mute and forlorn, in the middle of the road.

"Where have you been?" she finally managed to ask, working to control her feelings and her breath as she tried to bridge the emotional as well as the physical gap.

"Up there," Kristie said, pointing vaguely toward the mountain.

"On the mountain?" Sandy repeated, trying not to sound hysterical. She opened her arms, inviting a comforting hug. Kristie nodded a wordless affirmation but stepped back, avoiding the embrace.

"Why did you go up on the mountain?" Sandy said, trying her best not to scold, knowing she hardly needed to say it was against the rules.

"I don't know," Kristie said, still refusing eye contact.

Sandy wrapped her arms around Kristie, who didn't resist but didn't return the hug. "I thought you were lost," she continued, suddenly on the edge of anger. "I've been looking for you for over an hour. We've all been looking for you." She knew she had to stay calm. Anger would be the worst response at that moment. It would drive Kristie further away.

The sound of voices calling Kristie's name had become louder. The search party must not be too far away.

"Why are they calling my name?" Kristie asked stubbornly. "I'm not lost."

"They think you're lost. They're all very worried. You've made us all very worried." She pulled herself up short, not wanting to assign any more blame. Then another thought occurred to her followed by another pang of guilt. "You weren't trying to run away, were you?" she asked gently.

"No," Kristie protested. "Tony and Sean and Merrie were running away from me. They stole Merrie's hat and then they all ran away from me. It wasn't my fault." Her voice quavered, and suddenly all her pent-up emotions burst forth in tears. Finally, between sobs, she repeated, "It's not my fault. Everybody ran away from me." She paused to wipe her nose with the back of her hand. "And nobody came to the bus to meet me."

"I'm sorry," Sandy said, on the verge of tears. "I meant to be there," she confessed. "I should have been there."

"It's all right," Kristie said with a look of guileless forgiveness.

"So how did you get up on the mountain?"

Now it was Kristie's turn to hang her head and spill out her confession. "I went to the lake," she said, "and got my socks and my pants all dirty. I lost my lunch box and I fell into the stream and hurt my elbow. Then I went to look for the mountain man, but I couldn't find him. And then I was lost." She looked up as though to gauge the punishment to come. "I'm sorry," she said, her voice quavering. "I'm sorry for getting lost."

Sandy put her arms around her little prodigal, and this time Kristie returned the hug. "I'm sorry you had to get lost for me to find you again," she said. She looked Kristie in the eye again and said, "I bet I know who came to rescue you."

They both looked at Clyde, now sniffing in the brush beside the road. "Clyde loves me," Kristie said.

Sandy started to say, 'We all love you,' but instead said, "Yes, he does."

She got down on one knee and motioned to Clyde, who came over and licked her face. They now clearly heard voices just down the hill. In a moment, Austin and a few others appeared in the distance.

"Why don't you run down to see your daddy?" Sandy said.

"But he'll be mad at me."

Sandy looked her in the eyes. "No, he won't," she said. "You were lost and now you're found. Why wouldn't he be happy?"

Austin took the news of the rescue back to campus, then picked up dinner and brought it back to the house. For the next hour or so, the phone jangled as their friends called to be reassured that everything was all right. It was a wonderful outpouring of community concern but also, Sandy thought, a source of acute, if temporary, embarrassment. She realized the incident would probably become a permanent part of faculty lore. They got Kristie to tell her story again. It was all still a little jumbled but filled with more details than she had remembered earlier.

"I found your page of stickers by the roadside," Sandy said at the end. "You did a good job of printing your name. But what happened to your lunchbox?"

Now it was time for Kristie to make a final confession. "I left my lunchbox behind the church," she said. "Baby Heidi's picture is still inside." She looked up sheepishly. "I took her picture out and threw it away," she said and paused. "But I put it back again."

"Are you upset about having a baby sister?" Sandy asked. There was no reply. "You'll learn to like her," she said and tried to reassure her with a hug. "It'll just take time."

Kristie didn't seem fully convinced. "Will you still read to me?" she asked. They nodded in affirmation. "And sing to me at bedtime every night?" More nods of affirmation. She needed reassurance that they would fulfill the obligations of parenthood and the complicated contract of parental love. "And meet me at the bus, at least sometimes?" Kristie added. "Yes," they assured her, realizing that she and Austin would need occasional reminders of the contract as well. "As long as you promise not to take any more unsupervised walks on the mountain."

"I promise," said Kristie.

They heard a thud on the porch outside the sliding glass door. Clyde had just plopped down on the bed where he usually slept.

Kristie snuggled up next to the door, and Clyde looked at her through the glass with his great brown eyes.

"I love Clyde," Kristie said.

Sandy went over and opened the door.

"We do too," she said. "We'll let him sleep inside tonight if he wants."

TRADITION

I

The dining hall was almost empty when Jim Walton, Junior English and underclass dorm master, arrived for breakfast at 7:15. He came in the door by the conveyor belt that carried the food trays back into the kitchen, expecting to hear at least some of the usual clatter of plates and the muted roar of a hundred conversations echoing through the cavernous room. It was graduation day at Ravenwood Hall. The underclassmen were already gone, but forty-eight seniors- presumably excited and noisy- should have been eating their final plates of bacon and eggs after four years. The only ones there, however, were some of the faculty gathered at two tables. He got his breakfast, sat at the table where he usually sat, and gestured mutely toward the empty tables.

"Would you like to know where all the vandals of our esteemed senior class are?" asked Henry Hedgepath, Latin teacher and senior dorm master of Dewey Hall East, his voice poised to rise in vexation.

"I'm sure you'll tell him, Henry," said Andrew Baynes, chemistry teacher and assistant athletic director.

"Take a look out on the lawn and you'll see them picking toilet paper out of the trees. I only wish it were used toilet paper."

"Don't get your drawers in a wad, Henry," said Norm Weisman, American history and senior dorm master of Dewey Hall West.

"You probably like the new look of the landscaping," Henry shot back, "given the general squalor of your own quarters."

"I think their work shows unusual daring and creativity," replied Norm, refusing to rise to the insult. "It also shows their appreciation of the ancient ritual of pre-graduation Mischief Night."

"None of this would have happened," Henry went on, "if Headmaster had listened to my advice. I had a premonition about this. I heard rumors. But Headmaster always has been too trusting. He hasn't lived in a dormitory for thirty years like I have. Put duty teams on shifts to patrol the halls, I told him. Let everyone take a shift the way we used to do. But no, he said. 'This is one of our finest classes. We can trust them. Besides, I want our faculty to be well-rested for the ceremony.' Male adolescents are not to be trusted, I told him. They are only waiting to rebel. But he chose to ignore my advice."

"If you had a premonition," Norm said, pausing on the final word for dramatic effect, "why weren't you out on patrol? You! The Dragon of Dewey Hall. You had a reputation to uphold, and you let us down. For shame. You slept through the whole thing."

"I humbly accept the censure of Dewey Hall's Epic Snorer. Would any emergency ever awaken you?"

Norm absorbed the gibe, looking over the top of his glasses with an amused grin. Theirs was a long-standing rivalry that Norm loved to stoke on occasion before mischievously retreating.

"Well, Norman, I'll let you fill in the group on the rest of the shenanigans without me around. I'm sure you're dying to do so. I'll wait for the ceremony to begin by myself in my apartment. I've already told Headmaster I refuse to help with the clean-up."

He took his tray up to the line and headed out the door. After a discreet pause to allow the door to stop swinging, Norm cleared his throat, rubbed his hands together, and lowered his voice in mock conspiracy. Getting Henry's goat and telling humorous stories were two of his chief pleasures in life. Combining them was sublime. He just needed an invitation to begin.

"So, what's this about the canoe?" Andrew asked.

"Well, let me begin at the beginning," said Norm. "About five o'clock, I heard someone pounding on my door."

"Loud enough to wake the Epic Snorer?" Andrew asked.

"Loud enough even for that. Anyway, it was Henry, of course. His hair was standing straight up, and he had a frenzied look in his eyes. Like he usually does when he's patrolling the halls, only magnified by a hundred. 'Get dressed,' he shouted. 'There's been a riot on the hall.' When I got out, he led me right to the foyer in front of the dorm office. I have to admit, it was quite a scene of mayhem. Outside, of course, the whole campus was decorated in toilet paper. A regular blizzard of Charmin. In the hallway and sticking out the front door was one of the school canoes with a papier-mache effigy -of Headmaster, I assume- dressed in somebody's cap and gown, seated on the thwart, and pointing into the distance. Around his neck was a sign that said, 'Remember, boys, your voyage of life starts here.'

"I laughed, of course, which was not, however, the appropriate response for Henry. He grabbed my arm and led me down the corridor toward his apartment. It was all very quiet, of course, all the innocent lads pretending to be fast asleep.

"There, stuck to his door was a poster that showed a little man with his hair sticking up, big feet like Henry's, huge googly eyes, and a caption that read, 'The Master Never Sleeps.'

"At that point, I noticed a couple of the boys -looked like Butner and Gales- had dragged their mattresses out into the hall and were noisily opening doors and looking into rooms. Turns out they had been treated to an early morning bed bath. It was their shouts and their pounding on Henry's door that finally woke him up."

The listeners smiled quietly for a bit, fixing the little scene in their imaginations.

"These guys were good," said Chris Chapman, the drama director. He had already been out to inspect the chaos. "Everything was done with flair. Good props. Lots of wit. A real 'A' production."

"Anybody know who the organizers were?" asked Danny Stewart, the football coach.

"Nobody's confessed, or ratted anybody out," said Norm. "Henry's got his list of suspects, but there hardly will be time for an investigation. We sounded the alarm right away. Headmaster and some of the other administrators straggled over by seven to help supervise the clean-up."

"I must say I'm surprised," said Andrew. "I never thought these guys would be up to something like this. They always seemed so... compliant. Hardly risk-takers."

"Maybe we shouldn't be so surprised," said Peter Allswell, the school chaplain. "If you keep a bunch of adolescent boys on a such a disciplined routine and locked away from girls for so long, it's only natural they're eventually going to explode. They just need a few lords of misrule to organize the chaos."

"Well," said Norm, "I guess we better go out and help supervise. Remember, boys. Serious faces. No laughter. Everything's got to look good in a few hours when the parents begin to arrive. Andrew, you should lead the way. Everyone looks up to you as the very model of responsible and mature behavior."

"You guys head out without me. Henry stormed off without eating breakfast. I'll take a plate down to him. You know how he gets when he misses a meal."

II

The air was already warm by 10:30 as they gathered on the lawn for the commencement procession into the chapel. It was Jim's first experience of the pomp and circumstance of Ravenwood Hall. He could feel the sweat gathering beneath the black gown and the stole with his collegiate colors; he held his mortarboard underneath his arm. Amazingly, the lawn looked almost pristine. Just a few streamers of toilet paper hung limply from the upper limbs of the taller trees. He stood off to the side, away from the crowd of graduates, families, and friends already gathering in front of the red chapel doors. A little breeze off the lake cooled him slightly.

"Ready to march, my friend," said a voice behind him. It was Andrew. "Once we get all the ceremonial business over with, it's our time to party."

Jim gave him a questioning look.

"You did get your invitation to Headmaster's, didn't you?" Andrew continued.

"Sounds like a grand time," Jim said, with just a hint of irony. "Libations provided, right?"

"Headmaster does have a way with words," said Andrew. "But I think you'll be pleasantly surprised. The graduation party is always something to look forward to." He paused absently to scan the crowd. "It's good fun."

"So, what's going to happen?"

"Well, I don't know for sure. We never do. We always start the festivities the same way. And there are always some predictable events. Tradition, you know. But after that, we kind of go with the flow." He paused. "You really have to come, you know."

Jim gave a non-committal shrug.

"You haven't come to any of our parties. You must think we never have any fun." They stood quietly for a moment. "Also, you have to bring your lady," Andrew continued. "Martha's dying to meet her."

"I can't promise," Jim said. "I've invited her, but she's been totally wrapped up writing her dissertation. I don't know whether she can break away."

"Come on, Jim. We're all eager to meet her. We're just one big family out here, you know."

"Is that Rod Barton over there?" asked Jim to change the subject. "I've barely seen him since the middle of the year. I don't think he even knows my name."

"He moved off campus back in December or January after his

wife left him," Andrew said. Jim knew only a few details that had come through the rumor mill. "A pretty unpleasant situation," Andrew continued. "She got a job in town. Then came some out-of-town business trips. Turned out some of them weren't exactly for business. They seemed to be happy enough for the first few years they were here. But she never quite fit in and never really tried."

"Some people just aren't made for life in Grovers Corners, I guess," said Jim.

'You're probably right. It's probably what caused the break-up in Carrie Felton's marriage too. All in all, it's been kind of a rough year for marriages."

"Didn't I see the two of them sitting together this morning at breakfast?" Jim said.

"I hadn't noticed," Andrew said, his face assuming a look somewhere between mild surprise and sly satisfaction.

"How was Henry?" Jim asked. "I couldn't believe how upset he was."

It's been a tough year for relationships for him, too," Andrew said. "But just look at him hobnobbing just as if last night hadn't happened." Henry indeed was making his way among the assembled parents, meeting and greeting.

"He seems like such a contradictory character," said Jim. "One minute he's the martinet trying to force everybody to march in step; the next, he's all courtly charm and concern."

"He wouldn't see it as a contradiction. He's very old school. You know. Duty, duty, duty. And good manners. And always following the rules. But on the other hand, he's been a kind of surrogate parent to many of the boys over the years. Particularly the unpopular ones. They come to him with all their problems. It takes all kinds to build a community. I don't know what we'd do without someone so devoted to the boys. That's why the pranks really hurt his feelings."

"I thought he was about to have a stroke this morning he was so mad."

"He had calmed down a little by the time I got to his apartment.

He just needed a little more time and somebody to listen to him vent." He paused. "Despite the pranks and the hateful things he said, nobody will miss the boys more than he will. Unfortunately, a lot of them never figured out how to deal with him."

"How about you? Jim said. "Will you miss them?"

"Sure," Andrew said. "But there'll be a new bunch next year. Besides. I've got my own family." He stopped to consider. "I've learned to keep a little distance. Otherwise, the job would eat me up."

Norm spotted them as he left his apartment and made his way over to join the conversation.

"So how was Henry?" he asked.

"How do you think?" said Andrew.

"He certainly seems fine now schmoozing with the parental units."

"He's really mad at you, in case you didn't know."

Norm closed his eyes and clasped his hands together in a look of resignation. "He'll get over it," he said.

"But when?" Andrew continued. "He may sulk the whole summer, and Martha will have to listen to him complain."

"Don't be such a killjoy, Andrew," said Norm. "I'll humble myself and apologize later. Just let me enjoy his righteous indignation a little longer."

Andrew gave him a wry smile. It was obviously a little drama that had been played out many times before.

"Come on," Norm went on blithely. "Time to mingle a little."

Jim watched as they worked the crowd effortlessly. Was it a gift or a skill that he would acquire if he stayed for a few years. The former, he thought. Norm, in particular, had an easygoing manner that concealed the demands he made on his students. He somehow got them to like him as well as respect him, and all so effortlessly. He himself greeted a few of the grads, got introduced to a few families, but remained somewhat disengaged.

At 10:55 sharp, the academic dean, wearing a toque and bearing a mace, took his place at the top of the chapel steps. By ones, twos, and threes, the faculty and the students lined up behind him as they had practiced the afternoon before. They marched inside to the strains of Clarke's "Trumpet Voluntary," played on the chapel organ, and filed into the front pews. Chaplain Allswell read the invocation; they sang a hymn; then the dean seated them with a flourish of the mace.

It was all very solemn and impressive. The stone walls exhaled dampness and peace. Jim breathed the cool, still air and truly relaxed for what seemed the first time in weeks. He studied the row of heraldic banners mounted above the stained-glass windows. Each class -freshman, sophomore, junior, and senior- was represented by its own banner. The light, softened by the clouds, suffused the geometrical panes with rich color.

They stood and sang another hymn, then sat again. Two students read passages from the Bible: the first, the parable of the talents; the second, Paul's exhortation to fight the good fight. They were familiar texts he had heard more than once during the year's chapel services, dependable words to convey the school's mission. Jim eased back against the oak pew, listened with half an ear, and scanned the program. Next was the featured commencement speaker, a Ravenwood graduate and CFO of some company. During the speech, Jim took covert glances at the graduates massed in front him. Most seemed to be listening, or at least pretending to. Some stifled yawns. Perhaps they were the ones who had organized last night's mischief.

After the speech came the awarding of academic honors and scholarships. He smiled as he noted the last and most prestigious one: the G. Alvin Snook Award for Academic Achievement and Character, given in memory of the illustrious founder of Ravenwood Hall. Now let us praise glorious names, he thought. G. Alvin had to be a big achiever to overcome his own birth name.

After a brief speech by the winner, the students came up one by one to the chancel steps to receive their diplomas. Finally, it was time for Headmaster's valedictory speech. Jim had grown to like A. Bartlett Pennington. He was tolerant; he trusted his faculty to do their jobs; he ran efficient faculty meetings; and he had a Midas touch as a fundraiser. But he did have a rather sleep-inducing style as a speaker and an unfailing habit of drawing on his experience in the Navy for his themes, metaphors, and moral messages.

"Boys," he intoned, "I'm well aware that you have often heard me describe life as a voyage for which we've tried to prepare you. We have preached the importance of setting a true course. In your classroom studies, we have provided you with a helpful chart. We have encouraged you to pull together as a crew in athletic competition. In daily chapel, we have instilled faith in a Higher Power to be your navigational star in fair weather and tempests."

"Same speech as last year," he heard Alfred Murchison, chairman of the math department, whisper to his neighbor.

The address continued a while longer with no further nautical metaphors till the very end.

"Don't forget, boys," Headmaster concluded., "Ravenwood has been the vessel that helped launch you into young adulthood. Now let it be your anchor of tradition and your beacon of high ideals."

Speeches made and diplomas awarded, they marched back down the aisle to "Pomp and Circumstance." Outside, tables had magically appeared on the lawn; a buffet lunch was waiting. Jim watched the parents gather to walk through the line. They were obviously prosperous and well-preserved. Many of the women wore dresses and colorful hats that would have been suitable at Churchill Downs on race day. The men wore blue or black or gray suits, the uniform of upper-middleclass businessmen and professionals. They were already well along on their voyage of life and a little paunchy and subdued. He watched the new grads who were eager to doff their caps and gowns and head off to a beach somewhere to indulge in the ritual of bacchanal release. And he wondered if they would look like their fathers in twenty-five years.

III

By mid-afternoon all the BMWs and Lexuses were gone. The

food had been cleared away and the tables and chairs carried off. Everyone was milling around as though just released from self-imposed imprisonment but unsure of what to do with their freedom.

Jim was still deciding whether to join the festivities. He could go into town and spend the night with Jennifer at her apartment. They could go to dinner and a movie by themselves. It would be relaxing. But deep down he felt the urge to celebrate the completion of his first year by doing something out of the ordinary. Jennifer had tentatively committed to come to the party a few days ago though he thought she didn't sound too enthusiastic. She had been trying to finish a chapter of her dissertation that had been giving her fits. She probably would be grumpy and tired. But when he called, she was in a great mood. "Chapter's done," she said. "I'm free and ready to party."

"It'll probably be pretty dull," he said. "This tends to be a pretty buttoned-down group."

"Maybe you'll be surprised" was all she said. "Give me a few hours to get ready."

He joined a group of guys relaxing on the dock.

"I'm about to make a beer run into town," Danny Stewart bellowed to anyone in earshot. "Last chance to leave your order. Cash only, remember. I'll even make a stop at the liquor store."

Jim felt restless with nothing definite to do and took a long, slow run. When he got back, the dock was empty though someone had wound strings of lights around the railings. He sat and breathed and let his mind go blank. After a while, he felt refreshed and relaxed in body and mind. He took a shower, then got into his car and began the winding forty-minute drive into town, trying to think of a way to make his arrival special. He would get a bottle of wine, but that was predictable. Then he thought of a visit they had made recently to a jewelry store and a particular turquoise necklace they both had admired.

When he arrived, Jennifer was already dressed and ready to go. She was wearing a tight jersey top in pastel blue, shorts that hugged her long runner's legs and accentuated the tight roundness of her figure, and sandals.

"So how do I look?" she asked flirtatiously.

"You look marvelous," he said. "A true vision of loveliness."

"It seems like weeks since I wore anything except jeans and a tee-shirt," she said.

He reached into his pocket and pulled out the jewelry box. Surprised, she opened it. She was usually the spontaneous gift-giver.

"The necklace we saw last weekend," she said. "I love it." She took it from the box. "Will you help me with the clasp? I'm going to wear it tonight."

It was a good start for the evening.

They chatted idly for the first half of the ride, both relaxed but the slightest bit distant as though they had to get to know each other again, at least to enter this new environment. As they rode, she touched the turquoise pendant from time to time.

"So, tell me more about your friends," she said. "You never really have said much about them."

Where should he begin, he wondered. For simplicity's sake, he decided to tell her about the chaos of the morning clean-up followed by the stately formality of the graduation ceremony. She was amused by the pranks, by Henry's petulant propriety and Norm's skill at getting under his skin, by the familiar traditions of graduation and the proud parents. Then he told her about some of the couples who had made him feel especially welcome and some of the young guys he had coached with, played ball with, and hung out with. "Nice folks," he said. "Most of them aren't very exciting. Pretty traditional. I just hope you won't think they're boring."

"I'm envious," she said. "You know real people. Everybody I know is either spouting off great ideas or so wrapped up in obscure research that they aren't even aware of the rest of the world."

They drove deeper into the countryside.

"I told you it was in the boonies," he said.

"But it's so beautiful," she replied. "Do you know we haven't been out of town together in months? I didn't realize how much I was missing."

"Try to imagine what the drive back in the dark will be like," he said.

She gave him a sideways look. "Oh, I almost forgot," she said. "No shacking up in the dorm, right?"

"It's the rule," he said sardonically. "We're expected to set the proper example."

They arrived on campus just as the faculty were heading in small groups to dine in Headmaster's Tudor house. Dinner was left-overs from lunch, but leftovers from a feast meant to make the right impression on parents who might have younger sons to enroll or who needed a bit of stroking to keep contributing to the building fund. Plates of cold poached salmon and shrimp; scalloped potatoes, roasted potatoes, and wild rice heaped high on platters; roast beef in warming trays; a mound of asparagus; and a half-dozen trays of tarts and pastries, all were spread out on long tables in the dining room. And along with the food were the libations promised in the invitation: bottles of Chardonnay, Cabernet, and Pinot Noir; frosty beer; and bottles of gin and Scotch.

"Do you always eat this well?" Jennifer asked in mock-surprise. "No wonder tuition is so high."

They barely got in the door before the round of introductions began. Jim was almost surprised at how proud he was to finally be able to present his girl to his community of co-workers and -yes-friends. Jennifer responded to their warmth and friendliness like a flower opening in the sun. These *are* real people, he thought to himself. Just like she wanted to meet.

At first, everyone was a little subdued, feeling probably more than a little worn down by the whole year's busyness and especially by the final weeks' run to the finish. Jim figured it would be a pretty short night. They would have a good meal, drink a glass or two of wine, have some polite conversation, then head back to town. Maybe they would take a walk on campus by themselves and enjoy the stars.

But soon the noise began to pick up, and he could begin to feel the energy flow. There was a hint of expectation in the air. The food table, almost sagging under the load just an hour earlier, now had lots of near-empty plates. Even more significantly, most of the wine bottles had been opened and quite a few were empty.

Soon a piano in the nearby oak-paneled den began to sound. As though responding to some pre-ordained signal, people poured themselves another glass of wine and began heading over to listen. Norm, his glasses propped on top of his head, was regaling the listeners with tunes from the winter's musical, *Oliver!*. He rolled his shoulders and bobbed his head as his fingers glided up and down the keyboard and his feet stomped on the pedals.

"Sing, everybody," Chris Chapman cried over Norm's spirited playing. "You know the words."

The crowd hardly needed an invitation. The annual musical was a faculty as well as a student production; everyone did seem to know the words. Even Jim had been persuaded to sing in the chorus. "Consider yourself well in," they all sang fortissimo. "Consider yourself part of the furniture." Midway through the title song, Norm shouted over his own playing, "Libations for the piano player," and kept on banging away. One of the faculty wives brought a glass of wine to the piano bench, took his glasses off, mussed up his always neatly combed hair, then eased up onto the lid of the grand piano to join the song. Once the group had sung the repertoire of favorites, they went on to finish with a raucous, shouting reprise. By the end, Norm had worked up a sweat.

"Piano needs tuning," he said, getting up and taking his glass of wine. "Just like last year."

The crowd now began to move back into the living room, where Jennifer fell into deep conversation with Martha, Andrew's wife.

"We've been waiting forever for Jim to bring you out," Martha said. "He's such a shy thing."

"I didn't realize he was in the musical," Jennifer said. "I would love to have seen it. But he never mentioned it."

"Just like a man," said Martha, giving Jim a look of the mildest reproach. "If you want, I can keep you caught up on big events." They exchanged emails and phone numbers on cocktail napkins.

Meanwhile, the room had quieted down. Jim gave Andrew a questioning look.

"It's the annual year-in-review picture show," said Andrew. "I told you. The early part of the evening is always scripted. It's tradition. The musical revue is first. It kind of loosens everyone up. Next, it's the year's highlights. George Boykin has been taking pictures and videos all year; Martha as well. They put them together to present 'This Is the Year That Was.'

The feature presentation was just about to begin. Boykin, Senior English and assistant director of admissions, introduced it, as always, in the measured and grave tones of a Methodist preacher at a temperance meeting. But he always had a fine eye for the amusing and the ridiculous as well as the nostalgic and truly noteworthy. As Jim watched, he realized it had been a memorable and fulfilling -if sometimes frustrating- year. He gave Jennifer his own running commentary on the people and events. Many of the pictures drew groans, guffaws, and amused or satiric observations from the audience. They celebrated the great moments but didn't spare the embarrassing ones. Everybody sipped more alcohol as they watched and laughed and commented. But nobody left. It was tradition.

At the end, Jennifer asked, "Where's the infamous Henry What's-his-name? I at least want to see him."

Jim looked around for a while before he spotted him off in a corner in close conversation with the assistant headmaster.

"Would you like to be introduced?" he asked. "He's still speaking to me, as far as I know."

"It's probably not the best time," she said.

As if on cue, Headmaster, who had kept his usual low profile, took his place in front of the group. Short and slightly stooped, he looked like a wise Jedi.

"My friends," he said, "It's been a wonderful year, and a memorable graduation day...in more ways than one." He paused, smiling benignly as the group tittered. "But it's time for Irene and me to bid you goodnight. Please take any leftover food and wine as you leave.

"And remember," he continued. "Play safe." It was his traditional final blessing.

Everyone began to gather up whatever was portable.

"By the way," added Headmaster, "The kitchen staff has agreed to serve brunch from eleven o'clock till noon tomorrow. I suspect many of you will want to sleep in late."

"A cheer for Headmaster," someone cried, and on cue everyone gave a hip-hip-hooray.

"Well," said Jim to Andrew, "I guess Jennifer and I will be leaving. It's been a nice party. We really had a good time."

"What do you mean you're leaving?" Andrew said. "The party's just beginning. We always stay here till Headmaster gets tired."

"Then it's a movable feast," Norm added as he walked past them with two bottles rescued from the libations table.

"You can't leave now," said Danny Stewart, moving past them out the door. "We've still got a lot of beer to drink."

"I'm not eager to make the drive back to town half-loaded," said Jim.

"Why would you go back to town?" asked Andrew

"We both know the rules about women staying for the night."

"There are no rules tonight," said Andrew. "Even Henry won't be on duty. You can do whatever you -and Jennifer- like."

Martha returned with one of the other faculty couples.

"Why don't you two join us for the regatta?" she said. "It's very romantic."

Jim looked at Andrew, who responded with a look of amused resignation.

"Martha always decorates the dock. We paddle around the lake in canoes. It's a regatta." He paused. "It's Martha's favorite event every year," he added.

"We're going for a walk for a little while," Jim said. "Maybe we'll join you afterwards."

They went out into the final moments of twilight and stood

looking at the moon on the lake, deciding whether or not to stay. Nearby, on the lawn, Chaplain Allswell, George Boykin, and Norm had eased into Adirondack chairs. Norm filled his plastic cup with the remains of one of the bottles of wine he had carted off from the party.

"This is as far as my feast is going to move," he said. "At least for the time being." He ran his fingers through his mussed hair. "It's warm," he continued. "I think I'll take off my shirt if you don't mind." He stripped down to his sleeveless, ribbed tee-shirt and sipped his wine.

"Don't you think you've had enough?" said George. He was still perfectly sober in his blue button-down shirt, creased khakis, and wing-tipped shoes.

"Nonsense," said Norm. "I've barely had a sip so far." He looked over at George. "Is that Pepsi you're drinking? he said. "For shame!"

"At least have something to eat," said George. "Here, I brought the last bag of chips."

"Please, George, don't tempt me. I'm trying to keep my youthful figure."

Jim and Jennifer pretended to contemplate the moon while they enjoyed the overheard conversation. After a minute, Norm said,

"Reverend, it's nights like this that confirm my faith in God." He thought a moment. "A beautiful moon. A successful year. A bottle of fine wine. Good friends." Everyone remained silent. "Am I being irreverent?" he continued.

"Not to my mind," Allswell said. "You hit many of the essentials of the happy existence we believe the good Lord has provided us with. They're the reward for another year of good service in his Vineyard." He paused. "Speaking of which," he continued, "Would you pass the bottle? My cup is not overflowing."

They all saw Henry walking across the lawn to his apartment.

"Come, join us, Henry," Norm called, but Henry kept on walking. "Come on, Henry. Forgive and forget. Enjoy the night."

Henry stopped twenty yards away and faced them.

"My apologies, gentlemen," he said. "I've had quite enough for one day. Those of you who prefer can drink yourselves into oblivion. Just don't call me if someone gets hurt. I'm going back to enjoy the company of my cat." He headed on towards the dorm.

"His cat, and a fifth of Scotch, I bet," said Norm, and the three lapsed back into silence.

"Let's go to the lake," Jennifer finally whispered. "I think a canoe ride sounds lovely."

The dock was garlanded in lights. They took off their sandals and, stepping into the squishy mud, pushed off the canoe. The other canoeists were already well ahead of them, hugging the line of scraggly alder trees along the shoreline. With no wind, the lake was mystically calm. Jim gave the canoe an occasional stroke to keep them from drifting toward the center or getting snagged by tree branches, but otherwise let them drift along noiselessly. The one side of the lake was dimly illumined by lights from the campus, but as they rounded the far side, they passed into the deep shadows cast by taller trees. They could hear in the distance the occasional plash of a paddle in the water, muted voices, and the croaking of bullfrogs. A couple times the silence was broken by shouts that seemed to be coming from somewhere up on the mountain.

As Jim paddled on, Jennifer dragged her hand in the warm water. When the canoe ran aground, she cupped a handful and playfully tossed it back in his direction as he worked to push off. They emerged out of the shadows through a patch of moonlight and then back again into the shadows, where a few fireflies blinked on and off. From somewhere up on the mountain came the sound of raucous voices once again. Jennifer turned around and gave him a look of uncertainty.

"Just some of the local wildlife, I guess," he said.

"Or Pan and his satyrs," she offered.

At this point, they were approaching the dark little cove at the lake's far end. As they paddled into it, they noticed that one of the other canoes was already there. Jim looked into the darkness trying to figure out who was in it.

"It's only us," a voice called softly. "Temporarily marooned." The voice sounded familiar, but he couldn't quite place it. "We'll be along soon," it concluded.

Jim continued the circuit around the lake in the same leisurely pace, wondering at the tryst they had uncovered. When they got back, they rinsed their feet and climbed up on the dock. Jennifer put her arm around him.

"Martha was right," she said. "That really was romantic." They slipped on their sandals. "Who were the two we passed?" she asked.

Jim shrugged. "I'm not sure," he said, wondering about the magical effects the night of revelry was having on everyone.

They wandered about a bit longer, enjoying each other's company and the solitude and the darkness.

Back up the hill, Norm, George, and Reverend Allswell were still posted in their chairs like unofficial chaperones. Norm was a bit farther advanced in his cups. He ran his hand again through his unruly hair.

"What was all the shouting we heard?" Jim asked as they walked by.

"That was Danny and some of the boys," said Norm. "They always go up on the mountain at some point during the festivities. It's the call of the wild. Isn't that right, Reverend?"

"Or a primitive rite to celebrate the coming summer solstice," said Allswell.

Norm took a drink and gazed down toward the fieldhouse. "Lights are on down there," he said. "The young bucks must have gotten back already."

"What's going on?" Jim asked.

"It's field day at the fieldhouse. Activities vary from year to year. Go down and see. I'll be down eventually, if I can walk that far."

Jim looked at Jennifer, who gave him a 'why-not' look.

The door to the fieldhouse was propped open, and they could hear the sound of a bouncing basketball and the shouts of a game in progress. They walked over to join a group sitting in the bleachers. The action had paused because one of the guys had turned an ankle.

"We need another skin, Jim Bob," shouted Danny. "Take off your shirt and get out here."

"Jim Bob?" Jennifer said, with a smile of curiosity.

"Jim Bob Walton," he said, shrugging his shoulders. "Everybody has a nickname around here."

"I get it," she said with a smile. "The innocent new boy at school."

The game was a little wild. With all the beer, the guys were moving slowly and even more awkwardly. But conversely, the level of competition was even more intense than usual, the boxing out and the defense more aggressive. The testosterone was definitely flowing. Jim, however, hadn't had that much to drink. His head was clear; he was in the zone and not forcing anything. He hit a couple of short jumpers and scored on a tip-in, broke up a couple errant passes, and grabbed a couple rebounds. Within minutes, he had broken into a sweat.

The girls, meanwhile, organized spontaneous cheers. They were all feeling like cheerleaders with Friday Night Fever., shedding inhibitions as they shed years. Jim's team needed just one bucket to win a game of twelve. He hit Chris Chapman with a behind-the-back pass, and Chris finished with one of his patented driving, corkscrew-like lay-ups.

"Nice pass, Jim Bob," Jennifer said, with a mischievous smile, as he got back to the bench.

"Girls' turn to call the game," announced Danny's wife, Bonnie. "We've decided," she said, emphasizing the plural pronoun and looking to the other women for confirmation, "on hide and go seek."

There was a corporate groan among the men.

"It's her favorite game," said Danny by way of apology.

"No complaining," she went on. "We didn't play last year, and I think everybody was disappointed. Besides, it's a tradition.

"Now here are the rules for you first-timers," she continued.

"Couples only can play. Too bad for all you who came stag. All you men who are eligible to play have to go outside while we ladies hide. When the lights go out, gentlemen, it's your turn to come back in and start to seek. Once you find a lady, you can stay with her even if she's not your mate -just as long as she's willing. Or you can move on to find your own mate. Ladies, remember, no squealing when you're found. Once a rival has established possession in a lady's lair, no new arrival can stay unless the original possessor chooses to go back out on the hunt. The game ends at midnight, the hour of seduction. Anyone left without a mate is doomed to a loveless year."

"If it's so dark, how will we know when it's midnight?" someone asked.

"I've got my cellphone right here," she said. "I'll let Danny be the official time-keeper."

"She always tells me secretly in advance where she's going to hide," Danny informed them. "Just so she can be sure I know when to call time."

One final thing, gentlemen," Bonnie continued. "You are to mind your manners. No uninvited feelies are permitted."

Martha called over Bonnie and the other women, and they consulted among themselves for a moment. "All right," said Bonnie at last. "While we hide, you guys need to go out and," she paused delicately, "jump in the pool or whatever. Just to get the sweat off yourselves. We don't want you stinking the place up. And you can't come back in till the lights go out."

Jim looked at Jennifer, trying to gauge her reaction. She held her hands up as if to say, 'you decide.' Then she looked around and mouthed the place where she would hide.

Outside, the men rolled cans of cold beer over their bodies and dipped their heads into the pool. A wisp of night breeze evaporated some of their sweat. Danny brought a pile of towels from the locker room. A few covertly stripped and slipped into the pool. Then they all headed back inside for the hunt.

With the lights out, the fieldhouse was infinitely darker than

Jim had expected. He crept around to get oriented. The air inside was still and heavy, and the darkness seemed ready to suck all the oxygen from his lungs. Even in the familiar confines of the fieldhouse, he felt a hint of the kind of primitive terror a person must feel who gets lost in a cave. He heard other people breathing, whispering, and bumping into things, but he couldn't tell where they were. This innocent-seeming child's game was turning out to be more exciting than expected.

He banged his knee against what proved to be the bleachers. He bent down and felt his way along the bottom row, which seemed longer than expected. At last, he heard someone whisper, "Is that you, Jim?"

"Yes," he exhaled.

"Back here," came the answer after a brief pause.

He turned the corner at the end of the bleachers, and someone grabbed his arm and pulled him underneath. It was Jennifer. He got behind her and put his arms around her despite the suffocating heat, smelling her body lotion, feeling the rise and fall of her breathing, quietly waiting for midnight to arrive. Minutes passed while they remained in their sweaty embrace like two sardines tightly packed in brine.

"Who could have imagined hide and go seek?" she whispered.

Finally, the lights came on and couples began emerging one by one, rubbing their eyes. The last ones to come out -a little sheepishly- were Rod Barton and Carrie Felton. A light dawned in Jim's mind. Perhaps they were the mystery couple in the cove.

"Wasn't it exciting?" Bonnie wanted to know. "Pretty intense, wasn't it? Doesn't the darkness unleash all your primitive instincts?"

Meanwhile, Danny was ushering everybody out.

"Fieldhouse is closed for the night," he said.

Outside, everyone greedily breathed in the fresh air. It was almost tropically sultry. Norm, in his tee-shirt, long pants, and bare feet, was now reclining in a chair by the pool. Several of the couples began walking up the hill ready to retire for the night. Among them were Rod and Carrie.

"Very sweet," Norm said, without irony, as they left. "A summer romance begins."

Jim paused by the pool unsure what the next act in this night of revels would be.

"Pull up deck chairs, you two," said Norm. "The night is young."

"That's right, Jim Bob," Chris chimed in. "We won't be leaving till the games are over."

Jim began to make apologies in preparation to leave when Danny looked at Norm and said, "Where's Henry? I haven't seen him all night."

"He's gone to sulk in his inner sanctum," Norm replied.

Danny thought a moment, then wheeled around, cupped his hands into a megaphone, and began to chant: "Henry, Henry, come out and play."

The words carried with sonorous clarity through the night air. He turned around to the others who were left, mostly the youngest faculty members and their dates, and urged them to join in, like an athlete trying to hype the crowd. "Henry, Henry, come out and play" rang a chorus of voices. After a few repetitions, Norm, peering out over his glasses, said,

"Let him be, Danny. He's had a very terrible, horrible day."

The chanting stopped. Norm, as was often the case, had become the arbiter of how far things could go. Jennifer gave Jim a subtle look, and Jim conspicuously checked his watch.

"I think we'll be on our way," he said.

"All the love birds are flying away," said Norm.

As they headed up the hill, Jim heard someone -Chris, he thought- call out, "Is everyone ready for the swimming competition to begin?"

There was a moment of silence. Then they heard Danny reply,

"I'm for it. Norman, will you be the starter?"

"Honored, as always," they heard him answer. "Fetch me a beer before we begin."

They walked on quietly, hand in hand, the still not completely resolved question of where they would spend the night looming in their minds. Then Jennifer looked coyly at him and said,

"I've never had the thrill of spending the night with the master in an actual boys' dormitory. Seems like the ultimate forbidden pleasure to cap a night of revelry."

"We'll definitely be living on the wild side," he said.

"No rules tonight," she said.

"No rules tonight."

They wandered along the deserted corridor to his apartment.

"My place is a mess," he said.

"We won't turn the lights on, so I won't notice," she said. "The moon will provide all the light we need."

An hour later, as they lay close together in bed, they could still just barely hear the muffled shouts and the splashing from the pool. The party went on.

"Sure is a buttoned-down, boring crowd," she said. "I guess nobody ever has any fun around here."

"Who could have known?" he said, his voice trailing off. "Who could have known!"

Then they fell into a deep sleep.

IV

Brunch started off quiet and subdued. The families with little kids arrived first followed by some of the older faculty who had departed the festivities early. Jim and Jennifer were among the first of the revelers to arrive and lined up behind Martha and Andrew in the food line. Jim felt a little strange, as if part of his private life were no longer completely private. Jennifer, he sensed, felt that way as well. But Martha, in her welcoming way, quickly made them feel at ease. She seemed fairly well rested after the late night. Not so Andrew, who had bags under his eyes. Apparently, he had partied harder than might have been expected.

"We're so glad you two joined us," Martha said. "I hope you had a good time."

"Unforgettable," said Jim. "Truly unforgettable."

"It was a good party," Martha said. "They tend to run together over the years. But this one will definitely be memorable. At least in one way," she added a little mysteriously, giving Andrew a sidelong glance.

Norm, looking more than a little hung over, eased into line behind them. He gave Andrew a questioning look, but before he could say anything, Andrew said, "Patience. Patience. I'll give you all the details when we sit down."

They were unusually quiet as they waited for their food. As soon as they sat down among the other early arrivals, Norm said,

"All right, don't keep me in suspense. How is he? How long do they think he'll have to be in the hospital?"

The normal table chatter suddenly turned to hushed silence followed by a clamor of questions. What had happened? To whom? Whatever it was, it seemed that almost everybody was in the dark.

Andrew gave Norm a perplexed look. "He's not in the hospital," he said.

"Who's not in the hospital?" several voices demanded.

"Chris," Martha whispered, trying to act as go-between.

"But I got your message on the answering machine this morning," Norm continued. "You said they were expecting to admit him."

"I said," Andrew finally managed to get out after the voices quieted down, "that they were getting ready to discharge him, not admit him."

"Thank the Lord," said Norm. "What a relief!"

Right away the questions started up again. Andrew said, "Norm, it's up to you -and Danny, if he's here yet- to tell the first part of the story since I wasn't even there."

"Well," said Norm, hemming a bit in a rare moment of embarrassment, "it was all an unfortunate accident. We were having the traditional annual diving competition. All completely supervised, I might add."

"Just who was doing the supervising?" Martha asked, in a mildly accusatory tone. "Most of us wives had already gone home." By wives, she seemed to be implying 'adults.'

"We were all sober," Danny, newly arrived, interjected defensively as he pulled up a chair to join the conversation. "Even Chris."

Martha gave him a skeptical look.

"Let's say he was mostly sober," said Norm, taking back the narration.

"And we all know he's just a little crazy even when he's completely sober," Bonnie threw in for good measure.

"At any rate," Norm continued, "Chris had already made all his Olympic-level flips, flops, and cannonballs off the board and been judged the winner of the competition. But he insisted on trying his double back-flip one more time."

"The same one he almost killed himself trying to do last year," interjected Bonnie.

Norm gave her a look of strained patience. "He was standing on the very edge of the board, flexing it up and down -for a little extra drama, I suppose," he continued. "Then he fell -just like that- and smashed his forehead onto the end of the board." He paused as though calling the image back up in his mind. "It made a pretty sickening crack when he hit."

"He made it out of the pool on his own," Danny assured everybody. "But he was bleeding like a madman. I got some towels to try and stop the blood. But it was obvious right away he would need stitches. Head wounds, you know, are always the bloodiest."

"Since nobody at the pool was exactly in the best condition to drive him all the way into the hospital," Norm continued, "we had to wake somebody up to do the job."

"And that somebody, of course," said Martha, "was Andrew."

"It must have been incredibly nerve-wracking," Bonnie said, "driving him all the way into town all by yourself in the middle of the night."

"But he didn't go all by himself," Martha said, looking to Andrew to finish the story.

"No, I didn't," said Andrew. "The eyes of the Master of Dewey Hall East never close too tightly in sleep. At least not when the Master has a premonition of trouble."

"You don't mean you woke Henry to go in with you," said Danny.

"I didn't have to wake him. You know what an insomniac he is. He must have been at his window and seen Norm come up to the house. He must have been watching the whole time Norm was banging on the door to wake me up and the whole time he was explaining to me just what had happened. It was like he knew something bad was going on. Anyway, when I came out to get in the car, he was standing there waiting for me."

He paused as the revelation sank in.

"I have to admit that the trip would have been a whole lot more difficult without him. Chris was pretty agitated on the way in, but Henry did his best to keep him calm. Despite what happened this morning, he's usually rock solid in a crisis. I was really grateful to have him with us. Chris was still bleeding when we got to the emergency room. It was crowded with the usual Saturday night suspects, but they jumped us to the head of the line. They shone the flashlight in his pupils, waved an index finger back and forth for him to follow, and did all the tests to be sure he didn't have a concussion. Then they sewed up the gash with six stitches. Believe me, it was a little embarrassing explaining how the accident happened, but I guess they've heard lots of more bizarre stories. We finally got back on the road around five thirty."

"How was he on the way back?" somebody wanted to know.

"Pretty spacey at first, but after we got going, he perked up," said Andrew. "He had the most wonderful conversation with Henry. He went off on some real flights of fancy though that's hardly unusual for Chris. Henry, meanwhile, carried on as if the whole conversation was absolutely normal. He was the model of patience."

Everybody processed the details quietly for a while. Finally, Norm said, "And you're sure he was all right?"

"Other than a bad headache, he was all right," said Andrew.

"Absolutely all right?"

"Absolutely all right."

"And Henry?" Norm said after a pause. "How was Henry?"

"He seemed all right," said Andrew. "But it was hard to know." The question hung in the air with no ready answer.

Nonetheless, the little cloud that had descended on the festivities had apparently moved harmlessly on. Chris would be fine. Perhaps some of them would think of the incident next year when Headmaster counseled them to play safe. It would likely become part of faculty lore, a story that got recalled from time to time over the years.

Gradually, everyone began to feel enough at ease to start laughing about the amusing moments from the previous night.

Bonnie, staring wearily into her third cup of coffee, said, "It was a great party. I just wish we could skip the day after. It's such a downer." She sat quietly for a moment. "I did have an amazing dream though," she mused. "I was alone in a dark place when a big, muscular man in a loincloth and hair down to his waist came in and tried to ravish me." She waited for the desired reaction. "Well," she went on, "he looked just like Danny. Except for the hair, of course."

When she finished, they noticed that Rod Barton and Carrie Felton had just arrived. They got their breakfast and were heading to a table by themselves when Martha came over to invite them into the larger group. With noon only ten minutes away, a few of the youngest couples finally straggled in. Bonnie took a tally of the new arrivals, then said,

"I wonder how many new faculty babies will be born this coming March. It's true, isn't it? We have more faculty children with birthdays in March than any other month."

Just before noon, Norm looked toward the door, then stood up and announced, "Behold, the wounded Olympian has arrived."

Chris, with a bandage wound around his head, had just made his way sheepishly into the dining hall. A spontaneous round of applause greeted him, and he was quickly surrounded by well-wishers offering to carry his tray.

"I feel fine," he insisted. "Just fine. It was a great party." He thought for a moment. "A perfect subject for a one-act comedy."

Before everyone could finish all their breakfast, Chaplain Allswell stood at his table and announced, "It's Sunday, my friends, and especially appropriate that we offer the good Lord thanks for our food, for last night's festivities, and for sparing Mr. Chapman any further injury." After saying grace, he added, "As it is already noon, there will be no chapel services today." He paused. "However, I will be available to hear confessions after lunch. You may take a number and wait in line."

There was yet another round of laughter and applause for the day's official benediction. With the arrival of Chris, the gathering seemed complete, and everyone could enjoy the afterglow of the night of revels. Then Andrew put the slightest damper on their spirits.

"I wish I could say everyone is here," he said, "But someone still is missing."

"Henry, of course," said Norm.

"Somebody's got to go and get him," said Martha. "The celebration won't be complete unless he's here."

"I suppose he's still sulking in his apartment," said Norm.

"We can go down together and carry him back," Danny said, only half-facetiously.

"I'll go and take him brunch," said Andrew. "As a kind of love offering. Maybe I can coax him out again."

Everyone at the table quietly considered the plan.

"No," said Norm at last. "I'll go down to him and apologize. It's my turn this morning."

MODEST HEROES

I had just gotten home from World War II and was struggling with the turmoil from what I had experienced. Some days I'd wake up to joyful awareness that the fighting was over; other days to memories of disturbing things I'd seen or worse things I had been told by veterans who had survived the front lines. But other, vaguer things were bothering me as well.

By any comparison, my months of service had been easy. I had been a non-combatant, a chaplain at first stationed far behind the front lines. During my first couple months overseas, I spent my days in hospitals, listening to anguished stories from men who had waded ashore in the bloody waters of Omaha Beach or dropped bombs from B29s that destroyed munitions factories and civilians alike.

My unit was eventually moved forward in support for the final push into Germany. Along the way, I saw the physical devastation of the war on churches, townhalls, and shops. I saw civilians trying to rebuild their broken homes with their bare hands and their children searching for treasures in rubble piles and begging for food. It was a landscape of devastation populated by people trying to survive hunger and despair.

I was one of many who almost lost God in those ravaged places and was trying hard to get square with Him again.

I wasn't sure exactly what I wanted to do with my life. I didn't feel ready to serve a parish, organizing the programs that could keep a congregation enthusiastically engaged in the Lord's work and offering sermons and personal counsel to those struggling with their own spiritual uncertainties. My bishop, however, was patient and understanding. He believed that the ministry could still be my calling and that I simply needed an opportunity to ease back into faith and commitment. I needed a parish that wouldn't be too demanding and a congregation that would be refreshingly wholesome and free of spiritual complications.

As transition, he suggested a small country church, which I could serve as an interim pastor while the congregation began its search for a full-time man. The church was in a bucolic location in the heartland of Pennsylvania. Just as I had fairly well decided to reject the position without even seeing it, I received a letter from a Rev. R. Orton, introducing himself as the pastor I would replace. He invited me, "with eager and hopeful anticipation," to visit him at the parsonage. The letter, neatly handwritten, intrigued me enough to make a visit.

My destination about ten minutes beyond the outskirts of Gettysburg was surrounded by carefully cultivated cornfields, wheatfields, and pastureland. In the middle of these picture-book farms were red wooden barns and sturdy Pennsylvania fieldstone farmhouses. Even on the wintry December day when I arrived, a few hardy farmers were astride their tractors preparing, I guessed, for spring. It was a beautiful and peaceful place, perhaps right for readjusting to normal life. The countryside evoked the image of what I had imagined the heartland of Germany looked like before it was torn up by the war.

The church was a small, stone building, pretty, but of no particular architectural distinction. On one side was a well-tended cemetery; on the other, a small education building. Set well back from the road was the parsonage, which looked snug and habitable with a pleasing disharmony of turrets and chimneys and a wide front porch. My knock was answered by an older man certainly beyond retirement age.

"Reverend Orton?" I inquired, shaking his hand. "Matthew Forest."

"I've been looking forward to meeting you," he said, returning my handshake firmly. "Please, call be Robert." He was of middle height, trim, and erect in stature with light blue eyes that radiated warmth and beatitude. He spoke, as he moved, in a careful and thoughtful way as though considering each word he said.

He put on a jacket and took me on a tour of the sanctuary, whose echoing stone floor, oak pews and pulpit, and dim lighting felt almost tomb-like on the cold, gray morning. "We don't turn on the heat during the week," he said, "unless we have a special event. Sunday mornings I usually come over around seven to crank up the furnace."

He walked me up the nave to the chancel. "We have a part-time organist and choir director and a choir of about ten," he said, gesturing to the choir stalls directly across from the organ. "They're all getting along in years, but they provide us with traditional and, I think, inspiring music." He led me to see the altar and then peek into the sacristy. "It's a modest sanctuary," he said. "But when the heat is on and sun streams through the windows, it is very beautiful."

Next, we headed over for a brief inspection of the clapboard education wing. He filled me in on the various programs that currently made up the life of the church. "There are a few Sunday school classes for the children and teens," he said, "and one for the adults. They generally take turns teaching, though every so often they call me in as guest lecturer." He chuckled at the notion. "Their preference is almost always to study one of the books of the Old Testament. I would prefer discussing the Sermon on the Mount, you might say, but they prefer the Ten Commandments. It's a very conservative group.

"We have some young families, but not very many. The children who stay in the area usually end up taking over the family farm or marrying into another farm family nearby." He paused to let me take in the details. "Our members do most of the work of caring for the property and organizing the social programs. For most of them, the church is the center of their social life, and their recreational choices are pretty simple. I can vouch that they love their church suppers, and no cooks make better food than Pennsylvania farmwives." Our tour concluded with a walk around the cemetery, where he pointed out the graves of local Civil War veterans. "They're proud of their heritage," he said.

We headed back to the parsonage, passing across the wide front porch and into a long hallway. On one side was a large dining room complete with a table for eight, a massive china cabinet, and a sideboard. On the other was a formal parlor, stuffed with more massive, dark furniture, large oil paintings, and a threadbare Oriental carpet.

As we peeked in, he talked with amiable familiarity about his possessions. "The furniture is mostly family heirlooms," he noted, "none of which I intend to take with me when I depart." I gave him a look of surprise. "They're all too dated for my daughter and her children. You'd be free to do with them as you like, but at least you wouldn't have to worry about buying anything new till you get settled in. Then perhaps you can find an antique dealer who might see the value in them. I'll just hold on to Edward Bates over there," he said pointing to a large portrait. "He's my late wife's kin. He served in Lincoln's cabinet. One has a duty to care for one's illustrious ancestors."

Against the one wall in the hallway was a large, oak rolltop desk with pigeonholes bursting with envelopes. "Office central," he said. "I try to keep my study as uncluttered as possible."

The study was at the back of the house. It was spacious and well-lit with a bay window looking out over a small garden and a patch of woodland. The walls on one side were lined with bookshelves with two comfortable chairs pulled up in front. Against another wall was a small woodstove, stoked on that cold day with firewood. In front of the bay window were a table and two chairs. All in all, it was an exceptionally comfortable room. I had intended to stay just an hour at most, but suddenly this study seemed like a perfect place to while away several hours. I ended up staying till nearly evening.

"Have a seat at the table," he said, "while I bring in the lunch the housekeeper made. You might be able to negotiate with the church council to keep her on."

While he was in the kitchen, I browsed through his collection of books, believing that much can be judged about a man based on what he reads. The collection was varied. There were volumes on modern and ancient history, a set of Dickens novels and another of Faulkner, books on religion and philosophy, but also travel books, books on sailing and the sea, and a whole shelf of volumes on the Civil War. As I was making my way along the final shelf, he returned carrying lunch on a silver tray.

"That's only part of the library," he said. "It's yours, too, if you decide to take the post." I looked at him with evident surprise. "What can an old man like me do with so many books?" he said in response to my unspoken question.

"A man beginning retirement has all the more need of them, "I said.

"Re-entering retirement," he said. "I came out of my first retirement fourteen years ago to take this parish." This was just the first of many revelations about his life that he would soon share. "I'm eighty-eight," he said. "I took the call here back in 1932 during the Depression when the church was too poor to pay anyone. My bishop recommended me as the only one wealthy enough and foolish enough to do the job for nothing. The council has modified the terms somewhat since then, and they're quite willing to offer a comfortable salary to the right candidate."

He served our lunch of soup and sandwiches and after blessing the food told me a little more about the congregation. The main point he seemed to be emphasizing was that the people were wonderfully hospitable, sincere, and easy to work with, just so long as their pastor didn't insist on introducing any new and liberal ideas. The parish, he intimated, was a sinecure for someone with a reflective bent and no grand ambitions.

After that, he asked me about myself, my family, my growing-up years and education, and finally what had called me to become a pastor. I answered mostly in generalities. Only at the end did he ask how I was adjusting to being back from the war. I tried to be honest in my general way and he didn't press for any details, but I believe he sensed the crisis I was going through. As I talked, he listened with obvious interest. To keep the comfortable dialogue from becoming an uncomfortable monologue, he would occasionally interject an anecdote or observation of his own. I felt, as we spoke, that he was evaluating me, but not in an attempt to find flaws. Rather, he was looking for something specific in me, though I wasn't yet sure what. I was expecting that at some point he would ask the inevitable question of whether I could see myself serving this congregation. But he never did.

Our lunch finished, he suggested we move to the easy chairs for coffee. Once we had settled in, I couldn't resist asking him why he had stayed on for so long as pastor, using up his leisure years. It was in large part, he said, a desire to continue serving, to continue being useful in helping his parishioners maintain their spiritual life. But then, it was also a love for the area, the countryside, the town, and the history. "I never could resist living in a place steeped in history, Civil War history, in particular," he said, glancing at the shelf of volumes on the war. "So, once I moved here, I found it hard to leave."

"I take it that you haven't always lived in the area," I said.

"No. My family were not from around here. We were all Virginians. I was born on a medium-size farm north of Winchester. It was similar in size and appearance to the farms around here. But we were Southerners through and through. My mother's people had already been in the planter class for almost a hundred years though they weren't exactly wealthy. My father's people were newer arrivals to Virginia, who had found good, reasonably priced land to invest in. We owned about five hundred acres and twenty slaves." He gave me a look that was hard to interpret.

"Yes," he continued, smiling wryly at my look of unconcealed surprise. "We were a slave-owning family, shocking as that now seems. My father was a good farmer who tried to keep up with new farming techniques and equipment. But to make the farm pay he believed he absolutely needed slave labor. It was simply the way the system worked. He was a smart businessman, and he took an active part in local politics to help preserve the interests of our class. When the war broke out, he signed on right away with the cavalry regiment of Col. Ashby Turner, the son of one of Mother's old family connections."

As he talked, I made some quick mental calculations. "Then you were actually born before the war," I said, intrigued by the prospect of knowing someone whose life had spanned both sides of that epochal event.

He nodded, amused, I think, that he had surprised me again. "Yes, indeed," he said. "I was born several years before Fort Sumter. I expect I'm the first antebellum fossil you've ever met."

"You don't, by any chance, have any real memories of the war, do you?" I said.

"Mostly some vague recollections of my mother bundling us off to stay with different relatives a safe distance from the war zone. Our area was criss-crossed by soldiers from both sides, foraging for food mostly." He reflected a minute, sipping his coffee. "But I do have one particularly vivid memory from a time when I would have thought my mind was too unformed to retain it. It's my only real war story."

It didn't take much persuading to get him to tell the tale.

"The setting is the front yard of our farmhouse on a bright, chilly fall day," he began. "I can see the wind lightly rustling the trees and actually feel the sun warm on my shoulders. My mother is at the gate of our garden, her hair piled up on top of her head in a bun and only a shawl around her shoulders. She is talking to a young soldier. In my memory, he is wearing a blue coat though I can't be completely sure. He has a thin mustache, dusty boots, and a uniform that doesn't fit him very well. Behind him is a small company of soldiers standing by their horses. I can even see puffs of vapor coming out of the horses' nostrils.

"The officer seems to be giving her advice, which I can't hear. In my memory, he has a kind of homespun courtliness about him even though he has a chaw of tobacco in his cheek. My mother is reflecting on the situation when suddenly one of the house servants comes running out the front door, shouting that there's a fire in the kitchen. Sure enough, a plume of gray smoke comes curling out the window. There is a moment of chaos. My older sisters are screaming. A couple of the fieldhands have come to see what's going on. My mother stands mute and transfixed. But the officer responds quickly. He gestures and two soldiers lumber across the yard and into the house. In a flash, they're dragging a smoldering mattress down the steps and onto the grass. Shortly after that, they mount up and ride off."

He paused as though lost in the sights, smells, and sounds of the memory.

"I can't recall when this little drama worked its way back into my consciousness. At first, I wondered if the event actually had taken place or was just one of those vivid dreams that tries to nudge its way into actuality. Even more, I wondered whether my memory was playing a trick on me by picturing the officer in a blue uniform. For some reason, I never asked my mother to verify that the event actually happened. I guess I wanted to preserve at least the possibility that I actually did have a real war experience. And that the hero of the little drama was a Yankee, not a Confederate."

We talked for a while about the power of stories like his to shape whole periods of personal history and how the memory so often acts as a willful and sometimes whimsical archivist, preserving only tiny fragments of experience -happy and unhappy, significant and insignificant- while consigning the rest to an inaccessible storage vault in the unconscious.

"You must have been tempted," I suggested, "to play the novelist and throw in more vivid details and maybe add some drama to the ending."

"Actually," he said, "I didn't have to invent anything after all. Just before the First World War, my mother died, leaving me a farm and a house filled with many of the antiques you've already seen around here. I finally mounted the attic steps one Saturday morning to sort through boxes and trunks stuffed with family treasures: a wedding dress, my father's dress uniform, a box of tintypes and silhouettes, things like that.

"Last but not least was a diary. I opened it and recognized my mother's handwriting right away. Naturally, I wanted to read it, but at the same time I didn't want to discover any revelations about my parents that might alter the representation of them that I had created in my mind. Finally, I gave in to my curiosity and began to browse. The diary was carefully dated and written in a neat, feminine hand. It began in 1856 and extended through 1866. Most of the entries were of a very ordinary nature. She mentioned acquisitions of new silver and dishes, domestic problems, and problems with the slaves. She recorded the birth of two children, myself included, and described with some floweriness my father decked out in his uniform, mentioning how fine and manly a figure he was. The diary, in short, contained the expected sentiments and observations of a woman of the time.

"I was about to put it away when I suddenly remembered the burning mattress and the soldier with the mustache. I had long ago dated that memory to late 1864. I thumbed through the pages till I came to an entry for October 22 of that year. It was a long one that summed up a series of events over several days. Near the end was a single paragraph about the incident that had stirred my imagination over the years."

He got up a little stiffly, walked to the bookcase, and pulled a thin volume with a black cover off the shelf, thumbing through it to a particular page, which he read aloud:

Had a visit from some Yankees last Tuesday. They warned us about the coming hostilities. He strongly advised me to shut up the house, hide the livestock in the woods, and find some family or friends to stay with farther to the east. While they were in the yard the house near caught fire as a result of Ophelia's carelessness. But tragedy was averted partly with the help of the Yankee lieutenant. He was quite young but handsome with his little mustache. And he was a gent, and gracious. He introduced himself as George McVea from Pennsylvania. I wish I saw more like him We treated them to cornbread and apple cider by way of thanks. After they left, we packed ourselves, along with the silver and some other valuables, into the carriage, and headed out, leaving Lydie to care for the house. Nathaniel drove the carriage with Robbie sitting up beside him like a little soldier. The roads were mighty rough and the girls complained a good bit. Arrived at Brother's house in Charlottesville on Friday night after staying a couple of nights with Aunt Julia. Things on the Grounds were mighty quiet with all the boys off fighting.

"So, there it was -a memory and not a dream after all. It was an added pleasure to picture myself up on the carriage seat having a grand adventure. It was also at this point, I believe, that the mustache and perhaps a couple of other details became part of the mental picture. But what really stood out was the confirmation that the hero of this little drama of kindness and concern was, in fact, a Yankee. I actually tried to put my research skills to work to find the real George McVea, poring over enrollment lists of regiments from Pennsylvania. I tried a couple of different spellings of the last name and eventually found a few possible candidates, but none of them turned out to have fought in units stationed in the Shenandoah Valley. It was probably just as well to preserve the image of him as a young man that I had stored away in my memory. But it certainly would have been nice to know whether he had survived the war and been rewarded with a long and prosperous life."

He thought for a moment. "George McVea," he said. "He was probably the first of my modest heroes."

"Modest heroes?" I said.

"Just a term I coined for the ordinary people who do something generous or courageous or say something particularly wise at crucial moments in your life. The definition is imprecise, but you probably get the gist. My life fortunately has been filled with encounters with such people. Yours probably has been too. They're all around us if we just pay attention."

We talked about the idea a bit, but at first I couldn't think of any ready examples from my own experience. Then I recalled a little incident that was one of the happiest moments of my time overseas.

"Let me refill your coffee," he said. "I'd like to hear that story if you want to share."

It was a story I was eager to tell.

"It was April of 1945," I began. "We had finally pushed into western Germany and crossed the Rhine. My unit had just been called forward in support, and we were marching along the main street of a village somewhere east of the great river. The place had been badly torn up. Even though the area had technically been liberated by Allied troops, the people on the main street at first looked at us with distrust. The arrival of new Americans hardly seemed cause for celebration.

"We were moving along quickly when a boy -maybe eleven or twelve- with blue eyes and a tousle of blond hair fell in step with me. He was dressed just in a thin shirt and short pants despite the unusually chilly spring weather. '*Willkommen*, Americans,' he said with just a bit of an impish look. *Wie geht es dir,* I replied, assuming he was getting ready to ask for a candy bar or some other treat that Americans often had stored away in their pockets. He was pleased that I spoke his language, and we began to carry on a conversation as best we could while the column continued moving forward.

"He told me he was happy to see me and hoped the war would soon be over. He lived with his mother and his sister and said his father was still fighting, but he didn't know where. I asked him his name. 'Andre,' he said. 'Andre Griezmann,' -or something like that, though I can't be sure whether I heard the last name correctly. Half-French and half-German, perhaps, I thought, and caught in no-man's land between the two old enemies. He saw the cross around my neck and asked if I were a pastor. We carried on like that for a few more minutes -mostly idle conversation since my German was not especially good- till suddenly the column halted. We could see up ahead that the captain was in communication with a couple of the townspeople.

"Suddenly, he scampered up to the front of the column in search, I figured, of new excitement. Everybody in the unit seemed pleased for a chance to rest. We talked about lunch and speculated on how much farther we'd have to march before we stopped for the night. Suddenly, Andre reappeared and, without a word, took me by the sleeve and led me up to the front of the column.

"'*Er spricht Deutsch*,' he told the two townsmen, turning me over to them with a look of official pride.

"For the next ten minutes I did my best to translate a dialogue between our captain and the townsmen. There was a company of Germans, they said, that had been wandering around the area over the past couple weeks, killing livestock, ripping up newly planted cabbages and lettuce, breaking into barns, storehouses, and even homes. They were well armed and seemed ready to do whatever they considered necessary for survival. They had probably been caught behind the lines of the advancing Allied armies and considered themselves free agents in the war. Only that morning they had been spotted nearby by a couple of the townspeople as they were tending to their livestock.

"The captain quickly got on the radio to make contact with other units ahead and behind us. Then he dispatched a team of scouts to do reconnaissance up the road.

"As I translated, I glanced occasionally at Andre, who avidly took in the whole conversation. Within ten minutes, we were ready to move on. Andre accompanied me back to my place in line, chattering so rapidly about what had just happened that I could hardly follow a word he said. But it made no difference. I felt joy beyond all logical expectation at this unexpected friendship. I fished through my pockets for any treats I could find, but I believe he felt amply rewarded just by knowing that somehow he was helping protect his village. As we marched out of town, he walked along with me, but we didn't resume our conversation. Soon he dropped back and with a brief *auf Wiedersehen* disappeared.

"We marched on through the afternoon, halting frequently to let the radioman make contact with other units in the area. It was a tense time. Nobody in the outfit believed they would dare to launch an attack. We were too well-armed; our scouts were scouring the area. A dozen or so rogue fighters would have had little to gain and everything to lose by a surprise attack. It would have been sheer madness. But still, there was always that possibility. It was the only time I ever feared for my life.

"But I was just as anxious about the fate of the villagers and my friend Andre. Had our conversation been observed by prying eyes? If so, it was likely there would be acts of retribution after we left.

"Later on, we heard that some of our boys in another unit off to the north had flushed out a ragtag squad of Germans hiding in a barn. There had been prisoners taken and some casualties, but fortunately none to our boys. Details were sketchy, but I felt confident that my village at least was safe.

"The captain praised me for my work as translator, but it was really those villagers and my friend Andre who were the heroes of the story. Now whenever I look at photographs of towns devastated by the war, I see their faces. Then I feel blessed."

"A memorable story," he said. "You were fortunate to have seen the human face of war and witnessed some simple but true acts of courage."

"There's only one thing I regret about that experience," I said. "Later that day I realized that I had never asked the boy the name of his village. Now in my memory he simply comes from some nameless village east of the Rhine. I'll never know the next chapter of his story or the story of that town any more than you'll know about your Yankee lieutenant."

He got up, added a log to the woodstove, and refilled our coffee cups. Then we sipped our coffee in silence for a few minutes.

"My post-war life has been mainly uneventful," I said at last. "But what about yours? Your family must have faced challenges almost as daunting as the people in my little German village are facing."

"Actually," he said, "we were fortunate in living at the very northern end of the Shenandoah Valley. The area had seen its share of battles but nothing like the magnitude of destruction suffered by much of central Virginia. Most of the farms in our area were pretty torn up by armies marching back and forth. But Mother Nature proved amazingly forgiving. We were fortunate in being close to northern markets and areas where the railroads were being rebuilt. I'm no expert on economic matters, but it was obvious that recovery was going to be easier in our area than in most of the South. In addition, my father was determined and resilient. He hired on those of our former slaves who were willing to stay, and by careful management and some wise business decisions, he got the farm prosperous again fairly quickly.

"But in other ways, he wasn't willing to move on. Most Sundays he and a few of his old comrades would get together on our porch to drink whiskey and talk about the war, politics, and the prospects for the future. When I was eleven or so, I began to sit out there and listen. The men were all veterans of the Valley war, so much of their talk was about the campaigning from Harper's Ferry to Lynchburg. I soon got to know the names of Stonewall's famous victories - Winchester, Port Republic, Cross Keys, even Kernstown, where he violated his usual sacred commitment not to fight on the Sabbath.

"Their admiration for him rose almost to reverence. He was a stern disciplinarian who drove his troops on incredibly taxing marches. But they always showed up just where the Yankees least expected them and delivered a stinging defeat before escaping to set another trap. My father wasn't a church-going man, but he still admired Stonewall's almost fanatical religiosity. All his comrades were proud just to say they had served in his division.

"Paradoxically, they were probably even prouder to say they served under flamboyant Col. Ashby. He was a free spirit. His troops called themselves the Mountain Rangers, and the name was their badge of honor. Their job was tearing up railroad lines, capturing bridges, and carrying out reconnaissance for Jackson. Regular disrupters is how they liked to think of themselves. I remember Father and his friends talking about Ashby's phenomenal horsemanship, his superhuman stamina, and his flair for the dramatic. He had charisma and style of a very different sort than Jackson's, and the two didn't always see eye to eye. What was important to Father and his friends, however, is that both were winners. I remember my father describing to me Ashby's final moments during a skirmish outside Harrisonburg. They were retreating from a Yankee patrol when his horse was shot out from under him. Without waiting for help, he drew his pistol and saber and charged his Yankee pursuers on foot. It was his grand and final hurrah."

"The classic action hero," I said.

"He really was, and those who rode with him were guaranteed the opportunity to be part of heroic exploits. Father and his friends could trade stories for hours about their scouting missions and their hit-and-run attacks up and down the Valley. Their memories, of course, were highly selective. They didn't choose to remember the nights sleeping on the cold ground and the short rations. And they never mentioned the struggles their families were enduring while they were riding around confounding Yankees and gaining glory.

"At the end, they would always lament the premature deaths of their two heroes. Then they would go on to demonize the Yankee invaders, especially Sheridan. They hated him with particular venom for carrying out the Union's barbaric scorched-earth policy with such relentless efficiency. That policy starved out widows and orphans from one end of the Valley to the other. Then there was the total war being fought in places like Petersburg. To them, that was the ultimate horror. All the chivalry of battle was gone. After that, they would roll out the same list of post-war grievances: the injustice of Reconstruction and their hatred of Grant for enforcing it, the deviousness of carpetbaggers, and the Yankee attempts to destroy the proud heritage of the South."

"How did you feel as you listened?"

"Well, I knew that my father was essentially a good man. Hard-working. A faithful husband and a good father. And he was probably justified in carrying his grudge against men he saw as heartless invaders." He paused. "But even as an eleven-year-old, I was aware that there might be something wrong with the way he viewed the war. Later on, I began to see it as his moral blind spot. He could never quite see the underlying evil of the system he had fought so bravely to preserve. Only later still did I realize how much he must have dreaded the economic catastrophe that inevitably would follow the abolition of a system of labor that had existed unchanged for two hundred and fifty years. It made me a little more sympathetic. I'm not a strong believer in fate as an abstract notion. But a people's history bears with it a certain inevitability about their future."

"What about you?" I asked. "How did you manage to move forward?"

"Well, for one thing, I had to get away from home. Fortunately, Father had enough money to send me off to the University in Charlottesville. I think he always realized that I was too bookish to become a gentleman farmer. It always amazes me to think of how different we were. But I grew up in the generation after the war and that made a big difference. I sometimes wonder what I would have done if I had been forced to don a gray uniform and go off to battle. Fortunately, I ended up studying history instead of having to live it.

"After graduation, I went on to seminary, but the professors there were still teaching a theology that didn't seem very Christian to me. I did have one professor who had a profound impact on me, particularly as I worked my way through my thesis on religious life in the Confederate army. He had been a chaplain and thus became a valued primary resource as I explored the bizarre relationship between Christianity and Johnny Reb.

"It was a fascinating experience sifting through journals and talking to veterans and to chaplains who had served in the field and led the revivals that took place during the months in winter camp. The Baptists, the Methodists, the Presbyterians, the Catholics -all the denominations, in fact- were actively involved in saving the souls of the troops. Most of the boys had probably grown up with some connection to a church, but army camps are an easy place to lose your religion. The churches turned out pamphlets and tracts by the millions to pull back those in danger of falling into the abyss of sin. The emphasis was almost entirely on avoiding the terrible sins of gambling, card playing, drinking, and profanity. Those who didn't were doomed to hellfire.

"I was struck by the irony of the focus on those rather harmless sins for troops preparing to engage in wholesale slaughter. But Jehovah demanded righteous behavior in wartime as well as peace. I didn't see nearly enough mention of the loving Savior or words to console those who were maimed by horrible wounds or mourning the death of comrades.

"And many of the pamphlets laid out in some form the biblical justification for slavery. The South was America's equivalent of the Promised Land and fighting for it and for its institutions, including slavery, was doing God's will. Perhaps I shouldn't have been surprised. At first, I was morally outraged. Then, it occurred to me that the tracts were written by men who were probably incapable of thinking beyond the set of values that had been inculcated in them from birth. It made me pause before passing final judgment. But it also made me firmly commit to offer something different in whatever position I accepted after my schooling.

"As I brought back my findings, my professor and I discussed them in terms of his own experience, and he described the pressure on him to preach what to him seemed a perverted theology. Over the years, he had begun using his seminary lectures on Christian ethics to challenge the continuing prejudice and injustice of his time. Not long after my ordination, he either resigned his professorship or was forced to leave, no longer able to balance contradictory truths. It was an act of moral courage."

"Was he another one of your modest heroes?" I asked.

"Definitely so. And he had set an example that needed to be emulated.

"What was the effect on your own future?"

"Well, about that time, I had my moment of truth as well. I was at a crisis point probably not unlike yours. I had received a call from a small conservative church in a small conservative town and was wondering how I could possibly fit in. Serving that church would be a necessary first step toward positions at larger, wealthier, but probably equally conservative churches. I had to make a major career choice.

"I decided to apply instead for a position as chaplain and assistant professor of history and religion at a small college in the Fredericksburg area, and I ended up following that career path. They were quiet years. I married and my wife and I had a daughter. The pay in my new position wasn't very high and the expectations for advancement modest, but I was excited to be in the classroom each day to teach -and to learn -from new generations of young men moving out of the shadow of the war. Most of them were rigidly conservative. They had inherited a set of values and beliefs that they weren't necessarily willing to give up. But I kept trying, in my lectures and in my pastoral advising, to chip away at the old commandments they lived by.

"I was fortunate in one other way. My father died rather young but left my mother and me quite well off financially due to some wise investments he had made in the oil business of a young Yankee entrepreneur named Rockefeller. Father's bequest to me stipulated that the money should be used to further my education. In the end, I think he understood I was a different man in a new generation."

It was getting on into the later afternoon, and I knew I should be leaving soon. I didn't want to tire him out or feel as if I were intruding. But just as I got ready to thank him for his hospitality, he said, "All this storytelling has worked up an appetite. The housekeeper also prepared some delicious sweet rolls for us. Why don't I brew another pot of coffee as well?" It was an invitation I couldn't resist.

When he returned, we talked for another half-hour mainly about my long-range plans for the future. I realized as we did how vague they were, but how important it was to think about where I wanted my life to be in ten years, not just in ten months. Our conversation eventually turned again to both wars and their larger implications for that future.

"You've come home at a hopeful time in some ways," he said.

"We were fortunate to have been met by cheering crowds and general acclamation throughout the entire country," I said. "It's a blessing to feel certain that people are proud of what we accomplished. Despite the horrors, we all knew we had fought a just war. We knew who the good guys were, who the villains were, and what principles of civilized life we had fought to restore."

"In the history of human wars," he said, "that's a rare luxury indeed."

"And it was nice to have war heroes that everyone is proud of," I said. "Eisenhower, Bradley, MacArthur, Patton, all were exceptional commanders. They all had their individual flaws, but saints don't make the best generals to fight our necessary wars. In the end, they all made their contribution to the winning effort."

"It is an incredible irony," he said, "that even to this day the most celebrated hero of our great domestic tragedy came from the losing side."

"Robert E. Lee?" I asked.

"Yes, indeed," he said. "The hero worship he still inspires has intrigued me for years."

"What is it about the man that continues to call up so much devotion?"

He thought a moment, then said, "You've probably never seen the giant equestrian statue of him in Richmond, have you?"

I shook my head.

"I think it reveals the mystique of the man. He was the paragon of the Southern aristocrat -erect, commanding, self-contained. Every inch the noble warrior. He could be Marcus Aurelius reincarnated.

"And then there's his undeniable record of achievement in the war. It took strategic brilliance and willingness to take big risks to win all those battles. If we were to evaluate him just on his military record, he would certainly deserve the monument."

"We've had other military leaders who were probably as brilliant," I said. "What puts him in a special category?"

"I think it's the image of him as warrior champion of the Lost Cause that makes him so compelling." He sat back gathering his thoughts.

"Ultimately," he went on, "I like to think of him as America's great tragic hero. It's a useful idea and not just for those studying Shakespeare."

"Was he a victim of fate or flaws?" I asked, taking up his line of thought.

"A little of both, I think. In hindsight, we assume it was obvious that the peculiar institution was fated to collapse and take down the social order it was built on. But he probably wasn't able to accept that conclusion any more than most people of his time and place. In that regard, I guess, he was a victim of fate. But at the same time, we can never afford to ignore or apologize for a great man's flaws."

"His decision to cast his lot with his state rather than his nation was probably one of them," I suggested.

"Good insight," he said, "though we may not be able to fault him completely on that score. He lived in a time when loyalty to one's state often outweighed loyalty to country among Northerners as well as Southerners. And we can't forget that for countless generations his family had been bred to loyalty to the Old Dominion.

"Another flaw, of course," he went on, "was the same moral blind spot about race that afflicted my father. But even there, very few people, North or South, had been able to transcend the long history of prejudice."

"Do you see him in any way as an evil man?" I said.

"Not at all," he said. "I don't even see him as a bad one. He was honorable in his own way though he lacked moral vision."

He thought for a minute. "But for me he did have one major flaw. It was really the dark side of that fabled determination that would never allow him to quit. Even when final victory was completely beyond his grasp, he kept sending thousands more men and boys to their death. Great men must have indomitable will. Unfortunately, they're often unwilling -and probably unable- to admit defeat.

'I used to think his willingness to continue sacrificing so many young men was unforgivable. It was certainly another example of his lack of vision as well. Each of those young men had potential to accomplish something important to help rebuild their shattered land. Many of them were lost to families that would need to be provided for. They were all ordinary men -not great heroes- but they all had something potentially to offer to the future."

He paused, as though contemplating the lost achievements of a whole generation of men. "Yes," he concluded at last. "That I believe was Lee's real tragic flaw."

"You called his refusal to give up unforgivable," I said.

"I've changed my mind on that judgment over the years. He certainly wasn't a punitive or cruel man. I feel certain he took no pleasure in the death of so many soldiers on either side." He considered a moment. "In that regard, we have to remember how wide the amazing power of grace extends."

"In some ways," I said, "he was probably a victim of a fatal combination of character and situation."

"Another fine insight," he said. "And it doesn't apply just to great men. All of us are flawed in some ways, and we only need the right situation to persuade us to ignore basic moral principles and throw off restraints. Unfortunately, the more powerful the man, the greater the potential to create catastrophe in the wrong situation. In my darker moments, I sometimes wonder whether, on balance, the world wouldn't have been better off without the disruptive influence of great men. For every one who provides creative leadership that benefits many people, there seems to be another who willingly sows division and hatred that destroys as many."

After a pause, he said, "It is ironic that both sides were able to forgive Lee at a time when we were so absolutely unforgiving of each other and then to simply allow him to live out his life quietly."

"The final irony, though," I said, "is probably his transformation into heroic martyr for those who refuse to give up the Lost Cause."

"Quite right," he said. "Defeat left people in the South more strongly united than ever and in need a few great heroes to rally around in the ongoing struggle over race."

"It's hardly just a Southern problem," I said. I shared with him several instances I had witnessed of the enforced segregation of Negro soldiers during my time overseas and the difficulties they were already facing now that they were home. This got to the crux of some of my own uneasiness.

"We succeeded in liberating Europe," I said. "The next step, I hope, will be to complete liberating our own country."

"I don't want to be fatalistic," he said, "but the human heart and mind are terribly hard to change. We hold on to our prejudices very stubbornly and get more than a little satisfaction from following our instincts to defend them. You've seen how that sad truth applies in this country just as much as anywhere else."

He sat back and mused for a few moments. "I only hope," he said, "that we've survived the one and only civil war we'll ever have to fight."

After all we had just endured as a nation, the mere thought of another civil war was almost too terrible to consider. But, I realized, the potential was impossible to ignore.

"I don't want to seem gloomy," he went on, sensing my reaction, "but the fault lines are still there. We're still a society divided in many ways. It only takes the right situation and the wrong type of leadership to turn the tremors into an earthquake."

I had to admit he was right. "The one thing we have in our favor," I said, "is the sense of unity and national purpose that carried us through the war. If only we can act on that, who knows what progress might be possible on the domestic front."

"I'm certainly not without hope," he said. "At our best, we're a nation that values justice and the individual rights. I just pray that we can continue to act on our best instincts."

He thought for a moment.

"And I sincerely believe," he concluded, "that the best spiritual restorative is to be part of that social change. That's where someone like you can rediscover his purpose and his faith."

It was a little before four o'clock. We had finished our second pot of coffee and arrived at the point of conversational repletion. Robert graciously invited me to read or walk around the garden while he rested and then join him for dinner. I politely declined, but I assured him that I would never forget our day together and thanked him for his hospitality, his wonderful stories, and especially for his wisdom. He didn't press me to speculate on whether or not I would accept the position, but instead encouraged me to think carefully before I made up my mind. I was young, he reminded me, but my experience had matured me in ways that made my decision crucial to determining my future path.

Before I left, he asked if I had ever visited our greatest American battlefield. I shook my head. "Do so before you leave," he said. "For someone like you who obviously sees the value of studying the past as a guide to understanding the future, such an important historical site shouldn't be bypassed in the bustle of the present."

I decided to take his advice, drove into town, and checked into a small hotel. Then, bundled up against the bitter cold, I began by walking the length of Baltimore Street, beginning at the main square where Lincoln got off the train and spent the night polishing the address that would begin changing how men think. Very few people were moving about.

I stopped and bought a history of the battle and a battlefield guidebook complete with maps and old photos, then continued on toward the battlefield. I passed the Pierce House, where, according to the plaque by the door, the family had secretly sheltered wounded Yankees from Rebel patrols and snipers. At the far end, I passed the house where twenty-year-old Jennie Wade was shot dead while making bread for Yankee troops, amazingly, the only civilian casualty in a battle that engulfed the town as well as the countryside. Modest heroes, I thought to myself.

Though I had seen my share of war-scarred towns overseas, I had trouble imagining the devastation wreaked on this prosperous, staid Gettysburg street as troops rampaged back and forth.

Just beyond the edge of town, I got to the Soldiers' National Cemetery, where almost four score and seven years ago Lincoln delivered his brief, momentous address. I walked among the graves, some of them inscribed with the names of individual soldiers, others simply marked "19 Unknown" or "Delaware 15 Bodies." The final moments of sunset had colored the sky blood red. Silhouetted against the horizon was a statue of an officer in broad-brimmed hat and knee-high boots, holding a saber in his gloved hand. He was guarding the entrance to the cemetery but at the same time gazing off into the distance. I paused, wondering what vision of the future he might be contemplating.

Over dinner in a little tavern, I continued browsing the books. Right away, I was captivated by the extraordinary drama. One would be hard-pressed to think of any other battle in history -at least our history- so filled with heroic deeds, fateful coincidences, absurd decisions, and dreadful carnage. There were the little romantic tragedies of Wesley Culp and Jennie Wade. The wholesale sacrifice of the 1st Minnesota Infantry to stem a Confederate advance. The terrible, prideful blunders of General Sickles. Lee's fateful and fatal decision to launch Pickett's Charge against Longstreet's wise counsel. Was this the moment that Lee truly became a tragic hero? Every story was worth its own little morality play.

The history book portrayed it as a clash of grand armies in heroic struggle worthy of *The Iliad*, but the stark black and white Matthew Brady photos in my battlefield guidebook revealed a different story.

The following morning dawned gray and cold with snow in the forecast. After a hearty farmer's breakfast, I hiked back to the battlefield with my trusty guidebook in hand and followed it from point to point as best I could. I began at the north end where the fighting began on day one and ended with the Union troops in full flight to the safety of Cemetery Ridge. Next, I walked the length of unimposing, wooded Seminary Ridge along which much of the Confederate army eventually was ranged in preparation for the vicious fighting on day two and the fateful assault on day three. The battle lines were now occupied only by the marble and granite monuments erected to the soldiers from the various Southern states.

As I looked out, I found it impossible to imagine this gently rolling and fertile landscape crowded with a mile-long line of troops ready for the command to march or to hear the hellish roar of the artillery created by the one hundred and sixty Confederate cannons and answered by the one hundred Union cannons stationed on the higher ground of Cemetery Ridge. Even more I wondered what went through the minds of the rank-and-file soldiers as they waited for orders to attack. What did they have to gain by their sacrifice? What hopes for their future were likely to be dashed by injury or death?

"I walked across the open expanse, following my map beyond the Emmitsburg Road to what once had been Farmer Sherfy's Peach Orchard and Farmer Rose's Wheatfield, where four thousand men had been maimed or annihilated on the afternoon of the second day and the bountiful crops of peaches and wheat blasted to smithereens. There I found a memorial to yet another unlikely hero -Father Corby, chaplain of the Irish Brigade, who offered each of his troopers general absolution before they headed off to be killed. Now before me, however, was a rolling meadow unscarred by the battle. Nature had restored itself completely after eighty-three years. The bodies that hadn't been dug up for reburial had fertilized the soil.

I trudged on to Devil's Den, the aptly named tumble of boulders that provided cover for Confederate sharpshooters, who trained their rifles on Little Round Top, the hill that anchored the Union line. Each stop offered fresh stories of sacrifice, of senseless death, of ironic moments of fortune and misfortune.

Finally, I made my way to the little copse of trees referred to in the guidebook as the High Water Mark of the Confederacy. There, Rebel troops almost broke through Union lines during the final charge, only to be turned back and sent on a retreat that ultimately took them back across the Potomac. Standing there, I reflected on how the retreat had turned into a retrenchment and that the surrender at Appomattox had certainly not meant the final defeat of a whole social ethos. The charge had exacted an enormous toll to accomplish nothing.

It was getting late, and I was saturated with history and tragedy. I worked my way back to pay my final respects to the fallen in the cemetery, passing by Culp's Hill, where young Wesley Culp had returned with the wrong army to be killed. Though it was only a little after four o'clock, evening already seemed to have arrived. At the foot of the hill, I discovered I wasn't the only one on the battlefield.

A herd of fifteen or twenty deer were peacefully grazing just fifty yards beyond. They looked up as I approached, moved a little farther off, and continued grazing on the frozen turf. I stood watching them and enjoying the irony of the situation. It was deer season in central Pennsylvania and the battlefield, protected from hunters, was the safest place for them to be. They were oblivious to all that had gone on there in our violent human world not so many years ago. Now it was their refuge.

After an early dinner in town, I got in my car and headed home. On the way, along the quiet stretches of the Lincoln Highway, I made my decision not to take the pastoral position. I had been deeply moved by the serenity of the whole area. Being there would have offered me an opportunity to distance myself from my recent experience overseas and reset my inner compass. But the church and the town were too locked in their history for me at this point in my life. American society, I sensed, was getting ready for big changes. I wanted to play at least some small part in them and didn't feel Gettysburg was the place to do so.

Soon after I got home, I called the bishop to tell him I wouldn't accept the call. Then I wrote Robert a long letter explaining my decision and thanking him once again for the day we had spent together. A week later I received a letter in return. He told me that the church, as expected, had extended the position full-time to another man, older and decidedly more conservative. He said that he was already preparing to move back to Virginia to be near his daughter. Then he assured me he believed that I had made the right decision and concluded with these words: "Matthew, you need to be part of the future, not part of the past. Be one of the modest heroes. Help make the little, incremental changes."

Over the next few years, we stayed in touch with occasional letters. I had followed his example by pursuing a career in the academic world. Colleges were filling up with veterans seeking direction in their lives. A new generation of young men and women was in the earliest stages of reassessing our own history and the ways we had -and had not- lived up to the foundational promises of liberty and opportunity for all. It was an exciting time to be among the young, and Robert applauded my decision. Not long after I sent off one of my letters, another arrived, not from him but from his daughter, letting me know that he had quietly passed away.

One of the modest heroes of my life was gone. I will miss his wise counsel. I can only hope, in my own way, to help some young people to form a clearer vision of the future as he had helped me.

TALENT

I

After the workout and a shower, Bruno Kowalski wrapped himself in a towel and stopped in front of a mirror to examine a bruise between two ribs that he had sustained during the evening's hard sparring. He had a large-boned body and beefy shoulders and chest. Though he was fairly agile, he felt he conveyed the impression of awkward, ursine power. Tonight, he was giving himself the regular check-up for signs of age. Growing older had begun to worry him. He was approaching forty, and he wondered how much longer he would be able to tolerate the vigorous, three-times-a-week karate workouts. When he thought about giving them up, a great void opened in front of him.

As usual, he walked home. The dojo was on the fringe of downtown, not too far from his neighborhood. He didn't own a car and only took the bus when it was bitter cold or raining. The summer night was balmy, and the street was busy with people jogging, walking their dogs, and talking on their cellphones. He took his favorite route along Poplar Street with its funky boutiques and art studios. Most of the shops were getting ready to close up. It was in one of the little bookstores that he bought two of his prized possessions: a history of the samurai illustrated with woodblock prints and a book about Japanese gardens with color photos. Farther down the block was the little art theater where he had seen his first Japanese films soon after he became a serious student of the martial arts. He could still imagine Yojimbo pinning flies to the wall with a flick of his knife or the magnificent grove of trees where the seven samurai planned out the village's defense against the robber band.

He had first gotten interested in the martial arts during high school, watching Bruce Lee execute superhumanly powerful punches and gravity-defying kicks. Regular team sports had never appealed to him. But the martial arts intrigued him right away, and after graduation he decided to seek out a place to learn. He had been lucky in his first choice: Master Kim's Okinawan karate dojo. Master Kim was a martial artist of a different sort. He wasn't impressed by flashy, theatrical kicks and the special effects nonsense of movie brawlers. For him, the martial arts were truly art forms that focused more on self-discipline, conditioning, and proper technique than on combat.

Bruno lived not far from the dojo on the second floor of a rowhouse on a quiet street. His apartment was small, clean, and spartanly furnished. When he got home, he made his usual healthful snack and settled in to watch the news.

Tonight, the lead local story featured nearby St. Mary's Hospital, which was sponsoring a street fair to raise money for a new wing. Mrs. Foglietta, the wife of the neighborhood's city councilman, talked about "the hospital's vital service to the community." Just after the weather, the phone rang.

"Bruno, I'm glad you're home." It was his older sister, Louise. "I'm over at the ER. Sharon started running a temperature earlier today, and it went up to a hundred and four tonight. I got worried. You know, she's too old to be running a temperature that high. They told me to bring her in right away." Bruno wanted more details, but all she could add was that the girl had a terrible headache and ached all over. "The doctors don't know anything yet," she continued. "Or at least they aren't saying."

Bruno could tell she was getting weepy. "I'm all at loose ends," she said. "I called because I can't get in touch with Vito. I keep ringing the store, but nobody answers the phone. Would you go over and get him? She needs her father. You could come over too."

In fifteen minutes, he arrived at the huge home improvement store by the river. The manager steered him to the warehouse and loading area where his brother-in-law was checking inventory. The air conditioning wasn't working right, and he was in a full sweat.

"Hey, Bruno, what can I do for you?" he asked, wiping his hand and offering it to shake.

"It's not for me I came," Bruno said, hating to have to deliver the message. "Sharon's in the hospital with a high fever."

Vito's eyes darkened. "How could this happen now?" he said. "Last week it was the car. Now it's this." He threw the rag into the corner, and Bruno waited while he sorted out the situation in his mind. Finally, he looked up, embarrassed. "Don't mind me, Bruno," he said. "It's the heat, I guess. Tell me, what do the doctors say?"

"Nothing definite. Right now, they're doing tests."

"And Louise? How's she holding up?"

"So, so," I guess," said Bruno. "Polacks have always known how to suffer in silence."

Vito washed up and changed his shirt, then drove them over to the hospital. As they were on their way, he suddenly asked, "What's it like, Bruno, to be your own man? With no car payments, no house payments, no big responsibilities. Honest to God, I can't remember what that was like?"

When they got to the hospital, the girl's condition was unchanged. She had been given a sedative and was asleep. Vito suddenly became the family man again. After fifteen minutes of conversation in hushed hospital tones, Bruno realized his brother-in-law and sister had the situation in hand. He began to feel useless, even like an intruder in their personal problems. This was their crisis to be dealt with in the intimate unity of their own family. It was time for him to go home.

He tried to meditate before bed, but his mind was echoing with little voices that were carrying on a long conversation leading nowhere. As a result, he didn't sleep well and woke up in the morning stiff and sore. Walking to the subway, he could feel a twinge between the ribs where he had been bruised. As he sat on the rocking subway seat watching the darkness slide by, he wondered how much longer he could continue his training. He sometimes wished he had picked a softer style, but when he first discovered the martial arts karate was the only style he had heard about. Karate is a young man's sport, he thought, but he figured he would still probably choose it if he had to choose again. The subway got oppressive and stale-smelling as it filled with strap hangers, but he gradually ceased to notice. He had found the right frequency. When the train finally arrived at his stop, he was blissfully contemplating a garden with a pond in the center, a stone pagoda, an arching bridge, and a fringe of evergreen shrubs and red maples.

The morning passed smoothly. Up on his bulldozer, he pushed and leveled and smoothed a large area of a building site in tandem with his big yellow shovel. They worked together like a pair of dancers out of *Fantasia*. Before lunch, he went around the corner to the only pay phone that still seemed to exist and called the hospital. Sharon was doing much better, Louise assured him. The doctors still wanted to monitor her for another night, but she would almost certainly be discharged the next day. The nurses and doctors of St. Mary's had given her the best of care.

The news made him feel good, and he decided to join the other guys for lunch among the cinderblocks. As usual, they were talking sports. It was summer so baseball was usually the topic. Lately, a number of the conversations had been about money, especially the enormous salary packages and bonuses being offered to the stars. Today, it was a big-bucks acquisition, just before the trading deadline, of a closer who would be needed for the second half of the season. Bruno had heard the conversation before. Last week it had been a multi-year contract for the franchise quarterback and before that for a new shooting guard and before that for a designated hitter. "How can anybody be worth that much dough?" said Nick Oliver, one of the masons. "Especially a closer, who works, what, an inning every game or two?" The argument went back and forth. "Look what happened to our pennant hopes last September when we didn't have one," said one. "What about that worthless DH they traded for two years ago who rarely got a hit and never got his uniform dirty or even broke a sweat?" said another. "Too much money is making sports stink," concluded Oliver.

Bruno didn't follow pro sports, so they never expected him to get involved in the conversation. He was fine just listening. Nonetheless, he tuned in more closely when he heard Eddie Falcone mention the karate exhibition he had seen the previous weekend on television.

"Now there's a sport," he said. "Those guys were punching and kicking the crap out of each other in live matches. It was realistic combat, not like the stuff Jackie Chan does." He described a couple of the matches, adding a few imaginative touches here and there. "But the best part," he continued, "was when they started breaking boards and cinderblocks. You could watch them get this deep look on their faces. Then, all of a sudden, they'd give a little sound like an alley cat getting ready for a scrap, then shout, and smash the thing in two. After that, they'd give a neat little bow and a smile."

"Hey, Bruno," said Nick Oliver. "Do you still do any of that stuff?"

"A little bit," he said, not knowing how much they knew -or cared to know- about his sport.

"Can you really break boards and cinderblocks?"

"It would take me a little while to get my hands in shape and practice my technique, but I can do it," he said, half-expecting them to offer him a cinderblock.

But the lunch break was over, and they began gathering up their wrappers and soda cans into their lunch bags. As he climbed back up on his big machine, he tried to imagine himself giving a demonstration of well-executed punches and kicks and maybe even breaking some boards and blocks at the end. He usually didn't like this last activity because it seemed too theatrical. But if people wanted to see what karate is about, he certainly had the ability to show them.

II

That evening, he went to visit Sharon. He was worried when he first saw her. She was pale and seemed to have lost weight. Her long brown hair lacked its usual luster, and she had circles under her eyes. But the doctors said they felt she would be well enough to go home the next day. Louise said they first were concerned that she might have meningitis, but decided it was only a bad virus.

While he was there, mother and daughter argued most of the time, first about when she would be allowed to hang out with friends again, then when she would be allowed to return to the neighborhood pool. Louise had spent most of the day at the hospital, and they were getting on each other's nerves. Finally, they let their arguments lapse into embarrassed silence. As he got ready to leave, Sharon said,

"I almost forgot, Uncle Bruno. I had the weirdest dream last night. You were here in this room and I asked to borrow some of your strength. You agreed and handed me a box wrapped in brown paper. But just as I was about to open it, I woke up." She reached over and gave his arm a playful punch, then added, "I wish I knew what was in that box."

Louise called to him as he got to the door. "Don't forget about the cook-out at our house this Saturday afternoon, Bruno. You promised you would come. At least for a little while." Bruno wanted to escape without making a commitment, but she wouldn't let him. "Remember, you promised. You know you spend too much time by yourself." Sensing him weakening, she added, "You don't have to stay long. Besides, Sharon will need someone to talk to. She doesn't seem to have much to say to anyone else in the family right now."

He looked at Louise, then at Sharon, who held up her clasped hands and gave him a look of faux pleading. "All right," he said. "I'll stop in about two or so after my workout."

On the way out, he felt relieved to escape the drab paint and antiseptic smells. The old hospital building definitely needed a thorough facelift as well as a sleek new addition.

He worked out hard for the rest of the week, focusing mostly on stretching, strengthening his hands and forearms, and working on the heavy bag, but he didn't do any sparring. On Saturday morning, he had an especially good workout during which every pore in his body opened its floodgates. After a shower, he felt totally relaxed. His mind was empty of all annoyances and concerns. He was a pure receiver of the world. When he got home, he sat motionless on his front stoop, watching the children playing kickball, housewives walking home with bags of groceries, and neighbors waxing their cars. Time flowed by.

Then, he looked at his watch and remembered his promise to be at the cook-out. Ordinarily, he might have opted to stay right where he was enjoying the oneness with the world. But maybe Louise was right. Maybe he did spend too much time by himself. And if he didn't go, he would disappoint Sharon. She wanted him there. She needed somebody to talk to. Besides, he had a gift to bring her.

When he arrived, Louise was in the kitchen filling bowls with potato salad and chips and laying out cold cuts on a plate. She looked genuinely pleased to see him. Sharon, still looking pale, was curled up in a chair reading a paperback novel, but she gave a big smile of relief when she saw him.

"I brought you a present," he said, handing her a box wrapped in brown paper. She smiled with pleasure as she opened it. Inside was a white braided cotton belt. She gave him a curious look. "It's the first belt I earned after I started training," he said. "The white stands for purity and commitment to keep on training."

She gave him a look of quiet satisfaction, thought a moment, and wrapped it around her waist. "Thanks," she said. "I'm feeling stronger already."

"Why aren't you outside with the rest of the party?" he asked.

"Oh, everybody's drunk out there already, just like usual," she said. She had lately entered a stage of holding up adults for strict judgment.

"They are not drunk," Louise said, giving her an annoyed look but deciding to avoid a fight. "Bruno, could you," she paused, "and the princess help carry all these plates outside in a few minutes? No hurry though." She knew they liked to talk by themselves occasionally.

Sharon told him she was eager to get back to swim practices because her team had a big meet coming up with its big rival. As usual, he promised he would come to watch. She had been invited to a party the following week, and a boy she really liked was sure to be there. But her parents weren't completely onboard with letting her go. "Don't you think your sister still treats me like a kid?" she asked, but moved on fairly quickly to another topic without holding him hostage to an answer.

Then, she asked him how his workouts were going. Before he could tell her much, Louise called from the backyard. They -or at least the food- were needed. As they went outside, Sharon said, "You know, I'd really like to see one of your workouts sometime."

Bowls and plates in hand, they opened the screen door into the back of Leo Bertolli, Vito's recently divorced cousin. He was wearing a flowered shirt stained with great circles of sweat and Bermudas that exposed his white, hairless legs.

"Who the hell is that?" he growled, without looking around. "It's gonna cost them." Then he added, "Hey, Bruno, good to see you." He tried to slap Sharon on the behind as she passed.

"Pig," she said under her breath, fending off his hand.

He laughed and shouted, "Louise, this girl of yours just doesn't know how to respect her elders."

They put the bowls on the table next to the cooler of beer. With nobody her age to talk to, Sharon slumped into a folding chair at the fringe of the gathering of women. Bruno pulled up a chair next to Al Kubek, his old neighbor, and the other men.

Vince Costello was talking about the general contract for the new wing of St. Mary's, which had just been awarded. "Did you hear who got it?" he said. "Parisi and Company from over in Jersey. I started wondering why the job didn't go to somebody local and found out from a pretty reliable source that it didn't even go to the lowest bid. Rumor has it that one of the silent partners in the Parisi outfit is none other than the brother of our beloved Angela Foglietta."

Vito poured off his beer, then studied the empty glass for a moment. "I saw her the other night making the big push for funds. I wonder how much this little street fair will raise."

"Not much, I'm sure," said Costello. "It's just for publicity. The contract is big bucks, though. I bet your brother would like a little piece of the action on that job, Al," he added, turning to Kubek, whose brother owned a plumbing business.

"Those jobs aren't for little guys, Costello. The little guys get the little jobs. Fortunately, the world still seems to need some of us."

Kubek took out a cigar, chewed off the tip, and lighted it, surrounding himself in a quiet halo of smoke. He was a small man with a bald dome, a fringe of gray hair, and a scar that curled like a fine gauge wire above his lip. He and Bruno had become good friends years ago when Bruno was renting an apartment across the street from Kubek's barbershop. They had passed many an evening talking in the living room above the shop while Kubek's wife, a quiet woman who always smelled a little like pine disinfectant, brought Kubek beer and him endless glasses of iced tea.

The conversation moved on predictably to sports, this time to boxing. “How's your boy doing, Vince?” Kubek asked. “Is he still boxing?”

“He's doing pretty good. He won his last fight and got a preliminary bout at the Arena next month. His sergeant down at the precinct sets up his schedule to give him time to train.” He paused to drain his beer. “Vito invited him to join us this afternoon. Bruno, I thought you might like to meet him. He's interested in the martial arts too. Maybe you could tell him a little about the karate.”

A little later, the son arrived, making his entrance in a tight tee-shirt that showed off his big, sleek arms. He had gray, impenetrable eyes and black, wavy hair; everything about him exuded confidence. Leo shadow boxed in front of him at the head of his own imagined procession. “Hey, Vince, your boy's here,” he said. “Look at the arms on this guy.” Naturally, the son became the center of attention. Costello introduced him to Bruno. They talked a little about the martial arts, but Bruno didn't have the kind of ready information he seemed interested in hearing. Soon, the kid was talking about his own fighting career instead.

Bruno relaxed again knowing that he wouldn't be called on to take further part in the conversation. He went back through the morning's workout in his mind. After the class warmed up together, he had focused on his own technique by himself. The Master had come over to watch him and offer words of advice and encouragement. He was a quiet man, disciplined to speak only when he had something to say. He had praised Bruno's form and his concentration, saying he was truly becoming the master of his own body and his own mind. It was not idle praise. The Master never offered idle praise.

Bruno was jarred back to the moment by Leo's voice. “This party is getting boring,” he was saying. “We need something to liven it up.” Then, almost shouting now to get everyone's attention, he added, “I know what we can do.” He paused till he sensed he had his audience. “This is a great idea,” he went on. “A great idea.” He looked over to make sure all the women were listening too. “We'll have a challenge match. The boxer meets the karate expert in a battle to the death." He belched at the end, looking pleased with his suggestion. The kid smiled condescendingly while Bruno looked embarrassed.

"Come on, Bruno," Leo said, moderating his tone. "Just a little demonstration for the fun of it." He draped his sweaty arm around Bruno's shoulder.

"Stop it, Leo," Kubek said. "We can put up with you most of the time when you act like a horse's ass. But leave Bruno alone."

"But all I want is a little action to liven things up," repeated Leo, feigning wounded feelings.

Bruno stood up so suddenly that he tipped his chair over. "Look," he said. "If it's a demonstration you want, it's a demonstration you'll get. But not now. I've decided to perform for charity at the hospital fund raiser next Saturday. If you want to see the performing bear, you'll have to pay for it."

He stood the chair back up, walked over and tousled Sharon's hair, and left without saying another word.

III

It wasn't till he got home that he fully processed the implications of what he had said. His moment of pique over, he realized that he hadn't been really angry at all. Then why, he wondered, had he said what he did? Was he trying to impress Leo? Hardly. If anything, it was the boxer he might have been trying to impress. Or was it because he really did want to perform publicly, to do something he took pride in doing in front an audience for once? He briefly considered whether he dared back out of the commitment. But he felt instinctively that his words had come out not by accident but as a result of some deeper desire, some inner necessity to share himself -or at least one of his talents- with others.

The next morning Sharon came with some leftover cold cuts and potato salad and some choice words about Leo. "If I had been you," she said, "I would have slugged him in his big red nose. He's a disgusting slob even when he isn't drunk."

They talked a little longer before she asked, with what seemed like exaggerated nonchalance, "Are you really going through with that demonstration?" He asked whether she thought he should. "Yes," she said without hesitation. "I think you should show all those doubters just what you can do."

He didn't say anything or change his expression. "You can do this," she went on. "You know you want to." She paused. "But you're going to need my help." He gave her a puzzled look. "You need someone to advertise for you. I know you won't do it yourself, but if we want people to come out to watch, we've got to get out the word."

Bruno realized that she hadn't come over just to drop off leftovers. She laid out her strategy, which involved more than just posters and word of mouth. She would use the power of social media. As they talked, he also realized that organizing the exhibition would involve a lot more than advertising. It was the kind of thing he had never done before. But he suddenly felt that the effort would be worthwhile. For St. Mary's, for Sharon, and also for himself.

After she left, he laid out a basic plan of organization. First, he thought about what he would do for the exhibition. He wanted it to be educational, not showy. He would discuss some of the basic principles of the martial arts with spectators, then take them through the basic poses and stances, and highlight the exhibition with some punches and kicks. It would give people the essence of the martial arts. He recalled words he had just read in his book of Japanese gardens: "Exhibit the unadorned and embrace the uncarved block. Have little thought of self."

However, deciding on the routine, he realized, was probably the easiest of his challenges. First, he had to find a place for the exhibition.

During his lunch break the next day, he called the hospital to inquire. He was referred to Mr. O'Connor, the director of development. While he waited for the connection to be made, he tried to decide how to phrase what he knew to be an unconventional proposal. He started by saying that he was just a regular guy who loved his neighborhood and had a project to help the hospital. The man listened in official silence while Bruno explained his plan in somewhat confusing sentences. The man deftly felt the surface of the plan with a brief summary, probed it with a few concise questions, and then replied that, although the exhibition certainly had merit as well as an air of novelty, the hospital unfortunately did not have the space or facilities to accommodate it. If, however, Mr. (and Bruno had to supply 'Kowalski') could find a suitable location, the hospital would certainly be willing to have advertising posters displayed and would receive all contributions with heartfelt thanks.

Obstacle number one still stood in the way.

That night he went to the dojo to train, but also to discuss the details of his plan for the exhibition with Master Kim. The Master considered the plan thoughtfully. "I respect your commitment to teaching about karate," he said. "But don't forget. Most people want excitement. They think karate is crazy kicks and breaking boards and things. If you hope to get people to come watch and give money," he concluded, "you need to give them what they want." He saw Bruno's surprise. "Do you know why I have a night each week when students can break boards and bricks?" he said. Bruno had no answer. "It's because I need to do that to attract more students." He paused. "Not everyone is satisfied to be a purist like you."

They talked about the details of Bruno's plan. "I am pleased that you want to be a teacher and not just a showman," the Master said. "I think your audience will enjoy hearing some of your explaining. Then you can demonstrate your punches and kicks. But you should always end by breaking some things. People like to see martial artists break things." Bruno saw the wisdom in his advice. But where would he get materials to break?

The Master considered. "Your exhibition is a good thing," he said. "It's good for you and good for the community." He thought for a moment. "If I donate the materials to you, would you advertise a little for the dojo as well? That way the exhibition would be good for me too. Then everybody wins." The Master was also proving a master of practical wisdom.

The location still was a concern, but Bruno was already considering an alternative solution. That evening he stopped to see Al Kubek, whose corner rowhouse was just a block away from the hospital. Attached to the house was his garage, set back ten feet or so from the street. The space in front was just large enough for the exhibition. Kubek was glad to see him. They sat and talked for a while like old times. Then, Kubek asked Bruno if he still intended to go through with the exhibition and didn't seem surprised at the answer. He tried briefly to talk Bruno out of the plan.

"People won't understand you," he said, "and, as a result, they might laugh at you. I know your intentions are serious, but people may turn it into a circus." He sat back and lighted up a cigar.

Bruno knew he might be right, but he simply said, "Al, I'm committed to it now." He paused. "I came to you as a friend because I need your help. The hospital won't give me a place to perform." He hesitated to ask the next favor. "I'd like to use the space in front of your garage for the exhibition."

He watched as smoke rings coiled up from Kubek's cigar, shrouding eyes which rarely showed surprise or uncertainty. "Also, I would like to use your brother's truck one evening this week to bring over the materials I will use," he added.

"And this is the service you want to use your talent for?" Kubek asked. He occasionally had a curiously biblical way of expressing himself.

Bruno nodded.

"This whole hospital project stinks of graft, you know. Maybe worse than even Costello is aware."

"I guess so," said Bruno.

"So, what in the world is perfect?" Kubek concluded. "The garage is yours. And the truck also."

Bruno saw a large obstacle get up and move out of his path. He felt a nervous twinge at the realization of how possible -almost inevitable- the exhibition had become. As they talked a while longer about the details, Kubek's wife brought in sandwiches for them and retired again with just a deferential word of greeting. Finally, Bruno felt it was time to go. As he got to the door, Kubek said,

"Bruno, I wasn't sure at first that this exhibition was sensible or wise. But the more I think about it, the more it seems right for you. Let me know if there's anything else I can do."

IV

For the next days, Bruno was perfectly disciplined physically and mentally. At work, while he scooped, leveled, and moved back and forth across mounds of dirt, he played over in his mind the routine he would perform. At home, he ate training table meals of lean meat and fresh vegetables and hydrated himself with fruit juices and plenty of water. He gave up watching television, which filled his mind with interference.

At the dojo, he performed the carefully choreographed ritual of the kata again and again, perfecting the stances, strikes, and counters. He worked out on the heavy bag and sifted and squeezed the sand in the big sand jar to toughen and strengthen his hands. After the other students left, Master Kim invited him to stay and practice breaking objects. It was a discipline that Bruno rarely practiced even on the nights when the Master incorporated the exercise into the regular routine. As he always did before breaking sessions, the Master took Bruno through the mental and the physical motion of the strike. The goal was to rid the mind and the muscles of all interference. To break solid objects, one must strike through them as though they weren't even there. The mind shouldn't see the object, but the free space beyond it, the nothingness at the end of the completed motion of the arm and hand. That way the mind does not give conflicting orders, causing the muscles to work against each other and bringing pain and even injury.

Near the end of their first session, Bruno said, "I've already broken too many boards. I know you have to buy more for the rest of your students."

"If you want to be ready," the Master said without looking at him, "you have to practice." When Bruno started to object, the Master said, "Don't worry. This is my donation to the hospital. Remember, I am part of this community too." Thus, he continued to practice breaking boards each night under the Master's watchful eye and his constant reminders: "Take time. Don't rush. Stay focused."

On Thursday night, Sharon insisted on coming to his workout for moral support. He expected that she would be bored in ten minutes, but to his surprise she stayed a whole hour, watching the others, but mostly watching him as he went through the repetitions of his workout. Finally, when her interest seemed to have faded, he came over to talk. He told her what he expected to do. He would talk, demonstrate his punches and kicks, then break the solid world in half. She smiled her approval. He offered to call a cab to take her home, but she said her dad was already on the way to pick her up. As he walked her out to the street, it occurred to him that she had been invited to a party that evening.

"It's still going on," she said. "Mom gave me permission to go. She's been terrific lately."

"What about the boy you were supposed to meet?" he asked.

"He'll still be there, I suppose," she said. As Vito pulled up to the curb, she looked at Bruno with serious eyes. "You'll do great on Saturday," she said. "I know you will."

Friday evening after he and Kubek moved the truckload of boards and bricks from the dojo to the garage, he rested instead of working out. On Saturday morning, he felt invigorated. As he walked over to Kubek's, he saw the first evidence of Sharon's advertising. Tacked to utility poles were big, professional-looking signs that read:

Karate exhibition today – 11 to 5

Kubek's Barbershop – Corner of Collins and Thompson Streets

All donations to hospital fund

Before setting up, he walked over to see the attractions for the fair. There were a carousel and a tilt-a-whirl; games of chance and tables of pink, blue, and brown stuffed animals waiting to be claimed by the winners; charity bingo for the old folks; and more. He could smell the food already: popcorn, corn dogs, cotton candy, kielbasa, Italian water ice. It was all quaint and old-fashioned, but, he thought, right for the neighborhood. Even though it was after ten, there was almost nobody on the street yet. He went back to Kubek's and ate a couple energy bars and drank some orange juice, then slipped inside the garage to put on his loose pants and belted robe. He felt excited and a little nervous. Outside, he set up a scaffold to support the boards and bricks he would break. While he worked, an old man arrived for a haircut but, seeing the shop closed, walked off in a huff without saying a word. With all the preparations done, Bruno simply had to wait for the start of the event he had never imagined would happen.

A few minutes later, a few boys wandered over. He began by telling them that he was raising money for the hospital. Then, he told them about the wonders of the martial arts, the ancient masters, and the tradition of the samurai, but as he talked on, they stared blankly at him. Not to lose their attention, he demonstrated a series of stances, punches, and kicks. Then, he took a board, set it up, concentrated for a moment till he could feel the energy flow, and broke it neatly in half. The boys looked at him and at each other without any indication that they were particularly impressed, but they didn't leave. Instead of breaking more boards right away, he showed them a few more punches, blocks, kicks, and counters. They watched him impassively for a few minutes. Then one of them asked,

"Hey, mister, are you going to bust a few more boards?"

With a sigh, Bruno set up a board and then a brick, breaking one with his foot and the other with his hand. Finally, they seemed impressed. When Bruno reminded them it was for charity, they looked at each other and began to move on, but one boy with a buzz haircut fetched a quarter from his pocket and dropped it into the collection jar. At least, Bruno thought, it was a start.

At noon, Sharon arrived, looking fresh and well rested in a summer dress. She brought a girlfriend with her and introduced Bruno. He tried to open up a little conversation, but the girl didn't seem interested in talking. To break the awkward silence, Sharon said, "How about a demonstration, Uncle Bruno?"

He gave his talk and demonstrated the basic moves again; then he took a few boards and broke them in a variety of ways. Sharon was enthusiastic, but her friend betrayed no reaction. After he was finished, Sharon took out a folded ten-dollar bill and dropped it into the jar. "Go ahead, Lisa," she said, and the girl dropped in a dollar. After that, the girl left, but Sharon stayed on. They made a little small talk. She told him that the party had been great and that she hadn't missed anything by coming late. The boy she liked had been late too, and they had danced together at least three times. He smiled to himself as she talked and tried to think of the words to express his gratitude.

By then, the fair had begun to get crowded, and noise from the carousel mingled with scratchy voices over the loudspeaker, pings from a shooting game, and eager shouts from children. More people began to wander past on their way to the games, and some stopped out of curiosity. Bruno modified his speech, trying to make it as brief, entertaining, and enthusiastic as possible. Most of the spectators, however, were mainly interested in seeing him smash the object-world again and again. By noon, he had broken another ten boards and a couple of bricks. Sharon had kept track of the attendance and the proceeds and counted up the totals before she left to meet friends. So far, she announced proudly, twenty-five people had paid a total of $32.50 to see him perform.

Bruno kept himself going with another energy bar and some orange juice, but the combination of the talking, the demonstration of the stances and punches, and the concentration needed to break the boards was taking a toll on his energy. About twelve-thirty,

Kubek brought down sandwiches for him. He looked at Bruno and said, "You'll need these. You're beginning to look a little tired."

The activity along the street soon picked up even more as people made their way to the fair for lunch. More spectators stopped to see him perform. One guy, about twenty or so, arrived with his girlfriend in tow and began to ask Bruno about how he got his hand in shape and what live competitions were like. While the girl stood off to the side checking her cellphone, Bruno happily showed him a variety of kicks, punches, and blocks that were more elaborate than any he had demonstrated so far. Then he recommended his dojo as the best place to learn the sport. Perhaps he could win a new recruit for the Master. He broke two boards and then a brick for his finale. When the young guy left, he dropped five dollars into the jar.

Around three, the foot traffic slacked off as the heat became stifling. He sat on a folding chair and almost nodded off. Just as he began to wonder whether it would be worthwhile to stay any longer, Sharon reappeared, like the pied piper, with a group of her friends and their younger siblings. Bruno felt revitalized. He talked for a while before beginning the demonstration. They were not shy, particularly the young ones. One of the older ones asked a couple serious questions about the tradition. One wanted to know if he could break steel. Another wanted to touch his hand to see if it felt any different and asked if he thought he could beat Jackie Chan. The littlest one asked why he wore such a funny costume.

Most of all, though, they wanted him to break boards and bricks. He figured that he broke six or seven objects during the next twenty minutes. Most of them stayed for the entire time and dropped some money into the jar before leaving. At the end, Sharon stayed once again for moral support. Things seemed to be going so well that he felt almost triumphant, and he committed himself to stay till he had broken every board and brick.

Then, just before three-thirty, the thing that Bruno dreaded most happened. He was preparing to finish a demonstration before a small group by breaking a final brick. He felt tired and drank some orange juice for a shot of energy, but he didn't regather his focus afterwards. He brought his hand down on the brick but didn't strike all the way through it. He felt a sharp pain that shot along his forearm and past his elbow, then raced to register its message in his brain. He suspected immediately that he had broken a bone. As his audience dropped their small contributions into his jar, he slumped onto the folding chair still feeling the reverberations. Sharon, too, sensed what had happened.

Within a few minutes, she was back with a dish towel full of ice from Kubek's refrigerator. As he sat there, trying to freeze out the pain and feeling for any irregularity along the bone, he calculated whether it would be necessary to end the day prematurely. He flexed the hand as much as he could but felt a twinge of pain whenever he did. Meanwhile, Sharon sent away new spectators, saying he was resting for a while. After about ten minutes of silence, she said,

"Uncle Bruno, it wouldn't be good for you to go on with this any longer, would it?" He looked at her but wasn't able to decide on an answer. "Listen," she continued, "I'm going out to find my parents. They're probably over at the fair by now. Promise me you won't do anything till I come back."

He nodded in agreement and sat mutely on the chair, suddenly feeling completely exhausted. With his hand still wrapped in the ice and his head drooping, he fell into a waking slumber. When they finally returned, he wasn't sure how long he had been alone or what he had been thinking about. If any more spectators had come by to see him perform, they had left without asking.

As soon as Louise looked at the swollen, discolored hand, she pronounced it a serious injury. "I think we should go to the emergency room right now," she said. "After they x-ray it and do whatever else they have to do, we'll drive you home."

Bruno looked steadily at her through his glazed eyes. "I'm not going home or to the hospital," he said. "I promised myself I'd stay till," he paused and gestured to the pile of boards still remaining, "till I break all of these."

Louise tried to reason with him, to cajole him, and finally ended up lecturing him, but Bruno refused to listen. The decision to stay had been made by a power deep inside him and wouldn't be overruled. Finally, she said,

"Brother, I've always known you were a little different, and there's nothing wrong with that. But why are you trying to convince me that you're a fool?"

He had even more trouble dealing with Sharon, who had also set her mind against his decision. "I was proud of you today," she said. "But you've already done what you promised you were going to do. Look how much money you've collected?" She dumped the coins and bills onto the ground and counted them: $45.85 "That's more than enough," she said. "You've done your part. It wouldn't be worth it to mess up your hand for a few more dollars."

But he remained adamant. Finally, in annoyance, she said, "I swear, Uncle Bruno, sometimes you can be more stubborn than any adult I know." She noisily scooped the money back into the jar. Then, she and Louise, sensing defeat, gave up and left.

Bruno sat in a state of torpor for a while longer. The pain in his hand, however, had subsided to a dull ache, and he felt strangely revived. He took off his robe, stretched a little, then assessed the pile of boards. There were still fifteen to be broken. The object world confronted him accusingly. He had to break them all. He stacked the boards neatly next to the scaffolding and placed the top one in position. He concentrated for a moment then struck, breaking it neatly with his left hand. He had rarely used the off-hand and was grimly satisfied at how well he had coordinated the strike. Methodically, he reached for another and prepared to do the same.

He braced a third on the scaffold and broke it too with his left hand. For some reason, he decided he had to try another board with his injured right hand. He focused his mind, trying to think past the ache, but when he struck, the pain won out, shooting through his hand and arm even faster than when he first broke it. He had to call up all his self-control to keep from screaming. He felt the bone but could not tell if it had been further deformed. He kept telling himself not to think about the pain, but he found it difficult to think about anything else.

He put up another board, using his foot to strike through it with reckless ferocity and uttering a shout as some of the others at the dojo did. Then he took another and broke it with his left hand, reinforcing the strike with another shout. He sat back down and rested briefly, then went back to his task. Without his being aware, a number of people had begun to gather across the street to see what he was doing. They stood in silence as he concentrated and struck, then lifted another board into place, concentrated, and struck.

When he finished the first pile of eight, he walked back to the stack, trance-like, and began moving the final boards over to the scaffolding. He worked slowly, alternately using his left hand and his foot to strike. By then, the number of onlookers had grown. They seemed transfixed as his broke each object, then methodically and expressionlessly lifted the next into position. He made no attempt to communicate with the crowd or even acknowledge their existence. He was nowhere, giving the demonstration to no one. They, too, felt the distance, coming in silently to see the spectacle of this great bear of a man breaking things with his jackhammer fist or foot and then silently edging out again. The money jar stood near him, but no one came close enough to put anything into it.

Finally, as he broke the third-to-last board in the final stack, he felt a twinge of pain in his back. He had lost control of the basic mechanics of the striking motion. Though the pain was not nearly as intense as the pain in his hand, he knew he was finished and slumped into his chair. He looked up and for the first time seemed aware that people were watching him. They waited silently for another minute or two, fascinated by his sheer presence. As they began to shuffle off, he wondered what they must have thought of him. Would they, he wondered, be telling their neighbors about the big, trained bear they had seen breaking things with its paw?

Then, he noticed a man with a short beard and a hand-held

television camera coming toward him along with a young woman with a microphone. He heard her voice coming through as he held his head in his one good hand. She began to probe at the outside of his identity with questions. Who was he? Why was he putting on this demonstration? Was it connected with the hospital fund raiser? Was his hand severely injured? At first, he could think of no answers.

Suddenly, without warning, he began to cry. He cried because his hand hurt, but more because he had begun to fear what he might have done to it. He cried because he had made only $45.85 for all his hours of effort and because there were still several boards that would never be broken. But most of all, he cried because nothing people did ever seemed to come out as it was supposed to. When he was finally able to control himself, he gave answers -any answers- to questions he never remembered afterwards. Finally, the microphone and the camera seemed to have gotten enough and retreated. In the background, he heard a voice say, "This is Linda Folino, WSVI News."

After that, he dreamed, sitting hunched over in his chair. He didn't know how long the dream lasted, but the images came with amazing ease and clarity. He saw the garden again with the maple trees and the little shrine standing on the island in the middle of the pond; he could almost feel his hand dangling in the cool water. As he lay there, he thought he heard the voice of the Master say, 'Rest now. You did your best today.'

Then he felt someone nudging him. He came up out of his dream, trying to see who it was. Sharon was kneeling beside him with her arm around his shoulders, and Louise and Kubek stood behind her.

"Uncle Bruno, I came to say I'm sorry," she said. "I heard what happened. You were brave to stay."

He looked at her, mutely trying to find the right words of gratitude. "Don't be sorry," he mumbled finally. "Don't be sorry."

"The girl's right," Kubek said. "You did your best. You used your talent. You've got nothing to regret."

He nodded vaguely in agreement.

"We're going to take you to the hospital now to get your hand fixed," Louise said, sensing that he would no longer refuse. "Then we'll go home."

No part of him resisted. After all, the important ones had told him that he had done well.

TWO VIGILS

I

We were nearing the end of a remarkable year. It certainly hadn't been the best of times. Many were calling it the worst of times -at least in living memory. A pandemic threatened to shatter the health of the people, the health of the economy, or both. A looming election pitted those who feared the other side would tear apart the Constitution against those who feared the other side would turn us into a socialist welfare state. The Black Lives Matter Movement and the immigration crisis threatened to expose yet again the flaws in our image as the land of the free and the home of equal opportunity for all. The planet was warming at an alarming rate in more ways than one.

It was a troubled time indeed.

I sometimes wondered how we would survive.

My grandson, Randy, had just returned from college a week ago, one of the many students from campuses hard hit by COVID who would have to complete at least the first semester at home. It was a glorious early fall day, and we agreed to meet outside at our favorite coffee shop to catch up on life during his senior year.

I've always looked forward to these opportunities to find out what he has been doing. He has never been satisfied to be an academic grind or a fraternity party boy though he let me know on various occasions he hasn't exactly been a slouch at either studying or partying. He had devoted time to student government and political activism. During his sophomore year, he spent hours getting out the vote for the midterm elections and had been working hard on the campus campaign during the current presidential election. He was an organizer who thrived on being in the midst of action. It was his blessing and his curse.

We found a table in the early afternoon shade and settled in to talk. He had circles under his eyes, which he attributed mostly to outrage fatigue from too many hours on cable news and social media.

"Sorry I'm late," I said. "I tried to call, but I've been having problems with my phone." He was my tech guru and offered to fix it while I went inside to order our usual coffee and snacks. When I got back, he handed my phone back while he finished reading something particularly outrageous on his own.

"How much more can we stand?" he said, gritting his teeth but not commenting on the specifics of what he was reading. "How many lies and conspiracy theories, how much hypocrisy?" I nodded in sympathy. "And then with the pandemic, here I am stranded at home. I can't go to the gym. I don't feel safe hanging out with friends -present company excepted. I can't do any of the stuff that needs to be done. What else can I spend my time doing except studying and listening to the talking heads?"

"You can tune out," I suggested. "Watch a good movie. Go for a run. Listen to good music." I quietly noted his look of skepticism.

"I can't afford not to stay tuned in," he said, putting his phone in his pocket. "Nobody can. This is too dangerous a time not to be well-informed."

"There might be a difference between being well-informed and having information overload. Sometimes the latter gets in the way of thinking clearly."

"Well," he said, "I want to be well-informed enough to know when to take action." I made no comment, and he seemed to take my lack of a quick response as mild disagreement. "I know what you're probably thinking," he said. "What action can realistically make a difference in a society as divided as ours?"

"It isn't like you to be cynical," I said. "I know you're probably doing more than just listening to cable news and sampling the opinions on Facebook."

He admitted that he had already arranged to start volunteering in the local get-out-the-vote campaign. "This is the time when we need our people out on the front lines. We can't afford to let them grab all the airtime with their rallies. They're sucking all the oxygen out of our campaign." We sat quietly sipping our coffee, searching for a less upsetting topic. Then he looked at me with what seemed a mischievous expression.

"What about you?" he said. "Word is the young Paul Everett was politically active and stayed that way over the years. I bet you've attended more than one rally and marched in more than one demonstration during your time. I'd be eager to hear a few details." He had put me on the spot. At first, the request had seemed impromptu, but later it occurred to me that he may have been intending to ask for some time.

I did have some stories to tell. In retrospect, I was ambivalent about some of the details, but not unwilling to share. Like a good amateur historian, I had to begin by putting everything in context.

"I have to confess," I said, "that I wasn't engaged politically when I was young." He gave me a look of mild surprise but didn't say anything. "When I was in high school, of course, Vietnam was still in its very early years. The war was worlds away from football games, college applications, and school dances. Even Joan Baez was mainly singing folk songs then.

"Besides, I grew up in a family that didn't discuss politics. Whatever my parents thought about the war, they didn't talk about it, at least not to me.

"Typical of their generation, I guess," he said.

I agreed. "They were part of the Greatest Generation. After the country's heroic effort in World War II, they tended to trust that whatever the government did was in everyone's best interests. Still, I like to think that deep-down they opposed the war."

"What about college? You must have been debating the war while you were there. All your peers must have been wondering what was in their future after they graduated?"

"It seems strange now, but there was a kind of reluctance to talk, as though the war would quietly go away if we just didn't bring it up."

"It must have been hard to ignore all the graphic television coverage. I've seen some of the old film footage on *YouTube.* Jungle ambushes by the Viet Cong, guys mutilated by booby traps getting loaded onto helicopters, soldiers burning down Vietnamese villages. It was really hard to watch."

"Actually, I was spared most of that footage, at least during my early years in college. There still weren't many reporters embedded with troops in the jungle. Most of the information about the fighting came from carefully scripted press conferences and carefully selected film clips released by the military. At that point, the government was still able to manage the optics fairly well. Besides, there were very few televisions on campus. Nobody in the dorms had one. My frat house didn't have one. It was hard to be connected."

He shook his head in disbelief, trying to fathom a world without constant access to media of any kind. "What about newspapers? Or news magazines?" he said, probing. "You must have had some contact with the outside world through them."

"A lot of us chose to live in a cocoon," I admitted, "Particularly those who still had a couple of years of iron-clad college-deferment protection."

"So, there were no rallies, no demonstrations, no outcry against the war at your college."

"We were a fairly conservative school," I said. "The closest thing we had to a march was at the Homecoming parade. But there weren't many protests going on at most other schools either. At least not that I was aware of. The time wasn't ripe yet.

"The college administration, to its credit, did invite a variety of speakers to address the issue. One I remember had been in the State Department throughout the Eisenhower and Kennedy years. He was a fervent proponent of the domino theory. It all sounded so rational when he discussed it. It was our obligation to keep Vietnam from falling to the Commies and, in turn, taking down Cambodia and Laos and who knew which other countries. The world had to be kept safe for democracy.

"The other speaker I remember was a reporter for one of the major news organizations. He had just returned from weeks of covering the war in the rice paddies and the jungles, in the villages, and in Saigon itself. He was among the early group of reporters allowed full access with a camera crew. What he described made us all really begin to think about what we were doing there."

We sat back quietly for a few moments, each trying to focus his separate understanding. Clearly, he was having trouble fathoming a world in which so much was hidden from the public. He was used to having a swirl of misinformation, but not an almost complete lack of it. "What about your professors?" he asked at last. "You were taking classes in history and political science, weren't you? What discussions were you having there?"

"Here's another great oddity of the time. Even the professors seemed reluctant to bring up the topic for discussion. I don't know if they simply didn't feel well-enough informed or were unwilling or afraid to stir up controversy."

"So, there was a conspiracy of silence," he said. "An unspoken pact to perpetuate the illusion that the nation was not involved in a war that was literally tearing it apart."

"Almost," I said. "There was one student forum at the college that brought the raw emotions and the underlying conflicts to the surface. It was during my senior year. The school's tiny ROTC company challenged the tiny Students for Peace Committee to a debate. The college administration agreed to let the event take place in the fieldhouse. It ended up drawing a bigger crowd than most of our basketball games, and the discussion got more heated and competitive than most of them as well.

It was the only time during my undergrad years that I heard the pros and cons of our national argument so forcefully and nakedly debated. At one point, the two sides seemed ready to come to blows. Just because we weren't talking about the war in our everyday conversations didn't mean we weren't thinking about it."

"Where did you stand by then?"

"I'd like to say I had already taken a strong, principled moral stance against the war. But all that I can honestly say is that I knew I didn't want to have to fight in it."

"How about the guys you knew?"

"Well, I had a few acquaintances in ROTC who talked about being ready to go, though they probably couldn't have avoided it even they wanted. Some of them seemed to want the excitement and the chance to prove their manhood on the battlefield. They all seemed sincerely patriotic and could reel off all the arguments about the necessity of stopping the spread of Communism."

"And keeping the world safe for good old American capitalism," he added.

"I believe most of them were sincere," I said. "I really do."

"How about your frat buddies?" he asked. "How many of them were ready to go off to fight?"

"Let's just say we all were weighing our options. A couple of the guys signed up for the Reserves. Those units weren't likely to get deployed unless the Russians and the Chinese were ready to invade."

"How about you?" he pursued.

"I briefly considered the Reserves, but then just decided to turn over my future to fate or chance. Most of the brothers made the same decision."

We sat back for reflection.

"Were you ever worried about the threat of a worldwide Communist take-over?" he asked after a bit.

"No," I said. "Not really. All that talk seemed purely theoretical and likely to appeal only to certain kinds of people. Like everyone else, I felt surges of outrage at the Viet Cong. But I wasn't worried about the war in little Vietnam unleashing totalitarian Communism on the world."

"I can imagine what was on your mind instead," he said with a smile.

"No real mystery there," I conceded. "Like all my buds, I was mainly worried about whether my GPA was high enough to get into the grad school of my choice. And whether any of the girls I had the hots for had any interest in me. Not to mention who we were playing in the next intramural basketball game."

We laughed and mused over how little the world had changed. Life always was offering pleasant distractions even for a professed social progressive and committed political activist like him. I assumed he was ready to move on to new topics for discussion. But he returned to his pursuit.

"You still haven't told me anything about your years as a radical protester," he said with a wry smile.

"Well," I began, secretly pleased by his insistence, "my first real experience was way back in 1970, ancient history now, but one of the darkest years of Vietnam. I was a grad student in history at the University and living in an apartment in an old house just beyond the edge of campus. Actually, I should say 'we,' since your grandmother and I were already living together. She too had arrived at the big university from the shelter of a non-political family and a small, fairly conservative college.

"The neighborhood we chose to live in was really bohemian, with a mixture of grad students and undergrads and probably more than a few transients supporting themselves and their habit by dealing drugs. Fashions and hairstyles were pretty crazy. You've probably laughed at pictures of our generation in bellbottoms and psychedelic tie-dyes, Afros, micro-miniskirts, and muumuus. I had hair down to my shoulders; Nona's was halfway down her back. We were hippie wannabes, dabbling our toes in the counterculture.

"About the fighting in Vietnam and the anti-war movement, we were hardly what you could call radicals. But we were starting to educate ourselves, reading editorials condemning the war and articles exposing the emphasis on Viet Cong body counts and the failed attempts at pacification of Vietnamese villages. It had become impossible to ignore the horrors of what was going on over there. Nightly news reports no longer even tried to make it seem as if the war were going well. Walter Cronkite had come back after Tet disillusioned by what he saw in the war zone and called for negotiations and an honorable withdrawal. Secretary of Defense McNamara had a near mental breakdown before resigning. We found out about the disastrous assault on Hamburger Hill, the saturation bombings, the napalm, and, worst of all, the moral catastrophe at My Lai.

"Nixon, of course, had promised in his election campaign to begin withdrawing troops and winding down the war. As much as we disliked and distrusted him, we tried our best to believe the promise.

"Then, however, came his televised speech announcing the decision to invade Cambodia. Rumor had spread around campus beforehand that some dire new policy was about to be revealed. Your grandmother and I watched in stunned silence at the news of yet another front about to be opened in the seemingly endless conflict. For us that became the tipping point.

"Student demonstrations began almost immediately on campuses around the country, including at a relatively little-known state university in Ohio. Four days later, of course, was the massacre that triggered the most prolonged outbreak of violent protest since the Democratic Convention. For average, middle-class college students, it was probably Kent State that made the difference in their willingness to stand up and rebel. All of a sudden, it was our fellow college students who were getting killed, on a campus battlefield and not in Vietnam."

"Was it a George Floyd moment?"

"In a way. The University had already had some fierce rallies and built a reputation as a hotbed of the anti-war movement. Things had been quieter over the past year, but Kent State was an outrage that demanded a big response.

"The next day spontaneous demonstrations erupted all over campus. At first, most of the action was centered in the main Quad in front of the library. Students were parading around carrying home-made signs with memorials for the victims, peace signs, cartoons of Nixon with a noose around his neck, and calls to bring our troops home. Small groups began organizing anti-war chants; a few offered impromptu speeches calling for prosecution of the Ohio National Guard troops. By noon, the crowds had begun to swell in size and volume, and they got larger and noisier by the hour. That night a big crowd marched down Assembly Avenue, chanting and waving signs and smashing the windows of some of the businesses. It was getting really ugly.

"The following day the number of protesters grew yet again. Crowds gathered throughout the campus. Classes were disrupted. Academic buildings were surrounded by demonstrators. A few groups of counter-protesters showed up as well but quickly got driven from the field. The University administration, of course, was freaked out. The president consulted with the board of trustees, who agreed to call a halt to all classes. Exams were postponed and eventually canceled, and grades were awarded based on progress to that point. Undergrads were given two days to turn in late papers - no online submission in those days- and then leave for home. It was hoped those steps would settle everything down.

"But the demonstrations increased instead. Outside organizers from SDS were rumored to have arrived. The president saw the situation getting totally out of control and called the governor for help. Within hours the National Guard had been mobilized, and they began rolling in the following morning.

"The next couple days were full of sudden outbreaks of raucous protest and vandalism at unpredictable locations and times around campus. With no classes meeting and the library closed, there was nothing much for most of us to do but wander around idly. The Quad looked like a military encampment. The guardsmen, wearing camouflage fatigues and helmets and carrying rifles, were positioned in a semi-circle in front of the library, the old Armory building, and the administration building.

"Each morning, I went over mainly as an observer to get my historian's eyewitness view of what might happen. I took up a position along the hillside between the Quad below and historic Old Main above. I must confess I was still a bit of a fence-sitter. Though I was by then absolutely opposed to the continuation of the war, I wasn't sure how willing I was to get involved in an actual rally. Lots of other morning observers seemed to be feeling the same way. They were wandering around just as aimlessly and non-violently, enjoying the warm spring weather.

"The only action taking place seemed almost comical. More like a game of capture the flag than anything. From time to time, little groups of protesters -and I use the word loosely- would suddenly appear part way up the hill to take symbolic possession of one of the classroom buildings and spray paint an anti-war message on the wall. That would spur a counterattack by little squadrons of guardsmen who rushed up the hill with their truncheons in hand and occasionally fired some tear gas to chase off the pranksters, leaving a few lazy puffs of smoke floating across the blue May sky. The spectacle reminded me of photos taken at the First Battle of Bull Run, showing groups of well-dressed young couples who had ridden the train out from Washington to enjoy a picnic and watch the heroic contest of armies.

"A team of organizers began to fan out across the hill, handing out leaflets inviting everyone to a rally at nine that night in the Quad. There were to be well-known speakers, the leaflet promised, to offer a tribute to the fallen from Kent State followed by a peaceful march down Assembly Avenue. 'Bring Candles,' the leaflet concluded. For some reason, I decided at that moment that this event was the right opportunity to take a stand. It would be a chance to honor the martyrs. To join in a peaceful protest against a war that I believed was wrong. And to be a participant in some real, exciting history.

"I went home around lunchtime with the news, and your grandmother was all for attending. By the time we arrived at 8:50 that night, there was already a good-size crowd -a couple hundred, at least- and more arriving by the minute. The event organizers had set up a small stage with speakers in front of the library, and we could hear the crackles and squeals of interference as they adjusted the audio. We could also hear some rumblings of thunder and see a flash or two of lightning off in the distance.

A little after nine, the first speaker took the podium with a hand-held microphone. I could barely see him, but his voice came through clearly. He was well-spoken and serious, even reverent in tone. We had been called, he said, to pay tribute to the four martyrs of Kent State. He named each one, giving a few details to highlight the things they had already accomplished in their brief lives and the goals they were striving to achieve, all the bits and pieces of information that had appeared in the papers over the past few days. They were all, he went on, innocent victims of an unjust war. But, he continued, the memorial was for more than just the four students. It also had to be for the thousands of men and boys who had already given their lives in the jungles of Vietnam for an act of immoral aggression.

"He paused and very somberly lighted a candle and then the candles of the other three figures on the stage. The speaker now called on the spectators to take out their candles and prepare to pass on the light of remembrance. Then the four of them, now mainly four points of light on the makeshift stage, moved down among us. Those of us who had brought candles took turns receiving the flame from one side, then passing it along till all the candles were lighted. It was wonderful to be part of those quiet and reverent moments as row by row and section by section the points of light appeared.

"I remember thinking, as I held my candle, how morally casual I had been, how inconsiderate of the sacrifices required of our

American soldiers in Vietnam. Not to mention the lives of the countless Vietnamese victimized by the war. It was my moment of truth. After all our candles were lighted, the four martyrs' names were read again. We chanted the words 'shanti' and 'peace,' and sang over and over the famous refrain from John Lennon's classic anti-war song. You probably recognize it."

He nodded and together we sang the famous lines: 'All we are saying is give peace a chance.'

"Well, after that," I continued, "we just stood for at least another minute in silence. When those magical moments had passed, each of the other speakers had their time at the microphone, but not to mourn or memorialize. It was their job to whip up some different emotions to inspire the resistance. Each one got a little more radical than the last. It was time to refuse to serve, burn draft cards, pull all troops out of Cambodia, and make the bastards in Congress and especially Tricky Dick answer for their war crimes. The remarks were a little incendiary, but hardly a call to overthrow the government. The last speaker announced that the final part of the rally, the march down Assembly Avenue, would be the statement of our solidarity in the cause of peace.

"Whether the guardsmen had ever intended to allow the march is uncertain, but the speeches had certainly convinced them not to. As soon as the last speaker was finished, they came to life, surrounding the crowd on three sides. As if on cue, thunder and lightning started up in earnest over the downtown office buildings. The guardsmen had closed off entry to Assembly Avenue and began to herd all of us across the Quad into the narrow streets on the back side of campus.

"Nona and I maneuvered through the crowd as best we could. Behind us, a few small groups were resisting, trying to force their way through to Assembly Avenue or back up the hill toward Old Main, but the guardsmen were having none of it. Some had their truncheons drawn and were pushing resisters down to the ground and trying to club them. The speakers still had the microphone and at first were calling on everybody to resist, and then, when all order had collapsed, to run. By then, the air over the Quad was filled with pops and clouds of tear gas.

"We thought we had made it to safety, only to find more guardsmen were waiting in the tangle of dark streets. There were more pops of tear gas being fired off and a pall of smoke blanketed the area. Everybody was coughing and pulling their shirts over their burning eyes. With the tear gas and the darkness, we couldn't figure out which way to retreat. We heard more pops that sounded a little different, like they could be coming from rifles. Suddenly, we were scared to death that we might become the newest anti-war martyrs. Then the skies opened up, and the rain came pouring down. The positive side was that it neutralized the effects of the tear gas and helped soothe our eyes.

"We ran like a couple of terrified rabbits, your grandmother in her short shorts keeping pace with me with her long strides. We dodged around corners and splashed through puddles. I hydroplaned and tumbled into a bush a block away from our apartment. But we made it back alive. We were soaked through, half-drowned, breathless, and still choking on tear gas. Inside, we stripped down and dried off, then stood looking at each other shivering, and, for some reason, started to laugh. We had had our great adventure and were just relieved that we had escaped to tell our tale.

"For the next hour or so, we went back over the event, each of us adding little details, remembered shouts, guardsmen looming up suddenly out of the rain, the eerie sense of being lost in our own neighborhood. We speculated about the identity of the speakers, whether they had been arrested, and, yes, about whether anybody had been injured or even killed.

"Little by little, it dawned on us how grossly our basic civil right to protest peacefully had been violated and how easily we too could have been victims of a government ever more intent on shutting off dissent. Nonetheless, we felt proud that we had stood up for what we believed. Ironically, the details we talked about least were those of the vigil itself. After that, we got into bed and lay there, listening to occasional shouts in the distance till we finally fell asleep."

I sat back for a moment lost in the flood of feelings and images evoked by telling my tale. "Well, that pretty well ends the first chapter of my diary of a radical," I said at last.

"So, you really did make it to the front lines of battle after all," Randy said, not entirely unimpressed.

"It was hardly the front lines," I said. "Let's call it a minor skirmish."

"It wasn't exactly a game-changing event," he agreed. "But the important thing is that you were there."

"True," I said. "But when I thought about things later, it occurred to me that just being there had actually made no impact on anything. It was kind of depressing to realize how little our act of peaceful protest was likely to be noticed."

"At least you and Nona had a big adventure," he said. "It was a lot more exciting than any demonstration or march I've been in."

"Do I detect a little jealousy?"

"Maybe so," he said with a smile, then added, "It must have made an impact on you, though, if you remember it so well."

"You're right," I conceded. "In retrospect, our little act of protest wasn't totally futile. But it was the vigil that made the experience meaningful and not just an exciting war story. It was our chance to tune out all the angry background noise long enough to contemplate the senseless loss of life, at home as well as in Vietnam, all in pursuit of a goal we already knew we couldn't accomplish."

"The rally must have gotten some attention," he said. "Your voices must have been heard on the next day's news. They must have shown a little footage of the vigil. That certainly would have had a positive impact on the community."

"The sad thing is that there apparently weren't any news cameras or even reporters at our rally. They were probably covering rowdier demonstrations elsewhere in the city and on campus. The morning television news provided only skimpy details. There was no exciting footage of the tear gas and the fleeing crowd, much less our circle of lighted candles. The reported crowd size seemed underestimated. A few students and one guardsman were reported to have suffered minor injuries. No mention was made of the identity of the speakers or the main purpose of the rally to memorialize the fallen students.

The evening news aired a couple brief interviews with students who had been at other rallies and also a longer interview with the University chancellor. Though he came up short of condemning everyone at all the demonstrations, he did heap praise on the crowd-control measures by the guardsmen. They were portrayed as the heroes of the night.

"Our quiet little rally was one of the last events of that week of rage. The violence and vandalism dropped off significantly over the next few days. Though the paper seemed to be reporting the action as objectively as possible, citing criticisms of the guardsmen as well as the protesters, the letters to the editor increasingly were putting all the blame on the protesters for the chaos. The television station ran film footage, repeated rather frequently, of the looting from the nights before our rally and of rioting on other campuses. It was the kind of coverage that gets ordinary folks stirred up.

"The next few days were ominously quiet in expectation that there still might be more trouble. But it had been over a week since the massacre. All the undergrads and many of the grad students had left for vacation, and all the energy for the protest movement seemed to have drained away."

"The timing at the end of the school year wasn't in your favor," he said.

"True," I said. "Summer vacation certainly caused the anti-war movement to hit the pause button pretty much everywhere. But the timing was also wrong in the sense that it was still mainly young people who were demanding an end to the war. Most of the rest of the nation probably wasn't quite ready to go along yet."

We sat back, sipping our coffee and observing the conversation of the others from our socially distanced vantage point. "Actually," I said after a while, "chapter one does have an epilogue, a tragic one that did more than anything to quell the spirit of revolution in our university town.

"Your grandmother and I went separate ways to visit family for a few weeks, then got back in late July to begin preparing for the fall semester. We had a run of beautiful weather and spent lots of afternoons at the local parks or on day trips.

"We got back rather tired from one of those trips and went to bed early. We were sleeping peacefully when about two in the morning we were nearly blown out of bed by an enormous explosion. Within minutes, the air was filled with the wail of sirens. We looked out the window and could see the flashing lights of police cars and rescue vehicles streaming down University Avenue. We looked at each other, wondering what possibly could have happened. A gas main explosion? A plane crash? We didn't even think of a terrorist bombing.

"We threw on tee-shirts and shorts and went down to investigate. The street was already filled with people from nearby houses and apartments, milling around in confusion. All we could see were plumes of smoke rising against the night sky. The sound of the sirens was deafening.

Soon, a few people began walking cautiously in the direction from which the explosion seemed to have happened. More followed. We looked at each other and fell in line behind the crowd, but after only a few blocks we came to a police barricade. The site of the explosion was still out of sight, but it was obviously somewhere up on campus. We hung around for ten minutes or so, gazing down the street. Somebody near the front asked the nearest officer for details but got only the gruff reply: 'explosion.' We watched a while longer, but soon figured we were unlikely to gather anything more than rumor and contradictory speculation. Finally, we walked home and went back to bed, but we couldn't fall asleep.

"The next morning, we turned on the news as soon as we got awake to find out that a bomb had been detonated on the other side of campus outside a physics building, part of which was being used for military research. One young man, the father of several children, had been there working on an experiment unrelated to the military. He was killed instantly.

Over the next few days, we were glued to the television news coverage that showed pictures of the building, gutted by the force of the blast. Virtually every window in the nearby academic buildings had been blown out. Windows in the University hospital had been shattered, injuring some patients and staff. New details emerged each day in the newspaper about the suspects, all four of whom had escaped without a trace. One of them never was apprehended. After a couple days, we walked over to get a first-hand look, but the area was still tightly cordoned off by police and we couldn't get close enough to see much.

"The city remained in shock for weeks. Television interviews and letters to the editor revealed the deep well of sympathy for the victim and the outrage at the domestic terrorists. But they also revealed anger over the anti-war movement in general. It was time, people were saying, to reassert law and order. The bomb blast knocked the life out of the movement for the time being on our campus.

"When the rest of the students returned, any thought of restarting demonstrations was forgotten. Meanwhile, the war in the jungle slogged on. We were kept in the dark about the worst horrors of the bombing of Cambodia. The Pentagon Papers still hadn't been released, and Watergate was still just an office complex on the Potomac.

"So, when did the movement start to heat up again?" Randy asked.

"Things remained relatively quiet around college campuses for almost the entire school year. It wasn't till the following spring that the massive rallies started up again in earnest. This time, however, many of them took place in big cities, particularly San Francisco, New York, and Washington."

"Did you and Nona go to any of those?" he asked.

"We did go to the rally in D.C. in April. It was a peaceful, more well-organized affair. A couple hundred thousand people of all ages showed up to offer outpourings of concern and pleas to end the carnage. It was all about peace and love rather than defiance and rebellion. We all camped out in front of the Capitol, listening to speakers, enjoying the beautiful weather, in some cases smoking a little weed, and above all talking to each other.

"The big difference was that the crowd wasn't just college kids and flower children. There were folks from every age group, every social class, and every walk of life. Though we certainly didn't agree on all the changes taking place in America, we did agree that it was time for the war to end.

"But we didn't talk just about the war or even America's problems. Nona and I had some great conversations with a whole variety of people. I remember talking about the challenges of owning a small business with a plumber from Ohio, literacy problems with a teacher from Maryland, and Social Security concerns with a senior citizen from Florida."

"Was it a kumbaya experience?" Randy asked.

"In a way, yes," I said. "I like to call it a grand and wonderful be-in."

Before we left, we talked about all he intended to do in the run-up to election day. He talked about his worries that the incumbent seemed to be surging in the polls and that his huge rallies were threatening to unleash anarchy on a larger scale than anything seen in the sixties.

The sun was getting lower and the air chillier, and we had come to a good stopping place in our conversation. But before we left, we made plans to meet after the election was over.

"Keep the faith," I said. "Sanity and fundamental American good sense will win out."

I wished I could come up with something more convincingly optimistic.

II

Our next meeting didn't come for almost two months. It had not been a quiet time. The loser had whipped up outrage with claims that the election had been stolen. His followers were staging rallies as he continued to incite them on social media. Insurrection was in the air. In light of all the demagoguery, we went back to the topic of protests, rallies, and marches.

"I never thought I'd say this," Randy began, "but maybe there should be a limit on free speech and the right to protest. At what point do lies and hate speech no longer deserve First Amendment protection?"

We debated that thorny issue briefly, recalling the history of sedition laws and gag orders.

"We're in a real dilemma," he said. "After all the shameful events of the past month, rallies for any cause seem suspect."

I had to agree.

"After what happened following Vietnam," he said, "when did you and Nona go back to political action?"

"Not for quite a while," I said. "There wasn't even a true progressive movement to speak of during the eighties and nineties. The economy was too good, and we weren't seriously involved in any foreign wars."

"There certainly were plenty of underlying problems with racism and social inequality," he said.

"True," I said. "But after the gloom of the seventies, most people were too focused on making money and enjoying the good life to pay much attention. Your grandmother and I did attend a few rallies for presidential candidates in the nineties. Some were exciting, some were disappointing, but at least we had a sense of being involved. If anything, your aunt was the one who really got us motivated again, particularly about the women's rights movement. Without the megaphone of social media, it was hard for progressive voices to be heard. But little by little, average folks had begun accepting the changes that had started during the sixties."

"Grudgingly accepting them," he said. "Progress sure can be slow."

"I'm sure it seems that way to most young people," I said. "But it's probably accurate to say that progress has been on fast forward over the past sixty years, at least in comparison with the first couple hundred years of the Republic."

We debated the implications of generational change and the cycles of progress and regression and of evolution and revolution that have always characterized human society.

"I get it," he admitted. "Rapid change generally scares people, especially older ones."

"The election in 2000," I said, "was a referendum on the pace of change. A lot of Americans wanted leaders who would tap on the brakes. The result was deeply disappointing, particularly since the winner of the popular vote had lost the election. There was a lot of anger, but amazingly no sustained outcry of vote fraud or a stolen election after the Supreme Court declared in favor of Bush. Both sides eventually accepted that the people had spoken, even though they represented only an electoral majority."

"Then came 9-11," Randy said.

"Yes, then came 9-11. But more importantly the invasion of Iraq. When I think back, that was an event that truly deserved a loud national outcry of protest. It led us into a war that we were totally prepared to win militarily but totally unprepared to win in every other way. Even our stated reason for invading was deeply suspect. With no verifiable evidence, we were asked to believe we needed to destroy a massive stash of weapons of mass destruction.

But we were feeling a dangerous surge of self-righteous anger in the aftermath of 9-11. We had handled the crisis well as a nation up to that point, but we needed to prove our ability to rise from tragedy. We convinced ourselves that simply by invading and toppling a terrible dictator, we could set out the way for a smooth transition to a modern, humane, enlightened democracy like our own. It was an idealistic goal. Unfortunately, we lacked both the understanding and the commitment to accomplish it.

"You'd think we would have learned more from the hard lessons of Vietnam," he said.

"Certain ideas die hard," I said.

"And tend to keep getting resurrected," he added.

"From what I've read," he went on, "there certainly weren't many voices raised in protest during the lead-up to invasion."

"Precious few," I said. "A lot of individuals felt uneasy about the situation, but were reluctant to speak up, perhaps afraid of being thought unpatriotic. Besides the Administration did a great job of selling the invasion. It would be swift and surgical, they promised. It would be a demonstration of American greatness."

"What about you and Nona?" he asked after a moment. "Where did you stand?"

"We had strong reservations but weren't sure how to express them. It was hard finding a forum because the Administration had so carefully controlled the national dialogue."

"I don't imagine there were any rallies in our fair city," he said.

"Actually," I said, "there was one that I know of, one that your grandmother and I were involved in. It wasn't a march. We didn't chant angry slogans. We didn't carry any signs. It was probably the tiniest, but one of the most memorable gatherings of concerned citizens I've ever participated in.

"I was teaching history and civics at the high school and trying my best to interject, non-confrontationally, my reservations over what certainly seemed an inevitable invasion. During our discussions on current events days, I could tell that most of the kids -at least the most vocal ones- were convinced by the Administration's evidence of the existence of the weapons. Even I began to wonder how I could feel so certain of my opposition in the face of the public push for action.

"One day in December -as the Administration was building its case to the nation- I was about to have my last practice with the Quiz Bowl team before the Christmas break. They were a terrific group of young women and men. Smart, energetic, positive, committed to all sorts of things. Just like you, in fact. I got called away for a few minutes just as they arrived for the refreshments we always had at the beginning of practice.

"When I got back, I could see they had been talking together about something. We had a spirited practice, even more so than usual, and I was assuming it was because they were excited about the holiday break. When we concluded around 4:30, they all suddenly turned serious. They said they all believed they knew how I felt about the national situation -not Iraq, just the situation- and they wanted to invite me to join them downtown that evening at a gathering in the plaza across from city hall. It was impromptu. They had just found out about it themselves earlier in the day and all had agreed to go. Maybe it wouldn't make any difference in what the government decided to do, they acknowledged. But it would make a difference to them. Needless to say, I agreed to go.

"I made a quick call to your grandmother, who pledged to get out of work early enough to join us. We all caravanned downtown. It was already dark when we arrived, but the plaza was lighted up and decorated with its big holiday tree celebrating the season of peace and love for all mankind.

"By 5:30, a group of twenty-five or thirty had gathered around three of the local religious leaders. It was hardly a crowd to influence the minds and hearts of the nation's decision-makers. We formed a circle around the three organizers who introduced themselves as the rabbi from the city's synagogue, the leader of the Quaker meeting, and the pastor of a large downtown Protestant church.

"I remember only a little of what each of them said. The rabbi began by reading a passage from a psalm. He reminded us of the Jews' history of being conquered and oppressed, the age-old turmoil of the Middle East, and the unlikelihood that yet another foreign invasion could solve the region's problems. The Quaker spoke next, emphasizing the Friends' historic commitment to peace. Finally, the pastor read from the Sermon on the Mount. Then, he pushed the play button on a CD player and out came the strains of Mendelsohn's divine anthem, 'Grant peace we pray, in mercy, Lord; in our time peace, O, send us.'

"While the music played, he produced a bag of candles and the three of them began passing them to each of us in the circle.

We lit each other's candles and began passing on the flame till the ring of light was complete. When the anthem concluded, we stood for a minute in complete silence, maintaining our circle of hope. Then the brief gathering concluded with the great benediction from the book of *Numbers*: "May the Lord bless you and keep you..." and the words 'shalom' and 'peace.' We all wished each other a blessed and peaceful holiday season, then headed to our separate homes."

"I've been to my share of rallies and marches and listened to the appeals for justice and peace from lots of high-minded and sincere speakers. But no rally or march ever touched me nearly as much as those two brief vigils so many years apart. Of course, you know how much influence either of them had on a nation intent on war. But I believe they had a profound impact on all those who were there. It was our moment of grace."

He didn't comment, and I couldn't be sure how he felt about the story. He was young and probably not as moved by symbolic actions that didn't seem to move the needle of progress. But he respected the longer view of an older generation.

We talked for another hour or so after that. His work on the presidential campaign had paid off. He could breathe now and think about other things. He told me about his plans for graduate school in one of the big northern universities and his wish that, for at least part of his final semester, things would return to normal.

We agreed that our next opportunity to meet would probably have to be after the Christmas holiday. "We can toast the upcoming inauguration," he said, "And celebrate the return of sanity to the nation."

III

That day came just a couple days after the New Year. It was an unseasonably warm day, good for meeting outside, and our best chance to get together once more time before he was finally able to return to college the following week.

The national mood seemed to have calmed down a little over the holiday season. At first, he was in a talkative mood and eager, as usual, to discuss the political scene. He was pleased by the president- elect's cabinet choices so far. I didn't have too much to add on the subject, having made my New Year's resolution to wean myself from watching so much news coverage.

We shifted the conversation for a while to the upcoming BCS Bowl championship and the NFL playoffs. Sports always provided a useful neutral topic.

Finally, though, he navigated the conversation back to his hopes for the president-elect and the incoming Congress. The former was promising to reach across the aisle and work with the opposition on a few legislative initiatives where there might be at least a glimmer of hope for compromise. I offered extremely tepid optimism.

"I know," he said. "It's the usual promise that newly elected presidents have to make."

"It would be nice if some legislation gets passed, just as proof that the system still can work," I said. "But I don't want to be disappointed if nothing too much happens."

"It's probably a good idea for me not to set my expectations too high either."

"You look well rested," I said. "Not like back in the fall. What are you going to do to keep yourself busy on campus now that the election is over?"

"I'll be gearing up for more campaigning pretty soon," he said, only half-facetiously. "After all, mid-terms are just around the corner. We've got to keep the energy high and keep fighting the good fight. You never know what might happen in these times."

"You just never know," I said. "You never can predict."

"Are you feeling at all hopeful about the future?"

"I wish I could," I said. "But there's still so much noise. So much anger and negativity. People still aren't listening to each other. I'm a little...I guess you could say fatalistic."

"Yeah," he said. "The time is out of whack. I just hope we get to the inauguration in one piece as a nation." I pronounced a great 'amen' to that wish.

It had suddenly turned cloudy and a lot colder, and we decided to call it an afternoon. "Peace," he said, uncharacteristically, as we got to our cars. "I'll give you a heads-up, probably in a couple of months, when I get back in town. I know better than to text, but don't forget to check your email. We can get together and talk about whether any progress has been made."

"We can only hope the future is a little brighter," I said. "It hardly could get worse."

Little could either of us have foreseen all that would happen in the coming days.

ABOUT THE AUTHOR

Richard Tobaben is a retired teacher who used quarantine time during the pandemic to polish some stories written at various times over the past forty years and create some new ones as well. He lives in Winston-Salem, North Carolina with his wife Sandi.

Made in United States
North Haven, CT
20 March 2022